The Forbidden Kiss . . .

He kissed her before she could respond. Before she could put him in his place. She fought mightily to permit that kiss to have no effect on her. Her thoughts scrambled as the sensations swept her body and the secret regret burst out of her heart, together threatening to drown all good sense and rational, practical resolve.

We must not. It will ruin everything. Ruin me, I fear, far worse than going to Anthony ever would. Did she say it, amid the short gasps she made while his mouth burned her neck? She could not tell. He did not act as if he heard. Or else he did not care.

Always make them ask, Celia. Even with the first kiss. This man was asking permission for nothing. He never had.

His embrace felt too good. Too welcome. His strength proved too exciting. She had not chosen to succumb to this desire they felt for each other, but she could not resist either. His fire began consuming her will, much as the flames had that paper.

Sinful in Satin

MADELINE HUNTER

JOVE BOOKS, NEW YORK

THE BERKLEY PUBLISHING GROUP
Published by the Penguin Group
Penguin Group (USA) Inc.
375 Hudson Street, New York, New York 10014, USA
Penguin Group (Canada), 90 Eglinton Avenue East, Suite 700, Toronto, Ontario M4P 2Y3, Canada
(a division of Pearson Penguin Canada Inc.)
Penguin Books Ltd., 80 Strand, London WC2R 0RL, England
Penguin Group Ireland, 25 St. Stephen's Green, Dublin 2, Ireland (a division of Penguin Books Ltd.)
Penguin Group (Australia), 250 Camberwell Road, Camberwell, Victoria 3124, Australia
(a division of Pearson Australia Group Pty. Ltd.)
Penguin Books India Pvt. Ltd., 11 Community Centre, Panchsheel Park, New Delhi—110 017, India
Penguin Group (NZ), 67 Apollo Drive, Rosedale, North Shore 0632, New Zealand
(a division of Pearson New Zealand Ltd.)
Penguin Books (South Africa) (Pty.) Ltd., 24 Sturdee Avenue, Rosebank, Johannesburg 2196,
South Africa

Penguin Books Ltd., Registered Offices: 80 Strand, London WC2R 0RL, England

This is a work of fiction. Names, characters, places, and incidents either are the product of the author's imagination or are used fictitiously, and any resemblance to actual persons, living or dead, business establishments, events, or locales is entirely coincidental. The publisher does not have control over and does not have any responsibility for author or third-party websites or their content.

SINFUL IN SATIN

A Jove Book / published by arrangement with the author

PRINTING HISTORY
Jove mass-market edition / October 2010

Copyright © 2010 by Madeline Hunter.
Cover photo by Claudio Marinesco.
Cover design by Rita Frangie.
Text design by Laura Corless.

ISBN: 978-0-515-14844-2

JOVE®
Jove Books are published by The Berkley Publishing Group,
a division of Penguin Group (USA) Inc.,
375 Hudson Street, New York, New York 10014.
JOVE® is a registered trademark of Penguin Group (USA) Inc.
The "J" design is a trademark of Penguin Group (USA) Inc.

PRINTED IN THE UNITED STATES OF AMERICA

10 9 8 7 6 5 4 3 2 1

Sinful in
Satin

Chapter One

The funeral of a whore will be sparsely attended, no matter how celebrated and noble the whore's patrons might have been.

Celia Pennifold was therefore not surprised by the dearth of mourners at the funeral of her mother, Alessandra Northrope. Mostly women came, turned out in expensive black bombazine ensembles that would be discarded by day's end. Courtesans all, they knew that Alessandra would not expect them to wear mourning clothes longer than a few hours. There were protectors awaiting their company, after all.

A few men were present too. Five young bloods hung in the background. From their disrespectful grins and jostling, Celia could see that four of them thought it a great joke to be here. The fifth, however, appeared to truly grieve for the beautiful, fascinating woman in the coffin.

Alessandra had often received declarations of love along with generous gifts. She had been kind enough not to let those profoundly moved gentlemen know that she had

herself outgrown the need to cloak what she did in sentiment.

That was one thing that could be said about this particular whore, Celia thought. Dukes might write poems
to her and swains might sing songs to her, but Alessandra
Northrope had always known exactly who and what she
was.

Would that she had allowed her daughter the same secure knowledge of self.

"Five carriages," her friend Daphne's voice whispered.
The observation flowed below the droning prayer of the
vicar. "I wonder who they are."

Celia had noticed each carriage arrive. Hired and anonymous, their drawn blinds shielded their interiors from
curious eyes. "They are prior patrons, I assume. Or current ones. Men of note who do not want to be seen."

If prior ones, from how long ago? The possibilities distracted her from the ritual. She tried not to stare at those
dark coaches. She resisted the urge to walk over to them
and peer inside and see just who had arranged to say
good-bye to Alessandra in this secret, formal way.

"The sixth one does not hold her patrons from any
time," Daphne said. "Audrianna and Verity are within. They
are here for you, Celia, even if they do not show their
faces."

Celia appreciated the effort her dear friends had made.
Since both had recently married men of good society, Audrianna and Verity had to show circumspection in matters
like this. Even being known as a friend of Alessandra's
daughter could taint them.

Daphne, an independent widow, had neither a husband
nor a social circle to appease. Yet Daphne had not truly
shown her face either. A good deal of black netting flowed

from her broad-brimmed black hat, obscuring her moon-light hair and perfectly pale face. She had insisted on accompanying Celia, however, even though Celia had advised she not.

Celia peered at the five carriages again. She saw small slits in the curtains of two, and tried hard to glimpse whatever she might through the openings. They were too far away, and only darkness showed.

Daphne's hand subtly touched hers, reminding her to keep her thoughts on the prayers. Feeling guilty, Celia paid attention to the moment but not to the words. She allowed memories of her mother to come, some good and some painful, the most poignant ones those of the last few weeks. Alessandra's illness had brought them together after five years of estrangement. Any angers from the past, any resentments and scars, had not mattered very much during those last sweet days.

Except one.

When the service ended and the women drifted away, Celia permitted her attention to turn to the carriages again. She looked directly at each one as it rolled past, both to acknowledge the respects of the invisible man inside, and to try to sense his presence so perhaps she would recognize it later.

"He was here," she said to Daphne after all the carriages had gone. "I am sure of it."

"He probably was."

"He will perhaps write to me. Maybe now that she is gone, he will reveal himself."

Daphne wound their arms together and escorted Celia away. "He may indeed."

"You are only humoring me. You do not believe he will."

"He has not thus far, so, no, I do not believe he will."

Celia walked with more purpose. "It was cruel of her not to tell me. I have a right to know who my father is, but she dismissed my pleas."

"I am sure that she had her reasons, Celia. Perhaps you should accept that she knew best on this. Perhaps keeping her own counsel on the matter allowed her to pass in peace."

Celia blinked away tears for the woman she would never see again. "No doubt she thought she did what was best, in this as in everything else about my life. However, I will never accept that I will never know my father's name."

"It was just talk, of course. Vague rumors. I never believed it myself."

"But others did?" Jonathan peered through the slit in the blinds. Most of his mind assessed the mission that his uncle was giving him, but a small part of it remained alert to the little drama playing out near the grave.

"Perhaps some did. There was no proof, only patterns and coincidences. They caused those in power to be suspicious at a time when suspicions abounded, often without good cause. Hence the concern now. No man wants his name tied to hers too closely during those years, due to the talk, lest it cast him in a bad light unfairly."

Uncle Edward imparted the necessary information in a lazy voice that reflected how minor he considered the entire matter. He also made it clear that he assumed Jonathan would accept this little charge, as he had so many others over the years.

Jonathan parted the blinds a little more. Over at the

grave a clutch of women stood, all in black. Most of them would be recognizable to any man about town. Some were well-kept mistresses, and others were the most sought-after ladies of pleasure who chose their clients from among the ton. They lived on a little moon that closely circled the planet that best society inhabited, and formed a satellite world to which men of good birth traveled with some frequency.

Not all the women were notorious. Two of them seemed out of place. One, tall and willowy, remained invisible under veils hanging from the wide brim of her hat. The other, shorter and blond, wore no hat at all.

He squinted to see that second one's face better. The distance made her vague, but, yes, it could well be Celia. Had she come out of sentiment, as a dutiful daughter? Or as her mother's heir, the way Alessandra had planned and assumed? She stood proud and straight, and did not seem at all embarrassed to be surrounded by the kind of women who had been her mother's only choice of friends.

"And if the rumors were accurate?" he asked Edward, not taking his eyes off that blond head. "What if I discover that Alessandra did pass pillow talk to the enemy?"

"The war is long over. You are not being asked to investigate, let alone expose such things. Just discover if she left any accounts or such, with names that might be made public. Bring them to me if you do." He smiled a smile that had been the only warmth Jonathan had received from any of his blood relatives over the years. "It is very simple. A few days' work at most."

Jonathan finally gave his uncle his attention. "Why me, if it is so simple?"

"You knew her, didn't you? You were friends with her." Edward's expression remained impassive, but Jonathan knew the mind behind those regular features and dark eyes too well to be fooled.

"Friends, yes. Not lovers, in case you are assuming that. I do not know her secrets. I also saw nothing to give credence to these rumors."

"Of course not. Still, you can move in her world better than anyone else, since you were a friend." He gestured toward the window, and the women at the grave. The inhabitants of Alessandra's world. "They will all trust you for that reason alone. And also because people tend to anyway."

His uncle alluded to an odd truth, one that Jonathan had become expert in exploiting. People did trust him. For reasons unknown, their instincts told them to. He did not understand it himself, but it had made his missions for Edward easier. Somewhat ignoble too, and vaguely dishonorable, no matter how right the cause.

It was not clear how right this new cause was. Not that it really mattered. He had long ago stopped debating such things. A man could not make his way as an investigator if he took sides. Whether executing a duty for the Home Office, or tracking down the love nest of an errant wife, it behooved him to remain objective if he wanted to eat.

He peered out the window again. He wondered if he could remain objective this time. Alessandra had indeed been a friend. There was something distasteful in the notion of picking through her life and past. It felt like a betrayal of her.

He faced his uncle squarely. "Another man would be better for this."

"We want you. There is no telling what will be learned. We can't trust some runner from Bow Street."

"I don't like it. I had intended to go back to France anyway."

Edward tried to smile, but instead his mouth stretched in a thin-lipped line that spoke more worry than good humor. "You don't want to be leaving so soon. I am making progress with Thornridge. I intend to go down to Hollycroft myself next week and see if my efforts have borne fruit. If I am successful, you will want to be here when the goal is achieved."

He alluded to a long quest, one that Jonathan increasingly doubted fulfilling. Edward had been his only ally in that struggle of obtaining the family acknowledgment that would put the ambiguity about his life to rest.

Edward said nothing more, but an old understanding hung between them. Edward would help Jonathan, if Jonathan helped Edward. It had been his uncle who recruited him during the war, and who had always acted as the go-between for the Home Office when it came to the investigations on which he was sent.

Normally, the allusion to the great prize would make Jonathan set aside any misgivings. Today it did not. He was not sure why. Perhaps that sense of betraying a friend caused his ill ease. Possibly Edward's lure was losing its appeal. The bait had been in the water a very long time now, after all.

Then again, maybe it was because he had seen Alessandra's daughter today. Celia's vivid, bright, youthful spirit had always made him feel dark and murky and old beyond his years.

Edward's expression turned serious, as if he saw something in the face across the carriage that troubled him. "There is something else."

"What is that?"

"It is possible— I did not want to speak of it, because of this friendship you think you had, but there is some indication that the attack you suffered in Cornwall is tied to this. Just a pattern that can be traced; that is all. Nothing definite."

"You knew this and did not tell me before? Damnation, you know I have a debt to settle there. If you have any information about the man behind that I want—"

"I assure you it is all very elusive. Still—one of her early patrons was a French émigré, as you may know. He taught her style and manners. There have been hints he was linked to it, and we have reason to think that she continued to see him up until his death two years ago. Privately and on the sly."

So the rumors were not without some provocation. Jonathan did not believe that Alessandra would knowingly send him into a trap and to almost-certain death. He did not want to think such a thing of the woman who had been almost motherly toward him.

On the other hand, a person's choices could be harsh in this world. An agent with missions of questionable morality cannot afford a conscience that is too particular. He knew all about that.

The burial service ended. The women drifted away, leaving the blonde and her veiled friend near the grave.

"Will you do it?" Edward asked. "You must follow orders this time. None of that inconvenient independence you showed the last time up north."

"External circumstances intervened up north, as you well know."

"You should have found a way to put Hawkeswell off

when you learned he was sniffing around the whole matter. You should have—"

"I warned you that the stench was so big someone was bound to smell it. Do not blame me if the government has been embarrassed."

Their carriage rolled, and approached a part of the lane that cut closer to the grave. A blond head faced the passing carriages. As they drew near, Jonathan saw Celia's lovely face a mere ten feet away.

The pretty, golden child had grown into a very lovely woman. She appeared just as sweet now, though perhaps less innocent. She looked right at the covered window, acknowledging its invisible occupants.

The day was overcast, yet the world brightened just a bit all around her, as if she gave off her own radiance.

Jonathan turned away from the window and met his uncle's frowning impatience.

"Yes, I will do it."

Celia hopped out of Daphne's gig. She looked up at the three-story brick house. Like most of the others on this part of Wells Street, it appeared well maintained. It was the sort of house a merchant might live in, or a prosperous craftsman.

"It appears to be a decent neighborhood, and Bedford Square is only a few streets east," Daphne said. She had been inspecting more than the house. "You should be safe enough on your own for a few days."

Celia lifted her valise from the gig. She had not yet told Daphne that it might be more than a few days. That would come later, once she had settled her plans.

"I still think it is odd that my mother never told me about this property," she said. "It is much more modest than the house on Orchard Street. I suppose one of her patrons settled it on her, to be let for an income."

Daphne climbed down and tied the reins to a post. "Perhaps you should let it as well, rather than sell it."

"I may do that. I cannot sell until the estate is settled. Mr. Mappleton said that more debts might yet be claimed. If so, this will slip through my fingers like the other house, and everything else."

She plucked the key out of her reticule and fitted it into the lock.

"Thank goodness it is furnished. I feared you would be sleeping on the floor," Daphne said once they peered in the first chamber. "You will get a better price when you let it too."

Celia set down her valise and they strolled through the lower floor. There was a nice sitting room in the front, with a library behind it. Both sported upholstered furniture that was presentable, solid tables, and simple but tasteful carpets. The library even held an assortment of books. She examined the bindings and smiled at the little tomes of poetry. Mama had loved poetry and, in stocking this library, had assumed its tenants would benefit from her own taste.

They mounted the stairs to the next level and its bedchambers. The one in front looked over the street. Daphne lifted a coverlet on the bed. "There are sheets on it, and they appear clean. One suspects the last tenants left rather quickly. One step ahead of the bailiff, perhaps. Let us remake it anyway, so you are sure they are fresh."

Celia found sheets in a wicker trunk and they quickly finished with the chore. They took inventory of the other chambers on this floor, and found a second set of stairs at the back of the house.

"I will investigate the attic tomorrow," Celia said, leading the way down. "It appears all is in order here, Daphne. Do you feel better about leaving me alone now?"

"I did not object to your staying here for a few days."

Celia giggled. "You said nothing, but your eyes assumed that expression of forbearance that said you wanted to object, but are not allowed to."

They entered another sitting room, one of good size with cane chairs and a settee, at the bottom of the back stairs. The garden could be seen through its large windows. The view arrested Celia's attention.

"It faces south," Daphne said. "This is an excellent chamber. Even today, with such overcast skies, there is a pleasant light here, and the prospect of the garden is very refreshing."

"I suspect it will be my favorite place," Celia said. "Plants would take well to these windows." The seed of an idea that had been planted upon learning about this house now set down some growth.

They investigated the kitchen down below, then Daphne prepared to take her leave. She would drive her gig back to the property she had near Cumberworth, in Middlesex. Daphne had a business there, growing flowers and plants for the London market. For the last five years, that had been Celia's home too.

"We will miss you," Daphne said at the front door. "Promise me that you will take care."

"It is a good neighborhood, Daphne. I will be safe here."

"I suppose I should not think like a mother so much with you. I am only four years your senior. You must find my worries silly."

"You are not like a mother. You are the older sister I always wanted."

With something of a mother's worry still in her eyes, Daphne stepped out and untied her gig. Celia watched her dear friend drive away with the veils on her hat floating back on winter's breeze.

If Daphne acted a bit like a mother, it was because Celia had been a lot like a child when they had met. A confused, lost child, seeking sanctuary with a stranger whom she had heard possessed a kind heart.

She closed the door, and set about becoming accustomed to the property that was the only legacy Alessandra Northrope had left.

Well, not the only legacy. There was one other, should Celia choose to claim it.

Chapter Two

Celia spent the remaining hours of daylight in the light-filled back chamber. She took its measure with her eyes, and imagined it furnished much differently. That seed of an idea sent up a succulent shoot of stem. Leaves began forming.

At nightfall, she retired to her bedchamber. She did not build a fire, since she intended to sleep soon. She lit a single candle, changed into her warmest bed dress, wrapped herself in two thick knitted shawls, and sat looking out the window while she plotted her use of this house.

She trusted that any debts outstanding would be called within a reasonable time. She would have to ask Mr. Mappleton, Mama's solicitor and executor, when she would know this house was securely hers to keep.

The legalities had to wait, but the rest did not. She would clear out that back room tomorrow and assess whether her plans for it would work. Then she would go to the shops and lay in food supplies for the next week at least. When Daphne came in three days to take her home, she would explain that she would not be returning with her to that property outside London. She would break the news that she was striking out on her own, and intended to live in this house that her mother had left her.

Daphne would not like it. After five years, they had come to rely on each other more than most people guessed. It was time, however. Time to forge some kind of future for herself.

She looked around the bedchamber. The drapes at the window and bed appeared crisp and clean, but were sewn of simple white muslin. The furniture possessed elegant lines, but no costly carving. The house's lack of overt luxury contrasted with the other house on Orchard Street, the one where Alessandra had presided over parties and salons, and played a grand lady of the demimonde.

Celia preferred this one, she decided. She was glad it had not been occupied, so she could use it for herself.

Evidence indicated the last tenants had not been gone long. No dust cloths had covered the furniture. The larder even held some dry goods. On entering it today the space had not felt vacant. Rather it contained a pleasant atmosphere. Domestic—

She froze. Her senses shed all distractions. She listened hard to the quaking silence.

Sounds so subtle they might not exist whispered on little drafts of air. She wanted to explain them away, but the chilled prickling on her nape would not permit it.

More sounds, above now. Like a cat moving about. Perhaps a stray had gotten in.

The sounds stopped. She listened a long time for more, and half convinced herself that she had not heard anything of note after all. She had taken great care to ensure every door was locked. There was no way for anyone to get in.

A footstep atop the nearby stairs to the attic chambers made her jump out of her skin. There was no mistaking it, or the ones that followed. Whoever was up there was not even trying to be quiet. *And he was coming down the stairs right outside this chamber's door.*

Terror froze her for a horrible moment; then her mind raced. She jumped up, grabbed a poker from the cold hearth, and stepped quietly to the wall beside the door. Hopefully the intruder would leave as he had come, none the wiser that she was on the premises, but if not— She raised the poker, clutching it with both hands.

The boots reached the bottom of the steps and paused. She prayed they would move on, down one more level, then out the door.

To her horror they came toward her instead. They paused outside her door. She silently urged them to move on, away, down the stairs. *Be gone. Be gone.*

The door opened. Her heart rose to her throat. She caught her breath and did not move a hair.

A man entered. A tall one. He stepped inside and paced to the center of the chamber. She saw dark coats and high boots and the white of a collar and cravat. She glimpsed a profile with a dark eye and an intense expression, and dark hair pulled back into an old-fashioned tail. She saw all of that in a barrage of dim, golden impressions lit by the distant candle.

He stared at that single flame that indicated he was not alone in this house. Tautness entered his back, and alertness charged his aura. She gathered her courage and advanced silently toward his back, her poker poised to fall.

He swerved just as she brought it down, and caught it

in his hand. Then in a blur he caught her too, swung her around, and thrust her toward the bed. Shawls flew away and she hurtled onto the mattress.

Breathless with terror, she stared up at him from where she sprawled on the coverlet. She gaped at him while he gazed down hard at her, the poker still gripped in his hand.

She barely breathed in the tense silence that followed. His gaze drifted over her nightdress, down to where its hem had billowed to reveal her bare legs.

He moved slightly. She tensed, ready to fight if she had to. His change in position allowed the candle's dim light to wash his face. She took in the handsome visage it revealed, and anger abruptly replaced her fear.

"*Mr. Albrighton*? What are you doing stealing into this house and frightening the life out of me!"

His dangerous scowl cleared. "I apologize, Miss Pennifold. I did not know you were here. I saw no lights or fires. It is an odd time for you to be visiting this property."

"An odd time for *me* to be visiting? Not so odd as your presence, sir. I own this house, after all. What is *your* purpose in being here? Theft?"

"Hardly theft, Miss Pennifold. As it happens, I live here."

M r. Albrighton placed more fuel on the fire in the library. He bent to a small cabinet and removed a decanter of spirits. He poured a scant inch in a tiny glass and carried it to where Celia sat bundled in the shawls on a sofa.

She had invited him out of her bedchamber immediately. Now here they were, he dressed for a night on the town and she still in her bed dress, and far too conscious of her dishabille.

"I do not need fortification, Mr. Albrighton. I am not a silly woman who faints at the slightest provocation."

He shrugged and downed the spirits himself. He settled into a chair near the fire. Its light flattered him, and suited the impression of mystery and danger he imparted, whether he intended it or not.

Celia had always thought Mr. Albrighton an annoyingly enigmatic man. He had revealed little of his inner self during those occasions when he visited her mother's parties. One could put most of the other men on this shelf or that, each plank labeled by personality and intentions. One never quite knew where to put Mr. Albrighton. Since he had been only in his middle twenties back then, she had found his ambiguity disconcerting, and his entire person too dramatic.

There was something to him that appeared warm, almost intimate, however, which contradicted and confused one's reactions even more. A depth in his eyes caused one to think he would understand one's hurts or problems even if the rest of the world did not. But there was also much to him that spoke of things dark and hard. As a girl she had decided he was too complicated and more than a little discomforting. As a result, they had rarely spoken beyond greetings, except once.

Now he sat in that chair like he had a right to be there. Her whole body remained tight from the shock of his intrusion, but he lounged like a country squire home after shooting quail. Furthermore, he claimed that he *did* have a right to be here.

She both believed him and didn't. That was the problem with Jonathan Albrighton. One never knew what one actually had in him.

The silence turned awkward. For her, not him. He appeared prepared to sit there without any conversation, altering the atmosphere to his liking, just gazing in her direction while the flames cast dancing reflections on his polished boots.

"You do appear familiar with the premises," she said. "However, my mother's solicitor said this house had no current tenants, so I know you are lying about living here."

"First you call me a thief, now a liar. It is fortunate that I do not take insult easily."

"Do not expect polite inquiries from me, sir. To my mind, I am speaking to a criminal until you convince me otherwise."

"Criminal now."

She could not tell if she had truly annoyed him or not. Nor did she much care either way.

"I did not take the entire house," he said. "Only one chamber, in the attic. I have not used it much these last years, but my lease was legal, I assure you, and for a ten-year duration."

She could believe the part about not using it much. He had a way of coming and going from town, as she recalled. He disappeared from Mama's gatherings for several months during the year she had lived with her mother, only to reappear, briefly, right before she left herself. She knew from Mama that he had gone again right after that break.

"You had already left your mother when this arrangement was made, and I doubt she thought it worth mentioning if you saw her again," he added.

"You let that chamber from *my mother*?"

"Yes. I knew her as a friend only, in case you are wondering."

"I am not wondering." Except she was, a little. Who wouldn't? He was a handsome man in a smoldering, dark way, and he cut a tall, very fine figure. Alessandra had not been indifferent to a man's appearance, and would have surely appreciated this one's. "I already knew you were not a patron. You attended some of her parties during that year I lived with her, but I know my mother's standards when it came to business."

"Are they your standards too?"

There was no tone of insult in his question. He posed it like he might inquire on her health.

She would not pretend with him. There was no point. He knew it all, she was sure. Why she had been in the house at Orchard Street for a year, and the reasons she had left.

"Even though I left my mother's house, I did not dispute the lessons she taught me about life. Her standards will be mine if I should ever hope to achieve a similar success and fame in her profession."

He accepted what she said, as if they indeed discussed only her health. His face, amiable in expression despite the way the firelight emphasized the elegant harshness of its well-formed features and deep-set eyes, displayed no reaction. Yet she felt an intensity of interest emanating from him, and that odd sense of intimacy that he provoked, inviting her to confide.

She stirred in response to his direct gaze. There was no mistaking the little twinges of arousal. They were not unlike her reactions to him when she was a girl, and still carried an edge of danger and fear.

She had been too young back then to comprehend what

all that meant. She had assumed sensual responses required the provocations of kisses and flattery and declarations of love. Only with maturity had she acknowledged the power of subtlety, distance, and even silence in such things.

It was in him too. Alessandra had given important lessons on seeing it, even when hidden. Her profession depended on recognizing a man's interest, even when he did not admit it to himself.

She pursued the only topic that mattered, and tried to ignore how they had become too aware of each other, and how it altered the light, the air—everything. "So you had one chamber above, you claim. For when you chose to use it, which was not often the last several years. Who lived in the rest of this house?"

"Alessandra did. Were you not aware of that?"

No, she was *not*.

"She would retreat to this house when she tired of the game," he said. "A few days, most times. As long as a few weeks in late summer when the city emptied."

Celia glared at him. She resented the calm way he imparted news of this secret part of her mother's life. This man knew more about her mother than she herself did. She found that unseemly, and unfair. Why should a man who was almost never in London—and not even a lover!— share a part of Alessandra that her own daughter had not known?

She reined in her temper. Her anger was grief speaking, she supposed. And some guilt and regrets too. She had not lived with Alessandra long enough to learn everything, after all. Her childhood had been spent in the country, not here, and she had only come up to town when she was sixteen. Their time together had been very brief.

"I want to see the document that says you let that room up there."

"It is buried in my trunk. I will bring it to you as soon as I am able."

"Is not your trunk above?"

"I am only recently returned to town. I left the trunk with some friends and have not retrieved it yet."

"If this is your London home, why would you leave your property with friends? I think you are feeding me a tall tale and assuming I am too stupid to know it is all false. I do not believe you lived here. I am not even sure she did. I think that you were spying around for something tonight, and are spinning a lie so I don't lay down information with the magistrate."

"Is there something worth spying for? I can't imagine what that would be. I would say your mother's life was an open book. More than most women's."

His charming, vague smile distracted her enough that she almost missed the fact he had not denied anything. Now that she remembered, Mr. Albrighton had a talent for dissembling most elegantly. He had a way of not answering questions, but evaded them so cleverly one almost did not notice.

"Have you also visited the house on Orchard Street in recent days?" she demanded.

"I have no right to enter that house. Why do you ask?"

Again, no denial. "Someone was there, perhaps today during the burial, or before. I visited the house with the executor this afternoon, after the funeral. Her papers were too neat. I had never seen my mother's drawers so tidy."

"Most likely the solicitor organized them as he took inventory. Lawyers are tidy sorts by nature."

It was a good answer, but a wrong one. Mr. Mappleton

had not yet been through the property when she noticed this, and he had even been the one to mention the missing accounts. She doubted Mr. Albrighton would ever admit to having entered that house illegally if he had, though. Nor, she admitted, would he have any reason to.

The chamber had grown warm during their conversation. She wished she could cast off both shawls. Instead she carefully peeled one away while she made sure the other covered her sufficiently.

He watched, ever so calmly. His gaze left her feeling as though she had just done something scandalous and risky and deliberately provocative.

"Mr. Albrighton, you may have the lease you claim, but you cannot stay here. I have taken residence myself, and do not want the intrusion of a tenant, and a male one at that. I am sure you understand and agree with me."

"I understand, I suppose, but I do not agree. As I said, I have a lease. Paid in advance."

"I will repay you for the remaining years." She trusted it would not be too much money. She did not like to be laying out any amount from what she had saved.

"I do not want repayment. I require a pied-à-terre in London and made arrangements with the owner of a quiet house on a quiet street for this one. I expect to use it when I am in town. I am in town now."

"You are an unwelcome complication, sir."

"I do not require your welcome, only my bed."

"Surely if you consider the matter from my prospect, you will understand that I cannot have—"

"You will barely know I am here. I use the garden entry and I go up the back stairs. I require little housekeeping and am very discreet. I daresay most of the neighbors have never seen me."

"It is safe to say that some have."

"It is common enough to let rooms in a house this size, in this neighborhood. It will not affect your reputation, if that is your concern. My presence up there will mean nothing more than it did when your mother was in residence."

Had he just implied that his presence here could not hurt the reputation of a woman already tarnished beyond hope due to being Alessandra's daughter? She could hardly blame him if he did mean that. It was the honest truth, and with Mama's death, notoriety had found the famous whore's daughter even in Daphne's country home where she had lived in obscurity.

"As I recall, your visits to London are often brief, sir. If I acquiesce to this, will you be in town long this time?"

"I expect to be here a fortnight at most. And you, Miss Pennifold—will you be in residence here long? Or are you returning to wherever you lived before this?"

"I plan to stay here permanently. I intend to have a business here."

"You will live all alone?"

"I expect to have some other women in residence within a week or so. The privacy and quiet you so crave will be a thing of the past if you continue here." She tried to appear very worldly indeed, to encourage that he hear more between the lines than she meant in truth. "I expect many visitors too. It could become quite noisy, even in the attics. Especially at night. You are sure to dislike the changes."

He let the insinuations hang there for a long count while he looked at her. She trusted that he was concluding the worst about this business, and that living here would be dreadful, and too scandalous.

"It is not what she intended for you," he finally said. "Although I suppose such a business is more practical, and potentially more secure. When do you intend to begin?"

"Soon. So soon that it is hardly worth your time settling in again. The wise course would be to—"

"You misunderstand me. I am wondering if awaiting that day will delay my departure much."

"Delay? I would think that learning of such a pending development would encourage you to leave, not to stay!"

"And yet your plan tempts me to dally at least until the launch of your new endeavor. That probably has something to do with how charming your feet look, peeking out from the hem of that bed dress."

She quickly jerked her feet back under the hem, but her feet had little to do with this. She never expected this man to be so bold in announcing his interest. But he had, and now here they were, in a chamber that all but shook from the special power that could flow between a man and a woman.

She suddenly felt small. Small and vulnerable, and naked to his dark gaze. She stood so she would at least be free to move. To run, if necessary, although she doubted he was dangerous in that way.

Unfortunately, he stood too. She wrapped the shawl around her like armor and tried to appear formidable. What a muddle she had made of this.

"As I explained, Mr. Albrighton, I hold to my mother's standards regarding a man's birth and wealth."

He strolled around her, too at ease for her taste, far too tall for comfort. She kept turning to keep him in view. He ended up not far from her, near a wall. He casually rested his shoulder against it and assumed a very relaxed stance.

"If you seek to achieve a similar fame and success, you

said. You just spoke of a less illustrious road in that profession. Or did I misunderstand?"

Was he teasing her? Calling her bluff? She suspected so, but could not be sure. Partly she could not tell because he flustered her badly now, standing this closely, his gaze very warm and familiar and almost beckoning her to intimate confidences. Mr. Albrighton was far too self-possessed to leer when broaching such a topic. She rather wished he would leer, though. She could put him in his place, then.

She tried to assume a certain hauteur, the way her mother could when called upon.

"No matter what road I choose, and what profession, you would still be unsuitable. Dallying will gain you nothing," she said.

"I do not agree. Dallying here, now, for a mere five minutes, has already gained me something."

"I do not see what it could be, besides my vexation with you."

"Do you not?" He smiled so subtly she wondered if she imagined it. He pushed off from the wall. She held her ground with difficulty and masked the way fear caused her breath to shorten. No, not fear. Excitement.

"It has gained me evidence that dallying more might gain me more, no matter how suitable or unsuitable I may be." He reached over suddenly, and laid two fingers on her lips. She almost jumped out of her skin. She felt her lips pulsing under the contact. "You are not so sophisticated that your reactions do not show, Miss Pennifold, and I see more than vexation. There may be gentlemen who would not speculate on the possibilities present in this chamber tonight, but I am not that virtuous."

That special tension tightened even more with his words. He had just bluntly acknowledged that which she thought it better to ignore. Their gazes met across his outstretched arm for too long. She feared he was correct, and that she was not sophisticated enough to hide the way she stirred inside.

His hand fell. He smiled, to himself this time. "I will leave you now. I will bolt the garden door before I go up. Sleep well, Miss Pennifold."

Chapter Three

Celia's suspicion that someone had searched Alessandra's other property was not good news for Jonathan. Nor was her announcement that she intended to live in this house, no matter how much he had enjoyed last night's little contest with her. He was still assessing how both revelations would affect his plans when he rose from bed the next day.

He *had* entered that house on Orchard Street, before coming back to this one. He had seen the tidiness to which Celia referred. If Celia was correct, and the other house had already been searched before either of them examined it, there might be a rival for the information that Edward sought. That rival might have less benign intentions than ensuring Alessandra's past remained in the past. Any fool hoping to blackmail her patrons might risk illegal entry to find evidence of their names.

Or—and he did not want to think it, but he had to consider the possibility—there could have indeed been traitorous acts, and the man involved needed to be sure that Alessandra had left no evidence that pointed to him.

Jonathan thought of the lovely blond woman sleeping down below. Desperate men did desperate things. If Celia should chance upon an intruder looking for hidden evidence, or if someone concluded she knew too much about her mother's doings, she could be in danger. Just as well that he would be living here, then. She may not want his protection, but she might need it for a while anyway.

There was a different possible reason for another's interest in Alessandra's papers. It could have been someone hoping to ensure Jonathan himself would not find evidence that set him on a path of revenge regarding those events in Cornwall five years ago. It went without saying he would follow that evidence wherever it led if he came upon it.

His mind darkened as it always did whenever he remembered that disaster and its deadly outcome. Today it was worse because vivid images from that night had come to him in a waking dream, provoked no doubt by Edward's mention of it in the carriage. That betrayal had missed its mark, and instead caused the death of an innocent lad to whom he had paid a few shillings to guide his path along an unfamiliar section of coast.

He had killed enough in his life. He had seen others die too, some of them comrades. Yet nothing had prepared him for carrying that boy home to his mother, and seeing a grief so profound that it did not even care about blame.

Someone still needed to answer for that night. He really didn't give a damn if he found a list of Alessandra's lovers, or if someone else did and published it. He had agreed to this little mission for himself, and for the odd chance that he would finally be able to settle an old score.

As for Celia, this was another property that required a thorough search, but he could hardly do it in front of her nose. Last night he had given most of the chambers up here in the attic a quick inspection, but one had been locked. Now he could not break through the door across the passageway without Celia guessing just who had forced his way in.

No water waited outside his chamber door when he opened it. He thought it unlikely that his landlady would see to the linens either. Celia would make no efforts to accommodate his presence in her house, no matter what possibilities had been silently humming in the library last night. He judged that not only her desire to inconvenience him was at work.

He did not know where she had spent the years after she left her mother, but nothing about her suggested she had gone into service. The possibility existed that Celia did not know anything about housekeeping.

Left to do for himself, he went down the servant stairs. No sounds came to his ears as he passed the second level where she had her own chamber, nor as he descended farther. Only as he emerged from the stairwell did he see her, sitting in that bright back chamber with a sketchbook on her lap, concentrating hard on the windows and space and the drawing she made.

She wore a primrose-hued dress. Along with her hair and fair skin, she brightened the chamber like a beam of sunshine. She had appeared beautiful in the light of the fire last night, but now the sight of her made his breath catch.

She would be wasted as the abbess of a brothel. He believed that her insinuations about that last night had only been another attempt to encourage him to leave, but he could not know for sure.

She startled when he greeted her. Her blue eyes raked him from head to toe but she did not react to his dishabille. Since it wasn't his fault he had not shaved and wore little more than shirt and trousers, that was only fair. Yet he could not block the memory of a golden girl in her mother's other home, and imagine the lessons that Alessandra must have been imparting that year. Hiding any sense of fluster when a man looked like this was probably one of them.

"I came for some water to wash." The excuse sounded stupid to his own ears. The fact would be obvious enough when he returned with a bucket from the garden.

"Were you expecting me to bring it up to you?" Her tone implied honest curiosity.

"Of course not. You are not a servant."

"No, I am not. Certainly not yours."

"Linens, however, are customary when a single chamber is let." He had thought to put off this demand, but her resentful tone goaded him a bit. "I said that I required little housekeeping, but I do need bedsheets."

She just looked at him, then returned to her drawing. He went to the well and drew the water. Cold water. He carried it back, debating whether to suffer its chill or lose the time to wait for it to warm near his fireplace.

"Will you be going out today?" Her question found him at the bottom of the stairs.

"That is likely. In an hour, for a while."

"Good." She did not look up from the drawing.

Her distracted, dismissive "good" provoked the devil in him. He set down the bucket and strolled into the chamber until he could look over her shoulder at the drawing.

It showed the chamber itself, in good perspective, with

a system of shelves near the windows and low trays on the floor.

"You inherited your mother's talent," he said, while his gaze shifted to the intricate way she had dressed her golden hair. The angle of her head allowed tiny, errant wisps to show, like little feathers splayed against the nape of her elegant neck. He stood close enough to smell her lavender scent, and to move those tiny hairs when he exhaled.

Her pencil stopped on the page. She looked up at him, quickly enough that she noticed his eyes were no longer on the drawing, but on her.

Her color rose, but not too much. She glanced in his eyes for an instant. That quick, penetrating look acknowledged what he had been doing, and why, and displayed no shock or dismay. And so, as with last night, he did not try to hide his appreciation and interest the way he normally would.

Speculations about the possibilities began spinning in his mind. Pleasant ones. Erotic ones. Too complicated, though. She was beautiful and desirable, and the interest was mutual—that was certain—despite her feigned indifference. But whether she followed her mother's path, or indeed started a brothel, or just lived in virtuous isolation, she was not for him.

She returned her attention to her drawing, as if she had reached the same conclusion. "You knew her well, if you know she had a talent with art. I only realized it myself the last few months I lived with her back then."

"One only has to see one drawing to know if there is talent."

"And you only saw one of hers? Or did you see more?"

He hesitated. He was long practiced in revealing as

little as possible about most things, especially if they mattered to someone else and touched on his missions. Even casual comments could come back to haunt one and lead to problems.

"She would draw and paint when she came here," he said. "So I saw a few more than one over time."

"Are they here? These drawings?"

"I expect so."

She gazed around the chamber, and toward the rooms invisible to her beyond and above. "Perhaps I will see them too, when I have time to investigate the contents of this house. First I must see to other things, however. Like this chamber."

He almost asked what she intended for the chamber, and all those shelves. Instead he returned to his bucket, and mounted the steps.

Investigate. It had been an odd word for her to use. Whatever her reason for that kind of examination, it would be wise for him to make sure he investigated first.

Boot steps sounded in the stairwell, getting fainter as Mr. Albrighton carried his water to his chamber.

She had hoped that upon realizing she would do nothing to make him comfortable, he would take himself off to someplace where at least basic service would be provided. Instead he had not appeared to mind doing for himself this morning, and had continued to show more interest in her than was proper. He had also deliberately engaged her in conversation, as if to prove he could.

She suspected that if she were too obvious in her efforts to encourage his removal, he might deliberately stay.

He might decide it was a contest that he of course had to win.

She probably had achieved nothing by being rude this morning, and perhaps had only goaded him on in his plan to dally. A little more subtlety might be in order.

She did not like being rude and, she suspected, she had not even been very good at it. She certainly had not held the pose once he entered this sitting room. But then it was hard to act like a person hardly existed when that person made one's blood race when he stood right next to you, and his mere breath sent delicious shivers down your back.

She pictured him up there, waiting for that cold water to heat in a small attic chamber. How long had he been using that room while in London this time? Not long, she guessed, if he did not even have linens for his bed and washing.

She set aside her sketch and went up to her own chamber. She pulled cloths out of the wicker linen chest and made a stack of sheets and towels. She needed to protect whatever mattress was up there, after all. Nor did she want him dripping water all over the floor. Giving him linens was not actually accommodating his presence in this house, or acting like his servant. If she made him live like a prisoner, that chamber would eventually be as fetid as a prison cell.

She did not actually tiptoe up the front stairs to the attic, but she tried to make no noise. She would leave the linens outside the door and be gone before he knew they were there.

The attic had a long passageway. Three doors gave off one side, and two off the other. Three of the doors were open. She listened for any sounds coming across those three thresholds.

Nothing. Treading softly, she aimed for the other end of the passage, where two closed doors faced each other. As she passed the open chambers, she glanced in. All were furnished with simple beds and wardrobes. If she were of a mind to have more tenants, there was space enough for them.

She approached the top of the back stairs. As she did, she realized that one of those doors was not totally closed after all. A thin beam of light fell into the passage, indicating it was ajar. Cold air flowed out of the chamber too. No noise, however. No movements.

Angling her head, she spied around the doorjamb. For the briefest instant her gaze took in the open window and a desk piled with papers and books. Then Mr. Albrighton completely arrested her attention.

He stood with his back to her, facing the window, naked to the waist and with his hair still unbound. She followed the tapered line from his shoulders to his hips, captivated by the honed, lean strength that had been hidden by garments.

His arms extended straight out from his body on either side. In each hand he grasped a massive, heavy book. The strain of holding those books like that showed. His muscles had hardened from the stress into tight, defined, masculine forms, as crisp as if chiseled by a sculptor. His hands displayed an alluring strength as they reacted to the weight they bore.

She forgot her intentions to drop the linens and scoot away. She forgot *everything* while she watched him, fascinated. How long had he been standing like that? How long did he intend to continue? The books must grow heavier with each passing moment. They were of good size and probably close to twenty pounds each to start.

He slowly raised both arms until the books met over his head, then slowly, painfully, lowered them again. The muscles in his shoulders and arms corded in resistance. Then those in his back, and even, perceptibly, the ones in his hips. Even with the window open and the cold entering, a fine sheen of sweat showed on his skin.

He looked magnificent. Beautiful, really. She flushed deeply, thoroughly, in ways the cold breeze could not cure. Twinges of arousal moved in her like strings on an instrument being mischievously plucked.

He raised the books once more. They began their descent. This time they did not stop but continued the arc until he held them down by his thighs.

He turned around.

He saw her, of course. She had moved to get a better view through the opening. He looked right at her and it was clear he knew she had been watching him. And why. Dark amusement showed in his eyes, along with a dangerous awareness that she was bedazzled. She practically heard him debating what to do about that.

She forgot to be embarrassed. Forgot how to speak. She just stood there, holding the linens, looking at him because she could not look away. The same strength showed in his chest, and even now, with the stress of the books relieved, his body possessed those tight, hard lines.

"You are allowed to come in," he said. He dropped the books on the bed. She saw that it had a blanket at least. "It is your property."

"I—I brought some—" She lifted her arms.

He made no effort to come and get them from her. He just stood there, half naked, watching her to see—what?

She collected herself enough to pretend more composure than she felt. She stepped over the threshold and dropped the stack of cloth on the bed. "You will have to make it yourself, though."

"Of course."

She should leave now. Run for her life. Only he stood a mere foot away now and, dear heavens, he was something to behold. She felt he had pinned her in place with some invisible power that sapped her ability to will her legs to move.

She made a display of gazing around the chamber like the property owner she was, but his body was never really out of sight. Again she noted all those books and papers. This time she also saw the pistols. Three of them, lined up on the desk, along with the implements to clean them. What could one man need with three pistols ready for firing?

He noticed her interest. "They are not loaded."

"I suppose that is good to know. I thought perhaps you planned to kill someone."

"Not today."

He was teasing her. She hoped. Maybe not.

He seemed to see the question in her. "I am not dangerous to you."

She was still flustered enough to respond too pointedly. "Aren't you? I think you are."

"I suppose I am." He gestured to the pistols. "But not in that way."

No, not in that way. She struggled to shake off his power, so maybe he would not be dangerous to her in any way right now. It felt like lifting herself, hand over hand, up a dangling rope.

"You should have thrown on a shirt when you saw me," she said.

He stepped closer. She would have jumped out of her skin if she could move. His fingers were on her chin now.

Firm ones, a little rough, holding her, his dark eyes looking into hers deeply. Too deeply. Warmth and too much knowing in his gaze, beckoning in a subtle but ruthless seductive lure.

"You spent a year in Alessandra's home. You are no blushing innocent. Do not expect me to stand on ceremony as if you are. Do not expect me to treat you like an ignorant child instead of a desirable woman."

Her cheeks quivered from the contact of his hand. A hundred tiny thrills flowed through her skin and down her neck. She could only look up at him, at those dark eyes so close to hers. He was going to kiss her, she was sure. She should back away and cast him off. She should—

His hand left her. He stepped over to the fireplace and lifted the bucket of water. "You can stay if you like. Or you can run away if you believe you must." He poured the water into the wash bowl. He looked over his shoulder at her. "I should warn you, though. If you are still here when I finish with this, I will not let you leave soon after."

Finding a shred of sense, she left. Not soon enough, though. Not before she saw the way the sodden cloth he used to wet his skin sent rivulets of water snaking sensually over those muscles.

Celia's "good" upon hearing he intended to go out led Jonathan to conclude that his own investigating would have to wait for another day. He assumed she was glad he would be out of the house because she intended to stay within.

She might want no contact with him at all if he kept insinuating his inclination to seduce her. That was not part of any clever strategy on his end, however, much as he wanted to tell himself it had been. In truth his advances were impulses that had nothing to do with his mission, even if they might ultimately help it.

As he rode his horse west an hour later, he discovered he had miscalculated Celia's intentions for the day. Ahead of him he saw a cabriolet with a chestnut horse. The blond woman driving it wore a dress the same primrose color as Celia had worn today, beneath a lilac pelisse.

Nor did she wear a hat or bonnet, despite the crisp weather. Instead her golden locks had been dressed expertly in a style that he also recognized from the morning.

He slowed his own progress and followed, wondering where she went, knowing that he should return to the house at once and take advantage of her absence. The hair and back compelled his attention, however. He admired her poise, and enjoyed the secret glimpses he had of her face whenever she turned a corner.

She drove through backstreets, and eventually turned down a mews west of Hanover Square. He remained at their end, and watched while she stopped her little carriage, handed the reins to a man, and disappeared into a garden.

He paced his horse down the mews to where she had stopped. The garden in question surprised him. He knew this house very well. It was not one where he expected Alessandra's daughter to be received.

"Spying on me, Albrighton?"

The question emerged at the same time the man did from the carriage house on the other side of the mews. The man wiped his hands with a handkerchief while his deep blue eyes gazed up at Jonathan expectantly.

"If I ever do spy on you, Hawkeswell, you will never know it."

"You overestimate your subtlety. What the hell are you doing lurking at my back garden gate?"

This was one of those times when the less said, the better. "Cutting through."

The Earl of Hawkeswell smiled, which did little to soften the hard, critical expression in his eyes. "Now you overestimate my stupidity. Since you have not asked why I played groom to that carriage and horse, instead of allowing a servant to do so, I assume you know who was holding the ribbons. My reason for excessive discretion is not what you may think."

Jonathan experienced sharp annoyance at Hawkeswell's assumption that anyone would assume Celia's visiting here was for an assignation with the earl himself.

"I had no thoughts at all on the matter," he said belatedly, after he conquered the spike in his temper. "I was only passing through, I assure you."

"The hell you were." Hawkeswell pulled open the gate. "Tie up your horse and come along. I am being imprisoned by my wife in the morning room. You can have coffee with me."

Jonathan dismounted, tied his horse, and followed Hawkeswell into the garden. Its paths wound through attractive plantings, each of which presented itself as a private retreat. Finally they passed a conservatory, and mounted a few steps to the terrace. His host led him through doors directly into the chamber that served as the morning room.

Coffee waited. They sat on upholstered chairs, drinking as if they were merely old friends seeing each other after some time. The mood, however, was hardly that amiable.

"Our visitor is my wife Verity's friend," Hawkeswell said, breaking the silence. "Also a friend of Summerhays's wife Audrianna. They all three used to live out in

Middlesex with a woman named Daphne Joyes. The three of them are all in the library, talking about fashions and whatnot."

"The need for your discretion regarding this call is understandable, then. It is also unfair, but such is the way of the world."

"So you do know who she is. Damned if I did until recently. Even Verity did not know her history until the death of Alessandra Northrope. Imagine our surprise when the notice in one scandal sheet made reference to a daughter named Celia Pennifold. I should have insisted that Verity end the friendship at once, of course. But . . ." He shrugged.

But the Earl of Hawkeswell cared too much for his wife to command it, and his wife cared too much for Celia to make the break on her own. Jonathan had never met Lady Hawkeswell, but her loyalty spoke well of her, even if it was probably foolish.

"I am convinced that there is no reason to think that Miss Pennifold is like her mother," Hawkeswell continued confiding, the way so many others had confided over time.

At least this man knew to whom he revealed his thoughts. They had been at university together, and Hawkeswell was one of Jonathan's few friends, such as they were. Time, place, and duties had made the best of that friendship only old memories, but it still stood for something, in Jonathan's mind at least.

"It was generous of you to agree to allow the friendship to continue."

"Generous? Allow?" Hawkeswell laughed. "Hell, you don't know much about marriage, do you?"

"Not the good ones, no."

Hawkeswell turned his mind and attention away from

the topic, and onto his guest. Jonathan's instincts in turn grew alert, from long practice.

"I don't expect you will tell me why you were following her."

"If you are determined to think I was, just attribute it to a man distracted from his day's plans by a lovely lady." It was, he admitted, the whole truth.

Hawkeswell found that amusing. "One of your answers that says nothing. That means there must be a very good reason. One of your missions?"

"That idea is ridiculous."

"Indeed. Which is not to say it is wrong. After all, you are here and no longer up north in Staffordshire. There must be a reason for that too."

"I missed town life, just as you do."

"And you had also finished up there, hadn't you? I don't expect you to thank me and Summerhays and Castleford for our help."

Hawkeswell referred to a mission Jonathan had recently completed, the one in which Uncle Edward had accused him of too much independence. Hawkeswell's untimely and unexpected arrival in Staffordshire last autumn had almost ruined an investigation that had been months in the making. Jonathan did not mind that Hawkeswell and the other two men had ultimately solved the mystery more thoroughly than he had himself hoped to accomplish. He just did not want to talk about it. He could not discuss his work for the Home Office, or even admit he investigated for it in the first place.

"Was it you three who learned the truth behind that intrigue? Then, by all means, thank you."

"As if you didn't know." Hawkeswell dropped his probing, fortunately. "Will you be in town long?"

"Perhaps a month."

"Then we will all dine together. We will tell you how clever we were in exposing that crime, and you can pretend you are ignorant of the tale."

There it was again. Time to depart. Jonathan set down his coffee cup and rose to his feet. "I must take my leave now. It was good seeing you, even unexpectedly."

"If you are following Miss Pennifold around town, Albrighton, I expect that we will meet unexpectedly again."

Chapter Four

Late that afternoon, Celia paced through the elaborate drawing room of her mother's house on Orchard Street in Mayfair. Portly, balding Mr. Mappleton, the executor, detailed the bad news he had only outlined when they had met briefly yesterday, right before the funeral.

"As I indicated, this house must be sold, to pay off her debts. It and its contents should satisfy most of them. The coach will need to go too, but I calculate that you will be left with the cabriolet and the chestnut mare."

"And the house on Wells Street?" She prayed his final reckoning had not shown the need to sell that too.

"It still appears that will be spared. However, if any more debts emerge—well, as I explained before . . ." Mr. Mappleton patted his forehead with a handkerchief. Informing heirs that little would in fact be inherited distressed him. "Not much of a legacy, I am afraid. As her solicitor, I did advise less extravagance, I want you to know. Frequently."

"Please do not feel guilty for a situation not at all of your making. Nor should you think that my mother ignored your advice. However, her profession required much of that extravagance. Maintaining appearances are as important to a woman like my mother as to a duchess."

Celia examined the expensive raw silks at the windows, and the classical style of the furniture. A careful composition of blues and creams, each item had been chosen to reflect good taste so the gentlemen who visited would feel at home. There were important illusions to be maintained.

Nothing had changed in this chamber since she abandoned this house, and her mother, five years ago. She and Alessandra had met on occasion during their estrangement, but never here. Celia had not entered this house again until she came during her mother's final days.

"Is this property already in the hands of an estate agent, Mr. Mappleton?"

"I thought to take care of that after informing you of the particulars. I will come tomorrow and do an inventory, and see that full value is attained in the disposal of the property."

She paused her stroll near a mahogany table with a Chinese vase on it. She stood now in the very spot she had been when Anthony told her, gently but firmly, that she had misunderstood his intentions.

She had thought he meant marriage when he spoke of being together forever. She had thought he would save her. She had been a fool.

No, not a fool. Young and in love, but not a fool. Too innocent still, despite all her mother's lessons; that was all. One cannot teach experience about human nature, or the hard ways that the world forces compromises.

She closed her eyes and waited to experience again the desolation of that day. It did not come back, except as a small echo. She had long ago healed. Five years living in Daphne's house near Cumberworth had provided time for her to grow up.

She did not even blame Anthony anymore, and had not for years. Of course a man of good family and fortune did not marry the daughter of Alessandra Northrope. There were rules about such things. Celia not only knew them now, but she also accepted their power.

"Since the house is not yet for sale, I want to go through my mother's personal belongings more carefully than when we were here yesterday, Mr. Mappleton. I will not remove anything of value. However, if there are private papers and such, letters for example, I will take them with me. Is that permitted?"

"If you give your word that you will not strip the premises, that should be acceptable." He managed only a crooked smile at his own attempt at humor. "I have still found no account book among the business papers waiting for me in the library. If you come upon it, please leave it out and visible so we can ascertain just what is what."

She agreed to keep her eyes open for any accounts. "Will it be necessary for you to stay with me? I would like to say good-bye to her alone. The burial was a strange and foreign experience. This was where she lived her life, and breathed her last, and it is here that her spirit lingers."

Mr. Mappleton gazed at her so soberly that she worried he would weep. "I expect that I need not interfere with that good-bye. May I say, Miss Pennifold, that your mother was a wonderful, brilliant woman. If I did not attend the funeral to say my own good-bye, I hope that you understand that in no way reflects the esteem I had for her."

"I understood your absence, Mr. Mappleton. I saw no insult in it. Nor would she have done so. I thank you for your kind words."

He took his leave. As soon as she heard the door close, she went up to her mother's bedchamber.

She fought back the nostalgia provoked by the familiar scents and space. Most of the lessons had taken place here, in the privacy of this apartment. Mama would recline on that golden silk chaise longue and explain the world's ways, and so much more. It had seemed natural when the talk had moved from how to dress and how to entertain to how to touch and other intimate secrets.

More recent memories forced the old ones into a cloud, however. This bedchamber had also been where Mama had lain ill. There had not been much talking the last weeks, but even so Mama had managed a few more lessons, and voiced her belief that her daughter should take her place. She had regaled Celia with stories of glory, of triumphs and fame. She had extracted a promise that Celia would at least think hard about what she rejected before turning her back forever on the place waiting for her.

Celia checked the drawer in the small writing table. The contents were not notable in themselves, but their arrangement had made her pause yesterday, when she and Mr. Mappleton had done a quick search for those accounts.

Alessandra was not one to stack letters and papers like this. The spaces and trunks not cared for by her lady's maid were usually a tossed miscellany.

She stuffed the letters in her reticule, then went to the dressing room and opened the wardrobes. Alessandra's magnificent garments, all from the best modistes, shone like so many large flowers in the afternoon light. They, like everything else of value, would be sold now.

The dressing table also displayed uncharacteristic neatness, but then, Mama had not used it in several weeks. Its few drawers were neat as well, which was less expected. Celia examined the jewels within, and wondered if any of them had been gifts from her unknown father. None of their boxes gave her a clue.

The apartment offered no help with learning his identity that she could see. She ventured up to the attic, and found the storage rooms there. To her disappointment, they contained very little besides old furniture. One trunk held nothing but garments at least twenty years out of style. She had hoped, even assumed, that her mother's history would be evidenced in this house, documented by papers or objects.

She descended to the library and sat down at the elegant, inlaid secretaire.

She opened drawers to find little of interest besides a collection of old fashion plates, but again she noted the neat organization.

Had her mother done this, to get her affairs in order? Perhaps she did not want her solicitor to see disarray when he came to do his inventory after her death. It was one explanation, and the most likely one. It would have had to have been before Celia came home, and implied her mother knew the end was near.

However, Celia still could not shake the sense that someone besides Mr. Mappleton and herself had been in this house since her mother's death, and also examined the contents of her mother's private property.

Maybe it had been her father. If he did not want his identity known, he may have come, or sent someone else, to make sure no evidence of him would be found in this house. It saddened her that he might have gone to such efforts to thwart her attempts to learn the truth. He probably thought she would demand money or use his name badly if she knew him. The truth was she desired only to fill a void that she had carried in her soul all her life.

She continued searching the secretaire's drawers and nooks. When she poked deeply into one of the cubbyholes, her fingertips touched something. She extracted a folded paper with her name on it.

Curious, she opened it.

My dear Celia,

If you have found this, no doubt you are searching for money or jewels or, perhaps, evidence of his name. I can save you considerable time. You will find nothing here of value, and learning your father's identity will bring you no good.

Maintaining myself in the necessary style quite depleted the gifts I received over the years. As I have often said to you, your real legacy is in your education, not coin. You are more lovely than I, and more amiable, and you sing like an angel. You have already proven that you can fend for yourself. How you choose to fend in the future is your decision alone. I do not worry about you, and that is a great consolation to me.

Please know that except for one ill-advised affair of the heart, you were the only person I ever loved. It is my hope that you come home before this illness takes me, but if you did not, I understand.

Mama

She gazed at the letter. While she traced the elegant penmanship with her fingers, the grief that had eluded her for days finally shattered her heart. Her eyes burned with tears.

She *had* come home, briefly, finally. How terrible it would have been to read this letter if she had not.

She bent low over her palms and the letter itself, and cried out her good-bye.

"You must admit that my plan is a good one, Daphne. It will permit the business to grow with less burden to you," Celia said two days later.

Daphne pondered the offer that had just been made. Distraction claimed her gray eyes, but her delicate, flawless face remained serene below her simply dressed pale hair.

"The sense of your plan does not elude me. I had never thought to have a partner in The Rarest Blooms; that is all. I also thought I was bringing you here to stay for several days only, while you decided what to do with this property. However, now it sounds as if you intend to take permanent residence."

They stood in a back chamber of Alessandra's house on Wells Street. Sunlight poured in its southern exposure, emphasizing the translucence of Daphne's pale skin. Even on overcast days, this sitting room would be bright. And, as Daphne had noted that first day and Celia had clearly seen for herself, the windows and exposure made this chamber perfect for plants.

In the last year Daphne's trade, The Rarest Blooms, had prospered. Now some of the best houses in Mayfair contracted with Daphne to provide plants and flowers from her gardens and greenhouses near Cumberworth on a regular basis.

Transporting all that vegetation had become a hard chore, however. If there were an outpost of the business here in London, where the wagons could deposit blooms and greenery, the orders could be dispersed with less trouble.

"This chamber would be warm enough to hold plants for a few days, even in winter. Cut flowers could reside in the cool larder and basement in summer," Celia said.

"I agree that this property will meet our needs. If I hesitate, it is because I do not want you to assume the risk of a partnership," Daphne said. "We could do the same thing without that."

"I would prefer if you accepted the money I saved from my allowance while my mother was alive, and made me a partner. Even if I only have a small percentage, it will give me an income, which is what I need if I am going to live here. You will have the use of this house and I will see to the actual delivery of the plants."

Daphne lowered herself into one of the cane chairs. Normally she remained a carefully composed and beautiful portrait, but now her brow puckered and her eyes clouded.

"It is not your proposal that I resist, Celia. My mind knows it is a good one. My heart, however—" She gazed up sadly. "You are determined to leave us for good, then?"

Celia stepped around the chair, bent, and embraced Daphne's shoulders from behind. She laid her cheek against her dear friend's cool face. "I have been dependent on you too long. One year turned to three, and three to five. I will forever be grateful for the home that you provided, but it is time for me to make my own way."

"You are really doing this because of the gossip. I do not care what anyone says and I will not allow you to—"

"You cannot change the world, Daphne. Your business will continue being harmed as long as I am known to live and work with you. Our partnership will be a quiet one, and preserve both your trade and the reputation of your household, while it provides me with a living."

Daphne did not answer, and Celia knew her friend still fretted. Daphne did not like accommodating injustice.

"I am three and twenty, Daphne. I have this house now, and should return to the world anyway. I would have done this even if my name had never been linked to Alessandra's in the death notices. We will remain close in every other way, however."

"If The Rarest Blooms should fail, you might lose this house."

"We will not fail. We will flourish."

Daphne rested her hand upon Celia's embracing arm. Celia could not see her friend's face regain its composure, but she felt it within her embrace.

"It would be much easier to have one place to bring all the plants for dispersal," Daphne said.

Celia skipped around the chair, took Daphne's hands, and pulled her up. "You will not regret this. Neither of us will. You can take my investment and build another hothouse and we can sell fruit we grow in it out of season for ridiculous prices. We can bring in the wagon when there are extra blooms and sell to the girls at Covent Garden. We can—"

Daphne patted Celia's cheek. "First Audrianna left, then Verity, now you. I fear being all alone, Celia, and it was that which argued against your fine plan."

"We will see each other so often it will be as if I never left, and you still have Katherine and Mrs. Hill there."

"I suppose you are correct." Daphne picked up her

reticule. "I should go home to them now. I will write to my solicitor about this partnership and have it done as quickly as the settlement of your mother's estate permits."

Celia walked with her to the front door of the house. Daphne paused there. "I accept your reasons for living here, but I do not like your being alone, Celia. I wish I had brought my pistol and could leave it with you."

"I will not be alone for long, and I will be safe for the short while that I am." She felt a little guilty not telling Daphne about Mr. Albrighton. The revelation would lead only to more questions than could be answered, however.

Daphne departed with a kiss. Celia watched her step up into the gig.

Celia suspected that soon it would probably not be only Katherine and Mrs. Hill at the country property where The Rarest Blooms was housed. Daphne had a habit of finding and taking in stray women of ambiguous respectability and histories.

No doubt she would find more of them, although Celia sometimes thought it would be better if Daphne did not. At seven and twenty, it might be time for Daphne to step out of that sanctuary herself.

"Are you sure that you want the shelf like this, Miss Pennifold? It will be odd."

Thomas, a lad of fifteen, held the board for the second shelf, frowning at how the stepped levels in this structure would face the windows and not the chamber's space. This despite Celia explaining its purpose and showing him the drawing.

"Just like that, Thomas. That way the warmth and light from the higher plants will not shadow the lower ones."

He shrugged, and nailed the plank into place.

In the last few days Celia had made herself familiar to the shops in the neighborhood through her patronage, and had let it be known she had a bit of work for a boy who knew carpentry. Thomas's father, who owned a draper's shop, had been glad to lend him for the work.

Celia noted how Thomas used more nails for the plank than she had planned. She had bought sparingly and would have to get more. While she calculated how many, subtle noises up above told her that Mr. Albrighton was moving about.

He had insisted she would barely be aware of his existence. She was discovering, however, that his presence in this house could not be ignored. She might not see him often, but he was very much *here*.

She knew, for example, that he was above most of the time during the days. She would hear his footfalls making impressions in the floorboards. They served as little reminders that she did not enjoy either complete privacy or total isolation.

When she did see him, the experience contained a degree of intimacy that could not be avoided. They cohabited in the same house, after all. Their spirits shared this space even if their bodies rarely occupied the same chamber. And he had touched her twice now. That was like spilling oil that could never be mopped up completely again.

Every morning he came down to fetch his own water around ten o'clock. She had taken to listening for his steps on the stairs. After the first day he was never again in such dishabille, but he was never entirely dressed yet either. No cravat, of course, since he had not yet shaved. No waistcoat either. He would don a frock coat, however, so that he appeared only halfway disrespectable.

There was much of the bedchamber in the way he appeared at ten o'clock. Hair long and unbound, mussed and free, neck exposed, and new beard shadowing his jaws— even his very polite greetings unsettled her because he looked like that. His appearance reminded her that he had been close nearby while she had lain in her bed, both comforted by the safety his presence brought and dismayed by her awareness of him.

The steps sounded a bit louder. He would be making his little journey to the garden well very soon. He did not appear to mind the inconveniences of being a tenant here. Her hope that he would, and would leave as a result, was not bearing any fruit.

"I need more nails, Thomas. I misjudged how many you will use. Here is some money. Please go and buy twenty more from Mr. Smith."

Thomas set down his hammer. He held out his young, calloused hand for the money, then walked out of the chamber with the loose, gangling stride of a colt.

No sooner had he gone than the boots came down the stairs. Celia directed her mind to what color to paint the shelves. Green? White? She forced her thoughts away from how her blood thrummed with each footfall.

She had come to look forward to Mr. Albrighton's rare visibility, she realized to her chagrin. She wanted him gone but also did not. She did not mind nearly enough that he foiled her little plots to encourage his removal. She enjoyed their brief conversations and how sensual and dangerous he looked before dressing for town.

She laughed at herself. This silly anticipation was the sign of a woman too much alone. She would have to see to hiring a housekeeper soon, if only so she did not grow dependent on such insignificant congress as this.

"You are building something, I see." He stood at the
threshold, gazing at the two lower shelves. He walked
over and lifted the hammer. "Are you doing it yourself?"

"I hired a boy. I just sent him for more nails. Did the
hammering wake you?" She had let Thomas start at dawn,
specifically to discomfort Mr. Albrighton.

"No. I rise early."

"And do what?"

"If you are curious, you are welcome to come up and
see. I do not think you have set foot on that level since
your first morning here."

The memory of that morning flashed in her head, and
she felt her face warming. She had not forgotten how
badly she had acquitted herself then, or how mesmerized
she had been.

"I have been too busy." She gestured toward the shelves.

"Ah. I thought perhaps I had frightened you."

"Why would I be afraid of you?"

He shrugged. "Some women are."

Maybe they were afraid because of the way he was
looking at one woman right now. Her blood raced faster
from how his warm eyes gazed into hers.

She should not allow him to fluster her. That was his
intention. It amused him to tease her about that day. "Perhaps they are afraid because of your hair. It is so unfashionable as to speak of a reckless streak in you."

"Do you want me to cut it? I would not want you
thinking me reckless."

"Of course you would. But do not cut it on my account.
How a tenant's hair is dressed does not signify in my busy
life. I daresay even if you did cut it, I wouldn't notice."

"You wound me, Miss Pennifold. Here I was dreaming
that you waited to greet me every morning."

She felt her face warming again. He left her vexed that he had guessed that, and carried his bucket out the garden door.

He was correct. She had been avoiding the attic level of the house because he was there. What a conceited man to assume that, however. She would make it a point to go there soon, now that she had settled in. She needed to see what of her mother's property might be up there, in those chambers used for reasons besides housing Mr. Albrighton.

She watched him walk to the back of the garden and around a shrubbery, to where the necessary could be found. Then she spied his dark hair at the well. Bucket in hand, walking with a gait so smooth and fluid that the water did not slosh, he came back up the garden path, lost in his thoughts, ignorant of her scrutiny.

He was a handsome man; that was certain. Dangerous still, somehow, in the intangible depths he seemed to possess. The intimacy of an old friend waited in his warm eyes and playful teasing, however. It beckoned so effectively that she had to remind herself he was really a stranger.

Nor did it go both ways. For all their warmth and familiar lights, those eyes revealed nothing of the mind behind them.

Well, not nothing. The male thoughts were visible. She had seen the low burn of desire just now, set aside but still there. Not only *her* blood raced when their gazes connected.

He was good at hiding those lights. She always saw them, however, flickering through him and into the air at her. She saw them and felt them. She knew about male desire in all its forms and manifestations, and could sense it the way some people could smell rain on its way.

She had been taught by an expert to know it, feel it, and use it to her own benefit, after all.

Thirty minutes after Mr. Albrighton had gone above, a commotion poured into the house from the street. Shouting and whistles broke the day's peace.

Celia strode to the front sitting room and looked out. Thomas stood in the street, face red and body tense, surrounded by other lads. It was not clear if he wanted to fight or cry.

"In service to her, ya say," one of his tormenters taunted. "Or was that *servicing* her?" He roared at his own joke and his friends joined in.

"You've caught a fine one there, Tom boy," another teased. "Her mother was the expensive sort, we hear. Fancy carriages and such. I don't think you've got it in ya yet to appreciate such as her. You might need some help there." He wiggled his eyebrows and grinned lewdly.

They continued taunting Tom, not letting him out of the circle. It was just boys being what they were, but Celia's heart sank and thickened.

Someone in this neighborhood had realized who she was. Word had spread. Now everyone knew the daughter of the famed Alessandra Northrope lived among them. Everything would change now.

She closed her eyes and tried to conquer the desolation that hollowed her out. She had known for years that she was vulnerable to cruel judgments merely by her birth. She had never before actually experienced it, though. Certainly not while she lived with Daphne.

Not even while she lived with Mama, now that she thought about it. She had known it was happening while they rode the carriage through the park back then, but she had not actually seen it. However, Mama had warned that she would someday witness the scorn firsthand. Celia just had not anticipated how the reality would make her breathless from dismay.

Had Alessandra used a different name when she visited the shops here? Maybe she had never walked among these people at all, but only stayed in this house.

The ruffians began pushing Tom this way and that, toying with him, daring him to swing the fist that would result in a sound beating. She wished she could spare Tom this, and regretted hiring him. He was no match for these other boys, and could only try to break away to no avail.

Suddenly, out of the corner of her eye she saw another person approach. Not a neighbor, but a tall man dressed in gentleman's clothes, and boots that strode with purpose. Mr. Albrighton advanced on the little group like a man taking a brisk turn on these lanes.

He paused as he passed the clutch of boys. Their noise arrested his attention. At just that moment the boldest of the group broke away and walked with a cocky jaunt toward Celia's door. His friends lost interest in Tom and cheered him on.

An arm suddenly appeared like an iron bar, blocking the boy's path.

"Where are you going, young man?"

"I've business there, so be moving your arm if you don't want it broke."

"You have no business with this house if it is not your home. Walk away now."

"*You* walk away. We don't like strangers here. You're looking for trouble, and over a whore at that."

Mr. Albrighton's arm lowered. Sneering with triumph,

the boy took another step. A hand came to rest on his shoulder, stopping him.

Celia could not see exactly what that hand did. It appeared only to lie there. Yet the boy's eyes grew large and his knees buckled. His face contorted with pain.

In the next moment the boy spun across the street toward his friends, like a rag doll cast aside by a child. His friends caught him and he found his balance. Face white and teeth bared, he glared at the man who had bested him without even raising two hands.

"Damned whore," he snarled. "I've money as good as yours or anyone's and I'll be—"

"You will be doing nothing that insults whoever lives in this house. Now walk on, and do not come back here, or I will have to come back as well."

The boys shuffled off. Tom darted forward, palmed some nails and coin onto the step in front of the door, and ran away. Mr. Albrighton picked up the money and nails, then knocked on the door.

Celia swallowed her humiliation as best she could and opened the door. She could see the boys watching from down the street.

"These were left for you." Mr. Albrighton's smile tried to make light of the incident, but she thought she saw some pity in him too. That only embarrassed her more. She held her own smile with difficulty and summoned the illusion of good humor.

She took the nails and glanced to the boys. "It appears the whole world assumes that I am thoroughly my mother's daughter."

"Your tenant assumes nothing of the kind. And, unlike callow boys, he does not pass quick judgment on the choices a person makes in life, no matter what they end up being." He removed a calling card from his coat and handed it to her in a way that ensured the boys saw it. "If you have further trouble with them, you must let me know."

She fingered the card so it would not be missed by the eyes watching. He bowed and strolled away. The boys left too, and turned down a side lane.

She looked down at the card. Other than his name, it was blank. Opaque. The card, for all its quality, revealed almost nothing. A bit like the man who had just handed it to her.

Chapter Five

The coffeehouse near Gray's Inn was crowded at twelve o'clock. Solicitors and apprentices with chambers nearby read newspapers and smoked cigars. Cups hitting saucers added musical notes to the hum of conversation.

Jonathan spied Edward on a divan against the far wall and went to sit with him. Edward's greeting consisted of raised eyebrows forming an unspoken query.

"There have been a few unexpected elements added to my mission," Jonathan said. "The daughter has taken residence in the property on Wells Street. She rarely leaves. It may be some days before I can enter to thoroughly search whatever belongings Alessandra left there."

Edward did not know about that attic chamber. No one did. The vagueness regarding where he lived had begun as a caution during the war, and become a habit that permitted privacy. Jonathan preferred to meet people in their worlds, not invite them into his.

"You have made no progress, in other words," Edward said.

"I have looked in most of the attic. There was nothing there of interest."

"And the other house?"

"I went in the night of the funeral, but someone had been there before me. The daughter, for one, and someone else, she thinks. It is impossible to know if she is correct in her suspicions. The dearth of private papers there leads me to think she may be. Or else Alessandra did not leave anything of note in the house. She knew it would be searched by an executor, even if no one else did."

Edward sipped the thick liquid in his cup while his brow puckered. "Which do you think it was?"

Jonathan thought about the worldly woman with whom he had sometimes conversed. Like many, Alessandra had confided sometimes, but not anything that would bear on this mission. "I think that, knowing the end was near, she would either burn or hide whatever might reveal her true self. Even the account book is missing, if she even kept one, according to her daughter."

"That daughter has to leave the other property eventually, but of course you can hardly camp in the garden and wait for it. Odd that she has chosen to live there. I would have thought by now she would have concluded that running away like she did as a girl was a mistake. She could probably step into her mother's place with little effort. She was a very pretty girl. Men were lining up for when her mother would launch her."

"You know a lot about her."

Edward flushed to his hairline. "Please. Everyone knew about her, including you. Alessandra teased the ton for a year, showing the girl off, entertaining offers, expecting a fortune from the first protector. When she ran off—the daughter, that is—"

"Her name is Celia."

"Yes, Celia, quite right. When she ran off at the last minute, it was quite the *on dit* in my clubs." Edward set down his cup. "So she has returned to town, has she? I daresay that will be the *on dit* soon too. Several who were interested before probably still are, even if she is no longer a girl."

"It is a modest house, and it does not look to me that she intends to take up her mother's profession. From what I have seen, I think she plans to live quietly." He lied blandly. Actually, Celia had spoken of bringing other women to live with her. She had teased him with insinuations that she would start a brothel. At least he assumed it was just teasing, to encourage him to leave. Perhaps not.

"Give it a year, and she will probably be in silks at the theater, displaying her wares."

"As professions for women go, it is not a bad one if done Alessandra's way."

Edward found that amusing. "I keep forgetting that you don't have the normal sort of way of seeing things. Not even whores, it appears."

"As the son of a powerful man's mistress, I am hardly going to condemn other mistresses."

"Of course. I did not mean to imply . . ." Edward flushed again, and decided to drink more coffee.

"Speaking of powerful men, when will you see the earl?"

Edward tried to hide his chagrin, but Jonathan knew the answer as soon as the question was asked.

"Thornridge has put me off again. He guesses the topic I intend to broach, and does not want to speak of it."

"He has never wanted to speak of it. That is nothing

new. You must make it very clear that I am not looking for money."

"He will not believe it. We both know why he does not want to admit you are the last earl's bastard. He suspects this is only the thin edge of the wedge. He does not trust you to let it end there."

Jonathan kept his reaction to himself, but frustrated fury boiled in him. Thornridge's denial was inexcusable, and had never been made out of ignorance. He knew the truth, and had even executed the last earl's intentions regarding Jonathan's education. There had even been an allowance that Jonathan had repudiated years ago because its continuance required retreat. Thornridge remained determined to withhold the acknowledgment that would allow even an earl's bastard an easier path in life.

Edward had been the only member of the family to offer that acknowledgment, and even Edward's acceptance was a private matter, presented years ago as the first step in a long game.

The game had gotten very long indeed now.

"Perhaps I should not bother about the thin edge of the wedge, Uncle. Maybe I should go after it all with a blunt cleaver."

Edward grimaced. "I am sure you want to. I do continue to investigate in your behalf, however. You may suspect I do not, but I do."

"I wonder if my own investigations might not be more fruitful. I have become rather expert in such things the last eight years."

"It would be better if you did not. If he even begins to suspect that you are looking for witnesses to your father's intentions, he will destroy you. I will be unable to stop it."

"He does not have that power. No man does."

"You of all people know that some men do. After all, you have served as their agent on occasion."

Again a spike of anger, but it carried a world-weary quality. "For good cause only." For good cause mostly, not only, unfortunately.

"There are other men who are not so particular. Do not provoke him. Have patience, and allow me to do it my way."

Jonathan stood to leave before today's reserve of good will was spent. "For now I will leave it to you. It would be good to get the edge of the wedge in place soon, however."

He walked out in a dark humor that indicated that, for all his trying, he had not conquered the anger that the situation with the Earl of Thornridge always incited when he dwelled on it very long. A sensible man would have given up the chase long ago, admitted defeat, and found some peace.

Right outside the door, he almost bumped into a footman in elaborate livery who lounged against the building. The fellow snapped into proper posture upon seeing him.

"Mr. Jonathan Albrighton?"

Jonathan nodded. The servant handed over a letter. Jonathan examined the paper and seal and, surprised, tore it open.

Tuesday. Eight o'clock. Whist.

Castleford

Celia woke the next day to heavily overcast skies. She judged that she had slept later than intended. There were many things to do today. She should not have lain abed so long.

She donned an undressing gown and wrapped herself in her warmest shawl. Mr. Albrighton might have to fetch his own water, but she had to as well. She did not relish a walk through the garden on a day when the wind blew enough to rattle her window's shutters.

On opening the door to her bedchamber, she saw that a bucket waited, full enough for a good washing. She tested with her fingers. It had stood there long enough for the worst of the well's chill to pass.

There was only one way for this water to have gotten here. She thought the gesture both endearing and surprising. How would Mr. Albrighton know she had not risen from bed yet? She smiled at the notion that perhaps he looked for her in the morning when he came down those stairs, just as she looked for him.

While she dressed she heard the distant, rhythmic taps of a carpenter at work nearby in the neighborhood. They reminded her that she needed to find someone to replace young Tom. After the teasing yesterday, he would not be back. That was one more errand to add to a list of matters demanding her attention today.

Hair dressed, and bonnet and pelisse in hand, she descended the front stairs. With each step, that tapping sounded louder. She realized it came from the back of her house.

She ventured toward her back sitting room. As she approached she heard a woman say, "I still think she should have a joiner in."

"She decided nails would do," Mr. Albrighton replied.

"If used properly, perhaps they would," came the sweet, patient, but pointed reply.

That woman's voice belonged to Verity. What devil had devised that she should come here without warning, and while Jonathan was in the house?

Celia entered the chamber. Mr. Albrighton stood there in shirt and waistcoat, hammer in hand. Construction on the shelves had made good progress. Advising him, sitting aside with the drawing of the plan on the lap of her sapphire carriage ensemble, was Celia's good friend Verity, wife of the Earl of Hawkeswell.

Verity noticed her. "There you are. I found the garden door open and ventured in to see your new home. Your carpenter said you had gone above for a spell, so I have been helping him while I wait."

Celia walked over and gave her an embrace. "I hope that my friend has not interfered too much, Mr. Albrighton. You did not bargain for the sort of aid she sounded to be giving."

"It appears that I am barely competent at this task by the lady's judgment." Mr. Albrighton set another plank into place with a firmness that suggested Verity had been "helping" him for some time now.

"I only encouraged you to do better, sir. Any fool can bang two boards together if he has twenty nails to do the job. Since I have seen them forged one by one, neither the smith's labor nor my friend's money should be wasted."

Jonathan smiled at the scold. Thinly. Celia expected him to inform Verity that he had never hired himself out as a carpenter, but had tried only to do a good deed.

Instead he swallowed whatever he had been tempted to say. "You are correct, Madam. Your concern about my excessive use of nails is well-taken."

"You can perhaps excuse her, since she is a dear friend, Mr. Albrighton. Your critic is Lady Hawkeswell, and countesses tend to become particular about the particulars, so to speak."

"My apologies, Madam." He bowed his greeting. "Of

course, as a countess you are accustomed to more expert work than I can muster."

"As a countess I would not know the difference between expert and inexpert. If I am particular, it is the result of my youth in a very different world from where I now dwell."

He picked up one of the nails. "Another thirty minutes and all should be in order here. Miss Pennifold, if you want to entertain Lady Hawkeswell elsewhere, I will not mind at all."

Celia thought that an excellent way to end this prickly conversation. She put on her bonnet and tied it against the wind. "Let us take a turn in the garden, Verity, and escape the hammering."

C elia steered Verity deeply into the garden as the tapping began again. Verity kept looking over her shoulder at the house. Her brow puckered each time she did.

"Come and give me advice on this bed near the shrubbery," Celia encouraged, dragging her to the garden's rear.

"Your carpenter is not very good," Verity said. "You should have written so I could recommend one. Did you employ him because he is so handsome?"

"I clear forget what or who recommended him to me. Truly. Now, look here. I think bulbs must already be planted here, don't you?"

Verity glanced back at the house again. Another frown marred her snowy brow. She looked at Celia. She looked back at the house. She looked at Celia. Curiously.

"He was wearing very nice boots. For a carpenter, that is. His shirt and waistcoat too—"

"I trust you are not going to hold it against a man that he takes pride in his appearance."

"I am more concerned with how a carpenter with such poor skills can afford such things. I think we should not leave him in the house alone. He may be one of those fellows who presents himself as a tradesman only to gain entrance to houses to steal."

"You are being too suspicious. Now, the reason I think this must hold spring bulbs is because the trees above would shade other flowers once they leaf out. I should like to add some new ones come autumn, and need your help to decide just which ones."

Verity looked up at the tree line. Then she leveled her gaze on Celia most directly. "I do not think I have been too suspicious. However, it occurs to me that I may have assumed the wrong thing in thinking he was your carpenter."

Celia gazed down at the loamy soil. Stories and explanations lined up in her mind, each one more far-fetched than the idea that Mr. Albrighton was a carpenter.

"Who is that man to you, Celia?"

Celia heard the smallest note of merriment in Verity's voice. She looked up to see Verity's lovely face smooth of all frowns now. Impish lights dancing in her blue eyes.

"It is not what you think."

"More's the pity."

"Verity!"

Verity laughed, surprised at herself. "What can I say? He is very easy on the eyes, and a handsome man using his hands—even if not well at all in this circumstance— still compels my attention, my love for Hawkeswell notwithstanding." She glanced back yet again. "Tell. You must, or I will assume what I will on my own."

"He is a tenant. That is all. An awkward intrusion and an embarrassing nuisance. I inherited him, much like the furniture, and he will not leave no matter how uncomfortable I take pains to make him."

"Perhaps discomfort keeps him here, although perhaps not the kind you intended. It seems to me, now that I think about it, that he became even more compelling as soon as you entered the chamber."

So Verity had noticed the exciting energy in that chamber during their brief conversation. Celia had assumed it came from herself, and from the gentle thrill created when she saw Jonathan standing there, his forearms bare beneath his rolled sleeves and the general form of his body emphasized by the waistcoat and snug pantaloons he wore.

Verity hooked her arm through Celia's and encouraged her to stroll. "You really must bring an older woman into the house."

"I intend to. However, it is not my fault that I inherited property with a male tenant already in residence."

"No, it is not. However, you must take more care than most women who make such a discovery."

Celia thought about the altercation in the street outside her house the day before. "I am beginning to wonder if any care will be enough, and therefore unnecessary. You were good enough not to make assumptions about him immediately, and he was good enough not to comment on how you came to the garden door and not the front one, but the reason for both the assumptions and your entry is not to be avoided. I think there will be little difference in my reputation whether I repudiate Alessandra's biggest legacy or not."

Verity's face flushed. Her blue eyes moistened. "I did not assume he was your lover, Celia. Not ever. I was only teasing you. As for my discreet entry, I am sorry. I truly am. I will tell Hawkeswell that I intend to greet you in the park and have you call like any other friend. It is not fair that—"

"I will not have it. I do not blame you or your husband. Please believe that. I always knew how it would be. I am not angry with you about that, or at all insulted. Sometimes I get discouraged when I realize that I gain little with my virtue, and it vexes me. That is all I am saying. I have lost just as much of my good reputation as if I had indeed agreed to accept my first protector at seventeen."

She regretted her impulsive honesty immediately. It surprised her, then, when Verity did not express any dismay, but merely strolled on.

They returned to the shrubbery, near the well. Celia thought about the bucket of water outside her door. It had been very kind of Mr. Albrighton to do that when he realized she had not yet risen from bed. Kinder than she had been with him. Probably he felt sorry for her, after those boys had spoken of her as a whore.

Verity finally gave the flower bed in front of the shrubbery her attention. "This spring, after we see what comes up, we can decide which new varieties to add."

"*Now* you finally speak of bulbs, Verity? Have you nothing to say about the topic I indiscreetly broached?"

"I am still accommodating my discovery of your history, Celia. It is still news to me."

"I only informed Daphne. If anyone else learned the truth, it was by accident."

"I am not upbraiding you for not confiding. I am the last person to have any right to do that, considering the secrets I kept from all of you."

Verity referred to their time together, living at The Rarest

Blooms. There was a rule in that household that one did not pry into the histories of the others. Daphne said that women sometimes have good reason to leave the past behind, and that had been true of all of them, to one degree or another.

Verity, however, had been the most thorough in keeping her own counsel, to the point of assuming a new identity.

It had been a shock to all of them to discover last summer that the most quiet and circumspect among them had affected the most daring break with the past. It had also been a relief when, after that past found her, Verity had not only reconciled to it, but found glorious happiness.

"I am trying to explain how, since it is so new, I am still adjusting my own prospect, so to speak," Verity continued earnestly. "I do not see you differently, dear friend. I do, however, see you in a different place from before. And—" She bit her lower lip, shrugged, and forged on. "And I find that your allusion does not shock me at all. Nor do I think it would shock Daphne. I cannot guess about the others."

Celia laughed, weakly. "I do not know if I should be reassured, or insulted."

"Not insulted, I hope. I am not shocked because for all your good humor and optimism, you have always had a practical outlook." Verity slid her arm through Celia's so they walked closely side by side again. "I expect any practical woman would assess her possible paths very frankly. That is all I heard you doing."

Celia stopped their progress and gazed in Verity's blue eyes. No censure waited in them. They had learned to love each other without judgment at The Rarest Blooms, and it still informed the way they treated each other.

"The paths open to me are few, and mostly unappealing, Verity. I have been pondering them for five years now. I can remain forever in Daphne's sanctuary, away from the world's eyes and scorn but also away from the world's vitality, and risk hurting the reputation of every woman who lives with me. Or I can go far away, change my name, and hope my history never finds me. Perhaps, if I am willing to deceive a good man, I can even marry."

"Or you can live your mother's life, which was not without its allure, I expect." Verity smiled kindly. "Did you reject it as a girl because you thought it was wrong?"

"I rejected it because it required a practicality that proved stronger than I could muster at age seventeen. And because I do not want to give my father, whoever he is, even more reason to reject me." A wistful memory drenched her. She looked away, at the shrubs, the trees and sky. "And because there can be no love in that life. Affection, yes. But anything more is sure to break one's heart."

Verity gestured to the house and garden with a wide sweep of her arm. "So, my bright, happy Celia is blazing another path for herself. How like you to find a way to do so."

Celia laughed. "I suppose in a way I am. I had better blaze it quickly too, if those plants will start coming this week." She cocked her head. "The hammering has stopped. Perhaps Mr. Albrighton has finished."

Verity rolled her eyes. "We had best go and see the results. Your Mr. Albrighton means well, but I should have insisted he hand over that hammer, so I could have done the work properly myself."

They were almost at the garden door when Verity stopped in her tracks. "*Albrighton*. I knew the name sounded familiar when you first spoke it, and now I remember why.

A Mr. Albrighton called on Hawkeswell that day you came to visit me, when Audrianna was there too. Hawkeswell mentioned it afterward. This was the Albrighton who was the magistrate in Staffordshire when they had that unpleasantness recently. I wonder if he is related to your tenant."

"Actually, I think it is the same man." Jonathan had called on Lord Hawkeswell that day? They were in Verity's house together at the same time?

Was it possible that he had followed her there? There was no reason for him to do so. Yet the coincidence seemed most peculiar.

"The same? Oh, my." Verity spoke quietly, as if she feared someone in the house overhearing. "No wonder he has such nice boots. Not only is he not a carpenter; he is not even your normal sort of gentleman, Celia. According to my husband, Mr. Albrighton is the bastard son of the last Earl of Thornridge. He admitted as much when they were at university together."

Jonathan was gone when they entered the house. The hammer rested on one of the deep shelves he had just built. That he had bothered to complete this chore warmed Celia's heart, much the way the waiting water had. He really should not have done this, however. Gentlemen did not do work that might callous their hands, did they? Even the bastard son of an earl should be more careful.

"Let us examine your garden from the prospect of this nice window," Verity said. "We will decide what plantings must be removed so this view can be improved."

While Celia joined in the planning, a part of her mind mulled over Verity's astonishing revelation about Mr. Albrighton's parentage. An odd feeling took residence below her heart and dulled her mood.

Disappointment. That was what that sensation was.

She had rather thought . . . In truth, she had not actually *thought* anything. But she had experienced a fresh excitement in his company. She had enjoyed the undeniable attraction that flowed between them.

Now she could never experience that quite the same way again. If he was the bastard son of Thornridge, it would be normal for him to hope for more than he currently had, and for the social advantages that his blood could procure. He had tasted what that could mean while at school, and through being received in houses like that of the Earl of Hawkeswell.

Mr. Albrighton would not want to do anything that might interfere with crossing many other social thresholds that might open to him. He would not want to break any of society's rules.

Which meant if anything ever happened between him and her, if the silent thrum between them ever found fulfillment, she could not allow herself to pretend it was anything other than a gentleman amusing himself with a woman he saw as fit only for amusement.

The best she could expect was what Anthony had planned, and the worst could be much crueler. And, just as with Anthony, all that passed between them would be affected by her birth and by his.

Chapter Six

The day had started late, and Verity's visit delayed Celia's plans even more. It was close to four o'clock, therefore, when she finally tied on her bonnet and donned her wool, copper-hued pelisse. She walked through the garden and down the mews to the stable that cared for her mare.

She requested the horse be brought to her carriage house just as Mr. Albrighton arrived. He stood aside until the groom went away, but his high boots fell into step beside her as she left.

"Is it wise to take out the cabriolet so late, Miss Pennifold?"

"No less wise than your taking out your horse, Mr. Albrighton."

"My horse is faster than a carriage, and I am less vulnerable in its saddle than anyone in a small, open equipage."

"Your advice is well-taken, just as I am sure it is well-meant. However, I am determined to complete a necessary task today. I will take great care, thank you."

He did not turn back to the stable as she expected, but continued pacing beside her. "Allow me to accompany you. The streets are not safe at any time recently, and you may find yourself alone after sunset."

"I cannot ask such an inconvenience of you. You have already given up your morning to build those shelves. If you do more, I will be too much in your debt."

For the son of an earl, this man had a reckless streak. He risked his hands with a hammer, and now he seemed unconcerned about being seen in public with her. Perhaps he just assumed the latter would be interpreted as a man pursuing a liaison with the next goddess of the demimonde. Which, of course, was exactly what it probably was.

"It is no inconvenience, Miss Pennifold. I insist you accept my aid. You know that you should." They stopped at the carriage house. "Where are you going?"

She looked down the mews. The groom led her mare toward them. "Covent Garden."

"Now I doubly insist that you allow me to accompany you. I will not hear any objections. There was a large demonstration at the river near there yesterday, and tempers are still unsettled in the poorer neighborhoods."

True to his word, he did not hear her objections. Ten minutes later he snapped the ribbons from his place beside her in the cabriolet. They began the little journey.

"Where in Covent Garden are you going?" he asked.

"I am not sure yet. I will start in the square, however."

Was that a disapproving scowl that flickered over his face? Why, yes, she thought it was. She hoped Mr. Albrighton was not going to be an inconvenience now.

"It is not an area of town to wander aimlessly in the evening, Miss Pennifold."

"I will not be aimless. The person I seek will be in one of three places. I simply do not know which one."

"You do not seek a location, but a person?"

"That is correct. You should stay with the carriage, and I will proceed on foot once we are there. It would be better that way."

He appeared skeptical, but quizzed her no more until they approached the large square that was home to the market. Celia bade him stop the carriage; then she stood and surveyed the crowds that still thronged the plaza from her elevated perspective.

"May I ask, for whom are you looking, Miss Pennifold?"

She narrowed her eyes on the faces near some distant flower stalls. "I am looking for a whore."

"Allow me to help you. It is a bit early still, but— Ah, there is one, not fifteen feet from this carriage. Right over there, wearing the—"

"I am looking for a specific whore. I am sure you are not shocked to learn that the daughter of a whore has friends who are whores."

"You speak as though I should consider it not only unworthy of shock, but also inevitable. It is not, especially when the daughter in question is the friend of a countess. Why do you want to find this particular whore this evening?"

"I intend to ask her to come live with me." The silence beside her caused her to look down. "*Now* you are shocked."

"Not at all. I thought you were joking that first night, but if you were not, that is understandable."

She was not sure she would describe the secret weighing that she sometimes did as understandable. "Why do you say that? Almost no one else would."

"The only people who would deny the allure of security and comfort are those who are already assured of all three. It is understandable if you reconsider your prior rejection of that part of your legacy."

"That is very open-minded of you."

"I am the last person to pass judgment if you ultimately choose that path. My advice is of a different sort. It has to do with the standards you mentioned during our conversation in the library that night. You cannot raise up the particular whore you seek today, and she will only drag you down. I do not doubt that your mother explained all of this."

Of course Mama had. Just as she had explained that the social station of her first patron would go far in determining whether she plied her trade in silk-draped drawing rooms or beneath a bridge.

She turned Mr. Albrighton's frankness over in her mind while she cast her gaze along the flower stalls again. He was waiting for her to decide, perhaps. Waiting for her to conclude that the luxury, security, and comfort were worth the decision. Would he offer some arrangement then, and pursue this enlivening tension that existed between them even now, as she stood by his shoulder? Or did he also know that those standards she mentioned that night meant that he would never do, even if he had an earl's blood in him?

"There she is. I see her. Wait here, please." She gathered her skirt and prepared to climb down.

A hand clasped her arm. Her rump landed back on the seat with a smart thud.

"I will take you to her, and I will wait where I will not lose sight of you. It is not too early for the more dangerous denizens of the night to be about."

She thought his protective inclinations both charming and unnecessary. She had survived this neighborhood at worse times than this, and knew how to discourage those denizens from approaching her.

He maneuvered the cabriolet along the edge of the square until she told him to stop. He insisted on helping her down, but at least he did not attempt to accompany her to the flower stalls. She approached on her own, and stood in front of one for a solid minute before the flame-haired woman attending to customers saw her.

"Celia? I thought perhaps my eyes were deceiving me." The woman came out and embraced her with warm, motherly arms.

"It is good to see you, Marian. It has been some months, I know."

Marian pushed away those months with a flip of her hand. "If you have brought me some of your flowers, I am afraid it is too late for today. You can see that I've a good number to sell as it is and time is passing."

"I did not bring flowers, Marian. I brought a proposition."

Marian's green eyes reflected surprise, then humor. "You are a good girl to think of me, dear, but I'm too old and coarse if you have decided to take up the life after all, and are seeking other doves for your covey. My sympathies about your mum. I'd a been there, for old times' sake, but—"

"I thank you for your good thoughts, Marian. However, I am not recruiting the way you think. You did me a very good turn five years ago, when you told me about Mrs.

Joyes and her kind heart. I now would like to do you a good turn as well."

Marian gestured to the flower stall. "Already have, haven't you? That bit of money you gave me let me start this, and the leftover flowers you bring sometimes help more than you know. I've been able to get off my back, but stay in the lanes that I've known since I was born."

Celia worried that Marian's ties to this neighborhood would now interfere with the proposal. Nor did she believe that Marian had completely given up being a whore. Not forever, at least. Should the day's flower sales not pay for fuel and food, it would be too easy to sell something else instead that was always in demand. Even in middle age Marian was a handsome woman who could catch the eye of a man looking for easy pleasure.

"My proposal would require you to leave this neighborhood, but not go too far away, Marian. You would be able to visit often. I am in need of someone I can trust, and who better than the woman who befriended me when I was alone and lost?"

"Not lost, dear. But for the tears in your eyes, you'd a seen clear enough where you were, and that it was no place for such as you."

Those tears had blinded her not only to the danger of these streets, but also to the impossibility of what she had just done. Running away had been necessary, but also foolish, considering she had no idea where to go or what to do once she left her mother.

Nothing but hell on these lanes for you, dear. There's procurers waiting on every corner to spy for such as you, and that face and hair of yours will fetch one of them a good prize from the abbess who buys you. I've a bit of money, and we'll hire a carriage and you'll go home now.

That was what the red-haired whore had said, after shouting away one such persistent procurer. When Celia had refused to return home, Marian had told her about the beautiful widow who sometimes visited the flower sellers in Covent Garden, to give away the excess of her blooms to the poorest among them.

"I have inherited a house, Marian. I am going to become a partner to Daphne. I need someone to live there with me, and I thought of you at once. It will be a secure life, I hope, and I know that you will suit the situation perfectly."

Lights of interest sparked in Marian's eyes while Celia further described her plans. Toward the end they dimmed, however, as Marian gazed out over the crowds in the square.

"There is a young woman who would suit you better," Marian said. "I am doing fine now. This woman—Bella, I call her—is half-starving. It is only a matter of time before she finds a way to eat."

Celia's heart filled. She embraced Marian again. "I will not have her instead of you, but I will accept her along with you. If you care so much about her fate that you offer her as a replacement, then I hope that you will care enough to sacrifice the familiarity of these lanes to move a mere mile away."

Marian's eyes misted. Her fear of this change became visible, but also sad; desperate hope showed in the way she looked at Celia. "It won't be proper, you having a woman like me in your service."

"No one will know your history, Marian. You will only be the sensible woman who cooks for Alessandra Northrope's daughter. Whatever scorn descends on our house, I think it will be due to me."

Marian drew herself tall and straight, and appeared

as formidable as she had the night she faced down that whoremonger. "Is that how it has been, then? I'll put an end to that, if such talk reaches my ears. I'll be making a right understanding with them that speak against you."

"You must be with me in order to do that, so it sounds as if you accept my offer." Celia laughed, took Marian's hands, and pulled her into a little jig full of joy until Marian was laughing too. They bumped against flower buckets and danced until, out of breath, they fell into each other's arms.

"Let us go and collect your belongings, and get Bella too," Celia said. "I have a carriage here, and a driver who will help us." She pointed toward the cabriolet, and Jonathan.

Marian squinted in that direction. "Is he as handsome in the daylight as he is in the dusk?"

"More so."

"A gentleman, from the looks of him. What does he want with you?"

Celia urged Marian forward. "Nothing. I will explain it all later, but he did not want me to come here alone, unprotected; that is all."

Marian cast a sideways glance her way. "Trust me, dear, from the way he was looking at you a minute ago, he definitely wants *something*."

Jonathan arrived at the door near the western end of Piccadilly Street at quarter past nine o'clock. The house's stone façade loomed high above him, punctuated by rows of long windows aglow with lights that pierced the night.

The servants, decked out in wigs, hose, pumps, and the rest of Castleford's livery, expected him. One of them opened the door immediately upon his arrival and another right inside took his hat and gloves. A third, whose frock coat sported some gold embroidery that marked him as an important officer in this army, led him up the stairs.

Ceilings soared above, covered with gilt moldings and inset paintings of Greek gods at play. More paintings decked the walls. As if to emphasize that the Duke of Castleford was one of the richest men in England, a Titian oil showing Zeus and Ariadne—a painting that would be the prize of most family collections—hung on an obscure wall in the stairwell. The message was that the gallery and drawing rooms sported better works by the Renaissance master.

The servant escorted him through one of those drawing rooms, decorated, like the servants themselves, in the style popular during the earlier years of the king's reign. The current duke had not redecorated much upon inheriting the title and the house. Not because he was indifferent, although his habits might lead some to assume that. Rather Castleford liked the excess of this precious chamber, and the allusions to royalty and privilege it communicated.

Two servants swung two doors wide at the far end of the drawing room, giving ceremonial egress to another chamber of more intimate proportions and considerably less gilt. The large windows on three walls suggested this would be an airy retreat on warm summer nights, and have pleasant prospects of the town and river during the day.

The servants left him alone in the chamber. Jonathan regretted being only fifteen minutes late, instead of at least thirty. His attempts to ensure he would not suffer Castleford's company individually might have been in vain.

The letter had been more a summons than invitation, and as presumptuous as the man who sent it. Its mere arrival had been the surprise, not its imperious tone. There was unfinished business between him and Castleford, none of it good, and he had never expected the duke to address him again.

He busied himself by examining the paintings in this chamber. Crisply classical, and of newer creation, they presumably had not been inherited. For all the duke's personal flamboyance, he seemed to prefer very organized compositions in the art he bought himself.

"You are late, Albrighton."

Jonathan pivoted. Tristan St. Ives, Duke of Castleford, stood near the fireplace. One of the panels on the wall must hide a doorway.

Castleford always seemed to mock his own station and wealth, even while he thoroughly enjoyed both. Now his very stance subtly spoke of boredom as well as privilege, and expectations of the deference that he professed to find irritating.

Dressed in coats that probably cost hundreds of pounds, he managed, with his fashionably unruly mane of brown hair and his devilish, almost golden eyes, to remind one that among the rights enjoyed by a duke was the right to do whatever he damned well wanted, and anyone who did not like it could go to hell.

From what Jonathan had heard, mostly the duke still damned well wanted to whore and drink. He appeared sober enough tonight, however.

"It appears I am early, Your Grace. Not late. Whist, the letter said. The other two are not here yet, unless you intend to recruit your steward and groom to join us."

"The others are coming at half past nine. You received a special time."

"I am honored."

"It was not my intention to honor you."

"That goes without saying."

"If so, why did you say it?"

"To be polite."

"We are beyond such boring rituals, I would think."

"Then I said it to avoid an argument, if possible, while I pray that your other guests arrive very soon."

Castleford threw himself into a well-stuffed chair. His body and manner remained languid, but his eyes pierced Jonathan.

Better if he had been drunk, Jonathan decided.

"Hawkeswell will be late. He always is. He plans it, to emphasize that his title predates mine by two hundred years and he is not impressed by me. Summerhays is your best bet for a timely arrival, unless, of course, they are coming together."

"How good of you to bring us all under your very magnificent roof at the same time."

"Well, we all had our moments together years ago. Now, we were all a party to that business up north. We need to celebrate our success."

Jonathan hoped that was not really the goal of this evening's party. They all assumed he had been investigating when Hawkeswell stumbled upon him in Staffordshire a few months ago. He had been, but he could not talk about it. "I have heard rumors that the Home Office owes all of you a debt," he said. "The talk is that the matter was resolved much more quickly due to your help."

"Due to our interference, you mean. I suspect it would have ended differently but for us too. I don't think you were sent there to ferret out the truth, but to hide it, and perhaps even to aid it. What say you to that?"

"You may think what you please, and no doubt will, no matter what I say."

"Which won't be anything useful, I can see. Typical of you. By the way, one of our esteemed peers from that region saw fit to blow his brains out last week. It will be called something else, of course. An accident or whatnot. One last detail to clean up in that mess before coming to London, Albrighton?"

"Whatever you may think of me, I am not a murderer."

"Neither are soldiers. However, in the end, people end up dead by their actions. Do not misunderstand—I do not hold that last detail against you. Someone had to remind him of the only honorable way out. I was going to journey north myself to do so, if necessary."

"Why didn't you?"

Castleford stifled a yawn. "I did not think he would have the courage to do the right thing. Then what? It had to happen, for the good of England, but I did not fancy being one of those soldiers, if he required aid. It is a relief that he managed it on his own."

Except he had not managed any such thing, and Castleford had guessed as much.

The man in question had been unable to fall on his sword, and had expected that Jonathan would take care of it, just as he had taken care of so much else in that sorry business. Evidently Castleford and many others assumed the same thing. There were limits, however, to what any man could justify, no matter how good the cause. Even a murky soul had a few moments of moral clarity.

Jonathan's refusal had been a shock to a coward wanting to die in an "accident" with his good name intact. Jonathan did not know who finally pulled that trigger after he left the man, the pistol, and the library smelling of despair and terror— He guessed it had been a sympathetic servant, or even a wife.

"So you are saying that all is well that ends well, no matter how the end comes about." He did not like the world-weary bitterness he heard in his own voice. "I am delighted that you had me here early, so you could reassure me of your approval."

Those eyes fixed on him. The smile hardened. Castleford had not missed the sarcasm. "Actually, I had you here early so I could tell you that I do not blame you for what happened in France two years ago. There has been little chance to say so since then."

"You mean that you *no longer* blame me."

"Hell, I never blamed you."

"I hope that you do not blame yourself instead. There was no choice."

"There is always a choice," he snarled. Then he relaxed, and shrugged. "But duty called, and all that."

"Yes. All that."

Summerhays mercifully arrived then, not late at all. Castleford's spirits lightened immediately on seeing him. "I hope you brought plenty of money, Summerhays. I plan to pair with Albrighton here, and as I remember it, he never drinks at cards, so that mind of his will remain razor sharp."

"Regrettably, he can't play alone, but will be forced to contend with your own erratic play as his partner," Summerhays goaded. He greeted Jonathan warmly. They had not seen each other in years. Another old friend from Jonathan's university days, Lord Sebastian Summerhays, as the brother of a marquess and an important member of the House of Commons, had in the past known enough about Jonathan's activities to avoid asking about them.

"I am told you have been back from France for almost a year," Summerhays said.

"In England, yes. Rarely in London."

"But you will be in London awhile now?"

"Awhile."

Summerhays flashed the smile that made women swoon and men want to check their purse strings. "You must call and meet my wife, Audrianna. She has asked about you."

Jonathan could not imagine why. His confusion must have showed, because Summerhays added, "She is best of friends with Lady Hawkeswell, who knows a bit about you. Rather more than I do these days, from the curiosity being expressed in my home."

Summerhays waited for Jonathan to fill in holes and satisfy his own curiosity. Jonathan wondered just what Lady Hawkeswell had and had not said about her visit to Celia's new house.

The silent impasse was interrupted by Castleford. "Ah, here is Hawkeswell, so we can get down to it. You and Summerhays can just save time and put your purses in my money box, Hawkeswell."

The Earl of Hawkeswell hooted rudely in derision. "Albrighton, we can draw for partners if you want. It is unfair to force him on you, since you can ill afford the losses that will accrue due to his besotted intellect."

"He appears sober enough. I will risk it."

"Thank you," Castleford said. He lowered his eyelids haughtily at Hawkeswell. "It is Tuesday, or have you forgotten?"

"Oooo, Tuesday," Hawkeswell mocked, wide-eyed.

"Tuesday? Does it matter?" Jonathan asked.

Summerhays helped himself to some brandy offered by a servant, then took a seat at the card table. "Tristan here no longer drinks on Tuesdays. He gathers his faculties and concentrates on his duties then. The rest of the week . . ." He shrugged.

"Do not assume it will make a difference," Hawkeswell said. "The other days pickle him enough that one day's sobriety will hardly reverse matters. Expect bizarre play and huge losses. You really should demand we draw for partners."

Castleford took the teasing with good enough humor. But then, the duke had always relished his reputation.

Jonathan took the chair across from his host. "As I remember, even half of his brain was better than most that are whole, so I will take my chances. It was good of you to plan this for a Tuesday, Castleford, so I am not ruined without a fighting chance at least."

"Oh, he did not choose a Tuesday because of you," Summerhays mused as he dealt the first hand. "He did it because of the whores."

"Tuesday is the only day they are not about," Hawkeswell explained while he examined his cards. "On any other day a visitor is bound to run into at least one bared bottom somewhere in this house, poised for fornication on the chance our friend should wander by. Since Summerhays and I are now married, we would have to decline if he invited us here of an evening any day but Tuesday."

Castleford looked with resigned pity to his right at Summerhays, and to his left at Hawkeswell. Then he looked across the table at Jonathan.

"I have a most clever retort on the tip of my tongue, relating to wives and bare bottoms. Alas, I dare not speak it because—"

"Because it might get you called out," Summerhays finished.

Castleford sighed, dramatically. "See? They have become so boring it is a wonder I can stand them. The truth is that I will only entertain their company on Tuesdays because then I am somewhat boring myself." He smiled, a devil recognizing with delight the potential demon in another man. "You, however, are welcome to call whenever you like."

Jonathan had not expected this old, vague friendship to rehabilitate itself at all, let alone so easily and thoroughly. He thought he could be excused for finding it all a little suspicious. From the glances Summerhays and Hawkeswell exchanged, they did as well.

"I am honored. I do not know what to say."

"Your first bid will suffice. Make it a good one, so we can bury these two."

Chapter Seven

"So, it is settled, then," Marian announced. "I'll be doing the cooking and care for the kitchen, and Bella here will clean and help you with your dressing and such." She looked to Bella for agreement.

Celia did as well. Bella had not said much since they had descended into the cellar beneath a stationer's shop. Bella's attempts at creating a home there could not banish the dark and damp, and Bella herself could not stand against Marian's demand that she pack whatever she wanted to keep and follow them out.

Tawny haired, and thin and wan in ways that spoke of lack of food, she had obeyed, expressing neither joy nor resentment. Mr. Albrighton, who had led the way down into that dungeon, showed her great kindness, taking the little sack she made of her garments and gently speaking reassurances, as if he suspected she needed them.

Now Bella sat on a stool near the fireplace, her expression one of ecstasy from its warmth. She had not contributed to the discussions of the household, but she nodded at Marian's division of work.

"You and I should be going above soon," Marian said to her. "There's a good-size chamber that we can share, at the other end of the house from where that gentleman lives."

Marian had been startled to learn Mr. Albrighton resided here. Not given to trusting any man much, Marian would probably take on another duty now, as chaperone.

"Before you retire, I would like to speak about a few house rules," Celia said. "You may find them a bit odd, but my experience has been that they go far to ensuring peaceable coexistence among women. They were the rules by which we all lived with Daphne."

Marian nodded agreement. "If they suited Mrs. Joyes, I expect they will suit us."

"The first one is we do not pry into each other's histories or lives. Not the past, and not the present. That means, Bella, if you never want to tell me about your family, or how you came to be alone, I will never ask it of you."

Bella cocked her head, puzzled by this right to keep her own counsel.

"We will each contribute to the household as we can. You have both already agreed to that, in offering to help with its upkeep. And if we leave the house and intend to be gone more than the normal time, we will inform the others, so no one worries."

"That sounds sensible," Marian said, nodding away.

"As independent women, we must protect each other, and each learn to protect ourselves," Celia said, explaining another important precept under which she had lived for five years with Daphne.

"No problem with that. I'm well practiced in defending

myself, and Bella here once or twice. Ain't that right, Bella?"

"Then we are all agreed on the basic rules," Celia said. "There are a few others of less importance that I will explain later."

Marian stood. "I'll be fixing baths for us down in the kitchen now. Best to wash the past off, so we can start fresh in the morning."

"Yes, that would be good," Bella said. It was her first contribution to the conversation. Celia hoped it showed Bella had overcome her fear.

Bella started to follow Marian to the door, but faltered in her steps. She scurried back, took Celia's hand in her own two, and raised the little pile to her lips.

Her eyes closed hard while she pressed a kiss on the hand she held. Then she was gone, hurrying to catch up with Marian.

N oise from the kitchen below eventually gave way to giggles and footsteps on the back stairs. In the library, Celia set down her book and listened to Marian and Bella trod up to the attic passage and the room they would share.

There were other chambers up there, besides theirs and Mr. Albrighton's. One was used for storage. Celia had spied into it while she showed Marian the choices. She had needed to use her key to enter, and in the dark noticed only that it held an old trunk.

Tomorrow or the next day she would go up there, finally, and see what her mother had left in this retreat. Here, perhaps, there might be a clue about her father's name.

It had been a full day and a long night, and Celia knew that she should go to bed herself. Mr. Albrighton had not returned, but he would ensure the doors were secure when he did, if he returned at all.

The day's events made her too restless for sleep. The house, all but empty these last days, now felt crowded with the new spirits inhabiting it. Lifting her cloak from its peg, she bundled herself well, and left the house to take a quiet turn in the night garden before retiring.

She strolled down to the shrubbery, and the fallow bed stretching in front of it. Verity had probably taken one look at it and known exactly what to add to it in spring. Verity had found a true calling while living at The Rarest Blooms, first learning all she could from Daphne, then turning to books and journals and experimenting herself. Her earl permitted this avocation's continuance now, and Lady Hawkeswell's correspondence with horticulture experts all over England was always answered.

Verity had been too kind to mention that this entire garden showed neglect. Mama's brief stays did not facilitate regular upkeep, no doubt. There would be a lot of work to do here this spring.

She mused about that, and the improvements she would make. Her thoughts turned to Mama herself after a few minutes. She pictured the other house, and the afternoon salons that Mama liked to hold in the French manner, and the dinner parties at which she would have Celia sing.

The men who attended were all of good blood and high incomes, whether they had titles or not. She should have remembered that. Of course Jonathan must have had one or the other as well, if he had been included.

She tried to ignore how the thought of that made her oddly sad again. It was silly to react thus. She barely knew him. Yet the intimacy evoked by sharing this house now seemed ruined. The excitement would never be as carefree again. There were rules in the world he visited when he left this house. A man in his situation would probably calculate every act and smile with those rules in mind.

She forced her thoughts back to her mother's parties. Men came and went from those assemblies, but some reappeared again and again. She tried now to see their faces in her mind, and wondered if some had been coming for years. Was it possible that her father had not only been in Mama's past? Had she perhaps even met him at one of those parties?

She picked through the memories while she strolled back to the house. As she approached the garden door, a shadow shifted to its right, where a garden bench stood. Drawing near, she saw Mr. Albrighton sitting there, his eyes dark pools in the half-moon's light.

"It is too cold to sit in a dark garden," she said after greeting him.

"It is too cold to walk in one after midnight," he said.

"Have you just returned?" She gazed up the house, to the attics. "They are probably asleep now, if you feared the noise they would make in their excitement this first night."

"I have been here awhile. You walked right past me when you came out. You were so absorbed in your thoughts, I decided not to disturb you."

She sat beside him on the bench and bundled her cloak around her. "Not so absorbed. I often took night strolls where I lived before. The gardens were much bigger there because it was in the country, but not far from London at all. We grew flowers and plants for sale. My dear friend

Daphne owns the property, but we all helped her as we could."

"Is that where you have been since you left your mother's home?"

She nodded. "Then Verity joined us the last two years. And Audrianna—Lord Sebastian Summerhays's wife now—was with us for a spell too, before she married. That is how I know such fine ladies, in case you were wondering what an earl's wife was doing visiting me."

She found herself telling him about Daphne's greenhouses and gardens, and the odd family they had all created in that house.

"And now you have all left," he said. "Two to marriage, and you to—?"

She laughed at the inflection and question. "You did not even raise an eyebrow today as I collected Marian and her friend. Yet you must wonder what I am about. I all but invited the worst speculation that first night. Do not worry, Mr. Albrighton. You will not be living above a brothel."

"I did not worry about that."

Which was not to say he had not thought it might happen. "I am joining Daphne in partnership. That is what those shelves are for—plants." She described her plan. He listened closely. She could see his eyes as he paid attention.

He was very easy to talk to. It all just poured out, her plans for the house and the partnership, and her desire to forge a life for herself. "I joined Daphne when I was still quite young. I am no longer, and it was time to go. I think she understands that, even if she wishes I had stayed."

"It was good of her to take you in. She probably saw

that you were a lovely child, but a child all the same, and needed her help."

"Is that what you thought of me back then? That I was a child?"

"Yes. A very innocent, beautiful child. Too much a child for what your mother planned."

"At seventeen I was already older than some young women in that profession. It is considered a good age for marriage too."

"Some of the girls who become wives or mistresses at seventeen are too childish as well. Others not. It is not a matter of age."

Her face burned. She knew why he was saying this. "You remember me crying that day. My disappointment is why you think I was too childish."

She had bumped into him as she ran from Anthony. Mr. Albrighton had come to take his leave of Mama, because he was going away again. Blinded by her tears, she had careened right into him as she fled.

He caught her before she fell from the collision. He had sat her on the stairs, and asked why she cried. She had told him, this stranger who had an odd way of inspiring confidences. It had just poured out while he absorbed it with his fathomless eyes.

He did not pretend now that it had never happened, or that he had forgotten. "You can be forgiven that disappointment, no matter what your maturity, Miss Pennifold."

"My mother had just spent a year teaching me to have no illusions, and scolded me for forgetting the most important lesson."

"To have felt nothing would have meant you were already jaded. There is a lot of distance between a hardened heart and a child's view of the world."

"Do you still see that child sometimes when you look at me?"

He turned his head and looked at her quite directly. "Not at all. I only see a beautiful and desirable woman, who lights garden paths at night with her mere presence. The moon's glow finds you, like it finds a white flower. Even when you were back near those shrubs, you remained very distinct in the night."

"You were watching me the whole time, as you sat here? Why?"

"You know why."

Yes, she did. His admission changed everything and immediately gave their intimate chat new depths. That delicious tension pulled, full of sensual allure and forbidden excitement.

"Perhaps you regret I was not planning a different sort of business," she teased, to add lightness to what had suddenly become a mood pulsing with seductive potential. And yet, she still wondered if perhaps he had been waiting, to see how much of the legacy she would accept, the way he threatened that first night.

"Perhaps I do, somewhat."

Well, there it was. She could not say she had not been warned. Although, right now, with her confidences binding them and his warmth against her side, the implications of that did not seem very significant. He was too compelling, as Verity had described him, for her to think about them much.

He turned his head toward her again and she saw his smile fade into a different expression, one that sent a wonderful shiver down her body. She savored the thrill, and all of the other little responses to the power arching between them. To her relief it had not been ruined after all by the day's discoveries. There might be a social chasm between them, but that power seemed to bridge it for a while.

His hand began to move, hesitated, then reached toward her anyway. His palm rested on her cheek. His touch was warm and dry. Her breath caught at how this real connection intensified the enlivening, compelling invisible one.

Always make them ask. Never let them assume. Especially with the first kiss.

She ignored Mama's lesson. She sensed the kiss coming, and she did not make him ask because she did not want words to interfere.

His mouth took hers. Her heart leapt and all the excitements collected together to shout a chorus through her body. *Heed your body's stimulation. Savor the pleasure. Fight nothing, and it will not be a chore but the sweetest game.* She could not have fought or ignored any of it, even if she wanted to. She did not need to concentrate to find the pleasure. It inundated her.

A kiss. Long enough. Longer than it had to be, even for one stolen in a garden. One touch. That hand on her cheek, guiding and subtly controlling. A presence, dark and deep and unknown, but filling her and surrounding her and coaxing more response than it would ever exploit.

She knew that. Knew it would go no further, even though her body turned lusciously sensitive and hoped for more. Even while he mesmerized her, she knew this kiss had not been an impulsive accident, but a calculated step. A first step only, and perhaps there would be no more.

She was not surprised by what did and did not happen, by what he took and did not take. The kiss ended as it had begun, slowly and seductively, and without words. Finally that palm rested on her face and he only gazed in her eyes.

She was glad he did not speak. He did not say the required apologies that men say to proper women, as if those excuses make a difference. She was relieved he did not pretend she was other than who she was, and also did not act as if this kiss sealed her damnation.

He took his leave and left her there, sitting in the garden where he had sat. She held on to the happy warmth as long as she could, while she looked toward those black shrubs and wondered if the moonlight really did find her in the night.

J onathan woke in an ill humor. That single kiss had tortured him long into the night.

He had heard Celia finally come in last night, and climb the back stairs. He had not moved while he listened to each footfall, his body urging her to continue on, to this level and his door. He knew she would not, but that had not prevented his jaw from clenching until long after her steps had faded in the direction of her own chamber at the front of the house.

That had been, he decided as morning broke, the most ill-advised kiss he had ever given a woman in his life. Only she had charmed him totally, sitting there in the night garden, telling him about that place where she had lived and her plans to sell plants from this house.

He admired how she was trying to create a world for herself here, and establish an income that would permit her independence. It spoke well of her, and she had shown honest joy in her scheme. And in response he had told his better judgment to go to hell and kissed her for the simple reason that he wanted to. Needed to.

She had undone him with her fresh, vivid pleasure in that simple kiss. He did not think he had ever kissed before and been so aware that the woman knew no guilt, no hesitation, no fear, no expectations, and no regrets. He doubted *she* had stayed awake half the night debating the wisdom of it. He was very sure that if she had, she had not concluded it was a mistake. She would not think that way. She had not been raised like other women.

He found tepid water waiting outside his chamber when he opened the door. While not ideal, it was better than drawing cold water from a well himself. He wondered if it heralded that at least Celia did not mind his being here now.

As he reached for the bucket, he glanced at another door across the passage. A good-size lock stared back. He had been debating whether to pick that lock after all.

Celia had absented herself from this house enough that he had looked through the chambers down below. He had discovered no caches of papers or accounts, or anything else to indicate Alessandra had left a history of her lovers. This chamber across from his in the attic, however, probably served as storage. His mission would not be complete until he saw what it contained.

Celia had the key. He did not think she had spent much time examining the contents of the chamber either, but she had probably at least used that key to see what lay within. Perhaps one day soon she would enter the room again, perhaps with her two new servants, to clean it out. He really should get in there before that happened.

Red-haired Marian stuck her head out her own chamber door at the other end of the passage. A damp rag hung from her hand.

"That water be a bit cooled by now, Mr. Albrighton. Will you be rising this hour most days, sir? It is hard to have warm water for a tenant if one does not know his habits."

The water had not been Celia's doing. Of course not. It had been only one kiss, after all.

"I have been awake some hours already. I did not expect water to be brought, and did not check earlier." He had grown accustomed to waiting until ten o'clock to go to the well himself, to allow Celia her privacy in the mornings.

"Then eight o'clock will do for you? I will be waking with the dawn myself. I am not used to all the light we have up here." She walked down the passageway. "Bella and I will be doing the linens later today. We will come and get them and remake the bed if you want, or you can leave them outside the door if you won't be wanting us in there. All the same to us."

"Enter if you like, but do not touch the table, even to dust. I might lose something if it were misplaced."

She peered around him and into the chamber, and at the table against the window piled high with booklets and papers. "One of them studious types, are you, then?"

"More curious than studious."

She gave the chamber, and him, a critical inspection. "You've no manservant. I would have expected you to."

"I travel often. A servant would slow me down." A servant would have never accepted the conditions of some of that travel the last eight years either. Servants have standards.

"I expect you hire them as you go, then," Marian said.

"Bella and I can do for you while you are here, if you like. Washing clothes and such. Not so good as a manservant, of course. We won't be helping you bathe and shave, but for ten pence we'll scrub and iron those nice shirts of yours."

"That is better than bringing them elsewhere."

They struck a bargain on the laundry and other chores. As they finished, a commotion below broke the quiet in the house.

Marian draped her rag on the storage room's latch, then wiped her hands on her apron. "The plants must have come. I need to see if Miss Pennifold requires help."

Plants. Plants everywhere. Celia gazed around her back sitting room, excited to see her plan coming to life most literally.

Pots holding globes of green on upright stems crowded the landing below the back stairs. A palm as tall as herself flanked the entry to the back sitting room. Verity, decked out in a most becoming scarlet ensemble that complemented her dark hair and snowy skin, was taking pots carried to her by Marian and judging their best placement on the shelves by the windows.

Daphne stood in the center of the chamber with a journal book propped open in her arm. She had accompanied the wagons on this first delivery, to make sure all went well. Tall, willowy, and pale like the light of a winter dawn, her gray eyes watched the plants find their homes while she made notations in her book.

Boots thudded on the floor. A workman carried in a lemon tree in a deep, wide pot, straining from its weight.

"We should deliver that at once," Daphne said. "How will you ever remove it from here, Celia?"

"You said the Robertsons wanted it next week, not this one. I am going to have help, Daphne. I will not be carrying these plants myself."

The man brushed off his hands. "That is the last, Mrs. Joyes. Just the flowers left now."

"Put them in the front sitting room," Celia said. "It is chilled enough in winter to keep them there for a day. In warmer weather we will make use of the cold storage near the kitchen below."

The man trudged off to get the flowers.

Celia went back to moving pots onto the new shelves, all the while keeping one ear open and one eye on Daphne. Fate had conspired against her, and arranged for the wagons from The Rarest Blooms to arrive while Jonathan was in the house.

Verity caught Celia's eye. She glanced meaningfully at Daphne, then up at the ceiling, and raised her eyebrows. Celia shook her head. No, she had not yet explained about her tenant to Daphne. It appeared she would be doing so today, though, unless Jonathan decided to remain in his chamber for the next hour or so. He did that sometimes. There were days he never left. Perhaps—

Boot steps began a descent on the stairs. So much for *perhaps*.

Verity increased the noise of her movements and chatter. Marian began a loud conversation asking about the dinner menu. Beneath the growing commotion, like a drumbeat getting louder, those boots thudded in a steady rhythm.

Within the chamber's confusion, an island of stillness formed. Daphne was its center and its source. She looked up from her account book, to the doorway, and watched the stairwell, perplexed.

Jonathan stepped into view, dressed for riding, looking handsome as sin. Daphne just stared at him for a long count, then swung her inquisitive gaze to Celia.

"I fear that we have blocked your way with the topiaries, Mr. Albrighton," Celia said.

"I promise not to knock any over." Keeping his word meant a few awkward strides, but he emerged from the garden soon enough.

Celia asked him to join them. He entered, greeted Verity formally, and gazed around at their interior garden and the plants lined on his shelves.

"Daphne, this is Mr. Albrighton, a tenant. Mr. Albrighton, this is my dear friend Mrs. Joyes."

"He is one of Hawkeswell's friends," Verity chimed in quickly. "Isn't that a coincidence? My husband speaks very well of you, Mr. Albrighton."

"Thank you, Madam. I am honored to hear that he does."

Daphne smiled ever so graciously. Celia was not fooled. She saw her friend taking this man's measure most thoroughly, and being a bit suspicious about what she saw, no matter which earl had befriended him.

"A tenant, Celia? How enterprising of you."

"She inherited me with the house, unfortunately," Jonathan said.

"And you chose to stay, I see. It is so inconvenient to make changes of abode, isn't it? Although this is an odd location for a man such as you to have lodgings, Mr. Albrighton. Out of the way, and not especially fashionable. Would not the amenities of Albany suit you better?"

"I am not in London enough to own chambers, nor even

to justify having them at a better address. This neighborhood suits my purposes, but thank you for your interest."

"Quiet, obscure, and anonymous suits you?"

"It suits many people, Mrs. Joyes. Whether to a street west of Bedford Square, or to a small estate in Middlesex, there are many reasons why some of us prefer to retreat from society for a while."

Daphne's gaze sharpened. A touch of color rose on her cool white skin. He had surprised her with his own directness. Celia was sure she had never seen Daphne blush before.

"I am referring to Miss Pennifold, of course," he added. "She and I have this in common, this desire to retreat."

Daphne regained the fraction of composure that she had lost. "You also have this house in common now, it appears."

Celia began to think Daphne and Mr. Albrighton were going to have a row. Verity thought so too, from the way she watched the exchange.

"Your concern is admirable, Mrs. Joyes," Jonathan soothed. "However, Miss Pennifold has accommodated herself to my presence. If you are protective, consider that she is very safe with me here, and the ladies will not suffer the vulnerabilities most women face when they live alone."

He bowed and took his leave then, and disappeared down the garden path. Daphne watched him go, her lids low.

Finally, she turned away from the window and opened her account book again. "Small wonder that you no longer wanted to live out in the country, Celia."

"I did not move here because of Mr. Albrighton, if that

is what you are implying. I really did inherit him. His tenancy came as a complete surprise, and his continued residence a nuisance."

"I never doubted that discovering his claims on that chamber came as a surprise." She smiled. "Truly."

"He's an earl's son," Verity offered. "The last Earl of Thornridge's bastard."

"Verity, since you have found love with an earl's son, you may think they are all good men of high character. Regrettably, my experience has been that a title makes neither a fit father in and of itself, nor a reputable son without dispute. However, if our Celia thinks he is a decent man, and that she is safe here with Marian and Bella, that is all that signifies."

"I am safe. And while he is a nuisance, he is not as intrusive as I worried. Why, he is hardly ever around."

"How convenient, then."

"He built these shelves," Verity said, trying to help again by putting in a good word for him.

"That probably explains all those nails. He appears the sort of man who wants to make very sure things stand as he intends."

"I am tired of talking about him," Celia announced. "Today marks the beginning of our partnership, Daphne, and that is much more interesting. Verity, I think we should move these tall ones down one step."

Daphne watched as Verity and she made much of moving the plants, discussing each one's placement. All the while Celia felt her older friend's eyes on her.

"Has he trifled with you, Celia?" The question came out of nowhere a half hour later.

"Trifled? Who?"

"As if you don't know."

"Oh, you mean Mr. Albrighton. Of course not. I am not stupid, Daphne. I am not a child either."

"That is true—you are neither stupid nor a child. You are a young woman who has always viewed life with almost ruthless honesty. My question was one of curiosity, not criticism or judgment, or even a prelude to advice. I just wondered if that handsome man had trifled with you."

"Well, he hasn't." She was not sure what Daphne meant by *trifled*, but she decided that one kiss did not qualify.

"Pity, that," Daphne mused as she jotted in her account book. "I expect his trifling would be rather pleasant."

Celia gaped. She looked at Verity. They both looked at Daphne in shock. Then all three began laughing.

Chapter Eight

Celia mounted the stairs to the attic, holding a key of good size. She paused at the top landing.

The door she wanted was across the passage from Mr. Albrighton's chamber. This was the only space that she had not carefully examined in this house. Now that the plants had come, and she had arranged for a hired wagon to deliver them to houses during the next week, she had time to devote to this necessary chore.

Not only lack of time had delayed her, she admitted. She both craved to see what was stored here, and dreaded the potential disappointment. She might learn the truth about her father the way she hoped, or learn nothing at all. She could not bear to face the latter, especially when she had no other idea of how else to pursue the truth if her mother's own belongings failed her.

The chamber held the dry, dusty smell one finds in un-used attics. The chill, as winter's cold penetrated the small windows and roof, did not dispel that distinctive atmosphere.

She left the door open a crack to let in some fresher air, then surveyed the items stored here. There was much more than she expected. Not only that trunk that she had spied lived in this chamber.

A rolled carpet rested on the floor. She toed at its edge until she saw its pattern, and recognized it as an Aubusson that had once graced Alessandra's private apartment on Orchard Street. Her mother had been very proud of that carpet.

Two large framed watercolors rested against the wall behind the carpet. They also had once decorated the other house. Gifts from lovers, both represented airy sketches by French artists popular at the end of the last century. One was a painting of a nude model who looked a lot like a young Alessandra.

She stepped around some chairs and plant stands so she could investigate the largest of three trunks cramming the small space. She paused after she lifted its lid. A gorgeous fur mantle rested atop a pile of other garments. A quick examination said this trunk held a wardrobe far more valuable than the one left at the other house.

She went to the next trunk. There were more garments in it, but less grand. They cushioned small decorative items made of china and glass, and other personal belongings perhaps of sentimental meaning to the woman who owned them.

The third trunk surprised her the most. She gazed at its contents while nostalgia mixed with shock.

These were her own belongings. Her wardrobe, chosen so carefully that year, to be worn in the park and at those afternoon salons, lay neatly folded inside. Flipping through them, she also found dresses and gowns never worn, the ones ordered from modistes for a young woman's debut into a very special society.

Memories came to her of studying fashion plates, and choosing fabrics at the draper's. She pulled out the dinner dress that had been her favorite. At the last fitting, she had pictured herself presiding over a party as Anthony's wife. All the faces around her had been a blur in her mind, except his.

A sound startled her out of her reverie. She looked to the doorway and saw Mr. Albrighton there, his hand still on the latch.

He strolled into the chamber, his gaze quickly surveying its contents. "So this is storage. I thought perhaps you thought to let it to another tenant, or use it for more servants."

She refolded the dinner dress, and smoothed its liquid satin surface with her fingertips. "It was past time for me to see what lay behind this door. I expected a trunk or two, from my quick glance before. I never anticipated all that." She gestured to the end of the room farthest from the door, which was out of sight when she had stuck her head in.

He stood beside her and looked down. She saw him assessing the silk beneath her fingers.

"These are my things," she said, even though she did not have to explain. "When they were not at the other house, I just assumed she had sold them, or given them away."

"That is an unusual color. Like the fairest fawn."

His description was apt, and better than she would have managed. "It is one of the modest dresses, for public view."

"There are other kinds?"

"Oh, yes. I was not being groomed to be a bride. I knew that, and yet still allowed myself to pretend it could turn out that way, as you know."

His kind smile acknowledged her scathing disappointment that day. His deep-set eyes compelled her attention and she floated in their connected gazes for a timeless moment.

"For example, there was this one." She looked away and thumbed the corners of the garments until she reached a silk the color of geraniums. She pulled it out. "Hardly a demure hue, but fashionable and not scandalous in itself. However—" She held up the dress so it opened along her bodice and lap. The top of it consisted of lace and nothing more. "Only a fool would forget the future she would have if her mother buys her this, don't you think?"

"I think you did not err if you thought that lace might be appropriate no matter what life you would have. Not all husbands treat their wives like perpetual, blushing virgins."

She laughed, and set the dress aside. "Then perhaps I will give it to Verity or Audrianna. I have cause to believe neither one's husband will be shocked."

"Hawkeswell or Summerhays? I assure you, neither would be."

She rose to her knees to dig deeper in the trunk. "One for each, then. I am sure there is another of similar intention."

He dropped to one knee beside her and held out his arms, so she could place the luxurious fabrics on them instead of the floor. She stacked them up to his chin before she found the soft pearl-toned dress that she sought. She flipped it open to examine its low neckline and very sheer bodice.

"This would suit Verity, I think," she said. "Don't you agree?"

"It would be inappropriate for me to picture Lady Hawkeswell in it."

"You can at least admit the color would favor her."

"I think the color would favor you more."

She glanced at him, and in those deep eyes she saw the image of herself in this dress, surrounded by other luscious silks on pillows and drapes, and a tall dark man full of mystery admiring the erotic image she made.

She felt her face warming, and other parts too. She made much of turning her attention to folding the dress while the possibilities and expectations throbbed between them in the tense silence.

She began to reach for his stack of fabrics when something in the trunk caught her eye. Pushing aside a dove gray wool pelisse, she uncovered a folio flat on the trunk's bottom. She lifted the cover.

"Her paintings and drawings," she said. "It is very thick. Perhaps they are all here."

He peered in, interested. His angle brought him closer to her. So close she could smell the soap he had used to wash. So close she could see how thick his eyelashes were. Her heart beat more quickly and she feared stammering like a schoolgirl.

She took the garments from him, and quickly stacked them back in the trunk. She gazed at the other items in the chamber while she tried to ignore how he still remained down there with her on his one knee, too close really. She imagined him touching her again, and the next kiss, and—

Reckless thoughts. Stupid ones. He was not for her and she was not for him, at least not in any respectable way. And yet, her body was not caring much about that, and her thoughts were not very proper. Instead the things Mama had described kept presenting themselves, and some of them seemed appealing for the first time in her life.

She forced the scandalous images out of her thoughts. "I am supposed to inform the executor about these things, aren't I? That carpet is very valuable, and one of the trunks holds her furs."

He shrugged. "Send him the carpet if you would feel guilty not doing so. As for the rest, there is little value in used garments that may no longer be in the latest fashion. Not enough value to make a difference. You own the contents of this particular trunk anyway, so it is not part of her estate."

"I wonder why they are here. I would have expected it all to be in the other house."

"Perhaps it was her way to preserve what she valued most for you. If the executor did not know she lived here on occasion, he would never think to inventory this house's contents."

Could he be correct? Had it been deliberate, and a plan on Alessandra's part to hand down something at least, besides a tarnished reputation and a very specialized education?

"I think that I must take my own inventory, but it is too chilled in this attic to do so. I will move these trunks to my chamber and sort it all at my leisure."

He stood, and reached down to close the trunk. "Allow me. They are too heavy for you, even with Marian's help."

He followed her down to the second level and to her chamber. He set the trunk down. "Perhaps you should investigate one at a time. If all of them are here, you will have little room to walk."

There was some truth in that. This was not a large bedchamber, and the other trunks were of good size. "That might be best. Thank you."

His gaze had been taking an inventory of sorts as well, of the contents of her room. The last time he had been here it had been too dark to see much. It struck her that she had never had a man in her chamber before him. Not ever, even as a child. This one did not leave his masculinity at the threshold, and his intrusion created an intimate spell.

"It is not what I would have expected of your mother," he said, observing the crisp white muslin at the windows and serving as bed drapes.

"Perhaps you thought it would be red satin?" she teased, her voice steady even though she feared it would squeak.

"No, but more of the town and less of the country."

She fingered the simple fabric. "I find the anonymous simplicity of these hangings soothing, in part because they speak of no particular taste at all. They are very practical too, despite what one would think. They can be washed just like a man's shirt."

His gaze moved over those window drapes, then the ones on the bed, then the bed itself. Finally it settled on her. The chamber all but trembled from the degree to which his presence seemed to dominate it now.

"You think this chamber does not speak of its occupant now, Miss Pennifold? I find it whispers most eloquently about the woman who lives here."

She wasn't sure whether it was a compliment or not, although the way he looked at her suggested he had meant it to be.

They stood there longer than necessary, with the trunk that contained the remnants of her year with Mama between them. Or perhaps it wasn't long at all. Maybe the way her heart beat slowed time for her.

"Are you deciding whether to kiss me again?" she asked.

"Do you want me to kiss you again?"

"Of course not."

"Of course? Have you told yourself you did not enjoy it? And here I thought you were one of the rare women who does not lie about that."

He had her there. Her quick denial had been stupid, considering just how much she had enjoyed it. He hardly missed that part. "I only meant that I was not inviting another kiss."

He laughed quietly, enjoying her little fluster. "So perhaps you did enjoy it, but of course you do not want me to kiss you again."

"Yes—no—I am not sure," she admitted. "I wish I were sure, though. It was a nice kiss."

"Then I will not, if you are not sure."

She shrugged, and hoped she looked sophisticated and not as much the silly schoolgirl that she felt. "It was only one kiss. One more would have hardly signified much, even if I were not sure."

He reached out and laid his palm on her cheek, as he had in the garden. His thumb rose to brush her lips, creating a tingle that grew as it spread through her. Desire was in him. She saw it in his taut expression and felt it in the mystery exciting her.

One more kiss, surely. Now. He would—

"It cannot be one more, Celia. It can never be only one kiss again. Do not pretend you do not know that."

He left then. The chamber did not return totally to what it had been before. He lingered like a scent that would not quickly fade, as if the furniture and walls had absorbed some of his life energy and would quietly echo his invasion for days, reminding her of the excitement waiting if she *were* to be sure.

She looked at those crisp, pristine drapes. What had he seen in them that spoke of her? Virginal purity? Opaque blanks, much like his calling cards?

Perhaps he had seen only symbols of a woman still deciding what colors and patterns to add to her life.

Celia did not leave the house for the next two days. Jonathan knew this for certain because he did not either. He remained in his chamber, waiting for her to call for the cabriolet to visit friends or see to other business. With luck she would do so at the same time Marian and Bella went to the market, and he would have time to search without danger of interruption.

His vigil left him time to read the papers and journals that had accumulated during his absence from London. It was foolish to subscribe to such things when one would not have the leisure to enjoy them, he knew. However, the ones in France, while interesting and learned in their own right, only had notices regarding developments in England and Scotland, and he never regretted coming home to find the full reports.

The printing shop to which his mail was sent had been happy to see him claim the large stash that had accumulated. Now stacks towered in his chamber and he systematically worked his way through them. Most described experiments in chemistry or natural processes, but a few itemized new species found on long journeys and several reported industrial developments.

He preferred the investigations related to pure science, although its applications did not bore him. He had always found certainty more compelling than ambiguity, and progress in understanding natural law fascinating. The solidity of science, the small but sure discoveries that could be proven again and again, contrasted markedly with just about everything else in the world that he knew.

On the third day, he was forging his way through a lengthy treatise. It was badly written, but usually that did not deter him. Today, however, it encouraged his thoughts to wander, mostly to an image of Celia wearing that sheer silk dress.

He had no trouble seeing her in it, with her golden hair gathered into a loose, thick knot that begged for loosening, and the soft blush of the silk's hue complementing her pale beauty. The film of fabric stretched over her breasts, pulling tightly against dark tips that had hardened erotically. A man's hand, *his* hand, glossed over that silk, causing her breasts to turn heavy and firm and sensitive. Her eye color deepened with the pleasure and a million delightful sparks shone in them and she—

Sounds rumbled through the premises, shattering the fantasy. He heard Marian calling up the front stairs, telling Celia to come down at once and see what had arrived on the street outside.

Curious, he set down his reading and went to look himself, while feminine footsteps gently sounded on stairs below. His own chamber faced the garden, so he let himself into the storage chamber across the way. After he had carried that trunk down to Celia's chamber, she had neglected to relock the chamber, and he had not reminded her to do so. If she would just leave the house, he would finish this mission quickly.

Down below, in front of the house, a grand coach was stopping. It was the sort of conveyance intended to impress.

No more than a few hundred families who used such carriages would be residing in London in winter. A handsome matched pair snorted and stomped in front of it, controlled by a liveried coachman at the ribbons.

He opened the window in order to see better. The footman set down the carriage steps. A fair, Germanic-looking fellow got out, and set his hat on his head. Before the rim obscured Jonathan's view, he recognized the face.

Anthony Dargent was calling on Celia.

Chapter Nine

Celia quickly removed her apron and smoothed her hair. She posed herself on the settee in the front sitting room.

Marian entered with the card. Celia looked into Marian's eyes and recognized both the concern and curiosity in them.

"Bring him in, Marian. He is an old friend."

While Marian left to do as bid, Celia nervously eyed her surroundings. The upholstery appeared rather faded in today's light. She had never noticed that before. The furniture in general was quite humble in this house, compared to the other one Alessandra had owned.

She heard boot steps and her heart beat harder with each one. *Five years.* A good part of her life had passed since she had run from that drawing room that day, heartbroken and disillusioned.

Suddenly Anthony was standing in the threshold. Her nerves calmed at the sight of him. He had lost what had still been a boyish freshness in his countenance back then. Five years had matured him in the most flattering of ways, however, and he was even more handsome now. Even his hair had cooperated, darkening slightly to a color still golden but not so yellow.

She could be excused if she wished he had gone soft, she thought. It would help if his face had turned flaccid, and did not still possess such regular and finely sculpted features.

He bowed in greeting. He had always been a gentleman in his behavior, with Mama and her.

Then suddenly he strode forward until he stood right in front of her, gazing down so intensely that it startled her.

"Celia." He spoke her name as though he exhaled a word kept inside him too long. He abruptly took her hand in both of his and kissed it.

She extricated it from his hold as gently as she could. "Anthony. It is a pleasant surprise to see you. Won't you sit, please?"

He considered sitting beside her. She saw it and let her hand flutter toward a nearby chair. He followed her direction.

"How did you find me?" she asked.

"I assumed you had come to town, to settle your mother's estate, so I called on Mappleton to ask after you. Imagine my astonishment when he said you had taken residence here." He looked around, clearly not impressed by what he saw. "Where have you been? I kept asking your mother, but she would only say you were abroad. She never explained if that meant you were on the continent, or just abroad in England or even London itself."

"I was not far away. I have even visited town periodically these last years. And you, Anthony? Have you spent much time in town?"

"My duties result in long spells in the country. I have inherited the estate now."

"And married too. I read when it happened. My best wishes for what I am sure is a wonderful match."

His expression fell. Anthony had never been very good at hiding his thoughts or emotions. That was why she had been so sure he loved her. What else could all the pained, heartfelt, visible yearning have meant?

He flushed, and some of that prior boyishness returned. "It is an excellent match, for all the usual reasons. However . . ." His color deepened. "The truth is that you have never been far from my thoughts, Celia. Sometimes at night I hear you singing, the way you did that first afternoon Stratton brought me to one of your mother's salons. I find myself judging every woman's beauty against yours, and I always find them lacking. You have continued to captivate me for five years without even being present in my life."

It was a fine speech, especially for Anthony, who was not known for his eloquence. It was, Celia considered, the sort of speech that would sound very nice as the prelude to a marriage proposal.

Except Anthony no longer had the choice of making one, did he?

"You flatter me too much." She made sure her smile was kind but formal. "Better if you sought to be captivated by the good woman who *is* present in your life."

"That is not at all the same. She has my affection and respect, but—she is not like you."

"After five years, it is unlikely you know what I am

like, Anthony. If you hold fond memories, however, there is nothing wrong with that. We are all permitted those, no matter what our obligations."

He angled toward her, to bridge the distance made by the seat she had assigned him. "And you, Celia? Do you hold any fond memories?"

She did hold some, deep inside her, too bittersweet to examine after what had happened. They emerged now as he turned that earnest gaze on her. Yet it was only the memories that touched her heart, not the gaze itself. His eyes, so familiar once, seemed to be those of a stranger now.

He *was* a stranger, she realized. Five years was a long time in both their lives. Neither of them was the same person as before. She certainly wasn't that child anymore.

"The memories are a little vague now. They are from an old chapter in my life. It was kind of you to seek me out, to welcome me back to London, however. One can always use a friend or two in town to call on if problems arise."

A smile, indulgent and kind. The same smile he had given her when he explained her great misunderstanding of his intentions.

"I did not seek you out only to welcome you back to town, Celia. You must know that. Other women, with different mothers, can pretend to be coy, but it does not suit you."

His close proximity suddenly made her uncomfortable. She stood and strolled away. He began to rise as well.

"No, please, stay there," she said. "Let us set aside etiquette. It would be better if you remained in your chair. You mention my mother, and make assumptions about me. Yet you know that I left her home, and her plans for me. Why would you think I have changed my mind about that, and am now being coy?"

He smiled. He made a display of gazing around the chamber. "Because this does not become you. You should be living in Mayfair, not here. You should have a good carriage and pair, not the cabriolet you have been seen driving. You should be wearing silks, not that plain wool. You are no longer a girl. Surely you understand now, that marriages are economic choices. Love . . . may require other arrangements."

She almost laughed, but managed to swallow her bitter amusement. "Your high opinion of the luxury I deserve is charming. So is your reference to love. Do you think I have spent the last five years pining for you?" She offered her own indulgent smile. "But you are correct that I have come to accept the ways of the world. I do not hold against you what happened. What I wanted from you . . . what I thought you wanted too—well, it was naïve. If it is love you want, perhaps you should seek out another hopeful child."

He did not take it well. No man would. Mama had warned that many men, his kind in particular, thought they bestowed a great gift on women like them with their interest.

His lids lowered. Irritation flexed over his face. "I have waited too long to be easily discouraged."

"You should not have waited at all."

"I had no choice except to wait. You left, didn't you? After I had given your mother your first two years' allowance. She put me off about you, and the money, until I knew the latter at least would never be mine again. You, however—"

"You gave her money, and she did not return it after I

left?" The revelation came like a slap. The shock shattered her poise.

"She was sure you would return, she said. A brief delay, no more, she said." He gazed at her frankly.

Her stomach turned. *Oh, Mama.* Account book or not, there was indeed one more debt outstanding on the estate. No wonder he had arrived here so boldly, wearing his assumptions like a new hat, and broached this subject without much ceremony.

He again scrutinized the chamber. "In three months you will hate this house, and this neighborhood. You were born for better. I will take care of you, Celia. You will want for nothing. It will be as originally arranged, and as it was meant to be from the day you were born."

He articulated only what most of the world thought. She felt her face flushing, because sometimes she thought it as well.

"I was born as we are all born, Anthony. Naked and innocent. The daughter of a whore does not come from the womb with a mark on her brow and soul, inherited like the color of her hair."

"And are you still innocent, Celia? When last I spoke with Alessandra she believed you still to be."

"What—? You questioned her on—" They had discussed her, in the end as in the beginning, like an item for purchase. "How dare you quiz me, to be sure the goods have not been used, as if I am a—a— This is too much to bear. I must ask you to leave now."

"Please hear me out first. It is in your interests to do so."

"You have no right to assume you know what my interests are."

"You are foolish to insult me, Celia. You pledged your

innocence to me long ago because of our love, and can hardly be shocked at my curiosity about its preservation. I will attribute your behavior now to your surprise at seeing me again. I have perhaps been too impatient, but after five years, I can be excused."

His sense of privilege astonished her. "I must *insist* that you leave now."

He stood, but he did not leave. To her horror he advanced on her. She kept backing up until her back hit the wall. Then his hands were on her face, cupping it roughly, and he moved to kiss her. She twisted her face away as best she could and his mouth found only her cheek.

"Stop this, Anthony! Leave now, I implore you," she cried.

His hands tightened and began to forcibly turn her face.

"The lady invited you to leave, Dargent. If you are a gentleman, I am sure you do not want to distress her further, and will comply with her wishes."

Suddenly she was free and Anthony stood several feet away. Celia turned toward the source of the intruding voice.

Mr. Albrighton stood right outside the doorway, dark from his crown to his boot heels except for the glaring white of his cravat and shirt. Anthony faced him tensely, flushing from either ardor or anger. She could not tell which.

Mr. Albrighton's tone had been amiable. Yet Celia could not ignore how his presence charged the air in the room with a crackling force. Anthony looked as if he had just been threatened when no real challenge had been made.

"This is Mr. Jonathan Albrighton," she said. "He is—"

"I know who he is." He eyed Mr. Albrighton suspiciously. "What are you doing here?"

"I am a friend of the family, come to call on Miss Pennifold to offer my condolences about her mother." He casually stood aside. "Allow me to accompany you out, Dargent."

Irritated by the interruption, but well cornered all the same, Anthony strode to the doorway. He glanced at her furiously, then at Mr. Albrighton. "Friend of the family, I believe, since you are both of the same stripe, aren't you?"

Jonathan escorted Dargent right to the door of the coach. He barely resisted throwing the fellow inside with his own hands. He made sure that the coach left the street. Then he returned to the house.

Celia remained in the sitting room. She stood near a window, and had been watching the departure. The view of her there made him pause.

He searched what he could see of her expression for some regret, or heartbreak, regarding this man from her past. The light found her as it always did, and it made tears in her eyes and on her cheeks sparkle.

She did not look at him. She wiped the tears with her hand. More took their place. It touched him, this silent weeping.

"Thank you for saving me again." Her voice came slowly, and choked with her emotion. "It was going to become an embarrassing scene."

And a potentially dangerous one. "He is fortunate I did not give in to the impulse to teach him some manners."

"He did not believe he owed me manners. If he uses them with such as me, it is a condescension, not a requirement. I know that now, even if I did not years ago."

Such as me. He really regretted not thrashing the scoundrel now. "You are too forgiving. He is a conceited fool, and always was."

She wiped her eyes again, and took a deep breath. "He appeared afraid of you."

"He knew he was in the wrong and deserved a thrashing. Caught like that, he would be afraid of any man."

She finally faced him. He saw dismay in her eyes that said this visit had hurt her badly.

"You sound almost boyish, Mr. Albrighton. We both know that he came to propose a commonplace arrangement. Such negotiations are often frank and crude, and even physical, with the persuasions calculated to entice. I suspect the lures would have turned many women's heads."

"Are they starting to turn yours?"

He frowned when she did not immediately respond in the negative. The notion of her going to Dargent infuriated him.

"Luxury has its lures for me as well as most women," she finally said. "And, after all, I was taught that love is a commodity. In Alessandra Northrope's home, virtue was not considered virtuous." She laughed a little at her wordplay. Sadly.

It was a musical sound. Winter's light turned golden near the window, while lights sparked in her eyes. She was proving stronger than Dargent and his humiliating assumptions could defeat. Beneath it all, however, he still saw hurt and confusion.

He should leave now. Instead, he strode across the chamber, pulled her into an embrace, and kissed her hard.

Light poured into him as he did, rare and bright and almost painful. He wanted her so badly in that moment that he had to clench his teeth against his impulses.

Her expression undid him. No more shadows. Her face

glowed and her eyes revealed the arousal making her pliant in his arms. He kissed her again, knowing he should not today of all days. It lasted too long, too sweetly for his sanity. Summoning common sense from hell knew where, he resisted her encouraging mouth and stopped.

When he began to break their embrace, she wrapped her arms around his neck. "I know what you are thinking," she said, her breath feathering his neck. "That you risk insulting with actions worse than he did with words. It is not the same, however."

"It is more the same than you think. Desire is desire, no matter how the object of desire is pursued."

She laughed lightly. Musically. There were no sad tones in it now. Her face remained mere inches from his, their noses almost touching. His arms circled her more totally because there was no other response to the blue eyes looking into his so openly.

"There is all the difference in the world to me," she said. "He made me feel stupid, as if I deserved his insult. And you make me feel alive in the best ways."

She playfully ran one fingertip along the edges of his mouth. Then that artful finger teased along his jaw and up the edge of his ear.

Her mother had taught her that. It was easy to forget the education she had received, and the reason Dargent had come here today, but her little gesture reminded him too well.

She felt good in his arms. Warm and soft and ever so feminine. A better man would be content with that alone and hope it brought her distraction from today's visit. When she raised her lips toward him, however, inviting another kiss, he knew he was not such a man.

Passion's fever broke in him again. And in her. She

joined him, parting her lips so he could explore, encouraging more heat and aggression. Her hands tightened on his shoulders, then his arms, grasping him closer while she pressed her body to his. Time disappeared, then their surroundings, as they soared higher on kisses and bites and hot breaths.

He had to feel her, know her. He bound her close with one arm while his other hand moved to her waist and hip, following sinuous curves. Eventually he caressed the perfect roundness of her breast and she quietly whimpered with pleasure.

Hot now, burning for her, he sought to make her as lost as he. He ached more intensely than he had since his youth. He gave her pleasure and took his own and balanced on the brink of ruthlessness.

He smoothed his hand over her breast again, so she would feel it more. He rubbed the hard tip. She luxuriated in the sensation with closed eyes and parted lips.

"If he made me feel like this, I could probably lie to myself about the rest," she murmured.

Her mention of Dargent brought him back to his senses a little. Enough.

"And if there are no lies, but only this?"

"People always build some story around pleasure. The story of marriage or the story of love, or at least a brief tale of commerce."

"Not always . . . Sometimes it just is."

"Like now, you mean."

Like now. Only there *was* a story here, and he could not pretend there was not anymore. This was about Dargent's visit.

He stopped the caresses and embraced her closely. She tried to kiss him but he did not allow it.

"Forgive me, Celia. I have taken advantage of a kind of grief in you."

He released her and stepped away. The sight of her smiling, flushed and radiant, almost had him grab her again.

"If on a better day you conclude that virtue is not a virtue, I hope that I am the first to know." He walked away before her sparkling eyes changed his mind. "And if that scoundrel returns, or in any way insults you again, you must tell me."

Chapter Ten

Celia gazed around her plant room. The few remaining plants appeared forlorn on the shelves. More would arrive soon, but for now she had completed most of her task.

After three days of being very active, she suddenly found herself with little to occupy her. She went to the library to write to Daphne with news of how these first deliveries had gone. She would reassure Daphne that Mr. Drummond, whom she had chosen to help her, was proving to be a most agreeable and dependable employee.

The silence of the house pressed on her as she pondered the words to pen. Mr. Drummond had indicated that Jonathan had come down while she was out in the wagon arranging the plants' safest placements for their brief journeys. He had left the house, then. She was rather glad for that. At least she would not have to find ways to avoid him today.

Perhaps she would write him a letter too.

Dear Mr. Albrighton,

Thank you for your help the other day. I am sure you understand that I was not myself after the shock of Mr. Dargent's visit. I know that a worldly man like yourself would never put significance, one way or another, on a few kisses bestowed in a moment of extreme distress. All the same, what transpires makes the current situation in my home difficult. Surely you can no longer be comfortable here. I will not mind at all if you conclude you must leave and seek other chambers. Indeed, I have even taken steps to help you do so. Please note the advertisements in the paper that accompanies this letter, and the ones that I circled that speak of gentlemen's apartments.

She took some satisfaction in composing the letter, even if she would never write it. She liked how it sounded sophisticated, and so different from how she had acted and felt when last she saw him.

Once the shock of Anthony's visit passed, her humiliation over what Mr. Albrighton had overheard and seen, and how in her distress she then behaved with him, settled on her hard. Now it would not go away.

Nor would the memory of how devastated she had been when he returned to the house after throwing Anthony out. She had been dying inside. She had been mortified and afraid. She had called on all of Alessandra's training to regain some poise and composure.

Had he seen that? Was that why he had made love to her? Had he intended to comfort, or just allowed his inclinations to take advantage of her grief, the way he said?

What must he think of her, to have permitted him such

liberties—to have frankly encouraged them—after expressing shock at Anthony's overtures?

Sometimes it just is. That was how he had spoken of
that passion. One more ambiguity from a man full of them.

For men perhaps it could just be. For women, however,
the world imposes a story on sensuality if she is not brave
enough to write her own. And with Jonathan Albrighton,
there could be no story at all, she was very sure. She would
not do for a man in his situation, and he would never do
for her, no matter which life she chose to embrace.

She stood abruptly and walked to the back chamber.
She removed her gray pelisse from its peg and donned it.
She fastened it with quick, determined fingers.

She was done with the plants for now. She would no
longer hide from Jonathan, no matter what he thought, or
from anyone else. She would not allow herself to feel hu-
miliated about Anthony's visit anymore either.

She would take advantage of what had turned into a
fair day, and walk in the park. If anyone noticed her and
pointed and whispered that she was the daughter of that
Northrope woman, she would ignore them and hold her
head high the way she always had.

Hyde Park was not crowded, but a good number of
souls had come out midday to enjoy the sun and
calm breeze. Celia found a post to tie the horse and carriage, and began to climb down to tend to it.

Gloved hands reached for her horse's bridle as she did.
"Allow me, if you will."

The gentleman who owned those hands made quick
work with the tether, then came over to hand her down.

He was being polite, and kind to a woman without a

footman or chaperone. Yet Celia knew it had not been only a good heart that moved him to assist her. As she stepped down she saw the interest in his eyes.

Had he recognized her? Perhaps not. He might just be hopeful that she was the sort of woman who discarded proprieties in such a situation. If a conversation ensued, who knew where it might lead?

She had seen that speculative spark often before. Even while living with Daphne, even with men who had no idea who her mother was, she had garnered attention of this kind. Daphne always said it was merely because she was pretty, but she felt today that perhaps she had indeed been born with a brand on her forehead as she had insisted to Anthony she had not.

She did not want company, least of all of his hopeful kind. She thanked him and walked away, to enjoy the park on her own.

Soon the sun worked its wonders on her. She felt her spirits lifting under its warmth. She followed the path past the reservoir, watching for evidence of spring flowers beginning to poke green shoots from the ground. She examined the carriages rolling by, and the new fashions on the women of society who were taking turns together.

More at peace than she had been in days, she allowed her mind to turn to Anthony's visit. Not to the insults and the way it ended, but to what he had told her and what it all meant for the future. She was mulling that when a shadow blocked the sun. It moved with her for several paces before she looked up to see what had caused it.

A tall dark man on a large pale horse looked down at her while he paced his steed step for step with her own gait.

"Mr. Albrighton. What a coincidence to find you here too."

"It is an uncommonly fair day for the season," he said. "I decided it should not be wasted. It appears we think alike."

"Either we do, or you followed me here."

"Why would I do that?" He swung off his horse and came over to her, wearing a charming smile and leading his mount by the reins.

"Not a denial, I see, but one of your dodges."

She walked away. He fell into step. She let him know with a sharp glance and deep sigh that she did not want his company. He ignored her.

"I did follow you," he said. "I knew you could less easily avoid me in this public place than in your own home. That is what you have been doing, isn't it? Avoiding me?"

"You are more conceited than I thought if you believe that."

"Which is not to say it is not true. I am not the only one who dodges."

She stopped walking and faced him. "Yes, I have been avoiding you. I was not myself that day. I find your presence awkward now. Furthermore, I have come here to think over some matters of great concern to me, and not to entertain your company."

"Are you saying you regret that passion, Celia? If so, I will respect that, and apologize again for taking advantage of you."

She sighed at his persistence. He looked on her too kindly, and too seriously, for a clever retort to be fair. A handsome man, she thought, as she always did. Exciting. The sensual euphoria she had experienced with him had not been far from her thoughts these last three days, for all her confusion and embarrassment. Now it was in the air between them, subdued but present still.

"I was taught that regret is for fools, so it cannot be that, can it? But I know that there can never be any story between us."

He did not argue that last point. Of course not. She walked on. She did not have to spell it out for such a man. He would go away now. Maybe he would leave the house for good. That would be best.

That thought made her hollow inside, and a little sad. She scolded herself for that reaction. What a stupid girl she could still be sometimes.

She had progressed several hundred feet when his boots again found a pace beside her. His horse snorted behind them while they strolled in the sunlight.

"What matter of concern do you contemplate, if it is not me?" he asked.

"I am pondering my future, and how careless I have been with the lives of others for whom I have taken responsibility. I have discovered that there is a debt outstanding that may undo all that I have tried to accomplish. As a result, my independence may prove to be very short-lived."

"Have you been sneaking off to gamble, Celia? If not, I cannot believe this debt can be very big."

"I am sure it is bigger than I can repay. I learned that my mother owed Anthony Dargent a great deal of money, and if that debt is not settled, I am sure to lose the house."

C elia strode along and retreated into her consideration of this newly discovered debt. She displayed no ill ease being with him, for all her claims of awkwardness. Jonathan was glad for that.

There can be no story between us. He was fairly sure he knew what she meant by that. Her mother's training had taught her to view the world without mercy in this regard. He could be excused for wishing she were less sensible.

The path split up ahead. She encouraged their steps to take the direction less trod by others. He waited to see if, having sought some privacy, she would confide the rest about that debt.

"When my year in London with my mother was ending, she sought to arrange for my first protector. Perhaps you know about this," she said, as if answering his query when in fact he had asked nothing.

He knew. All the younger men of society knew, and more than a few like himself who collected at its edges. Edward had been accurate in saying Alessandra had teased the ton for months with Celia's imminent launch.

Alessandra had guessed he did not approve, and had in turn teased him about his scruples. It had seemed a sin to him to send a girl into that life when she was so fresh and innocent. Her mother had explained—patiently, considering she spoke to a young man about nothing of his concern—that it was the freshness and innocence that would ensure Celia's triumph.

"I knew about her intentions regarding you, yes."

"Well, Anthony was the one chosen. That was how that horrible conversation with him started. The one right before I left my mother's house. He was telling me with great glee that she had given her nod. That was how I found out that he did not intend marriage at all."

He had not known Dargent had been chosen. Celia's comments after Dargent left the other day made more sense now, and took on more meaning. However—

"He has wealth enough, but I would have expected her to choose a peer for you, or an heir to a title."

"She would have preferred that, but she firmly believed that I should have a voice in it. She knew I loved him, so she accepted his proposition, which was a very generous one."

"It was convenient that you loved one of the appropriate candidates. I assume that she would have never accommodated your voice if you had fallen in love with a man lacking great expectations."

"Alessandra had many months to explain why, whether it be a lover or a patron, it could never be someone with no fortune."

Which, of course, was one reason there could be no story between the two of them.

"When Anthony visited me the other day, he said those negotiations had progressed much further than I imagined. He claimed to have given Alessandra my first two years' allowance, in advance."

"Did she return it when you left?"

"He says not."

"So this is the debt that troubles you, I gather."

She nodded. "I should have waited, I suppose, to begin with the plants. I should have definitely waited before giving Marian and Bella a home. Now I either lose the house when he makes a claim against Alessandra's estate, or I involve them in a life other than I promised. Quite the opposite, in fact."

"Are you convincing yourself that you have no choice except to work off that debt?"

He regretted his sharp tone as soon as it was out, but her little debate infuriated him. He resented the way she had made him a party to it, as if he had no right to mind. Which he didn't, but that did not mean he liked this. He could almost hear her mind weighing, judging, and all the while coming to very practical conclusions indeed.

She stopped walking, stung. "I am trying to determine what my choices are, both the good and the bad."

He'd be damned before he allowed her to talk herself into going to that fool. "I wonder if you truly comprehend the good and bad of what he is offering. Security, yes. Luxury even. A better house and more servants and even a type of status in his world. I am sure your mother explained all of that."

"She did little else."

"Did she also explain what happens when the silks are removed and you are a man's sexual slave?"

She glared at him. "I am hardly ignorant. Alessandra did not fail that part of my education. She taught me how to keep matters dignified."

He almost laughed. Of course Alessandra had not been too specific about what happened when things went very wrong. "You asked for my advice. Well, hear me now, as you debate your choices. There will be men who will encourage your illusion that you are in control of matters, because they anticipate the pleasure they will have in breaking you. Not all gentlemen are gentlemen in this area. Just so you know."

"Thank you for the lesson, *Mr. Albrighton*." She turned and walked away, retracing their route.

He easily caught up with her. He bore her brittle silence and told himself he had not been so blunt for his own purposes, but only to warn her.

Except it had been in part for his own purposes. The

thought of her going to Dargent—willingly, no less—made him want to kill the man.

He marshaled his next argument to dissuade her from feeling any obligation for this debt. Before he could speak, a little drama began unfolding in front of them. A woman he recognized was walking toward them on the path. Tall and dark-haired, she wore a green promenade ensemble with a fur-trimmed mantlet over its velvet pelisse. A more humbly dressed woman accompanied her; a maid, from the looks of it.

The dark-haired woman stopped in her tracks at the sight of Celia and him. She immediately looked down at the muddy grass on either side of the path as if seeking a quick escape. Realizing that leaving the promenade was unwise, she straightened her back and continued on, wearing a face of stone.

Jonathan took unseemly pleasure in closing the space between them. He caught the eye of the woman despite her best efforts to avoid it. In response she looked right at him and Celia, then tossed her head dramatically as she walked past, her nose pointing to the clouds.

Celia flushed deeply, but a steely glint entered her eyes. She did not speak again until he had returned her to her cabriolet.

"Your advice on my problem is well-taken, Mr. Albrighton, even if I thought it an unnecessary lesson, such as one might give a child."

"It was not my intention to speak to you as a child, but as a woman adding up future gains and costs."

"Then that lady's direct cut was not fortuitous to your purposes, reminding me as it did that I am paying costs while receiving *no* gains."

He handed her up, then swung onto his mount. "That

cut was not aimed at you. She probably does not have any idea who you are."

"Are you saying she was being deliberately rude—to you? Do you know her?"

"I know her well enough. That was my cousin."

"I am curious about something, Uncle," Jonathan said. "It may bear on my search."

They sat in Edward's library, in front of a fire that toasted their boots. Edward's wife had retired after dinner, as she always did when Jonathan visited. She could not refuse her husband his demand that she entertain Jonathan, but she did not extend herself beyond the formalities, which, while she was present, remained very formal indeed. Long ago she must have decided that staying in Thornridge's good graces was more important than staying in her husband's.

Jonathan did not much care. The very private meals mattered to him far less than the conversations after them. Edward was hardly the warm family that Jonathan had yearned for as a boy, but Edward was all there really was.

"What would that be?" Edward asked, reaching over to pour more port.

"Anthony Dargent. What do you know of him?"

Edward shrugged. "Good family out of the Midlands. Lots of money. His grandfather dabbled in more trade than he ever admitted and stuffed the coffers. Wool. Cotton. Slaves too, probably. Dargent is probably worth seven thousand a year."

More than enough to keep a mistress in style. Alessandra had expected a princely sum for Celia, and there were few young men who could afford that. *She believed I should have a voice in it,* Celia had said. How convenient to Alessandra, and potentially fortunate to Celia, that the one she wanted could actually afford her mother's demands.

He wondered if Alessandra had intended to keep that allowance for herself all along. More likely not. When her daughter had left, it probably just leaked away as time went on.

"Is there any trouble attached to his name?" he asked.

"None that I know. He is a good-natured fellow, suitably boring and stable. He married the daughter of an equally good, boring fellow, who in turn had married the sister of a viscount. So I suppose Dargent rose up a bit in the world with that."

"And his father? Was he also good and boring?"

"Less so." Edward lit a cigar and watched its smoke drift. "But it is not what you think."

Jonathan did not think anything yet. Damned if he was going to tell Edward that. "You are sure?"

"His father was very religious. Unusually so. The idea that he may have had some kind of liaison with Mrs. Northrope is absurd."

Jonathan had never had that idea. Clearly someone had, however, so now it became an interesting line of thought. "He was busy in the government during the war? The father, that is."

"Informally. He had spent three years in France as a young man, acting like some kind of missionary to French peasants who were none too willing to listen. They already had their priests for that, didn't they? But he learned the lay of the land very well in certain provinces. The army would consult with him now and then. You know the sort of questions: Does this river flood in spring? Is this line on the map a good enough road to move cannon?" He shrugged. "Nothing dramatic."

Except those questions might give some indication of the army's potential movements. The army asked twenty questions to learn the answer to one, in order to bury the true interest, but anyone who knew military developments on the Continent could probably decipher which question had mattered.

Dargent's father may have been too religious to have a liaison with Mrs. Northrope, but the son was not so fastidious about his soul. Perhaps Alessandra had another reason to pair Celia with Dargent besides Celia's preferences and the young man's considerable expectations. Maybe she intended her daughter to serve as another pair of ears for those useful tidbits men tended to drop when they were very contented. Alessandra may have even thrown Celia and Dargent together with that end in mind.

"I saw Miranda today," Jonathan said, leaving one topic for another in the way of chats by the fire.

Edward's relaxed expression firmed. "Did you? Where?"

"In the park. We almost walked right into each other."

"Did she acknowledge you?"

"If the cut direct is a form of acknowledgment, then yes."

"Do not pretend you were surprised, or even truly insulted."

"Not at all. However, she rarely comes up to town unless her brother is here as well. Is Thornridge in London?"

A deep puff on the cigar. A deep sigh. "I believe he is."

"I would like you to obtain an audience with him, for me."

"That would not be wise."

"Not wise for you?"

Edward's annoyance began showing. "For either of us."

"I disagree. I think it is long past time I spoke with him. I can simply call on him, I suppose."

"He will not receive you."

"I will give him reason to. I will say I am calling on behalf of the Home Office, and am investigating all the influential men in government during the war who visited a certain Venus. He was there at least several times. I saw him."

Edward sighed with resignation. "If you do that, you will force an issue before it is necessary and achieve nothing. If you insinuate he was at all disloyal, you will give him the excuse he wants to destroy whatever life you have built for yourself."

"Allow me to weigh my own risk and rewards."

"The hell I will. You want me to bare my chest to the blade too, after all."

Jonathan had always wondered if Edward was afraid of Thornridge. He had long suspected that this uncle's easy use of his bastard nephew had been a way to protect the other nephew who was an earl. Now he regretfully concluded that was correct. Whether out of fear or calculation, Uncle Edward would probably never speak or act for Jonathan in ways that might anger Thornridge.

Why should he?

Edward appeared weary and chagrined. A weak smile of appeasement heralded a change in topic. "Where are you staying these days?"

"I have let a chamber in a house during my visit to town."

"Hell of a thing, the way you have no real home. What if I need to contact you quickly?"

"Just use the usual mail drop."

Edward exhaled a large cloud of smoke. Jonathan added his own. The two clouds hung there above them, then drifted away on the air currents, going their separate ways.

Chapter Eleven

"I only said that you are most curious about Mr. Albrighton, Celia. I did not imply anything else," Daphne said. Her smile, however, implied plenty.

"I was not expressing curiosity about him, but about that woman who cut him so cruelly. And why should I not be curious about him? If I were, which I am not. He lives in my attic, after all."

"If she is his cousin, it could be Lady Chesmont," Verity offered. "She is proud enough to have done it, but otherwise rather sweet, I think. A little dull, and married to a viscount who only has his title as a distinction."

Verity had fetched Celia on Wells Street, and had not waited in the mews either. The coach had been hired and was anonymous, and Verity had not left it at all, but it had come right to the front door.

Now they sat in Daphne's back sitting room, at her house near Cumberworth, enjoying the good light coming through the window behind the sofa. Through its panes Celia could see the greenhouse, and Katherine inside tending to some pots.

Katherine was the latest addition to Daphne's household, but she had absented herself when the guests arrived. She knew the women who had left this house sometimes wanted to share old times and old memories with Daphne. It was not a slight to her when that happened.

"As for your excuse for being curious about him, I remind you that I lived in the chamber beside yours here, and you were not curious about me," Verity added.

"Oh, tosh. Of course I was curious. I just never asked because we all agreed not to. I have no such understanding with Mr. Albrighton, and he is worthy of a good deal of curiosity, if you ask me."

"Every handsome man is, I suppose." Daphne added some fuel to the fire, then returned to the sofa and gave Celia a very direct look.

Celia felt her face warming under Daphne's inspection. "It is not because he is easy on the eyes. He is a cipher. He is friends with Verity's husband and Audrianna's husband, he is educated, and Verity says he is the bastard of an earl. Yet he might have popped out of the ground fully grown for all the sense of family and history one has of him. He is not employed in trade, but he does not appear to be wealthy either. I think it is very normal for me to find all of this too mysterious for comfort."

"I am willing to discuss Mr. Albrighton if you wish," Daphne said. "However, before you go on, did I mention, Verity, that Mrs. Hill tried a new kind of trifle the other night? It had a bit of lemon in the cream."

"It sounds delicious," Verity said. "I do favor trifle

myself, so I must ask her for the recipe. I wonder if trifle is called *trifle* because it was once served on trifle? That is what my father called our everyday pewter when I was young. *Trifle*."

"How interesting. One could serve trifle on trifle to a man at dinner, who later trifles with—"

"Could we return to the topic at hand?" Celia interrupted pointedly.

Daphne looked innocent. "I did not realize we had left it, Celia."

Verity snorted. She and Daphne had a good laugh. Then Daphne took her hand. "Fine, let us return to discussing handsome, too-mysterious-for-comfort Mr. Albrighton. Other than his cousin's name, you will learn nothing here, I am afraid. We are as ignorant as you are."

"Do you think so? I do not. I cannot help but notice that one person in our company is avoiding this conversation completely, and carefully."

Celia glared right at that person. Daphne and Verity turned their gazes in that direction too.

The silent object of their attention sat a little straighter in her chair beside the fireplace. Lady Sebastian Summerhays's green eyes widened like a child caught stealing a piece of sugar.

"Is Celia correct, Audrianna? Do you possess information of interest regarding Mr. Albrighton?" Verity asked.

Audrianna's glance darted from one to another. Her color rose. She absently felt her chestnut hair, a habit she had when nervous.

"I may," she murmured. "I should not tell you, though, Celia. Mr. Albrighton might be displeased if I did. Sebastian said as much."

"Did Lord Sebastian forbid you to tell us?" Verity asked.

"He did not forbid it. He only expressed the opinion that it would be better if I did not repeat what his mother told me."

"He was wrong." Celia giggled and leaned toward Audrianna. "What did she say? Stop teasing me and tell."

Audrianna resisted only a few more moments. "His education was paid for by the Earl of Thornridge. He admitted as much while in school with Sebastian."

"Well, that explains that, at least," Celia said. "The family has taken some responsibility, then. They recognize that his is not a baseless claim. And yet his cousin was deliberately rude."

"The last earl died before Mr. Albrighton was born," Audrianna explained, warming to the subject. "His mother was carrying him, though, and the last earl knew that and made some provisions. Hence the education. You can see how ambiguous it all was, however. The title passed to the earl's nephew, who denies the relationship."

"That must chafe," Daphne said. "It would be hard to live knowing that one nod from one person can change your fortunes considerably. Even as a bastard, if he is acknowledged by the family to have their blood, many doors will open."

Celia turned this over in her mind while her friends chattered on about which doors might, should that acknowledgment ever come.

This information explained much. Why that cousin had cut him so cruelly. Why he appeared so rootless. The lack of acknowledgment must indeed chafe. He would want it, she was sure, even if it did not open doors. Anyone would, no matter who the family was too. People were not intended to live severed from all family ties. It was not normal.

"Perhaps he has been acknowledged, in a way. Maybe one door has opened," Verity said, her snowy brow puckering while she thought. "That business up north, near my home. He was a magistrate there. That is not a position that a man comes upon by accident, especially if he is new to the region. Someone had to use influence for that to happen."

The conversation stopped. The oddity of Mr. Albrighton obtaining that position teased at Celia's mind. Nor had he remained in it long.

"Perhaps that is why Sebastian thought Mr. Albrighton would not like me talking about his background," Audrianna said. "See how quickly we have discovered a mystery. It could be that Mr. Albrighton rather depends on no one looking too closely at his past and his present."

"Perhaps we should leave the gentleman well enough alone, then, and speak of other things," Daphne said. "Audrianna, when you wrote to say you would join us, you mentioned some news. Pray tell us what it is."

Audrianna blushed, and smiled girlishly. "I have the best news. Sebastian and I expect a happy event come early summer."

Mr. Albrighton was forgotten in the excitement that followed. Talk turned to babies, good health, and preparations. Yet even as Celia joined in, a part of her mind continued to mull over what she had learned today.

Jonathan did not hide his father's identity. He had informed Lord Sebastian and Hawkeswell of it years ago. Yet he also did not publicly claim it. Nor could he if the family refused to do so as well. He must resent that. He would not be human if he did not.

Was that what he was doing in London now, plotting how to gain that acknowledgment? When he went off in the evening, was it to pass through the few doors that had opened privately, while all the rest remained closed? He did not strike her as someone who would accept the situation as it now stood.

Oh, yes, he had expectations, and not quite what she had assumed. He was not a man looking to appease society in order to hold on to the thin edge of advantage that his birth had given him. He was a man still fighting to get that edge firmly in his grasp. He had more to gain, and more to lose, than she had guessed.

No wonder he had not disagreed when she said there could be no story between them. At the moment neither one of them was suitable for the other. And if she ever followed Alessandra's path, he would never do as a protector, even if he achieved all he hoped to win.

Itemizing these hard realities dulled the day for her. She did not dwell on it, but the smiles and laughs and gossip with her friends felt hollow, even distant, after that. It was a kind of hell, she decided, to find a man so exciting and stirring, but also to know that one dared not do anything about it.

It was not until she was in Verity's carriage, riding back to London in the late afternoon, that the melancholy lifted enough for her to realize that her absorption over Jonathan's birth had made her stupid.

The other information about him, and that odd business about him serving as magistrate, had actually been much more important. Mr. Albrighton might be more useful than she had guessed. She was sure that he would agree to help her if she asked the right way. Which she probably shouldn't.

On the other hand, while there could never be a story between them, a tiny bit more trifling might be excusable if it was all in a good cause.

Chapter Twelve

The letter came up with his hot water in the morning. Its penmanship clean and feminine, and its paper crisp and folded, the note carried an invitation from Celia. Would Mr. Albrighton care to dine with Miss Pennifold this evening at nine o'clock?

Intrigued, he penned an acceptance and sent it down to her.

That evening he dressed as if he dined with a table of twenty in Mayfair. He tied his cravat with infinite care while he wondered if she would greet him in one of those silks. It might be an informal dinner, of course, in which case he would appear a little ridiculous. He risked it, however, and counted on Celia to know how to stand on ceremony when it was required.

This dinner had a purpose, of course. She wanted something from him. He could be excused for wishing the reason was the most welcomed one instead. It would be very nice if she had decided that virtue was not a virtue, and now wanted more than stolen kisses.

Laughing at himself, he went down the front stairs. He halted as he walked past Celia's chamber. Feminine murmurs penetrated the wall and door. On an impulse, he knocked.

Silence fell within. Then the door opened a crack and Bella stuck her head out.

"Tell Miss Pennifold that I have come to escort her to dinner, Bella."

Bella looked over her shoulder. Soon Celia came into view through the narrow opening. Bella scurried away.

"What a gentleman you are, Mr. Albrighton," Celia said. Her hair had been dressed in an elaborate style with tiny, intertwining braids on her crown. She wore the fawn satin gown from the trunk, the one she had been studying when he came upon her in the attic chamber.

She looked stunning. Sophisticated and elegant and very feminine. She had dressed in a manner designed to drive a man to distraction.

She definitely wanted something.

So did he. He doubted that they wanted the same thing. His mind turned to seductive strategies, so he might ensure they were of like mind by night's end.

"Bella, my shawl, please."

Bella's hands showed behind her, holding a Venetian shawl with a cream ground scattered with deep blue sprigs of flowers. Celia wore no jewels. He calculated whether, if he sold everything he owned and spent the rest of his life in dun territory, he could afford sapphires to adorn the soft skin below her neck.

She waited patiently for him to stand aside. Coming to his senses, he offered his arm.

"Marian is cooking, so do not expect a French meal," she said as they descended the stairs. The fluid satin of her skirt floated, floated, brushing his legs. He felt the texture caress him even though his own garments meant no fabric touched his skin.

"I am sure it will be much better than my usual dinners."

"Were meals part of your lease, and I have been neglectful? If so, you must excuse me. I did not know, since I have never seen that document." Her eyebrow arched high over one eye in a meaningful glance.

"I will bring it to you tomorrow."

The dining room had been decorated with some of the plants and flowers that remained from the Cumberworth shipment. Lighting came only from two candelabras set near the plates that waited. Celia had gone through some pains to create a restful and alluring table.

Bella and Marian served, decked out in clean aprons and acting like sober servants. The turtle soup was probably quite good, but he did not notice its taste much. Celia appeared beautiful in this light. It made her eyes appear even larger and deeper, as though if he looked long enough, he could see right into her soul.

"I heard a rumor about you," she said while they waited for the next course.

He had been pouring some very nice wine that she said she had found in the cellar. He focused on the flowing red liquid. "I am hardly notable enough to attract rumors."

"It has to do with the woman in the park—your cousin—who snubbed you. She is the sister of the Earl of Thornridge, isn't she? Lady Chesmont."

Marian arrived with fish in a nice citrus sauce. It appeared a few of the fruit had been removed from that orange tree before it was delivered to the Robertsons.

"Have you been talking to Summerhays? Hawkeswell?" He had never asked them not to reveal his relationship to Thornridge, but it would still surprise him if they had. "Their wives?"

"Then it is true. It is very cruel of them not to acknowledge you."

"They have their reasons, I suppose. Nor is it cruel. Inconvenient to be sure."

Her expression softened. "It was cruel when you were a child at least."

"Perhaps. I don't remember." Except he did remember. The rejection by that family was not something one would forget.

"Then they all do know about you?"

"Oh, yes. They know." He should let it be, but her blue eyes invited confidences, and the wine and her presence urged indiscretion. "It was only cruel once. I was nine years old. It was long ago."

"What happened?"

He did not answer. She waited, very serious, very interested.

"My mother brought me to Hollycroft, Thornridge's estate. She asked to speak with my cousin, who had just reached his majority. He refused to see her. We had traveled a good distance, and she would not accept his repudiation. She sat down in front of his door, and declared she would remain there until either he saw her or she died. I sat with her."

Her expression turned troubled. "Please do not tell me that he let her starve there."

"Not quite, although it did nothing good for her health, which was already poor. We sat there for three days and three nights. Finally Thornridge relented. He expected guests for a house party, and did not want the embarrassment."

"So you met him then?"

"It was the only time in my life that I did. I remember little of it. She made demands. He was cold as stone. Accusations flew from her and insults from him. In the end, however, she obtained his agreement to educate me. There was a small allowance for some years, conditional upon my not claiming any relationship."

He returned to his meal, to indicate there would be no more details. He remembered more of that meeting between his mother and his cousin than he said, however. Over the years bits of it had come back to him, especially what his mother had said and the claims she had made. No, not claims. Threats.

Celia considered him while he ate the fish. She puzzled over what she saw with a vague frown. "How do you live, if that allowance ended? I see no employment."

"You are very inquisitive about me. Is there a reason?"

"I am curious. That is all."

"Because I kissed you?"

"Because you live upstairs. And because of that business up north, and your being a magistrate there. I knew about that, you see. I recognized your name in a paper's story that Verity showed to me months ago."

So, she had begun piecing things together. He pretended she had not, and waited to see where this went. It was an excuse to watch the nuanced changes in her eyes and expression, and the way the candles' flames cast moving lights over her skin.

"It occurred to me that important men would have to intervene for you to have that position," she said. "You had never even lived in the region before, I believe, so important recommendations would have to be made to the locals there. Then I remembered how you used to go away suddenly and come back unexpectedly during the war, while I lived with my mother. I have developed a theory about all that."

She smiled smugly. Her eyes teased him

"If your theory gains me invitations to private dinners at which you wear satin dresses, I am unlikely to declare it wrong."

"Don't you even want to know what my theory is?"

"Not really. I think that you will tell me anyway, however."

She pouted adorably at his refusal to play the game. Then, as he expected, she did tell him anyway.

"I think that you are one of those men who spied and such during the war over in France. What do you think about that?"

"I am relieved that your theory did not make me out to be boring, at least."

"Then I think you were sent north to find out what was happening up there. Sent by important men. I think that you are now waiting for them to tell you to go somewhere else to do things like that once more."

"You possess an active imagination."

"There is more. I think you came by this unusual employment because someone important heard the rumors too, years ago, and opened this one door for you when most others remained closed." She tilted her head back and gave him a haughty gaze. "What do you think of my imagination now, Mr. Albrighton?"

Marian arrived to serve fowl in a rich sauce. After she had left he poured Celia more wine. "I only went to France a few times. Most of my missions were right here in England. Mostly along the coast. You are correct about the last part too. One important man opened one door." He raised his wine in salute.

Her eyes widened. "You mean I have it right? I guessed it all?"

"Most of it." She appeared so astonished that he regretted not dissembling. One good feint and she would have probably dropped the entire topic.

Only he had not really wanted to lie or distract her after she had turned her mind to the matter so well. That she had even bothered flattered him, and perhaps opened its own doors, in a manner of speaking.

She gazed at him so clearly. So frankly. Merriment sparkled in her eyes, but there was nothing of the child in her regard. "Are you spying now, with me?"

He had not expected that. Damnation, she was far shrewder than he had realized. He hid his surprise with a laugh. "You have found me out. The leaders of the nation's horticultural societies petitioned the Prince Regent to send me to discover the secrets about your plants."

She laughed, musically. "I am happy to learn that you are employed with such trifling duties right now. You see, I would like to hire you."

She surprised him again. His guard was down due to wine and a woman's beauty. Which, of course, had been her plan, and the reason for this dinner to begin with.

"I will have to decline, Miss Pennifold."

"You do not even know what I want you to do."

He was not so besotted that he did not know that trouble lay ahead. "You cannot afford me. Paying my fee would impoverish you."

"You cannot be that expensive. You live here, after all.

Not on Park Lane. You might at least listen to my request before turning me down."

He nodded, resigned. "Forgive me. I have been rude. Tell me what you require."

"It is very simple. I want you to find out who my father is."

"To what end?"

She rolled her eyes. "Do I need an end? I just want to know. Wouldn't *you* want to know? You are a bastard too, and you *do* know, but I do not."

"My father acknowledged me, even if his relatives do not. If your father chose not to acknowledge you, he probably had his reason, and will not welcome any prying."

"His reason is the same as everyone's reason for everything where I am concerned. He assumed I would follow my mother's path, and did not want his name associated with that. However, if I do not enter her profession, he may feel differently. Nor do I expect you to let him know you are prying, so his welcome or lack of it will not signify."

If I do not. The question still had not been firmly decided, then.

"I cannot conjure information out of thin air. Tell me what you know already, and I will decide if there would be any chance of success if I agreed to this."

"That is the problem. I know nothing. I had hoped to learn some hints in her papers and belongings, but she removed everything that might lead me to him." Her expression turned sad. Her entire posture did. "I only want to know his name, so half of me is not this blank. It was unkind of her to make sure I never would see him, even across a crowded park."

Only that in itself was telling. Alessandra would not have been so careful with an unimportant man's identity. Nor could an insignificant man bring to bear the power that demanded such discretion.

Celia watched him earnestly. All flirtation had left her manner upon speaking of this. It mattered to her, finding this man's name. He could understand why. She was correct. He was a bastard, but at least he knew his parentage. He tried to imagine what it was like not to.

Celia was twenty-three. Her conception had been early in Alessandra's career. The father might be that French émigré Edward had spoken of. Or an early lover after that, one who had reason to be discreet in his affairs.

He might well find out her father's name without even trying, as he pursued his other mission—

She frowned in reaction to his silence. Determination entered her eyes. She rose slowly, and the candlelight warmed the pale fawn of her dress. Satin ripples moved over her body as she walked around the table.

She stood beside his chair. The scent of lavender flowed over him and her satin touched his hand. She cupped his face in her smooth, soft palms, and bent down to kiss him.

A deliberate kiss. Artful. Expert. Her tongue slid into him and played, teasing and arousing. This was not an impulse like on the day Dargent had come. That had been Celia, acting out of both joy and sorrow.

Tonight, the daughter of Alessandra Northrope bestowed a favor.

If the goal was to drive him delirious, it worked. His body reacted savagely. This courtesan drama was a calculated, controlling taunt, however, and he'd be damned if he settled for it.

He pulled her onto his lap, into his arms. Her studied

expression shattered into one of astonished surprise. She
even stretched away when he began to kiss her, but as
soon as their mouths touched she melted, then circled his
neck with her arm.

She met him as an equal in that kiss, giving, taking,
swinging between abandon and restraint. The velvet of
her mouth, the warmth of her body in his arms, the in-
stinctive flexing of her hips against his lap, pressing his
erection like the softest squeeze, made him senseless. His
mind narrowed on the feel of her, the taste, her gasps of
girlish surprise and her moans of wanton pleasure.

Her scent, floral and musky . . . Her mouth and
tongue tantalized him, implying pleasures he doubted she
understood. . . . Her breast, so soft and womanly beneath
that satin, rose into his caress as if she ached for the
touch, filling his hand . . . Her body moved, moved, in a
gentle flex, maddening him as they both lost themselves in
sensations . . . Light, white and pristine and fresh, surrounded him, filling him and making the pleasure joyful
and perfect.

No thought interfered. No considerations. He teased at
her breast and she cried soft whimpers of need into the
crook of his neck. The beautiful, feminine sound sparkled
through the light, changing quickly to needy notes, then
desperate ones.

The dress was designed to be discarded. He had no
trouble loosening the hooks that closed it. He took her
mouth, ravished it, while he slid the satin down slowly,
then pulled the chemise less carefully.

He had to look at the ivory skin beneath his hand. She
did too, with her lips parted and her eyes two pools of
stars. They both watched his fingers circle her breast, their
impatient breaths merging together. The barest smile spoke

her pleasure in the tease, and her breast, pale and brown tipped, rose to encourage that caress while her hip pressed down and made even the light dim for a moment.

He touched lightly, tantalizing her. She closed her eyes and sighed deeply. Her face showed ecstasy as he circled and rubbed. His consciousness narrowed on the heat making him tight and hard and on her willing passion and on what would come, had to come now, soon, when he took her, claimed her, and bound her to him so that light and joyful pleasure would never be lost.

Whispers now, in her madness. Breaths of assent and clipped gasps that begged. He kissed down her neck to her chest, and used his tongue as wickedly as he could so she would know the ragged desire he knew, and the hunger howling through his essence.

Sweet, too sweet, even with the painful need. He saw himself with her, holding all of her, satin gone, feeling her skin against his own and tasting her, all of her. His caresses followed his mind's eye, to her legs and the watery satin, then up the silken flesh beneath. Her melody of astonished breaths quickened, faster, faster, wondrous now, urging him on—

Noises, loud ones, from somewhere in the distance. Golden candle flames swallowed the white light, leaving deep shadows and a table. Celia's hand grasped his arm, her blue eyes sightless, her cries swallowed in a deep breath.

A cough nearby. A loud one, as a woman cleared her throat so gutterally it shook the door behind him.

They stayed there, immobile as the chamber and the world and the woman demanding attention settled into their consciousness. Primitive fury roared in him, at the interruption and the evidence he would be denied.

Celia's expression checked that reaction. She looked

down at her naked breast, surprised, as if her loss of control dismayed her. She clumsily tried to put her arm through the chemise, blushing hotly now, blinking rapidly as though the world had not righted itself yet.

They got her dressed somehow. She moved back to her chair. As if on cue, Marian opened the door, carried in a tart, and served it.

When she left, Celia gazed across the candle flames at him, her eyes full of awareness of what had happened. He looked back, and imagined her undressed from head to toe, and bent over this table so her pretty bottom rose to him.

T hings had gotten a bit out of hand with Mr. Albrighton, Celia admitted to herself. *Remain in control. Do not yield too easily. Have an understanding on the arrangement before it progresses beyond a caress or two.*

Alessandra must be turning over in her grave.

Her daughter was forgetting everything. She had yielded far too much at dinner, and might have yielded everything if Marian had not made so much noise and brought them back to their senses.

Celia waited that night, for the man who would probably be at her bedchamber's door after the household went to sleep. She debated what she would do if he came to her. He could be excused if he thought she would accept him.

She tried not to imagine the rest, but she remained excited and enthralled as she lay in the dark, half hoping he would be so bold. Her breasts ached, sensitive to every movement she made. A soft dew covered her skin. She sensed him, above, deciding, wanting.

When it was clear he would not come, her body mourned

but her mind found some relief. It was better, of course. There was no understanding. No arrangement. Nor did she really want one, if she were honest and viewed it sanely. He would never do as a protector, should she choose to have one. In such decisions, one must be practical and think of the future.

And yet—it had been delicious. Unearthly. Nor had she been forced to find the pleasure within herself, or remove this man from her mind to do so. He had commanded it in her, and she had no choice in responding. The sensations had teased and lured and overwhelmed, and just thinking of his gaze while they ate that tart made her warm and moist again.

Chapter Thirteen

Jonathan presented himself at the door of Castleford's home. The duke had invited him to call anytime, and he was about to find out if in fact he could.

He had made sure it was not a Tuesday. He did not want to find Castleford too busy for a good talk. He also did not want to find him too sober to be indiscreet.

The ritual ensued with the liveried servants. This time the captain bore his card away on a salver and left him to wait in that nice chamber with the windows, where they had all played cards.

Alone, with nothing to occupy him except the paintings on the walls, his thoughts turned to Celia. He had been avoiding that. He had kept very busy all morning specifically to that end.

The titillation of desire could not keep away darker reactions to the memories of the dinner last night. Nor could images of her joyful, even enthusiastic, acceptance of pleasure. The truth was he was trifling with her, and did not even know why. He found her beautiful, and fascinating in her unusual view of life; that was true. But he had no interest in a liaison, let alone one that could set her on a path toward more men in the future.

He told himself that if she had not kissed him, things would have never gotten that far. Only he knew that he would have lured her into it anyway. As soon as he saw her in that dress, those caresses became inevitable.

He saw the dress sliding down her shoulder, drawn low by a man's hand. His hand. This time. The dress suited her too well. Alessandra had known it would enhance all that Celia was when she ordered it.

"One of the public dresses," Celia had called it. Restrained. Almost demure. Devoid of excess in every way, and more than modest enough. Yet that fabric flowed like water over her body, and hinted at her form more than a man could ignore. No man could see her in it and not imagine her naked, even though the garment offered no scandal.

Like Celia itself, the dress combined innocence and worldliness, modesty and the most sophisticated sensuality. A schoolgirl's dress, but for a girl schooled by Alessandra.

"His Grace will see you, sir."

The summons brought him back, to the chamber and the windows. It promised the welcomed reprieve of other things to occupy his mind besides Celia. He needed to complete Edward's mission quickly; that was clear. It was time to leave London, before he followed the impulse to seduce first and assess the consequences later.

He followed the white wig up the stairs to the duke's apartment. It sprawled on the level above the public rooms. The wig ushered him into a huge dressing room where Castleford was, surprisingly enough, dressing.

Two valets fussed around the duke. He stood there like a knight being encased in armor instead of a peer being sheathed in superfine. Jonathan took a seat on one of the many chairs and watched the show.

"Good of you to call," Castleford muttered, with his chin high so valet number one could fix the top button of his shirt without creasing the collar.

"You remember inviting me to do so, don't you?"

"Of course. Why wouldn't I?"

"Some men only remember sober utterances when they are sober." Which Castleford was not at the moment. He stood straight enough and his speech did not slur, but his eyes were those of a man who either had already imbibed today, or still carried the effects of the night before.

"I remember everything. The only difference with me is whether I give half a damn, or none at all."

Valet number two offered Hessian boots for approval. Castleford signaled they would do by sitting in a chair. With smooth moves that belied the effort, the servant slid the boots onto the waiting long legs.

The other man approached with coats in hand, but Castleford shooed him away and told them both to leave. Then he sprawled, hooked one booted leg over the arm of his chair, and smiled at Jonathan like the devil eying the next soul he would steal.

"You came too early. You are supposed to come at night. Ten o'clock would be good, tomorrow. There is a pugilist match to see, and we can find some whores later. I hope you like common ones. I have never understood men paying a hundred pounds for what can be bought for a shilling."

"I don't like them too common."

"I do. Common and lusty and fun. No sad stories of

being driven to sin by poverty either. There's plenty who like the trade." He eyed Jonathan thoughtfully. "Little Katy would do for you. You've spent a lot of time in France and have probably learned to use your tongue well. She fancies that." He yawned and stretched. "Tomorrow night, then, unless you are occupied with your current mission."

That was the problem with a man half-drunk. He was wont to speak indiscreetly. Only this indiscretion had been planned, Jonathan suspected.

"The war is long over. There are no more concerns about the coastline."

"There is always a use for men with your skills. Only it isn't the Home Office this time, which intrigues me."

"How do you know whether it is or not, if there is any mission at all?"

"I asked. They don't like when I do that. It flusters so many people. However, I always get an answer. You would think I was a royal duke, the way it pours out."

"Perhaps they are afraid that you will kill them if they do not answer."

"Perhaps so." He thought about that, and burst out laughing. "I think you may be correct. And here I thought it was deference to my title."

"It is useful that you collect all that information that you should not have. You probably know more political gossip than anyone."

He shrugged. "It is more amusing than the twaddle in the drawing rooms about whose fool of a daughter allowed herself to get compromised."

"It occurs to me that you may know who has set me on a mission, if not the Home Office. Not that there is one, of course."

"Of course. No, I do not know just who it is. I have not

tried to find out. I haven't decided if I give that half a damn yet, you see."

Jonathan hoped he would. If Edward did not have him poking into Alessandra's past on behalf of the Home Office, then for whom instead? He did not like learning that he did the bidding of a man whose name he did not know.

"I can see that I came at the wrong time," he said. "Before I go, I wonder if you could dig into some of that useless information your curiosity has accumulated, and answer a question for me."

Castleford looked to the ceiling and groaned dramatically. "You sound like Summerhays. He is always boring me with his political questions."

"I promise it is only one question. Do you know anything about Anthony Dargent's father?"

"Dargent? The father left his family to do missionary work, didn't he? Probably why Dargent turned into such an ass. Chased after that Northrope woman's girl some years ago. There were some who thought he'd marry her, he was so besotted. There were others annoyed he seemed to have too clear a field."

"That was generally known, was it?"

"I remember it well. All these men salivating over the pretty virgin. I have never understood the fascination with them. Virgins. For dynastic reasons it is wise to marry one, but that first night has to be clumsy."

"So you were not interested yourself?"

"Hell, no. Nor in the mother, although she had something to her. You could tell she knew her trade. But if I wanted to swive a woman who subjects me to salons and assemblies and expects diamonds for the effort, I would just get married."

"I have heard that many others felt differently. Mrs. Northrope was famous for a reason."

Castleford leveled an unexpectedly direct gaze on him. "So that is what you are doing. Cleaning up after someone's bad indiscretion. Only it sounds as if you aren't even sure who he is, and that makes no sense."

"No, it does not, which should tell you the idea is ridiculous."

"It certainly is, but that does not mean I am wrong. As for the many others you cleverly encouraged me to remember, I assume they were all titled, like the ones who pursued her openly. Or from families of peers. It was said she was very strict about that, and only gave herself to the best blood."

"That leaves a lot of men in the pile."

"In the queue is more like it. And some of them had her while you and I were still boys. Unless she kept a list, you are on a fool's errand."

Perhaps not, since the errand was to ensure there was no list. Jonathan had his own reasons for wishing one existed, however.

"If Mrs. Northrope's patrons were your reason for calling, I am sorry that I have been so useless." Castleford's tone did not carry the sarcasm that Jonathan expected. And so he pushed forward when he might have retreated.

"That was mere curiosity, provoked by some coincidental meetings I have had recently. I really came to ask a favor of you."

"Of course you did." His eyes glinted with both curiosity and resignation. "The price will be a good rout tomorrow night."

"The boxing and drinking only. I will pass on the common whores."

Castleford sighed. "It isn't as if their vulgarity is catching, Albrighton. It is a hell of a thing that a man has to be a duke before he can freely follow his inclinations."

"It is not vulgarity that I fear catching, Your Grace."

That caught Castleford up short. The moment of sobriety passed quickly, however. "What is this favor? Will it amuse me, or be a boring chore?"

"I want you to obtain an audience for me with Thornridge."

Castleford's eyes lit with surprise, then dark humor. "So you are going to confront him? Finally?"

"I want to have a conversation with him. That is all."

Castleford swung his leg down and looked at Jonathan long and hard. Jonathan got the sense that the duke was deciding his impulsive condescension toward the bastard had been inspired after all.

"A conversation. Of course." He grinned. "What fun. I will set my mind on how to trap him, but only if I can be present when you have this chat."

T he next day Celia left the house early. More plants would be coming tomorrow, so she wanted this day for herself. She took her cabriolet and drove it east, toward the City. There she called on Mr. Mappleton, as he had written and requested.

Some papers related to her mother's estate required her signature. After she had completed those formalities, she inquired about the resolution of the debts.

"All are covered, I am delighted to inform you," Mr. Mappleton reassured.

"No others have come to light? No indications in her records of others possibly outstanding?"

"Not to my awareness. As you know, I never found any account books. It is possible, I suppose, that she simply kept it all in her head." Rosy tints spotted his pale cheeks. "More discreet."

"How did you know about the debts now being settled?"

"The lenders and shopkeepers sought me out. They presented documents. In most cases, your mother had her own copies. Even if she did not have an account book, she did have papers."

"But if a debt is presented to you as executor, how do you know it has not been paid already?"

"Only a fool pays off a debt and does not procure documentation of the fact."

And Alessandra was no fool.

She took her leave. As she emerged from the building, a tall, blond man approached her, smiling.

Anthony removed his hat and made a deep bow. "Celia, what a happy coincidence."

She glanced down the street. His carriage waited fifty feet away.

"Too much a coincidence, Anthony. I think that you have had someone follow me today, and perhaps other days. I will not tolerate that."

"I would never be so rude. I merely called on Mappleton, and learned that he expected you today." He smiled the smile that she had once considered warm. "I thought to call on you again at Wells Street, but after the interference the last time— I do need to talk to you, Celia. I also want to show you something."

"It looks to rain, Anthony. I really must return to—"

"I want to show you the little contract your mother signed with me. I have not given it to Mappleton, or pressed for repayment yet. I thought you and I should talk about it first."

She had been enjoying her day, but now he had ruined it. She wanted to walk away, but if he spoke the truth, she dared not.

He swung his arm toward his carriage, by way of invitation.

"I have my own, thank you. I would prefer to follow you, so retrieving it does not inconvenience either of us."

"As you wish. I will tell the coachman to proceed slowly, so you do not get lost."

The coach stopped on a street of tall houses just north of Grosvenor Square. Celia pulled up her carriage behind it. One of Anthony's footmen hopped down and came to take her reins.

"Do you live here now?" she asked Anthony, angling her head so she could gaze up the pale façades.

He half smiled and half nodded, and escorted her to a door. He used a key to enter, which she thought odd.

She understood as soon as the door swung open. The house was empty. Its high-ceilinged chambers echoed with their footsteps.

"It is a fine house, in the best neighborhood. Your wife will find it very suitable," she said.

"She does not care for town much."

"Then you will find it suitable."

"I hope to."

She strolled through the library, then on to a chamber that would make a good morning room. It was not a huge house, but large enough for entertaining. One would not host balls in it, but dinner parties would work well, or more intimate gatherings. Its arrangement of chambers reminded her of Mama's house on Oxford Street. It even had a chamber near the drawing room that would serve for a music room.

She felt Anthony watching her reactions. She paused by windows with good prospects of a nice garden.

"Have you purchased it?" she asked.

"It is my intention to."

"Please do not on my account, if that is your thinking."

He did not respond. He did not move. She dared not look at him. The atmosphere in the chamber stilled in the worst way, as if the whole house held its breath.

"Are you expecting me to pursue you, Celia? I remind you that I have already done so."

She turned to face him. "I expect nothing from you. I want nothing from you. I explained that."

"This house will be in your name, Celia. I will be settling a good deal of money on you as well."

Her gaze drifted to the ceilings and walls. She wished the proposition held no allure, but it was a very fine house, worth a good deal, and she was a very practical woman. *Property, jewels, and money, Celia. Always demand things that last.*

"Why, Anthony? You could set up a mistress in style for much less. There are many women who would be happy to play the role, I am sure."

He advanced on her in that intense way he had. She stiffened and stepped back. He must have seen her caution, and it checked him. He stopped ten feet away and looked at her face as if he had to memorize every inch.

"You were my first great passion, Celia, and still my

only one. I have imagined our first night together for years, and time did not quench that desire. Rather the opposite. I said we would be together forever, and that is still my hope and intention—to be your first lover, and your only lover."

Pretty words again. She heard each one, and many more not spoken that were much less loving. "And if you are not my first lover?"

He reacted as she guessed he would. His expression flexed in a vain attempt to hide his anger. It mattered to him a great deal, that *first and only* part.

Mama had told her about men like that. In fact, Mama had counted on their competing to have the daughter of Alessandra Northrope. Only now this one had become rather fanatical about her virginity. That might not bode well for either his affection or his treatment of her after that first night.

"Are you saying that there has been another?" His voice sounded more dangerous than mere anger could explain. "I asked at your house, and you avoided the question."

"As I intend to avoid it now. Does it truly matter, Anthony? You spoke of love when you called on me. If I am your only great passion, surely this is a little thing."

His lips folded in on each other. "I have a right to know."

"No, you do not, because I am not swayed by this house or the settlement." She should have said that right away, of course. Only it was a good house, and considering his zealous ardor, she could have arranged a very handsome settlement before she accepted him. One had to give such things at least a little thought before rejecting them. She had even promised Mama that she would.

He did not see it her way. Face flushing from insult and

anger, he reached in his coat and withdrew a folded vellum page. He snapped it open with a sharp flick of his wrist, and handed it to her.

"You are not responsible for it, of course. Your mother was, however, which affects her estate."

She took the page and read the scribner's elaborate penmanship. She sickened at the words, and silently cursed Mama's carelessness.

It was not a bill of sale. Anthony had been too clever for that. Instead it took the form of a loan to Alessandra, for eight hundred pounds to be repaid in coin or in kind. Celia's favors no doubt would be the "in kind."

"It appears you are not above coercing me to get your way, Anthony."

"It has nothing to do with you. I will go to Mappleton and settle it with the estate."

She imagined telling Marian and Bella that the house was lost. Marian would survive, and return to the lanes she knew so well, and perhaps to her whoring. And Bella— they could both go to Daphne, she supposed. Two homeless, helpless women looking for sanctuary among The Rarest Blooms.

She had been happy there, and probably could be again. She should tell Anthony to do his worst. She should tell him to go to Mappleton, and then to go to hell.

She looked at the vellum, then at the fine moldings on the chamber's ceiling. She pictured the years passing in Daphne's home, while other women came and went but she stayed there, suspended like an insect caught in amber.

"I need to think about this, Anthony. Give me a week to do so, please."

Chapter Fourteen

J onathan turned the last page of the journal he read. As soon as he did, the shadows closed in again.

He did not doubt that Castleford would find a way to put him and Thornridge together. Uncle Edward would be furious, but it was time to settle that matter one way or another.

The expectation of that meeting kept conjuring up memories of the last time he had seen the earl. He had been hungry and tired and chilled to the bone by the time his cousin had agreed to see his mother.

In a library of massive size, Thornridge had listened to his mother's demands and threats, looking much older than his twenty-one years with his hard expression and cold, dark eyes.

Jonathan set aside the journal and walked to the window. Most of that meeting was a blur now. A few other things remained vivid, however. He remembered all the books in that library, their bindings like so many jewels, row upon row. He recalled the earl agreeing to provide the education his predecessor had promised. And he remembered some of those threats his mother made, which had made no sense until he thought about them years later.

So now he would force his way into another audience with his cousin. He had not decided yet if he would issue his own threats this time.

Weighing that choice occupied him as he stood in the light of the window. It distracted him enough that he barely noted the movement in the garden until Celia was almost at the house. Once he did, all thoughts about the pending meeting with Thornridge flew from his head.

He could not see her without wanting her. Even now, from this distance, memories of her joyous passion made him hard. He was not accustomed to the incomplete sensuality they had shared, and she was driving him mad.

She appeared to be thinking as hard as he had been, and about something just as difficult to decide. He doubted she noticed any of her surroundings as she walked slowly, almost stiffly, down the path toward him.

She stopped, and removed her bonnet as if its bow constricted her. She raised her head and looked at the house, inspecting it with a sad expression.

Then her gaze drifted down. A profound distraction claimed her. She did not move. She just stood there, and, instead of the light finding her, it seemed that the garden's shadows did.

He watched, waiting for her to reclaim herself, looking for the joy of living that transformed her face even when she did not smile. Instead she remained immobile, looking more like her mother than she had ever looked before.

* * *

The house and garden appeared strange to her. Foreign. The sense of home that she had experienced in it had disappeared.

She did not belong here. The decision to make this her residence and join Daphne in trade had been an act of confusion, not clarity.

She was not like Daphne Joyes or Audrianna. They did not share the same history or upbringing with her. Daphne's elegant frugality had been learned over half a lifetime. Her good birth and breeding elevated even a penurious existence to something genteel.

The daughter of Alessandra Northrope had been raised for other things, and with different expectations and values. Her gaze took in the house's proportions. She thought of the slightly worn upholstery. For a year or so all of this might satisfy her. The excitement of independence would sustain her for a while.

She had been schooled for a different kind of life in other ways besides material things, and their promise had always proven to be stronger lures. Even infamy was a kind of fame. The last five years she had experienced a virtuous nonexistence in obscurity. She had tolerated it because it was temporary.

Now, as she looked at the house, she wondered if she might not be better off fulfilling Mama's plan and accepting Anthony as her first protector. She imagined herself ten years hence, moving plants around inside this house while she wondered if Mr. Albrighton might return to London this year.

Promise me that you will think about your future, and what you forgo and what you gain from any choice. Promise me that you will weigh it all fairly, without pretending you are other than my daughter.

It had been an easy promise to give a dying mother. She thought that she had fulfilled the pledge too. Only now, with the gain and loss so clearly defined for her, she realized she had not.

"You appear lost, Miss Pennifold."

She startled and turned. Jonathan stood not far from her. She had not even heard him approach.

"Perhaps I am," she said. "The bishops would say my thoughts might lead to the worst kind of lost, even if I believe they would be wrong."

"Are you wishing that you believed they were right?"

"It would perhaps make my choices easier." She had to smile as she admitted that. If she could believe that Anthony represented damnation of her soul, she might not be debating her path.

The warmth in his eyes beckoned her to confide. She felt the words swelling inside her. He did not really have a friendly face. She would even describe it as harsh, in a sharp way that had not been softened by the effects of too many society feasts the way it was with many men his age. A handsome face, to her at least, but perhaps too seasoned by life for a man who could not be much older than thirty.

Those eyes, however, changed his general countenance. She saw friendship in them, and the promise of discretion, and true interest, as if her next utterance would be all that he heard in the world.

"I am thinking about my legacy, as I promised my mother I would. It is past time to do so. Before I go too far down one path, I should give fair judgment to them all."

A few shadows gathered around the edges of those eyes. "I hope that my inexcusable behavior is not the cause of this."

"Hardly inexcusable. We both know that I gave you the

best excuse. I promise that you have not led me astray. However, your words the day Anthony came here do cause me some confusion."

"Which words?"

"*Sometimes it just is*, you said. You revealed a man's view, I think. A man's preference. My mother's patrons probably just wanted it to be, many of them. Others, of course, wanted to play out a great love affair on the world stage. But she would never let it just be. She insisted there be a story that required all those expensive gifts. Without a story of some kind, a woman gains nothing."

"If you believe that, you are still ignorant, for all of your mother's lessons."

She found that charming, and so masculine in the touch of insult it revealed. "You have no idea how thorough my mother's lessons were. You are speaking of pleasure being what a woman gains, I assume. But I know that I do not need a man to experience that, any more than you need a woman."

Her insinuation appeared to shock him a little. Enough that she had to bite back a giggle. Her throat unaccountably burned in the next instant. It had felt so good, that urge to laugh, that its contrast with her mood pained her.

"Your mother did not only offer those men pleasure. They could have paid a woman a few pence and been done with it, if that was all they sought."

"Ah. So I am wrong. Perhaps they wanted the story even more than she required it." She made a face. "I am not sure that I want the silly dramas and pretense, although I suppose I can live the lie if necessary." She certainly did not want the story of first and forever that Anthony expected. Which did not mean she could not play the role if required.

He appeared rather formal suddenly. The warmth turned shallow and the gaze distant. "I expect you are correct. Even with me, it would probably not just be."

"With you? Goodness, are you propositioning me, Mr. Albrighton?"

She spoke in a flirtatious tease, but he did not take the cue.

"If you conclude that you are willing to entertain propositions, I could never afford you. You will do it the way she taught you. The smart way."

Of course she would, but she did not think he had to say it so baldly. Whatever had started between them, it had not ended yet. Or had it, right now in this garden?

She pictured herself preparing for her first man. For Anthony. She could do it. She could even know pleasure, the way Alessandra had taught her. She would not experience excitement, however. Or joy. Whatever she felt, Anthony would not be a part of it, only its agent. She imagined what her heart and soul would feel waiting for Anthony, and it was the calm calculations of a very practical woman.

She set that boring speculation aside and considered the man in front of her now. Her blood hummed just on seeing him. He had aroused her that first night, and ever since. Their affair would have been brief and strangled with discretion, but at least it might have been an adventure.

She moved closer to Mr. Albrighton. To Jonathan. To his warm eyes and dark enigma. She wanted to bridge all of the distances he had created here in the garden, for a final moment at least.

He looked down at her, his expression hard now, maybe angry. She laid her fingertips, no more, on his cravat, very lightly.

"It can never just be, unfortunately," she said.

He captured her hand against his chest, and held it there tightly. She felt his body beneath her palm, hard and pulsing with the heart within. She could not extricate her hand now even if she wanted to.

"It sounds as if your debate with yourself is well along. Far past the question of whether virtue is a virtue, Celia."

The warmth of his gaze drew her in, as it always did. A warmth so in contrast to the brittle danger he could project. It was a world away from chilly practicalities concerning Anthony. Regret strangled her, and it was hard to respond.

"Yes, it is well along." Further than she had realized until this instant.

"And you will go to that fool?"

"He is as good a fool as another, and will be more foolishly generous than most."

"The hell you say." The danger emerged in him, and the darkness.

She tried to remove her hand from his grasp. He clutched it tighter, so she could not. The hard heat of his body entered her through her touch. She could not ignore the arousal that flowed with it, teasing her like so many wicked licks.

She had been trained to feel such things to their fullest, not deny them. She ached for more contact, more pleasure, and for the happy melody playing in her blood to become a soaring aria. Once, at least once, before she chose any path forever, it would have been nice to know all that sensual pleasure could be when it was truly shared.

He was angry now. Coldly furious. "I'll be damned before I see you do this."

"The decision is mine alone. You have no say in it."

"The hell I don't."

He looked at her darkly, intensely, but he said nothing more. She stretched up to kiss his cheek, in a gesture of friendship and to acknowledge what they had shared.

He moved his head away, so she could not. "A final kiss, Celia?"

"A friend's kiss, Jonathan." But, yes, a final one too. For herself, to remember.

"I told you it could never be one kiss again. Whatever your decision, that has not changed."

He walked away. He left her alone in the garden, sadder and more dismayed than she had ever expected to feel.

Many men will think it is like a horse auction. You must make it clear that you will not merely award the prize to the highest bidder, and that any liaison will always be your choice.

Your choice. It appeared that she had just made hers, for good or ill, despite what Jonathan believed. It had been inevitable, once she acknowledged her place in the world, and the brand of her birth. Once she stopped fighting the rules of the world. Alessandra had always known she would reach this decision if she gave the truth a fair hearing.

She should be content, and confident in her choice. She should be anticipating the gowns and luxury, and the comforts of that fashionable house, and taking joy in being able to save this home for Marian and Bella and maybe others like them.

Instead grief burned her heart, and tears blurred her sight so badly that she had to turn away from the sun.

* * *

He had to leave the house. There was no staying there that day. He was too aware of her presence and her spirit and every distant sound she made. He was sure that his hunger and anger filled the whole building like an invisible mist. Every minute inside those walls was torture.

He went out and called on Summerhays. He barely heard what the man said during the hours they talked. As a result, however, Summerhays and Hawkeswell joined him when he met with Castleford for the boxing match.

The duke was not happy to see he was not alone. "Why in hell did you bring the two aunties?"

Summerhays laughed.

Hawkeswell did not. "We are not going to interfere with your fun. You can drink until you drop, and we will cheer you on."

"It won't be the same."

"What ho? Are you saying that the presence of half-way responsible individuals makes your total lack of that quality embarrassing?"

"I am thinking that with two angels harping in Albrighton's ear, it will drown out my speaking in his other one."

They positioned themselves to see the match well. Standing among the other shouting men, they laid their bets with the roving keeper of the books, bought glasses of spirits, and lit cigars.

Summerhays flashed that smile of his. "Are we here as angels? Your invitation to come along was pointed, now that I recall."

"Not angels. Excuses, perhaps, to prevent this being a party that lasts until morning." He looked at Castleford, who had recovered from his pique and was busy explaining to Hawkeswell which of the pugilists would win. "Perhaps I was wrong in assuming that marriage sends you home before dawn."

"Not always, but knowing what Castleford intends for those last hours, we will be taking our leave much earlier."

"As will I. I told him so, but he did not believe I could not be swayed."

"Do you need us to sway you?"

"Not at all." These friends might keep him from leaving so early that the duke was insulted, however. He did not want to be here at all. Most of him wasn't, but instead back in his chamber, suffering the titillation of the close proximity of a woman who had told him today that their passion did not fit with her plans.

If she thought he would accept that and just stand down, she was much mistaken.

"He does know his whores, if one is of a mind to have one. I daresay he could write a book on them," Summerhays mused.

I don't want one of his whores.

Castleford overheard. "That is a splendid idea. You always preach that I should use my station for the greater good, Summerhays. I think you have hit on a way for me to do so."

"Sort of a *Sites and Monuments of London*, only *Venuses, Abbesses, and Soiled Doves*?" Hawkeswell said.

"I would need a better title than that," Castleford said. "Something less obvious and more poetic."

"If you are too poetic, the average man coming up to town will not know the value of the tome."

Castleford put his mind to it. "The title can wait. The form of the content occupies me most intriguingly, however. There is no point in including the most celebrated courtesans, since the men who would buy my book have no chance with them. To be truly useful, it must only be women accessible to anyone with the coin."

Hawkeswell looked at Summerhays and Jonathan. "Damnation, he almost appears sober all of a sudden. I think he is seriously contemplating it."

"Of course I am. Such a book would be a great boon to mankind. I wish someone had given one to me when I first went seeking women in this town."

The notion distracted him all through the boxing matches. Jonathan wondered if Castleford was choosing the chapters despite his vocal cheers of the pugilists he had bet on. The duke's eyes did appear more sober than earlier, as if the better part of his mind remained on this new literary endeavor.

Jonathan's own remained on something other than the blows being exchanged in the center of the room too. As time ticked by he imagined the women in that house going about their normal routine. He saw Marian serving the dinner, then Bella cleaning the dishes. He saw luminous, beautiful Celia, presiding over it all and making them laugh.

The last match ended after midnight. Castleford cajoled him to play on, in the games waiting to fill the hours. He refused, and slipped away with Summerhays and Hawkeswell. They went home to the certain satisfaction waiting with their wives. Jonathan rode toward a woman he was determined to seduce.

Chapter Fifteen

Celia put a little more fuel on the fire, then began folding the satin dresses strewn on her bed. Her examination of her scandalous wardrobe had been most practical. She had indulged in no sensual pleasure in the fabric's feel this time. Instead she had scrutinized each garment for any need of repair, while reciting the lessons her mother had taught her.

A clean sheet of paper waited on the small writing table. An inkwell stood at attention beside it. She gathered her resolve, left the dresses, and sat down. It was time to write to Anthony.

She penned a simple note. She invited him to call on her, and signed her name. As soon as he saw it, he would understand that he had won.

She looked around her chamber. Would it happen here? He would not want to wait. Her mother's voice chanted in her head. No, not here. Not yet. The arrangement must be settled before she gave him what he wanted. She would make him purchase that house in her name first, and furnish it. And when it happened *there*, finally, that indenture her mother had signed would be waiting on the mantel to be burned as soon as it was done.

Once all was agreed, there would be no turning back. There would be other letters to write then, to Verity and Audrianna, and probably even Daphne. They might still see her very privately and very discreetly once she did this, perhaps. She prayed they would. If not, those friendships would be the true loss and true cost.

An odd sorrow filled her heart. One too encompassing to be relieved by mere tears. Much like grief, it just sat in her, to be accommodated in the days ahead as she lived the reality of who she was and released the illusions of who she had tried to be.

She returned to the bed and finished folding the dresses. As she did, the silence of the house changed just enough to arrest her attention. Subtle sounds from below came to her softly. Movement. Steps.

Jonathan had returned.

She paused and listened to those sounds of his presence. They brought her comfort, although they should not. She closed her eyes and saw him in the garden today, angry. His image changed to his face before he kissed her the first time. So sweet that kiss had been.

She startled out of her reverie. The footfalls were not following the normal path up to the attic. They came closer, down the passageway on this level. Panic scattered her thoughts.

Boot steps, near her door. They stopped. Then, silence. No knock. No voice. She felt him through the wood. Felt that energy he exuded and that intensity.

She waited. Nothing. Perhaps he had rethought whatever his reason for coming here. She all but held her breath as the time pulsed.

She walked to the door. Taking a deep breath to steady her nerves, she opened it.

He stood there, arms crossed, shoulder resting against the ridge of the threshold.

"Were you going to stand there all night?" she asked.

"I did not expect to."

He knew she would hear him if she was still awake. She wanted to think he had not knocked or called out of consideration, but he did not appear very thoughtful and kind right now. Rather the opposite.

"Did you want to say something to me? Why are you here?"

He crossed the threshold. She stepped back instinctively. She saw his face in the firelight as he entered the chamber. He answered her question with one direct glance that required no words. *You know why I am here.*

His gaze was drawn to the silks on the bed. He went over and lifted one. The soft satin flowed down like a waterfall, so in contrast to his masculine hand in form and color. "I thought there were only two such gowns, and that you were giving them to your friends."

"There were more. I saved them for myself."

His gaze drifted down her body, sliding over her breasts and hips much like the flow of the silk that he held. She instinctively touched the lawn fabric of the undressing gown she wore.

"I would like to see you in one someday. But not tonight."

She should tell him to leave. That went without saying. Yet he commanded this space so totally that she could barely form the words. Compelling, Verity had called him. If only she knew how inadequate that word could be. Like now. He appeared dangerous, but in the best ways. Her traitorous blood thrilled in reaction to his masculine force.

He moved near the writing table. The letter resting on it distracted him. His head angled while he read it. Then he turned to her, with the paper in his hand.

"You will not do this. Not now. Not yet."

Dear heavens, he had come to talk her out of it. *To save her.*

She found her own presence again, despite the way his dominated this chamber. *Her* chamber. She resented that he was going to make her explain herself, about what was a decision about *her* life.

"I will do whatever I decide to do, as I said this afternoon. You are the last person I expected to judge me about whatever the decision might be. You even said several times that you would not."

"I am not judging, Celia. I am saying you will not accept this fool's arrangement now." He waved the letter.

"I will not allow you to—"

"*No.*" He cast the letter into the fireplace. Flames immediately ate its edges and began to digest the rest.

She strode over to him, furious. "A fine gesture, and a meaningless one. Your overbearing manner is presumptuous and your criticism is offensive. I am not some stupid woman who struck on a fast way to accumulate new garments one afternoon, Jonathan. I have been thinking about this for more than *five years.*"

He gazed down at her, his expression tight and hard, his eyes warm, fathomless, and full of intensities that made her breath catch. He pulled her to him abruptly, and held her face just as he had that night in the garden. "I am not saying no to the decision, Celia. I am saying it will not be that man."

He kissed her before she could respond. Before she could put him in his place. She fought mightily to permit that kiss to have no effect on her. Her thoughts scrambled as the sensations swept her body and the secret regret burst out of her heart, together threatening to drown all good sense and rational, practical resolve.

We must not. It will ruin everything. Ruin me, I fear, far worse than going to Anthony ever would. Did she say it, amid the short gasps she made while his mouth burned her neck? She could not tell. He did not act as if he heard. Or else he did not care.

Always make them ask, Celia. Even with the first kiss. This man was asking permission for nothing. He never had.

His embrace felt too good. Too welcome. His strength proved too exciting. She had not chosen to succumb to this desire they felt for each other, but she could not resist either. His fire began consuming her will, much as the flames had that paper.

He caressed her body, her breasts, his firm hands claiming and possessive. He held her so she molded against him. His kisses insisted she burn with him. Pleasure sang in her. Not a melody but a primitive song, pulsing and hot, its rhythms getting more rapid with every moment.

She could not deny that pulse. She could not pretend she was not glad to know this glorious passion once more. She should not indulge—for so many reasons she should not—but she could not care enough now to stop it.

She gave up the fight with herself. She surrendered, and her heart soared with relief and joy when she did. Yes, once, just once, she deserved to know what this could be.

You must remain in control. You must keep it dignified.
She had no dignity, no self-possession now. She controlled
nothing with this man. She never had. She should have
sent him away somehow. She should have never—

His hands left her body to hold her head to a kiss, hard
and ravishing. She flew into a fevered daze and lost hold
on her thoughts and the remnants of resistance. She pressed
closer, closer, so she might feel more of him and more of
everything.

She reached high and released the tie on his hair so it
fell along the sides of his face, making him look roguish.
She caressed from his nape to his chin, then plucked at his
cravat. The kiss turned feral and she gasped for breath
when he broke it, and gasped again and again as he heated
her neck and chest with bites while his hands found her
body again, and caressed with a touch that implied the
fabric had disappeared.

Wonderful pleasure. Delicious excitement. The sensations piled one on another, making her want to groan and
cry and sing. A special hunger took hold of her body and
mind and she kissed him back, aggressively, so he might
not delay too long in answering that need.

A storm of insanity caught them both. A whirlwind
of heat and hardness and no thoughts at all. When he
moved her toward the bed, her hunger rejoiced, trium-
phant, and her body silently begged for him to throw her
down and fill the aching void that pulsed, pulsed, almost
desperate for relief, so much it maddened her.

Instead he released her, sat on the bed, and removed
his boots. She stood there, unsteady, shocked by the evidence he was not nearly as impatient as she.

He cast off his coat and pulled her to him, not so patient after all. She climbed on his lap, facing him with her

knees flanking his hips. They were in the eye of a storm but nothing had changed. The winds of desire still howled in her, and in him too, she could tell. There was no need to rush, however, and his gesture had reminded her that there were rituals to enjoy.

She finished with his cravat. He let her, and caressed her legs. The undressing gown rose with those firm, skimming hands until it was skin on skin. By the time she removed the linen from his neck, the fabric pooled between them like so much water, and his hands explored her thighs.

That distracted her enough that she handled his waistcoat and shirt with less panache. She finished with the shirt's buttons while his touch slid up and down her inner thigh. Each time he teased close to her vulva, her breath caught.

She pushed his shirt off his shoulders and leaned forward to kiss a line from his ear to the top of his arm. She flicked her tongue to taste the flavor of his skin, then leaned back so she could caress his chest. It was a fine one, she decided. Lean and muscular, as if he lived an active life. Stronger than one would guess at first, if seeing him in his coats. She slid her fingertips along the planes and ridges, fascinated.

He eyed her undressing gown. "It closes in the front."

"That will make it easier for you."

His caresses moved very high on her thighs. "I am busy."

He wanted her to do it. She clumsily worked the closures, too far gone to be artful. An odd shyness tinged her madness, one she knew she was not supposed to feel. It mattered to her, she realized—what he thought and whether he was pleased.

She parted the bodice, so her breasts showed. A moment of profoundly intense sensuality passed between them, with his hands firmly caressing her legs and his gaze capturing hers. She nestled deeper on his lap, so the bulge of his erection pressed her. The pressure tantalized her.

His hands cupped her bottom. "Up."

She rose on her knees, took his face in her hands, and kissed him with all the skill she could muster. His hands worked at his garments, and when she sat back down he was naked and her gown was high, bunched around her waist. He pressed against her directly, hard, giving a vague relief that also made hot thrills coil deeply between her hips.

Caresses on her breast, too wonderful, so enlivening. A daze of sensation built in waves, each one more exciting, each one making her more sensitive. Soft fabric slid high, blinding her as he drew off the gown. Then she was naked, facing him, filling her gaze with his intense expression and hard, taut body, fascinated by the look and scent of him, trembling from what he was doing to her.

She almost could not contain the way he aroused her, but she feared it ending too soon, too fast, ever. She leaned back and braced herself with her hands on his knees so he would caress her breasts more fully. He did, in smoothing strokes that made vibrations thrum down her core, to where that coiling tightened, then sent bright jolts of pleasure even lower.

Kisses now, on her body, her stomach. The tightness in him palpable, a thrilling tension that she felt in the air and his touch and kiss, in the way he handled her.

She floated in the sensuous haze, feeling it all as fully as she could, wondering if there was a way to feel like this always. She forgot herself for a timeless spell as the pleasure filled her and his hands moved over her in possessive strokes, so masculine and firm, making her want more and more.

Alessandra's lessons whispered. It was not right to only take pleasure. She was supposed to give it too. She sat upright again, unsteady, aroused beyond shame or restraint. She looked in his eyes directly, into hard lights of male need that carried so much potential danger.

She looked down at where their bodies met, at his lap and her mound. She moved back enough, and took him in her hands. She knew how to do this. It had been the easiest thing to learn.

She stroked the shaft softly, then harder. She circled the tip, then enclosed it entirely. She watched his face flex within its tautness, and the line of his mouth firm, and those wonderful eyes deepen, deepen.

Up again, but he did not ask this time. He grasped her bottom and lifted her high enough that he could take her breast in his mouth. His phallus rose along her thigh, but it was his hand that pressed her now, his palm on her mound and his fingers farther back, touching swollen, sensitive skin that shrieked from the contact.

Helpless, she grasped his shoulders and wept from it all. From the hard way he sucked at her breast and the stunning, screaming pleasure he gave with his hand. Nothing else existed but her body and his and the insistent need he made her feel.

She could barely remain steady. The daze closed in and the hunger made her insane. She heard herself whispering, begging, asking for more, always more, offering herself, her body, her soul, anything, if he just gave the relief he had made sure she wanted.

Firm hands grasped her hips, lowering her slowly, so slowly, too slowly at first. Then she felt the hardness push and she knew why, but still her impatience made it torture. Filling, stretching, hurting, but the daze never shattered and the hurt almost felt good. Gasping at the end, she clutched his arms and pressed down even more.

She huddled against him, within protective arms holding her close. She fought through the haze so she could feel it all, him inside her and around her, the breath carrying his reassuring murmurs, and remember it forever. He allowed the respite of poignant restraint, but she sensed the need waiting in him, and it would not be denied.

Holding her hips, he moved, and moved her too. Then she felt him, again and again, filling her body and her senses, defeating what was left of her hold on herself. And she knew in her soul, as intimacy drenched her heart and left her defenseless, and as his strength made her weak, and as she gave far more than her virginity—she knew that Alessandra Northrope would never have approved of how much her daughter had relinquished to this man.

She had been a virgin.

He wanted to believe he had been surprised. He could find reasons why he might have been. Only he had guessed as much, and it had not stopped him.

He should feel more guilty than he did, most likely. There were things he should say now too, if he had any claim to being a gentleman. In the white bliss of his contentment as he lay with her atop him, her knees still pressed to his hips and their bodies still joined, the notion of saying them actually seemed a good idea.

He sat up with her still bound to him, and stood enough to cast the satin gowns from the bed and pull down the bedclothes. He laid her down, then put more fuel on the fire.

She gazed at him when he returned to the bed, her eyes

still glistening, her face radiant. It would be a while yet before she decided whether this had been a mistake.

She appeared so beautiful there, all pale and gold. He joined her and gathered her satin warmth into his arms so the lightness he experienced inside would not pass too soon.

"Did I hurt you?"

She turned in his embrace so she looked down at him. Her fingertips lightly stroked his lips. "Not very much. I expected worse."

That was something at least.

Her eyes saw into his mind. "You were not sure, but you were not surprised, were you? Nor deterred. It was safe to say that no matter which way it went, I was no innocent, after all."

"Officially you were."

"And now you have made sure that officially I am not. You have made sure that there will be no arrangement with Anthony."

He did not miss the note of accusation in her tone. "Was your innocence essential to that arrangement? He is more a fool than I thought."

"You do not sound sorry that you have ruined everything. Perhaps your conscience will speak differently when we are all thrown out of this house."

"He is not going to take this house."

"It isn't as if you can stop it."

That remained to be seen.

"I am not sorry at all, Celia. If you want that life, I cannot stop you, but at least you will not go to *him* now. The last of my thoughts is concern that I interfered with your decision on that. He was blackmailing you into it." That sounded harsh, so he added, "You said it must be your choice. And it was tonight, and your choice wasn't him."

"No, it was you, with an unfair amount of encouragement on your part."

He'd be damned before he apologized for that.

And yet . . . he *had* seduced her. There was no other word for it. And she *had* been an innocent, in the way that mattered in these things.

She rose up on her arm and looked down at him. His heart almost stopped at how beautiful she looked in the light from the fire. But he also saw that the daze had passed, and she was thinking now, and assessing what had just happened.

"Do not speak what you think you are obliged to speak," she said, as if she saw his deepest thoughts. "Do not get tediously proper and guilty with me, when you did not bother with such things an hour ago."

"I was not thinking clearly an hour ago. I knew nothing except that I wanted you."

"And now you have had me. It changes nothing. I will still choose my own path. I do not want you to twist things around to create any story for me now. There isn't any that is suitable for the two of us. This just *was*, the way you said it could be sometimes."

Most men would kill for such uncomplicated intimacy. He would have often enough in the past. So why did he want to argue with her now, and explain that in truth it could never just be, unless two strangers met in the dark?

Content that she had absolved him of any inconvenient guilt, she nestled down beside him. "I wonder if Marian is going to scold."

"Perhaps, if she guesses. She will probably say that you have been reckless."

"At least she will not talk about sin. As for reckless, it is not the word I would use."

"Brave?"

"I suppose that is apt, in a way. But it was not foremost in my mind."

He rolled, so his body pressed against hers and she looked up at him. "Seductive, then."

"I was not the one who was seductive. Remember?"

"You were very seductive. You have been from the start. Quietly, subtly, and very effectively."

She thought about that, and gave a little shrug, ceding the point.

"Seductive, and enchanting, and brilliant," he said. "I do not normally lose all sense over women, Celia. At least know that this is no common desire."

She appeared to flush. "Brilliant now. An odd word."

"It speaks of both your mind and radiance."

"Well, thank you, Jonathan. That is very poetic of you."

He would have laughed if she did not look honestly touched. No one had ever called him poetic before; that was certain.

She watched his face very closely, while she ran her fingertips down the side of his cheek. She studied him as much as he had ever been studied, while her expression turned earnest and serious.

"What are you thinking?" he asked.

"I am making sure I remember, Jonathan. How you look and how I feel. I want to remember everything about how it just is, while it just is."

He did not like her matter-of-fact assumption that there could be nothing more between them. Nor did he like thinking about where she would go when she ceased being brilliant with him.

He lowered his head and kissed her thoroughly. Then he cast aside the bedclothes. "I will go now, so there is no danger of falling asleep and being discovered here by Marian or Bella."

"You can come back tomorrow night, if you want."

Oh, he wanted. He was glad for the invitation, but he did not think he would have waited on one if it did not come. He wanted her again right now, but it would be inconsiderate. She said he had not hurt her much, but he had hurt her some.

She lay on her side, watching him pulling on his garments. She was unashamed of her nakedness. The line of her body from shoulder to knee formed a sinuous, entrancing curve. He looked long and hard, at that line and her breasts and the face that always reflected good humor. At her brilliance.

He bent and kissed her, and stayed there, hovering over her upturned face with his hand cupping her chin. All kinds of erotic images of her entered his head. He almost reached for her, to make at least one a reality. Instead he tore himself from the bedside, and went above to his monk's cell, to be tortured until tomorrow night.

Chapter Sixteen

Marian knew.

The next morning she brought Celia breakfast in bed, which she had never done before. Face impassive, she placed the tray on a table, glanced at Celia's naked shoulders above the bedclothes, then surveyed the satin dresses that had been thrown off the bed the previous night.

"Pretty things," she said, bending to pick some up. "Too costly to be in a heap like this."

"I was examining them for repairs when . . . when . . ."

"When you became a bit distracted, did you?"

"Yes. Distracted."

"Peculiar, that. Must be something in the air. Mr. Albrighton looks this morning like someone suffering from distraction too." An impish smile played on her lips while she folded the satins.

"How odd."

"Speaking of the distractions, Mr. Albrighton is bathing in the kitchen. We'll be heating water for you next."

She draped the discarded undressing gown on the foot of the bed.

Celia was glad she would not have to pretend with Marian. When the bath was ready, she went below. The house seemed different today. Something about the light had altered, and the way her body moved through the spaces. Of course it was not the house that had changed, but rather her.

As she approached the stairs to the kitchen, someone grabbed her and pulled her around the stairwell's wall. Jonathan pinned her against it while he looked around the corner and listened. Then he kissed her in a way that showed last night had done nothing to diminish his desire.

"You look beautiful," he muttered, between kisses. "I favor that undressing gown."

"It is hardly attractive," she said, laughing between gasps.

He looked down at it. "I'll be damned. You are right. Let's get it off you again. No, wait, that won't do here. Marian and Bella. Is it wrong for me to wish they lived elsewhere?"

"It can be excused by the moment, I think." She met him in a less frantic kiss that went on and on. "Now, I need to have my bath, as you had yours."

"I'll come and help."

"You will not. You will go about your day, as I will go about mine."

"I will be useless. Send them away, and come above with me and we will spend the day in bed."

She gave him a playful slap on his chest. "The wagon is coming from The Rarest Blooms early this afternoon. Do you want Daphne to find us up in your bed? She owns a pistol."

He kissed her once more, then reluctantly stood back and let her free. "Off with you, then, to your bath and duties. I will find some way to survive. Perhaps I will not think about you for a few minutes at least."

Happy that he had found her, glad that there had been no awkwardness when they met again, pleased that he had conjured up some romantic words, she made her way down to the kitchen and the tub.

The water's warmth stirred her senses again. A memory of pleasure lapped over her along with the liquid eddies. For the first time in her life, she mentally thanked Mama for the education that had taught that a woman should feel pleasure without regrets. There were sins in the world, great ones to be sure, but sensuality was not one of them.

A pleasant daze of happiness suffused her for the next few hours. Thoughts of Jonathan and even Mama, of the night's initiation and of the night to come, all mixed in her mind. In an odd way, she felt closer to Alessandra today than she ever had. More her equal too, perhaps, now that she was no longer ignorant.

In late morning, while Celia waited for the wagons and plants, she opened the trunk that had been brought down from the attic by Jonathan. The dresses and other garments had long ago been inspected and stored in her wardrobe.

She lifted the large folio-size boards that rested on its bottom still. She had glanced through the top images days ago, but now she wanted to study each one, and imagine her mother drawing or painting it. She wanted to feed her nostalgia about Alessandra, and perhaps know more about her from her artistry.

"What do you have there?" Marian asked, entering the

chamber with clean sheets over her arm. There had not been much blood, but there had been some.

"My mother's watercolors and drawings." She set the folio on the writing table near the window and turned back the cover. "She made all of these, over time."

Marian looked over her shoulder. "That one could be in a shop window."

"She was very talented." The watercolor in question showed this house's garden in late summer, she realized. Mama must have sat on the little terrace when she painted this.

"If I painted that good, I would have sold some," Marian said.

"Perhaps she did. There is so much I do not know about her." She turned the sheets, one by one, and admired the little landscapes and views with Marian.

"There be a lot there," Marian said. "I'll be leaving you to look at them. I'm taking Bella to the shops, and making her do the buying. She has to stop being so shy about such things."

Marian left, and Celia continued admiring her mother's artistry. The watercolors gave way to drawings, most of them landscapes but some quick sketches of people. Halfway to the bottom of the stack, however, a very different kind of painting faced her.

It was a coat of arms, carefully drawn in pencil and colored. The next sheet held another drawing of similar subject, without the watercolors. Curious, she thumbed through the rest of the sheets. All of them showed coats of arms, some of which she recognized. Ten of them were colored.

One by one she turned them. As she flipped one, she realized that there were numbers on its back. She checked and discovered numbers on them all. There were a few numbers on some, long columns on others, but only two on the colored ones, one number at the top and one at the bottom.

She frowned at those numbers, each six digits long. Then suddenly she realized what they were and what they meant.

The discovery startled her. She perused those drawings again and again, until Marian called up that the wagons had arrived.

"Follow me. I must show you something." Celia issued the command after the plants had been brought in and arranged. She led Daphne up to her chamber. Verity and Audrianna, who had visited today so they could see Daphne too, followed.

"What a pleasant chamber," Verity said upon entering. "It is very fresh in its simplicity."

"Can you believe my mother decorated this?" Celia asked. "It is so different from the house she lived in most of the time."

"Perhaps it reminded her of her childhood," Daphne said, fingering the muslin drapes. "If so, she came from simple folk. Country, it would appear."

The observation startled Celia. How like Daphne to comprehend this house in ways Celia had not. She thought of her mother as the Venus, because that was what she had known. But Daphne was possibly correct, and this house represented the real Alessandra, who lived inside that famous woman. The woman her daughter had never met.

She gathered them around the writing table and opened the large folio. Most of the watercolors and drawings now

rested on her bed. Only the coats of arms were inside it
now. "Look what I have found. See here, on the backs. I
am sure those numbers are dates."

They flipped through a few, all of them peering down
with their heads together.

"Is it a record?" Audrianna asked, her sweet face showing astonishment. "Like a journal, do you think?" She flipped
one back and forth. "This lord, on these nights? Goodness, I know some of these crests. It may be hard to keep
a straight face when I call on some ladies with Sebastian's
mother now."

"It was very apparent it was a record once I realized
they could be dates," Celia said.

Verity lifted one of the sheets. "Oh, my. This baron is
known as very upright and fastidious about not sinning.
He is always making speeches about it." She turned the
sheet and perused the numbers. "He appears to have slipped
up a few times seven years ago."

They all looked at one another, and bit back laughs.

"Won't this be the talk this season if this gets out,"
Audrianna mused. "Look here. Do you think it was the
father or the son?" She pointed to one of the sheets.

"That is a good question," Daphne said. "Perhaps we
should not assume it was the peer. It could be the heir."

Audrianna giggled. "You are no fun, Daphne. I rather
like the thought that this particular viscount erred. I don't
care much for him; he is so arrogant. I expect his insuf-
ferably conceited wife would be most shocked to learn of
it. She is very sure he adores her."

"We can enjoy all of those later," Celia said, gesturing
to the drawings. "These are the ones that interest me. They
are colored. Special. And the only ones without a list of

dates. See, only two. One at the beginning, and one at the end. I think these were ongoing affairs, and those dates mark beginning and end."

She spread out the colored sheets, then removed some and set them aside, leaving only three. "These three were the ones from around the time I was conceived. I think one of these represents my father."

They all gazed down on the expertly rendered heraldry. Verity's pale finger pointed to one. "This is the coat of arms of the Marquess of Enderby, Celia. He is of the right age." She touched another. "This is the Baron Barrowleigh. This final one, I believe, is the Earl of Hartlefield. He is no more than forty-five now, but he inherited when very young."

"I cannot eliminate him on account of his youth. At the time, Mama was not much older."

"How do you know all this heraldry, Verity? I recognized Enderby, but not the others," Audrianna said.

Verity's mouth pursed. "I was required to memorize many of them. It was part of my education. My cousin's wife wanted to be sure I did not miss any opportunity regarding my betters due to ignorance."

"How will you find out which one it is?" Daphne asked. "Three are still two too many. Nor do you know for certain that the correct man knows that he fathered you."

"I believe he does. I think he made Alessandra promise to keep it a secret." She put the other drawings back in the portfolio and closed its cover. She faced her friends. "I thought perhaps you could help me a little, however."

"Of course we will do what we can, Celia," Audrianna said.

"I am relieved that you in particular are agreeable,

Audrianna. Summerhays's mother likes to gossip, and she was a formidable woman in society back then. She may have heard things that she will share with you, if prompted."

"She does not think of it as gossip, but instruction," Audrianna said. "It will mean planning whole days with her, and suffering her company in the effort to create intimacy. However, if she remembers any rumors, she will share them, to help her son's common wife chart a proper course in society."

"I will see what emerges when I mention these names among ladies who call on me too," Verity offered. "Also, Hawkeswell's aunt will be coming to town to order dresses for the season soon. She may know something."

"I regret that I will be useless," Daphne said. "I have no female relative to pump for old gossip."

Celia hugged each friend in turn. "It may all come to naught, but it is a start. I am optimistic for the first time in my life about identifying him."

"And when you do?" Daphne asked.

"I don't know." Except she did know, in her heart.

The excitement in her, born of this small progress, would allow only one outcome after she knew his name. This man might be lost to her for the rest of her life. He might repudiate the connection for all time. But she would have one conversation with him, as daughter and father, before that happened.

*I*t just is.

The words kept returning to Jonathan's head as he moved through the day. They chanted while his mind saw Celia last night, opening that gown to expose her breasts, her eyes glistening and her arousal both innocent and wicked.

He risked going mad waiting for the night to come. Forcing some control on his thoughts, he sought diversion without much success. In the early evening, however, diversion found him.

He was walking down the Strand, giving his body something to do rather than torture him, when a grand coach suddenly careened out of the flow of carriages and made a difficult stop just ahead. He noted with annoyance that in the hands of any other coachman, the equipage might have missed its mark in that broad swerve and killed him.

As he approached alongside, the door to the coach opened.

"Get in."

He peered in to see Castleford sprawled on the seat with a woman wrapped around him.

"Perhaps another time, Your Grace."

"Oh, hell, get in. We are done, if you are going to become a vicar on me today." Limbs and garments jostled in the dark. Some coin flashed. "Here you go, little dove. My man will see you into a hackney."

"You said you would take me home," a woman's voice complained. "You promised me a ride in your coach."

"And you have had one. I must speak with this fellow here. You will still go home in style."

A pretty face emerged from the coach, followed by a voluptuous body dressed for evening. A footman slid past Jonathan to help the woman down.

Once out, she turned and spoke into the darkness. "You promised I'll be in that book, remember? You aren't going to forget?"

"You are on your way to having your own chapter, dear lady. Now, off with you. I will see you soon."

Satisfied with whatever bargain she had struck, the whore

marched away with the footman. Jonathan climbed inside the coach.

"Convenient seeing you on the street just now," Castleford said by way of welcome. "I have news."

The duke still sprawled, slouched low, barely awake from the looks of him. What had happened in here scented the carriage enough that Jonathan reached over to open the blinds and glass.

Castleford noticed. "How rude of me. I should have let her stay so she could—"

"That was not necessary." The vague reference was enough to make him hard. But then, he had been at half-mast due to memories and anticipation all day. "Your news?"

Castleford scratched his head, which only mussed his hair even more. No valet had attended him today. He looked like he had slept in his clothes. Three empty wine bottles rolled on the floor.

He noticed Jonathan's raking glance and laughed. "I have been in here all night and day, in case you are wondering. It is research for my book. Did you know that you can swive a woman six different ways in a coach without hurting yourself or causing anyone much discomfort?"

"Six, you say. I am impressed. I can only think of three, and four if we are very liberal in our meaning of swiving."

"I thought so too. She told me she had done it six ways, though. Of course I had to know if it were true."

"Of course."

"Do you disapprove, Albrighton? You looked a little like my tutor just then."

"I have sinned enough in my life to have no right to disapprove of most men, and least of all if they swive women."

It was the truth, especially on the latter point. He could not ignore that the man across from him might spend twelve hours fornicating in his coach, but he had never seduced an innocent. Which, for all intents and purposes, Jonathan had now, and planned to continue doing.

Nor, he suspected, had Castleford, for all his use of whores, ever been the man who set a woman on the path to selling herself. Which, perhaps, Jonathan had also just done last night.

None of which would matter tonight, or the next night, or for as long as Celia opened her bedchamber door to him. But if he appeared a little like a tutor right now, it was not due to Castleford's behavior.

"The news?" he prompted again.

Castleford yawned, and closed his eyes. "Why were you walking? Imagine my surprise to glimpse you out the blinds at the crucial moment of ecstasy. Where is your horse?"

"I left it at a tavern up the Strand. I wanted to take a turn for exercise. What were you doing looking out the blinds at such a moment?"

"Making sure she was not pretending. They do that sometimes. Oh, yes, they do. Seeing you was a complete accident. The blinds moved a bit."

Jonathan laughed. "Forgive me, but I am imagining you in your climax, seeing something despite the considerable distraction, and yelling to the coachman to stop the horses."

Castleford appeared startled at the notion. "No wonder she shifted like that at the last moment, then went still like she had died. Damnation, she thought I was yelling at her." He doubled over laughing. "Over, man, over!"

"Rein it in at once!"

"Stop immediately, damn it!" He wiped his eyes. "Poor woman. She definitely gets a chapter. I may have to write this in the form of a memoir to do her justice."

He called to the coachman to move on. "We will turn around and bring you to that horse."

They rolled forward. Jonathan waited a minute before prompting again. "The news? Is it about Thornridge?"

"Not yet. The fellow is slippery. He went down to the country again. That may have to wait a few weeks. This is about something else. Now, what was it?" He frowned while he picked through the sober half of his mind. "Ah, yes. Dargent."

"Father or son?"

"Both. Father Dargent was indeed talking to the military during the war, advising them on terrain. The news is that Son Dargent often accompanied him when he did so. The father knew he was sick and was handing things over the way it is done, and wanted any future appreciation of his help to fall to his heir along with the estate."

"Was this well-known?"

Castleford shrugged. "I expect it was known to anyone paying attention. It was not a secret, but it was not published in a broadside either."

So Anthony had heard those questions being posed to his father. That had been careless of the government, but not entirely surprising. Father and son were honorable and loyal, and who would expect any trouble to come of it? It was not as if the military laid out its strategies through those questions.

All the same, it was not news that Jonathan wanted to hear. How much better if Alessandra could have had no ulterior reason for throwing her daughter at Anthony. He reminded himself that the suspicions and talk had been that and nothing more, but his soul and his instincts—the parts of him that he ignored at his peril—took a big step away from that belief now.

He had assumed his investigation would exonerate Alessandra, or at least leave the question open. He did not think that would happen anymore.

Chapter Seventeen

He decided he would wait until eleven o'clock before going down to Celia that night. He made it until ten.

He heard Marian and Bella going to their chamber. He listened for their door closing. After that every minute felt like an eternity.

The discretion was perhaps unnecessary. Marian clearly knew what had happened last night. The way she offered to prepare that bath in the morning with her bland, blank expression, had said it all. He wondered if she had scolded Celia for recklessness. Perhaps, having been a whore, she did not think she had any standing to do so.

He went down the back stairs and walked the hall to Celia's chamber. He had been burning all day, and with each step he cast off his normal restraints. Desire was slicing him into pieces by the time he reached her door.

He did not have to knock. Her voice quietly said his name as soon as he got there. He opened the door to see a scene of alluring comfort.

Celia sat near a high fire that warmed the chamber, wearing one of her special satin gowns. Its lovely shade of pink gave her skin a rosy hue. The bodice consisted of a filmy, transparent fabric and her breasts were visible through its hazy mist. Her hair was down and brushed, her face washed and glowing. Another chair waited near hers, and a bottle of wine rested on a small table.

"Sit," she invited.

He did not want to sit. He wanted to grab her and throw her on the bed and—

He sat. She poured him some wine. He drank. Submitting to the domesticity of the situation dulled the most ragged edges of his need. He realized, as they sat there sipping the dark liquid and the fire danced, that she had intended just that. He kept forgetting that the knowledge of centuries regarding men had been passed to her.

She seemed to know when the tempest became more manageable. She set aside her wineglass and stood. He began to reach for her, but with a gentle gesture she stopped him. "Stay there, Jonathan. All that you want will be yours, and more."

She stepped back, out of her slippers. It was, he was sure, one of the most erotic things he had ever seen a woman do.

She unbuttoned the gown's two fastenings at her shoulders, watching him boldly as she did so. Her gaze carried a frank acknowledgment of what she was doing to him, and of the teasing pleasure her slow movements created. Finally loose, the shining fabric slid down her body until she stood naked in front of him, washed in the fire's golden light, her eyes large, as if the moment amazed her.

Again that erotic step of her pretty bare feet, forward this time, not back. She stood right in front of him, beautiful and ready with the subtle scent of arousal too close to ignore.

"I have sat here two hours, thinking of nothing except your being here tonight," she said.

"I spent most of the day thinking of nothing else." He reached up and slid his fingertips from her shoulder down her body. To his surprise she covered his hand with hers, and moved it to her mound.

"Just a little," she said, parting her legs. "Just enough."

He turned his hand and stroked her slowly. Pleasure trembled through her, transforming her expression. She allowed him to watch, demanded he do so, and his own arousal built until the storm howled in him again.

She surprised him then, for the last time perhaps. Gracefully, elegantly, she knelt in front of his chair and his legs. Her fingers plucked at the buttons of his shirt until she bared his chest. She leaned forward, with her lovely breasts nestling in his lap and her naked back curving down to the alluring flare of her hips. She kissed his chest, then caressed and licked while he turned taut and hard and mindless.

Her caresses moved lower and her fingers worked again, at the buttons of his trousers. A flash of hope turned to ruthless determination and single-minded need. Her first caress sent him careening into pure sensation. Then her kisses lowered too, and her mouth enclosed him, and he closed his eyes and submitted to her perfect torture.

"How did you come to know her? My mother."

She propped herself on one arm while she asked the question. Jonathan was naked now, his garments discarded in the lazy aftermath of his pleasure. They lay in her bed beneath the bedclothes, skin to skin. The fire burned low, sending dancing pale lights through the shadows.

"Why do you ask?"

"Do you never simply answer questions, Jonathan? Do you always dodge them? I ask because I have been thinking of her a lot today."

"Because of me?"

She laughed. "My, you are conceited." She knew what he meant, though. And what he feared, she supposed. "Perhaps because of you, a bit. I have come to realize, however, how little I really knew about her. This house, for example. Her past."

He pulled her back into his embrace. "She knew my mother. When my mother became ill, she visited. When my mother died, Alessandra was one of the few to attend her funeral. She informed me years later that she had told my mother that it was fine to love the earl and to be his mistress, but that she must demand a settlement first. My mother had ignored her, rather deliberately, it appears. I do not know why."

I do. His mother had not wanted to be the earl's whore. She had either hoped for more, or she had preferred it just be an honest liaison.

She would not explain that to him. He really did not need to know.

"After I left university, Alessandra wrote and invited me to call on her if I ever needed a friend. So I did, since I knew few people in town then."

"She offered an unusual entrée into society, but one of sorts, I suppose. You were able to meet all those men of the ton at her parties and dinners."

"That was how she saw it. It was kind of her to even remember me all those years later."

It explained much, Celia thought. Why this young man was there even although he would never be acceptable as a patron. Why Alessandra had let him that attic room. She had been helping the son of an old friend who, in the name of uncorrupted love, had foolishly not provided for him herself.

"Did she know about your work for the government? On the coast and such?"

"I think she guessed. She never asked where I was going when I took my leave of her, which is why I think that. It was as if she knew not to ask." It was his turn to prop up on one arm. His other hand began caressing her. "You have been thinking hard about this. Too hard for the night. You require distraction, I think."

His slow touch made thinking impossible soon enough. She closed her eyes and allowed the pleasure from that hand flow through her.

"Who taught you to use your mouth the way you did, Celia?"

She opened her eyes in surprise. "She did."

"You never did that before in reality?"

"Are you going to be jealous if I did?"

He watched his hand while she watched his expression. "Yes."

She could not decide if that was charming or annoying. She decided the former, but then, the teasing pleasure encouraged such a view. Better he feel jealous than guilty, though. She suspected he had the potential for the latter. They probably taught men all about guilt at university.

His gaze speared her. "You are not going to tell me?"

"It is undeniable that you were my first man in one way. It could hardly be hidden. The rest is not your business to know."

The vaguest smile formed. Humor warmed his eyes. "You are not as clever as you think, Celia. That alone tells me much. The rest I can see in your eyes and hear in your cries. It is one thing to know about these things, and another to be experienced in them. Do you think I can't tell the difference?"

"I don't think you are noticing much one way or the other."

He lowered his head and kissed her breast. "Oh, I am noticing. If you were taught I would not notice, an error was made." He took her two hands and raised them above her head. "I will have to be sure that you are noticing too, in the event you were taught to ignore the man you are with."

How did he know that lesson? Perhaps he just guessed that it made sense for many women. It was possibly a necessity for most of them.

He did not have to make sure of anything. She could not ignore who she was with. She saw him in the beautiful firelight, his hair falling along his face, while he caressed her. Even with her eyes closed, even when he made pleasure shriek through her as he used his mouth on her breasts to arouse her and his hands moved over all of her, even when the whole world became a dark place of excruciating need and impatient, pulsing desire, he was there.

He held her hands together above her head the whole time, so she could only feel and submit, so she barely could move to relieve the building fury. In the end he held down her legs with his own while he caressed into her cleft, making sensations burst in her, each one more intense, until she was mad, lost, crying, and moaning. She grasped him to her when his body covered hers and he positioned her knees to accept him.

Heaven then. Perfection. She could not believe how good it felt, how the fullness and pressure and rightness astonished her. When he moved in her, braced above her, when his strength dominated her and commanded new thrills to tremble through her completely, she could only accept it, and cry for more, for relief, for the frightening drive of the pleasure to find the finish it seemed to demand. When it did, when the crescendo reached its peak and broke apart in its climax, then, and only then, was he not there. Nor was she in truth, nor the world, nor thought, nor even her body.

His own hard finish was like a salve after that. She loved the feel of him in her so hard, so strong, and the way relief flexed through him at the end. She wrapped her legs around him and held him to her, his hard breaths on her hair and his tight muscles within her embrace. She held him like that as long as she could, with all of her body touching him, and allowed herself to feel all of him, all of it, even the aching poignancy that carried danger within itself.

They pretended the next day that the night before had never happened.

Jonathan found it a little ridiculous to do so in front of Marian. Bella was another matter. She appeared to be a frightened mouse of a young woman who had, he suspected, seen a hard life. She idolized Celia, and it probably was just as well that they maintained discretion around her.

That was hard to do. Neither he nor Celia could keep merriment out of their eyes when they greeted each other upon his coming down the next day. The formalities became a joke.

"The table here is clean, and Marian still has the breakfast pans out, if you want something to eat, Mr. Albrighton." Celia gestured to a little table in her back room while she handed some plants to Mr. Drummond.

"I was not expecting board, Miss Pennifold."

"It is a wise man who does not expect anything not paid for, sir. An unassuming manner makes generosity all the more welcome."

"I was just thinking last night how you are nothing if not generous, Miss Pennifold." He availed himself of that generosity this morning, much as he had last night. He sat himself and watched her deal with Mr. Drummond, and issue commands on which of the pots of forced bulbs were to go where.

The food arrived just as she completed her chore. She sat with him while he ate. She did not speak, but it was impossible to keep the night out of the gazes they exchanged. The memories hung between them without a word being said. All the same he felt words were needed. They had been trying to form since before he left her side at dawn.

"Are you going out today, Mr. Albrighton?" Celia asked while Bella cleared the plates away.

"I thought to."

"Perhaps, before you do, you could spare me a few minutes. I would like to show you something."

He politely followed her to the library. She closed the door after they entered, then rose on her toes and kissed him.

That was not enough. It never would be now. He took

advantage of their privacy to embrace her and kiss her properly. "You will have to show me something in the library several times a day," he said.

"It was not a ploy for some secret kisses, Jonathan. I really do have something to show you. Look over here."

She took his hand and led him to a table. A folio rested there, the kind made out of two taped paperboards covered in marbleized paper. She opened it to reveal a stack of papers of good size. The top one bore a watercolor view of the house's garden. She lifted it and a stack of the rest to reveal what was below. More drawings, each of which depicted a coat of arms.

"These were in Mama's trunk. Remember that day I found them in the attic, at the bottom? These were beneath those watercolors of the garden and such. I think they contain a clue about my father. You said you might be able to help if I had more information. Now I do."

She pointed out numbers on the back and explained her theory that they were dates. She showed how the ten colored ones seemed to imply long relationships, with three covering the year before she was born.

He stared at those crests, and their dates, and the identities that they revealed. Damnation. Celia had stumbled upon the list of Alessandra's lovers that Edward wanted him to find.

"Do you think this will help?" she asked.

"Help?"

"Help you find out which one is my father?"

"I will take all of this above to my chamber and put my mind to it."

She cocked her head to one side, puzzled. "Why would you need to do that? I know who these three men are.

Enderby, Barrowleigh, and Hartlefield. Verity identified the
coats of arms. As for the rest of them—" She gestured to
the larger stack without color. "They do not signify."

Oh, they signified. He needed to spend a good amount
of time with those drawings, and their dates, and some
books on heraldry. He wanted to see which ones had dates
much more recent than Celia's birth. Dates from around
five years ago, when he went to an ill-fated mission on the
Cornish coast. He needed to—

He realized that Celia was watching him closely, as if
she saw more than he knew his expression ever revealed.

He looked in her quizzical, concerned eyes, then at the
drawings. Answers rested in the stack of coats of arms,
he was sure. The truth about Alessandra, and probably the
clue to the man whose indiscretion had resulted in that
trap. With these drawings, in a day or two he might know
it all.

Then what? The question presented itself starkly.

He pictured the lovely face in front of him, disillusioned when she learned it all too. What would she think
and feel if she discovered that her mother had betrayed
this country, and perhaps even her own daughter, during
those negotiations with Anthony?

"If they do not signify, perhaps you should burn them,"
he said.

"Why would I do that? They are like her journal. They
are by her hand. She left me very little, especially of herself."

"They are potentially embarrassing to some of the men
with whom she had liaisons."

A twinkle entered her eyes. "Only if the wrong person
sees them, and comprehends those numbers on the back. I

doubt that will happen." Her delicate fingers came to rest on the top colored drawing. "Now, about these three—"

"You think that you have narrowed the field, but you cannot be sure."

"Let us assume that I have. Can you help me, with this smaller field?"

He flipped through the three drawings. They were names, for all intents and purposes. That was more than he usually had for some of his missions.

"If I do help you, what will you do if you learn who he is, Celia?"

"I told you. I just want to know his name."

"You think so, but it will not be enough when the name is securely yours. I think that you will be compelled to speak to him."

She stiffened, and looked on him less kindly. "Are you going to refuse, to prevent that?"

She did not deny how he thought it would go. Which meant she already knew he was right. "If you confront this man, you will probably face insult from him. I fear that if I help you learn who he is, in the end it will break your heart."

Her stiff poise wavered. Her eyes glistened now, but with tears. "That will be *something* at least. He will have to speak to me in order to do that. He will have to meet me, and see me, and admit I am his in order to repudiate me in that way. I will risk the heartbreak, Jonathan, for a few minutes of that most basic acknowledgment from him that I am alive."

He wanted to argue, to dissuade her. He wanted to tell her that it was not worth it. Only he knew that he would do the same thing. Knowing that his own father had acknowledged him as his son provided an anchor to his history, to who he knew he was. Celia's need to know this man's name for certain was not a small thing that could easily be put aside.

"I will see what I can learn," he said.

She rose on her toes to kiss him. "Thank you. I do not ask that you do anything that would be obvious, or cause him to hurt you. I just thought that perhaps you can do your investigating, and learn things quietly."

He embraced her, doubting that he could ask many questions before the men in question learned of it. Still, it was possible a conversation with Uncle Edward would eliminate one, or hopefully even two.

As he held her soft warmth and let it distract him from misgivings about the final cost to her of his agreement, he saw those drawings on the table behind her.

"Leave the folio here, Celia. I want to look at your mother's drawings more closely. There may be more to be learned from them."

Chapter Eighteen

"I need your advice, Jonathan."

The words drifted through the night, infiltrating the profound contentment he experienced lying in the dark holding her. His body wrapped hers from behind and his hand cradled her breast. Her climax had been violent, abandoned, and she had pulled him along with her until he shattered at the end.

Her voice now helped the pieces gather together once more, but the ecstasy still remained, too vivid to be a memory yet. Words formed to describe it, words that had been impossible a few minutes ago. Perfect. Astonishing. Pristine. It had been full of something that a man did not relinquish easily.

"About your plants?" he murmured. "I am no more a gardener than a carpenter, I am afraid."

"About a friend. I received a letter from Audrianna late yesterday," she said. "She requested that I call on her to-day. However, she left out the instructions about arriving discreetly. Surely she can't mean for me to call on her as if I were like her other friends."

"It sounds as if she does."

"I do not want to cause trouble for her, with either her husband or his mother."

"Perhaps you should allow her to decide if you would cause trouble, and how much she wants."

She went quiet for a spell. He sensed her fretting about this invitation.

"She found out about my mother by accident, soon after she was married," she said. "I remember the day she came to The Rarest Blooms and told me that she could no longer be my friend in a public way. She cried terribly, but I expected no less, of course. I thought it generous that Sebastian would even allow her to know me at all."

"If she obeyed him then, she would not stop now. Sebastian appears to have had new thoughts on the matter."

"Or she has convinced him to." She giggled. "I wonder how she managed that."

"Perhaps she was unusually generous." He kissed her shoulder. "I was thinking of calling on Sebastian today. Why don't I escort you there?"

She turned in his arms and looked at him. "Would you? I admit that approaching that door alone— I picture what might happen if I misunderstood and . . ."

"You are as worthy of approaching that door as any of the other women she knows. She is saying so, and it is true. We will take your carriage and go this afternoon."

"That will be too visible. If you are seen too much with me, your name will be linked to mine."

"No one will notice two obscure bastards riding in a cabriolet, Celia. Nor, at your age, will it compromise your reputation if they do."

"It is not my reputation that concerns me, Jonathan. Your expectations are better than mine will ever be. You are the one who must be careful."

He moved so that he lay atop her and could stare down at her face. "My reputation will not be damaged by being seen with you. That is absurd."

She began to speak, then stopped. She turned her head, and avoided his gaze. The dying fire gave little light, and her expression was not clear, but he thought she appeared more sad than angry.

"Nevertheless we will go in a hired, closed carriage. Perhaps that way the world will not even know how foolish you and she are both being."

"How kind of your tenant Mr. Albrighton to accompany you," Audrianna said that afternoon, after she had received Celia and Jonathan.

They were alone in her private sitting room. Jonathan had asked for Sebastian, and both men had left at once for the library.

"He has become more than my tenant . . ." Celia said.

Audrianna smiled. "Well, as lovers go, he probably is not a bad one, I would think."

"You are supposed to be shocked."

"Yet I am not. Imagine that."

"Because of my mother?"

Audrianna's face fell. "What a stupid question, Celia. The reason I am not shocked is because you are a woman and he is a fine figure of a man, and because for as long as I have known you, your views on sensual intimacy have carried a certain . . . how should I put it . . . irony?"

"Forgive me. You are correct; it was a stupid question.

Ever since it became public knowledge that I am the daughter of Alessandra Northrope, I have been too quick to see insult, sometimes when none exists."

Now Audrianna's sweet face showed concern. "And sometimes it does exist?"

"Of course. I am grateful that you received me openly today, but I am afraid you may pay the price." She looked to the door. "Is your husband's mother aware that I am here?"

Audrianna's hand went to her chestnut hair and dabbed and poked at a few curls while she tilted her head. "As it happens, she left this morning for the country. I doubt she will return until the season starts."

"Then you are spared the costs of receiving me."

"Oh, she knows. We had a big row yesterday, before I wrote that letter to you. I had been asking her questions about your mother and the old gossip, and she finally realized my interest meant that you are still my friend, and, well—" She shrugged.

"That is what I mean! Our friendship has been causing you trouble even while we have been discreet. How much worse if we are not—"

"No, quite the opposite! Let me tell you what happened. She drew Sebastian into that row, which was very foolish of her, as she should know by now. He sided with me and said that I would be receiving you in the future and she should either accept that or leave the household." Audrianna decided her hair was in sufficient order. Her hands went to her lap and she gazed over innocently. "So, in a manner of speaking, Sebastian commanded that I receive you, and all but ensured his mother would leave the house by doing so."

"I see. How convenient."

"Yes, wasn't it? I believe Sebastian has been congratulating himself on his stroke of brilliance."

"Speaking of your mother-in-law—before her departure, did she happen to remember any gossip about my mother?"

"She remembered more than I expected, but then, the men were of high interest, weren't they? She mentioned in passing that Hartlefield had neither heir nor daughter, despite having had three wives by the time he died."

"Although it is possible that he had the bad luck of marrying three barren women, it would appear . . ."

"There are some who think it can be the man's problem, due to such evidence as this. If so, it appears, if you are correct about those drawings, that the man you seek is either Barrowleigh or Enderby."

"Did she say anything interesting about those two?"

"She said that Enderby's liaison with Alessandra was intense but brief, due to his falling in love with another woman, whom he subsequently married. As for Barrowleigh, the *on dit* was that he wanted to marry Alessandra and the world be damned, but she would not have him as a husband. Perhaps he proposed because he knew she carried his child?"

"Perhaps." Not necessarily, however. It was not the only proposal Alessandra had received over the years. Pleasure could induce men to impulsive declarations.

Barrowleigh or Enderby. She would have to learn what she could about each one of them. It excited her to be so close now. Perhaps she would not even need Jonathan's help.

"She knew other things too, Celia. Other rumors." Audrianna's tone had lost its lightness.

"What other things?"

She sighed. "It was said that one of your mother's earliest lovers was French. An émigré. It was thought by some that he kept his ears open for the French during the war." She reached over and placed her hand on Celia's and gave a gentle squeeze. "It was also whispered that her ears listened for him too."

Celia looked at her friend's troubled expression, then at the hand grasping hers in reassurance and comfort.

She could not help herself, and started laughing. "Alessandra a spy? Audrianna, that is ludicrous. Why would she do that? She was from Yorkshire, for heaven's sake. You could still hear it in her voice, much as she tried to mask it. Why would she do such a thing?"

"Money. Love."

"I don't believe it. This is just the harpies spinning wool out of nothing. The very notion is beyond ridiculous."

"I thought so as well. I am sure it is all wrong. I was not even going to tell you. However, I thought that you should know this, as you seek out your father's name."

"You think that his silence on his paternity may have nothing to do with me, but this other business?"

"Consider it, at least. Perhaps he also heard these rumors, and does not want his name linked to hers in any way. Men of good reputation would not want to be explaining that she heard nothing from them to pass along to her French friend, would they?"

Most likely not. This explanation carried some logic, no matter how outraged she was that her mother's name had been slandered with whispers like this.

If Audrianna was correct, if this was the reason her

father's identity had become a secret, he might not mind so much if she discreetly made herself known to him.

"You are not going to tell me what you are doing, are you?" Sebastian asked the question from where he read a book on the library sofa. He did not even look up when he spoke.

"I am researching some heraldry, out of idle curiosity," Jonathan said while he turned a page. There were hundreds of crests, many very similar. A single color could indicate a different person, and he had no colors for certain, only crude sketches that he had copied off Alessandra's drawings.

Celia had seen him copying the colored ones the afternoon she revealed her theory, then left him alone. She had no longer been in the library when he turned to the others and sorted them by those numbers into a chronology of the lovers Alessandra had seen fit to document.

"It is a good thing Castleford is not here. He would tell you that you are being boring."

"And rude too. You are too good to make either scold, however. That is why I am using your library and not his."

"I am also too good to point out that if you have questions on heraldry, there is a place to learn the answers more quickly than in any library."

"I doubt the College of Heralds would receive me and give those answers, least of all on matters of idle curiosity."

"What else do they have to do?" He looked up from his book. "Unless you cannot share your curiosity for some reason, that is. Unless it is not as idle as you claim."

Now, that was pointed. And informative. "Do you have reason to think it is not idle?"

"None at all, other than it not being a subject that a man interested in scientific investigations would normally dabble in."

"I dabble in many things."

Sebastian laughed. "You do indeed. I am normally aware of what, in a vague way. Not this time. Someone is being extremely discreet."

Apparently so, if neither Castleford nor Summerhays could learn the truth, even vaguely. It was time to ask good Uncle Edward just who that very discreet person was.

"It was kind of you to allow your wife to receive Miss Pennifold," he said, thinking a change of topic, away from himself, was in order.

Sebastian gestured lazily with his hand. "I doubt she is the first person with her background to walk through the front door."

"Decidedly not. I have been here before, for example."

Sebastian smiled ruefully. "It is not really the same."

"Why? Because my mother attached herself to one man and remained invisible and hidden?"

"Because there is no suggestion that you will take up a profession that will irredeemably mark you. That unlikelihood of permanent blemish is not a confirmed fact with Miss Pennifold. That year she spent with Mrs. Northrope has not been forgotten."

"I have killed in my profession, Summerhays. If that does not mark a person, I do not know what does."

"If your point is that the world is harder in its assumptions regarding the Miss Pennifolds than the Mr. Albrightons, I can only agree. However, rumors surround both your and her histories and future prospects. Hers are of the worst kind, while yours are the best. That does factor into the difference, I expect."

Jonathan could ask why Summerhays assumed better prospects for him, but he did not have to. Castleford must have been indiscreet about the scheme to meet with Thornridge.

Just then the ladies entered the library. They had tied on their bonnets and wore their pelisses. Jonathan rose to greet them along with his host.

"The sun is fully on the terrace, and I told Cook to send up some tea," Lady Sebastian announced. "Would you gentlemen like to join us?"

Jonathan gave Lady Sebastian his attention, but he watched Celia too. Her attention shifted all around the library, while she took in its size and appointments, its books and tall windows. Just as Sebastian was accepting his wife's invitation, Celia's gaze passed over the books near where he and Sebastian had been sitting.

He sensed an alertness pass through her. As they strolled out to the terrace, he was sure she had noticed that the book near his chair concerned heraldry.

Jonathan went out that night, as he usually did. For the first time Celia wondered where he was going.

There had not been nearly enough curiosity about him on her part, she decided.

She sat in her room after dinner, trying to write to Daphne, but a jumble of impressions from the day distracted her. Audrianna's information was the most troubling. Sebastian's mother's memories of social gossip from more than twenty years ago could not be discounted. That woman might be a trial for her son and his wife, but no one could fault her expertise in such matters.

Had Alessandra done it? Collected indiscretions from the important men who sought out her favors, and given them over to her French lover? Or to someone else, another man? If so, did she do it out of love, or for money? Perhaps there was a very good reason the account books had gone missing.

Celia pondered the matter at length, far longer than needed, she knew. She finally accepted that she was avoiding other memories of the day. In particular she did not want to contemplate that book on heraldry that Jonathan had been consulting in Summerhays's library.

He did not need it to identify the colored crests in her mother's folio. She had handed him those names. He might have been confirming the accuracy of those identities, of course, before doing whatever he did when he investigated. She wished she could believe that. She wanted to very much.

She went to her writing table and opened the folio. The watercolors still rested atop the other drawings. She worked her way down to the crests, the ones not colored, and began turning them. Perhaps there was something in these that he thought would be useful in helping her too. She wondered what it might be.

She watched the shields and bars move by, and those numbers stack up when they joined the pile that showed their versos.

At the bottom, when she was almost done, she noticed something that made her heart sink. The last five all had numbers from five years ago. They were together now, but she was sure they had not been this morning.

These crests had nothing to do with her paternity. They were far too recent. Yet Jonathan had found them of interest.

Enough interest that he had separated them out. Had he then used Summerhays's library to investigate the men to whom they belonged?

The implications of that pressed on her. A surprising pain speared her heart. A good deal of humiliation joined the hurt. She shielded herself with anger, but it did not obscure the disappointment.

It had been stupid to think that any passion could be free of the accountings that marked women's lives and hearts. She had been naïve to believe she had nothing to lose in this affair.

She had probably been sharing a story with Jonathan from the first night she saw him in this house, even though she had not realized it. It was time to find out what that story was.

Jonathan entered the house through the garden door, as he always did. There had been no lights visible from within, however, when he looked up the street while on his way to the mews.

Silence greeted him. Not only that of a household that had retired, but one more still and pervasive. He paused on the first landing of the back stairs and listened. Normally sounds of life came from Celia's chamber. Tonight not even a floorboard creaked.

He had stayed too long with Castleford. The duke's condescension came with demands, especially for the likes of Jonathan Albrighton. Tonight Castleford seemed determined to ensnare his guest in his excesses. It had taken considerable finesse to escape the debauch that had been planned.

He lit a candle in his chamber and removed his coats,

all the while musing about the duke and his women, and the oddity of this renewed friendship. Perhaps Castleford had concluded that since both he and Jonathan Albrighton were bound for hell, it would be less lonely if they went there together.

He untied and slid off his cravat. As he did the air in the chamber moved. Immediately alert, he looked to the door.

Celia stood there, with a single taper in her hand. Her golden hair was down and brushed, flowing in its soft waves over her shoulders and chest. She was still dressed for the day, however, and the glint in her eyes was not one of anticipation.

Anger flowed to him, and disappointment, and an emotion so poignant that it twisted his gut. She tried to act casual as she closed the door. He knew in that instant, however, that this night would not end like the others.

She blew out the flame on her taper, and the shadows flooded her. Then the light from his own candle and the window found her and she became again, as she had always been for him, an oasis of golden light in a desert of darkness.

She strolled over to his writing table and its stacks of journals and papers. She perused a few titles. "You have varied intellectual interests, Jonathan. That does not surprise me. Although discoveries on chemical compounds seem a little obscure to me. Then again, perhaps some of them have practical applications that you find compelling. Poisons, for example."

So it was going to be like that tonight. He could not really blame her, if she had learned something to indict him and the life he had led. He did not have to like it, however.

"I have never used poison," he said.

"I have heard it is unreliable, so that is probably wise."
She poked at a few more journals. "Nothing on heraldry. I
thought it was one of your fascinations."

He reached for her, to stop this. To soothe, or to distract, he was not sure which. She raised a hand to block
the embrace, and warned him off with her eyes too.

"I should have come back here long ago," she said,
gazing around the chamber, at the artifacts of his life. "I
should not have allowed you to remain a mystery."

"I am no longer one to you, and you know it."

"Would that you were, perhaps." Even anger could not
harden the sweetness of her face, but a good deal of it was
in her; that was clear. "I thought you were visiting London for a spell, before going elsewhere. I thought that you
were here between missions or investigations. I think now
that I was stupid to assume that."

He could admit it, or he could lie. Or he could say nothing. The last option was his common choice when pointed
questions were asked about his activities. He made it again
now.

Fury flared in her eyes. "Will you insult me by refusing
to speak of it? Will you ignore my questions as if I am a
whore you dallied with and expect to be gone once the
coin is paid?"

"I have not insulted you. You have asked no questions.
You are angry but I do not know why." Except he did. The
sense of pending loss inside him said he did. It astonished
him, how hollow that truth felt, and how it wanted to grow
until it emptied him out.

"Don't you?" She stepped close to him and looked up
at his face. She peered at him so hard one would think she
had never seen him this closely before. "I learned from
Audrianna that there were whispers about my mother years

ago. About her and a French lover, and about her loyalty. Do you know of this?"

"Yes. They are rumors only. Nothing more."

"Rumors are enough in this world." She searched his eyes, as if she had to work hard to see anything at all. "Jonathan, are you here because of a mission? Are you investigating my mother? Or me?"

"Not you. Not even her, in truth. Not investigating. That is the wrong word."

"What is the correct word?"

"I was asked to see if she had left a record of her liaisons. The goal was not to harm anyone, but to protect the innocent."

Her expression fell. She turned her head away, dismayed. "It is true, then. Oh, dear God." She paced to the window and looked out at the night garden below. "Audrianna's mother-in-law told her about these suspicions. They made no sense to me, but if you also—"

"There is no proof of it. No reason to think it was true."

"And yet you are here."

"I was only asked to ensure no man was tainted by association to such rumors."

She nodded, but he wondered if she had even truly heard him. She seemed to calm, however. He was not sure that was a good thing.

"It was not about you, Celia," he tried. "It was to be a minor mission, to avoid embarrassment for men who were discreet and who counted on discretion in turn. She gave such discretion while she was alive. I was to ensure it continued now."

"Of course it was *about me*." She glanced over her shoulder at him as her anger bit the air. "You are here, aren't you? You were in this house that night, and you stayed so you could do what you were sent to do, and deceived me in order to accomplish your goal. You have what you wanted, those names of her patrons over the years. I daresay that you have made a list from the drawings." She looked away. "Since your mission is finished, I expect that you can leave now."

She stilled then, with her back to him and her face to the window. She became a statue of stone.

"If you wish it, I will go." They were hard words to say. He almost choked on them. He wanted to argue with her instead, but knew it would be hopeless to do so.

She did not even respond.

He donned his coats again, and took a few personal items from the table. He would get the rest later.

"Did she really give you this chamber, Jonathan? I never saw that document."

"She did, but there is no document."

She finally turned and looked at him. He waited, standing near the door, hoping she would say something else, but knowing if she did, it would not be what he really wanted to hear.

"What happened five years ago?" she asked. "You had a particular interest in the drawings from then, and in the men they identified."

He saw himself finishing with that folio that afternoon in the library. He had been careless, and left the most interesting crests all together. Celia had noticed, when most people never would.

"It is a personal matter," he said. "A private interest, related to one of my last missions during the war."

"Yet you thought those crests might help you in this personal matter," she said. "That means you think the whispers about my mother might be true."

She gazed at him long and hard. She no longer appeared angry. The chamber lost its cold, brittle atmosphere.

"That is something, at least," she said. "This personal, private part. It makes more sense to me, and less a calculated betrayal somehow, despite the implications for the conclusions you are drawing about the rumors."

He opened the door. Her expression turned sad, but she said nothing. He walked over to her and his heart thickened with every step.

He took her face in his hands and looked at her in the moonlight. He memorized the feel of her skin beneath his palms, and the way she illuminated this space all by herself.

"I am sorry that I disappointed you, darling." He kissed her, and let the brief contact brand his soul. Then he walked away, knowing that she would not speak again.

Chapter Nineteen

"You look like hell, Albrighton. Wake up, and my man will get you cleaned and shaved."

Jonathan opened his eyes at the command that intruded on a very restless sleep. Castleford loomed above him. The duke was dressed for the day and appeared far different from how he had looked the last time Jonathan had seen him.

Clearing his head a bit, Jonathan noticed that he was sprawled on a sofa in the duke's dressing room. Memories of the previous night rushed into his head.

After leaving Celia, he had retraced his steps to this house, and been brought back to these chambers by the servant. Castleford had taken one look at him and guessed that he had not returned to join the debauch still under way. To Jonathan's surprise, Castleford had summarily ordered the woman in his bed to depart, had thrown on a robe, and had brought his new guest to this dressing room for a long conversation punctuated by too many silences and many glasses of spirits.

He ran his fingers through his hair. And froze. "What the hell—" He groped around his head, trying to make sense of what he did and did not feel.

"I had my man cut it while you slept," Castleford said. "It looks much better now. He did a fine job of it."

Jonathan glared at him. "You go too far."

"I can't be seen around town with a man whose hair is so unfashionable. You will thank me once you see it. The women will be swarming you now."

Jonathan gave the short locks one final touch. His ire thinned, diluted by the hazy aftermath of all that drink.

"What time is it?" he asked, peering at a window.

"Nine o'clock thereabouts."

Jonathan groaned. The decanter on a nearby table caught his eye. They had finished that off only two hours ago at best. "You have not slept at all, have you?"

"It is, regrettably, Tuesday, so I have not. And if I do not, neither do you. Bad enough you interfered last night, showing up with a funereal countenance the way you did."

"I expected you to be finished with her by then."

"I try never to finish so quickly. Now, up with you. I'll not have another man lolling about in my chambers when I can't."

"It is rude of you to just throw me out, and even ruder to have cut my hair while I was unaware. I thought dukes had better manners." He sat up, amazed at how full of wool his head felt. And how, with consciousness, that sick hollow in his gut returned.

Castleford gazed down, then sat and studied him. It occurred to Jonathan that he should either resent or fear that scrutiny, but he was too dead to care.

"You left here last night your normal, inscrutable, dodgy self, and returned so distracted I could have stolen your purse while you stood there. What happened in the interim? Did you find out that you really are only a middling sort of bastard, and not that of an earl, the way your mother led you to believe?"

The question sobered him faster than a bucket of cold water or a punch to the face. He stared at Castleford, thinking about punches to the face in a less metaphorical context.

"Ah. So it wasn't that. And here I was going to banish your gloom by reassuring you the resemblance is notable." Castleford suddenly looked bored. "It must have been a woman. Threw you over, did she? Probably because you are, I regret to say, *no fun*." He stood. "I must attend to my duties now. As for throwing you out—there are at least thirty empty chambers here. If you lost your bed as well as your woman, you can stay in one of them."

"That is very generous."

"Yes, it is. It is the epitome of the sort of thing a kind, magnanimous duke would do. Be glad it is Tuesday."

"You should know that I probably will not be any more fun if I stay here. I will not be going to hell with you."

Castleford smiled, like a parent might with an innocent child. "Of course you will, Albrighton. Eventually. We both sold our souls long ago."

A gentle jostle jolted Celia awake. Light blinded her eyes when she opened them. Then she saw the window was not the one in her chamber.

She looked at the angled ceiling and stacked table. A thick misery instantly lodged low in her stomach. She must have cried herself to sleep.

She had been unable to say the words to stop Jonathan

leaving, but the worst sorrow had immobilized her after he did. It had tortured her to remain in this chamber that was so full of his life and his spirit, but she had been incapable of walking out. And so she had given in to her emotions here, her face buried in the pillow that carried his scent.

She had not thought it possible to feel so horrible. Even after Anthony disappointed her as a girl, even when that truth had been thrown in her face, she had not been this desolate.

Marian stood beside the bed, her eyes full of concern. Celia sat up and wiped her face of crusty, dried tears. She saw through the open door that the chamber across the passageway was open too. Soft sounds came from it, as though an animal poked around in there.

"This door was ajar," Marian explained. "I did not expect to find you here when I brought water to Mr. Albrighton this morning."

"He is gone, Marian. There will be no need to bring water tomorrow."

Marian sat down beside her and embraced her shoulders with a motherly arm. "I wish I had something to say to make you feel better. The truth is that men are pigs by nature, and not known for constancy, and this one was no worse or better than others on that, I expect."

She rested her head on Marian's shoulder. "Insult men all you want today, my friend. Just do not tell me I was a fool. I feel enough of one already."

That was not really true. She did not feel too much like a fool this morning. Not the way she had last night while she waited to hear Jonathan's steps on the back stairs. Now she only felt tired, spent, and numb, and full of a special kind of grief.

She guessed this was true heartbreak, this terrible feeling echoing in her emptiness like a raw hunger, making her want to weep again.

It appeared that she had built more romantic illusions than she had thought around Jonathan. Despite her resolve to the contrary, she had let him touch more than her body. She had not used Mama's lessons in the most important way. She had not remained in control of their passion and what it meant to her.

She gazed at his belongings. They would be removed soon. She would return from visiting a friend one day, and this chamber would be as empty as she felt right now, and he would be completely gone from her life.

She had known it would be brief with him. Just not this brief. Nor had she expected betrayal to taint what had been. Now she could not even indulge in memories, without wondering what he had been thinking the whole time, and wondering if every single moment had been affected by lies.

The sounds from across the hall got louder. She looked in their direction.

"Bella is cleaning in there," Marian said. "I told her to move everything to the walls, and give the floor a good scrubbing. Come warmer weather we will air it out and—"

A loud thud interrupted her, followed by Bella's exclamation.

"Did you hurt yourself, Bella?" Marian called. "I told you not to try and move the furniture without my help."

"I am not hurt," Bella said while she emerged from the chamber. "I lifted one end of that big rug, to move it, and this fell out. It was tucked inside the roll a good ways." She entered the chamber, carrying a flat wooden box.

Celia took it from her. She placed it on the bed and moved the simple latch to open it.

Inside were brushes, pens, and vials of colored pigments. "It is my mother's paint box. Look, this little mortar and pestle is for grinding the pigment more finely. These tiny bowls must be what she used to mix the paint."

"I saw one of those in a shop window once," Bella said. "It even had a little drawer for paper." She knelt down and peered at the back of the box. "Here, like this." She caught an edge of the back wood and pulled open a shallow drawer.

It did hold paper, several sheets of different textures, all of them heavier than one might write on. Bella took them out, fascinated. In doing so she revealed what lay beneath them.

Celia lifted out a thin, hardboard journal, such as sold in stationers' stores. She opened it to see rows and rows of numbers in her mother's neat hand.

"Fowl, flour, salt," Marian read over her shoulder. Marian was not truly literate, but every woman knew these words. "It is a household account book, looks like."

Celia scanned the pages quickly. It was not only an account book of what was bought. It also included income. She raised her eyebrows at some of the figures. Alessandra's entertainment had not come cheaply to the men she favored.

A pattern caught her eye. A regular expenditure, with her name by it. That must have been the money sent to the country, to keep Celia with the two spinsters who raised her. Each debit came right after a credit, however. A similar amount had come in right before it went out.

Another name was always with those entries too,

unlike the other payments Alessandra had received. It was a name that she recognized. It belonged with one of the colored crests. That of the Marquess of Enderby.

She flipped the pages, month by month and year by year, and saw the money coming in and going out. It could not be a coincidence. This must be money from her father, and not in return for favors. He had been paying for a daughter's support while she was a child.

Her mind raced with her excitement at the discovery. She would have to tell Jonathan when he—

Her joy disappeared as quickly as it had come. Last night's sorrow settled on her again. There would be no telling Jonathan now. She certainly was not going to show him this journal either, and allow him to pick through this more detailed accounting of her mother's life.

Bella was admiring all the items in the paint box, lifting each vial of dry pigment and holding it to the light of the window.

"You be putting those back now," Marian scolded.

"Let her play with them," Celia said. She closed the cover of the box. "Take it below, Bella. You can use the brushes and pigment if you want. I will take this book, however, and decide what to do with it."

*   *   *

Dear Mr. Albrighton,

I am told by friends that you now reside with the Duke of Castleford, and I trust this letter will find you there. I am sure that you have every comfort in His Grace's fine home and I am happy to know that you must be content.

I want to inform you that there is no need for you to do the favor which I requested of you. I have found the evidence that I seek in my mother's account book, which was recently discovered. It includes regular payments to her, for my support, from one of the men I had already identified as likely to be my father.

Do not be disheartened by your failure to find the account book before me, or think that it speaks poorly of the special skills that you were sent to employ in this house. It was well hidden, and it contains nothing that you do not already know from other investigations that you pursued the last few weeks.

It appears my little quest will be completed soon. I wish you well in finishing yours. In the meantime, do you not want your personal property? If you fear interfering with my day, or having an unexpected meeting, be advised that I will be leaving town, and will not be at home for some days.

Miss Pennifold

Jonathan folded the letter and held it to his nose. She had not scented it, yet the lavender water she often wore lingered subtly.

He had to smile at the letter's directness, and at the way she could not resist pointing out that he had failed to find the evidence he sought when it had been in the house all the time. *You betrayed me and did not even make a good job of it.*

The rest of the letter was less amusing. Especially the part about regular payments. Celia might assume those were for her support, but there were other explanations too.

Removing himself from Celia's presence had given new life to his own little quests, as she put it. He had been analyzing what he had learned about Alessandra the last weeks. He was still of two minds about whether the whispers had been true, but if she had been receiving regular payments from someone, especially from an old lover who no longer had a liaison, it was not a certainty those payments were to support a love child. A man could have been buying Alessandra's silence about indiscretions, or even be the agent for whom she had worked.

The various possibilities occupied him while he rode to the park. Edward had written to the mail drop, demanding a meeting. The impatient tone of the summons indicated someone somewhere was getting annoyed that Jonathan's mission was not being fulfilled quickly enough.

As he sought out his uncle near the reservoir, he pictured Celia confronting the man who she now assumed was her father. She would do it, he was sure. Discreetly, perhaps, but that would not be welcomed any more than the boldest approach.

And if the man was not her father, but someone with other reasons to pay Alessandra down through the years, then what?

Edward hailed him and he trotted over.

"You are unhorsed, Uncle. I did not see you."

"The physician said I must take long turns every day. Tie your mount and join me. This is tedious and too time consuming."

Jonathan did as bid, and fell into step. "Are you ill?"

"Just aging. It takes its toll in dozens of ways until you are dead of it." Edward kept a sound pace, swinging a handsome walking stick to the rhythm of his stride. "I have not heard from you in some time. I thought I should find out what is happening."

"Is someone impatient?"

"You are merely unaccountably slow. Is there a reason?"

A very good reason. He had avoided telling Edward about those crests, in part to protect Celia and in part to have time to learn what he could about a few patrons from five years ago.

"If I told you that I had learned it all, and had a list of her patrons, what would you do?"

Edward stopped walking. He studied Jonathan's face, with his own expression serious and sober.

"Do you have such a list?"

"I do not. However, I wonder what you will do with what I learn. I have discovered that this mission did not come to me the normal way. The Home Office did not send you to me this time. I am curious who did."

Edward walked on, faster now. His eyes burned beneath his hat brim. "Who told you that? I'll not have some fool interfering—"

"I was told by someone who usually receives accurate information."

"You told him, whoever it was, that you were doing this? Have you gone mad?"

"I revealed nothing. My activities have not escaped notice all these years. I am not completely invisible to others besides you in the government. I can see that my question has agitated you, however, so let us forget I asked."

"Damnation, I should say so."

They walked on and Edward eventually controlled his temper. "I wanted to ask you about the daughter," he said.

"Celia."

"Yes. Is it possible that she found something that you did not?"

"It is always possible, I suppose. Not likely. Even if she did, how could she know anything from it?"

Edward chewed that over, frowning.

"Why do you ask?" Jonathan prompted.

"Rather suddenly, Alessandra's long-past history has become a topic of some interest among ladies of a certain age, my wife tells me. One would think a history of the gossip surrounding her is being compiled. Summerhays's mother quizzed a few old friends, who in turn queried others— Well, it is peculiar."

"It was probably only her recent death that caused it. Perhaps two ladies had an argument over a few points in their memories, and sought to be proven correct."

"I don't like it, however it happened." Edward speared him with a hooded gaze. "You know her? The daughter?"

"Celia. Yes, I know her. I have spoken with her as part of my investigation."

"You need to find out if she has learned something. Be very firm with her. Offer her some money if you must. That sort will respond to either pay or threats with little trouble."

Two ladies approached, holding a close tête-à-tête. Jonathan let them pass while his annoyance with Edward simmered.

"What do you mean, *that sort*?" he asked, once they again had privacy.

Edward stifled a groan of impatience. "I am in no mood to mollify your delicate sensibilities about such women, Jon. I am not speaking of your mother. It is not the same. Even if it were, it does not matter what I meant. This is serious, and you must think about your duty first and do what is necessary to find out what is needed from her." He tried a smile of appeasement. "You know how it must be."

"I know how it must be when the mission is for England. We are a long way from the days when a vulnerable coast excused so much, Uncle. I don't even know who has given me this damnable mission. There are limits to what things I will do in executing it, and insulting or threatening or hurting Celia Pennifold is beyond them."

Edward's face flushed. He directed a beady stare right at Jonathan. "You doth protest too much, dear boy. What is this woman to you, that you are so defensive? Has she seduced you? She has, hasn't she?"

"She has not."

"Then you seduced her. Do not deny it; I can see it in you. Perhaps others cannot, but you are not such an enigma to *me*." He tapped his walking stick impatiently, in a quick staccato of vexation. "Are you mad? A liaison with such a woman is—"

"You do not know her, so stop referring to her that way. Such a woman. That sort of person. Damnation, it is enough to make me—"

"I do not need to *know* her. I do not care if she prays night and day. Her mother precedes her, she was groomed for the same life, and no man in society has forgotten. If you have any hope of the acknowledgment you seek, you will end this affair at once and hope no one is the wiser. That is all your cousin would need, to have one more excuse to deny you—"

"Hell, he is going to deny anyway, so don't throw that old lure into the water. I don't give a damn what Thornridge will think."

"Don't you, indeed? I see she has turned your head

completely. Well, her mother could do it, and no doubt she can too." He drew himself straight and sniffed. "For my purposes, I can see that she has compromised you too much."

"What do you mean?"

"I no longer trust you with this mission. You are released. I will find another who will not allow a pretty face to divert him. My instincts say she knows something, and I intend to find out what it is."

Edward marched on, his stick spearing the ground and his back straight. The military strictness of his bearing did not bode well for Celia. Evidently this was not such a small matter, the way Edward had claimed that day in the carriage.

Jonathan caught up with him. "Hear me now, Uncle. Do not miss one word of what I say, or doubt my resolve. It is not war time, and the acts of those years have no justification if committed now. Not by you, and not by your master on this, whoever he is. If you send another man, and he does anything to harm or impugn or even insult Celia Pennifold, I will make sure that he pays for it. She is under my protection, in all that means."

Edward stared at him, astonished. "You would not dare."

"I would dare. And when I am finished with him, Uncle, I will then deal with you."

He left Edward gaping at him, and strode back to his horse. A half hour later he called on Lady Sebastian Summerhays, to see if she knew where Celia had gone.

Chapter Twenty

The manor house intimidated her. Tall, gray, and sprawling, with a drive it took her cabriolet twenty minutes to traverse, it spoke of power and exclusion.

Celia gave the reins to a groom and accepted his hand down. Her carriage rolled away and she faced the monstrous edifice. Her heart beat too fast and a terror of excitement paralyzed her. She forced the panic down and approached the door.

A servant bore her card away. She waited in a nice little chamber near the reception hall for a long while. Long enough that she counted the tiles on the floor, and noticed that the plantings at this end of the drive, visible out the small window, could use better care.

Eventually the servant returned, to convey regrets that the Marquess of Enderby was not at home today.

"Do you anticipate his return soon?"

"We have no anticipations at all."

"I am willing to wait. It is not a social call."

"Waiting is not advised."

In other words, Enderby was at home, but had chosen not to receive her. Normally that would not be surprising. However, she was sure he knew who she was to him. He knew that he turned away his own daughter.

She sat down on a chair. "Please tell the marquess that I have come a long way. I am not inclined to leave until I have met with him on a matter of utmost importance to us both."

The servant appeared disconcerted. He was not accustomed to people who did not obey the rules. After some fluster, he wandered off.

He returned a quarter hour later, accompanied by another man. She knew what that meant. "Did he tell you to throw me out the door?"

One had the decency to flush. "We are here to escort you out."

It was the same thing. She half decided to make them do it bodily. However, since there was no audience, and no one to think badly of the marquess for it, it did not seem worth the drama.

Good to their word and their orders, they escorted her to the door, over its threshold, through its portico, and down the steps. One of them signaled to the waiting groom to get her carriage.

She gazed up that gray façade. Was he watching up there? Looking down on his bastard daughter who dared to want one conversation with him? There should be a law that required he receive her. No man should be able to father a child and not even look that child in the eye once in his life.

He expected her to leave now, knowing her place, accepting his repudiation. She would be damned first.

"Tell the groom to keep the carriage. I will not be needing it yet."

She went to the steps, marched up three of them, then sat on the top one. She glanced to the threatening skies, and tucked her cloak around her more snugly.

"Tell the marquess that I will not move until he grants me a short audience. Five minutes is all I require of him, nothing more, now or later. If he sees me this once, I will no longer darken his door until the day I die. Until he does, however, I will not move from here."

B y the time dusk gathered, Celia was concluding that she did not like her father much. Whatever girlish hope she had brought on this journey had been chilled out of her by the cold that permeated her rump from the stone on which she sat.

As if heaven itself sought to punish her for hubris, it began raining then. She opened her parasol so the water dripping off the portico would not drench her.

The grooms took shelter. She sat there alone, discouraged. What had Jonathan told her that night about the time his mother had done this? They had sat in front of that door for days, he said. Celia had not really expected her father to make her do that too.

Up ahead on the drive, the gathering shadows moved. She squinted to see if it was an animal. That would be some distraction at least.

Instead a horse paced into view. A tall white one with a man astride. He drew nearer, and she realized who it was. She wanted to cry, from relief and the cold and the slicing shards of a broken heart not yet mended.

Jonathan brought his horse right to the portico and

gazed down at her. He did not appear to mind the damp at all, or even notice the drizzle rolling down his hat and greatcoat. He appeared magnificent, she had to admit. Cold and wet and other elements of nature were small matters to such as he.

"How long have you been here, Celia? All day?"

"I arrived just after noon."

He dismounted. "Thank God. I feared you had started this yesterday."

"I took a room at an inn last night, so I could start fresh today. How did you find me? Did you just guess which one was my father?"

"I went to Lady Sebastian, who said you had gone to visit Mrs. Joyes. When I arrived at The Rarest Blooms, I was told that you came here."

"If Daphne told you, I must have worried her."

"She appeared relieved to learn I would follow you." He propped one booted foot on the step beside her and leaned closely toward her. "He is not going to see you, Celia. Not tonight and not tomorrow and not the day after. Come with me now."

She shook her head. "If I go now, it will never happen. He will have to relent if I stay, just as Thornridge did with your mother. Tomorrow, if he has any decency at all, he will—" Her voice broke. She clenched her teeth for composure.

Night was falling fast now. Jonathan handed her his handkerchief, then shed his greatcoat. "Stand up."

She wobbled to her feet on cramping legs. "You cut your hair. I like it."

"Since you do, perhaps I will too." Gray wool floated out in a wide arc, then came to rest on her shoulders, over her cloak. He bundled and wrapped her in the coat's swaths, then fished in a leather bag on his saddle. He returned to the step with a piece of paper and a pencil and sat beside her.

Turning to use the step as a desk, he scribbled away. He folded the paper and walked to the door.

A servant opened it.

"Please give this to the marquess. Tell him it is from an agent for the Home Office."

He came back and sat beside her again.

"What did you write?" she asked.

"I told him that you have evidence he made regular payments to Alessandra Northrope all during the war, and if they were not for the purpose you think, then I must assume they were for another purpose and would be obligated to report that to my superiors."

"Perhaps he never heard the rumors about my mother. Then your note will make no sense."

"I am assuming a marquess hears everything of note."

Despite her tears, she laughed. "Jonathan, you *threatened* him. That was very bad of you."

"Very bad." He reached for the parasol, opened it, and held it so she was protected. "Do not pretend you did not know I had it in me."

She took his other hand in hers. "Thank you for trying to help me."

"It may take a while, but it should get that door open."

It took a good while, so long that she doubted it would work at all. They sat there, silent in their companionship, their row the last time they were together miles away and a matter for another time. She found amazing comfort in his presence, and regained some of her own strength from the intimacy blanketing them both.

Eventually the door did open again. Jonathan stood and helped her up.

"Miss Pennifold, the marquess will see you," the servant said.

She turned to Jonathan. "Do I look hideous?"

He slid his greatcoat off her shoulders. "You could never look hideous, Celia. You are always beautiful."

She fussed with her damp skirts. "He is going to be angry, isn't he? Because I forced this. Because of what you wrote."

"He will be very angry. Do not take what he says to heart too much."

"I will try not to. I will—" She licked her lips. "I am suddenly terrified."

"You will be fine. I will wait for you here." He smiled reassuringly, and walked her to the door.

Then suddenly she was inside again, alone.

The servant brought her deep into the house, to a small chamber near its back stairs. She dripped on marble and wooden floors the entire way.

He left her there, in a small sitting room with very ordinary appointments. She had expected better of a marquess, and of this house.

A large cupboard against one wall had one door slightly ajar. She peered in. Steely reflections glimmered back. She understood the furnishings then. This was not a chamber used by a peer's family. This was the butler's pantry, where the silver was stored and counted.

That hurt her, more than she thought anything so small could anymore on this miserable adventure. She also wanted to laugh, however. He hardly needed to remind her of her place this way. She was here only because she had sat on a stone step for five hours, after all.

He let her wait again. No refreshments came. No hot liquid to warm her. No servant arrived to build up the fire.

The goal, she guessed, was to emphasize he had been forced into this meeting and that she did not deserve it. She should probably be frightened, or insulted or sad. Instead she had to work hard to contain a building excitement.

Once he was here, once they were face-to-face, none of this would matter. Surely a parent could not be cruel to his own child when they met. Once he saw her, in the privacy of a chamber where no other eyes could see, he would be glad she had come.

Despite her efforts to control it, her anticipation reached a high pitch by the time the door moved. She held her breath as a man walked in. He faced her squarely from a spot just inside the chamber.

He was not what she had pictured all those years when she wondered about her father. He proved to be shorter than in those fantasies, and a bit portly now. His hair was almost white but she guessed it had been golden like hers years ago.

She noticed his eyes most of all in that first glimpse, however. They held the anger she expected, and a good deal of impatience and disdain. She did not care, because they appeared very familiar to her. They were the same eyes she saw in a looking glass.

Her heart filled with joy, and another emotion so anguished that her composure wobbled. She longed to reach for him, if only to have the physical connection of touching the sleeve of his coat. Perhaps he would reach for her too, the way she always hoped, and they would embrace, and his anger would disappear as a father's emotion drowned it in better sentiment.

He took out a pocket watch and scowled at it. "You have five minutes, Miss Pennifold. What is it you want?"

"Nothing. Just to meet you."

"You must think me a fool if you expect me to believe that. I know who you are. I know your name well." His expression twitched, unpleasantly. "She gave her word that she would never tell you about me. It was part of the arrangement. How dare you come to this house."

"She never told me. She was good to her word. I discovered things in her papers that led me to you."

"She wrote it down?" The idea appalled him. "I was assured she had not. I was told she left nothing to point to me."

"Nor did she, the way you fear. I saw the payments in the account book. It was hidden, and the man you sent to search her house for it would never have found it."

He did not deny he had hired someone to do it. "The book shows my payments among those from many others, I assume." He laughed. It had a harsh, angry sound. "How many did she bleed with the threat of scandal? I was newly married to a woman I loved or I would have never agreed to pay that money with which she played the grand courtesan. She said her child was mine, but she probably told a dozen men the same thing and got money from them too. With such a woman there can be no knowing the truth, can there? Hell, I still don't know, even if it is in your interests to think you do."

"I do not just think it. I know for certain now." She stepped closer to him. "Is your looking glass so distorted that you cannot recognize the resemblance?"

For the barest instant his gaze resentfully acknowledged it, then turned cold again. "I only see the bastard of a whore who found a way to extract money from me long after the favors ended. Nothing more."

Celia felt slapped by every word and insinuation, every distasteful grimace. Her temper strained a bit more with each insult.

"Since I expect never to see you again, Papa, I should disabuse you of your errors now, while I can. If she knew you were my father, it must have meant there was no other patron during the short weeks of that affair. I assume you demanded that of her, and Alessandra was an honest woman. As for your payments, they went to my support. Every penny. Her account shows it coming in and going out."

"So you say."

"If Alessandra Northrope intended to bleed you, she would have demanded much more than the paltry amount she received from you twice a year after the affair ended."

He eyed her suspiciously. "You think she should have gotten more, do you? Have you come to try and get it for yourself now?"

"I can see that I inherited my intelligence from Alessandra, and not you, sir. I did not have to see you to ask for money, or face your scorn in order to threaten scandal to get it. I came so that for once in my life I could look upon my father's face and hear him address me. I came so that I would know the truth of my parentage, even if you claim you do not."

He softened not one bit. The scowl never left his expression. "Indeed, I do not. I cannot help what fantasy you have concocted in your mind, nor do I care. I see nothing of myself in you, I am relieved to say. Now, this audience is over. Do not dare to try to repeat it. Do not approach me or my family, and do not spread rumors. If you do, I will use the influence of my station to see that you are made most uncomfortable, and prosecuted as a blackmailer."

That repudiation was his final utterance. He walked out the door, five minutes after he had arrived.

As soon as he departed, her indignation left her too. Then all that remained in her was scathing disappointment and humiliation.

The opening door jolted Jonathan out of his thoughts. Most of them had been on Celia, and the passing time, which he hoped indicated this meeting was going better than he had dared expect.

Celia stepped across the threshold and the door closed on her, blocking the light from within. She stood there, a dark, unmoving form, so quiet and still that his instincts sharpened.

He held out his hand to her. She seemed not to see it. He went over and, arm around her shoulders, guided her down from the portico. Her carriage came around the house as he did.

He helped her in, and tied his horse to its back. Then he sat beside her and took the reins.

"I want to go home," she whispered, in a tone so flat and distant that it chilled him.

"London is too far, Celia. I will take you to an inn and—"

"Not London. Home."

She must mean Mrs. Joyes's house near Cumberworth. "It is at least four hours, perhaps more with the weather. You are cold, and—"

"Please, Jonathan. There are people who love me there, and who have never scorned me the way that man just did."

Nor have I. He did not say it. It did not matter now, nor would she believe it. She had let him help her today, but that did not mean that she had forgiven his deception.

"If you catch a fever, I am going to regret this."

"If I catch one, it will be from having sat on that stone, and his fault, not yours." She spoke listlessly. "At least I will be home if I do. I can't bear the thought of suffering an illness in a strange inn."

He stood and removed his greatcoat, and wrapped her in it again. At least the rain was stopping. With any luck the clouds would break and permit some moon.

He took the ribbons again, and began what promised to be a long, bitter journey. Celia sat tensely and silently beside him, so unhappy in her thoughts that he doubted she would notice any part of it.

M rs. Joyes entered the library where Jonathan dried his sodden self near the fire. He had not seen her since she answered his pounding on her door an hour ago. After handing Celia over to the women here, he had found shelter for the horses and tended to them, then let himself back in and built a fire here.

She surveyed his chair and the table near it. "I am relieved that Katherine finally saw to you, Mr. Albrighton. I know that you will forgive my own lack of appropriate welcome."

"I am more comfortable than I expected, under the circumstances." He lifted a glass of the brandy that the quiet, dark-haired young woman named Katherine had found in a low cupboard. "Is Miss Pennifold more herself now?"

Mrs. Joyes sat nearby, and to his surprise took another glass from the tray and poured herself an inch of brandy too. Her long pale hair fell over her blue undressing gown, and her distinctly beautiful face displayed little emotion.

"She is not at all herself. I feared illness had taken her, but she is cool enough, and shows no chill. If she has any malady, I think it is one of the spirit. She expressed great relief in being here and yet—"

He waited for her to finish if she chose. She appeared to be finding her thoughts, or her judgment.

"I do not think she has found the comfort that she sought," she said. "Certainly my company has not pulled her out of her melancholy."

"Perhaps once she sleeps, she will feel better."

"Perhaps. Or not. Celia has always lived life with few illusions, you see. I would have said she had none at all. It appears there was one in the end, however."

"Do you mean that you fear that she has little practice in overcoming disappointment, and may not conquer this one?"

"How well you put into words the concern I feel in my heart."

One had to look deeply into this woman's eyes to see any concern at all. It was there, however. He guessed her cool composure was a mask. Perhaps she removed it for Celia, and the other women in this house.

"She has known more disappointment than you think, Mrs. Joyes. In the past, and perhaps recently. It grieves me that she now knows this one, but I believe she will overcome it."

"You know her better than I on that point, it appears. Your words reassure me, especially since I believe you have experienced something similar in your own life, and know of what you speak."

He had not expected that. He did not know where this

woman was going with this conversation, but he suspected he did not want to join her in the journey. "I have, and I would have spared her if I could. As would you, I am sure." He set down his glass. "Now I must take myself off to an inn. I will call tomorrow if you will permit it, to see how she fares."

Mrs. Joyes considered him, while her slender, long fingers turned the crystal glass that she held with both hands. She stood and set her glass back on the tray.

"It is well past midnight, Mr. Albrighton. Allow me to give you a chamber here, and spare the innkeeper being woken at such an hour. Please do not object. It is no trouble, and the least we can do after you have shown such considerate care of our dear Celia."

Chapter Twenty-one

The familiarity of her old bed comforted her. So did this chamber in which she had spent five years. Nothing had changed here since she left. Perhaps Daphne had believed she would be back eventually.

She could not blame the house or its occupants if arriving here did not provide the sanctuary she had expected. The house had not changed, nor had the women in it.

She had, however. That must be why coming home had not provided the balm she needed. She had remained a child here, for all of the worldly, practical advice the others gave her credit for giving. She had not lived enough experiences to speak with true authority on the ways of the world, though. She had only been reciting lessons learned from Alessandra.

No more. Her brief time away from here had aged her soul with some bitter lessons. Today's had perhaps been the most hurtful. She avoided reliving the humiliation only by wrapping her consciousness in a thick, obscuring blanket.

She wished the total escape of sleep would come, but awareness of the chamber and herself, of the window and the house, floated above the deadening mist in which she drifted. And so she heard the sounds in the chamber beside her own.

She struggled to more alertness. Raw hurts began paining her as she did, and she almost retreated. The sounds intrigued her, however. That was Verity's old chamber next door. Had Verity come for a visit? Surely Daphne would have said so.

Perhaps she had. Everything Daphne had said while getting her out of those wet clothes had sounded far away. It had been almost like listening to a conversation taking place between two people in another room.

She listened to the sounds, relieved that they permitted her to feel normal somehow, but also served as a distraction. She found them increasingly curious and interesting.

Casting off the bedclothes, she padded to her door, opened it, and looked out. The rest of the house was silent. No noises came from Daphne's chamber on her other side, or the one Katherine used down the passageway.

She opened the door to Verity's chamber. She looked in. Relief poured through her, one so profound that her spirit ached from trying to contain it.

Jonathan stood at the washstand, stripped to the waist, cleansing himself of the road and rain. He appeared as beautiful to her as he had that morning after she moved into the house on Wells Street, strong and lean and, for all their intimacy, still mysterious enough that her heart fluttered. She had learned that his mystery did not always hide good things, but tonight she did not think about that. She cared only that his presence warmed her in so many

ways right now, and revived the Celia who was young and
sensual and not afraid of the world.

She watched him while he dried himself. Arousal purred
through her, bringing her joy.

He turned, damp, dark locks falling about his brow,
and looked at her.

"I heard sounds in here. I thought perhaps Verity had
come to visit," she said.

His dark eyes were as they always had been—too knowing, too seeing, and offering a compelling intimacy that
might only go one way.

"You did not think it was Verity, Celia."

Perhaps not. Maybe she had hoped the chamber was
being used by the one other person who did not belong in
this home tonight.

"Did you not hear me open the door, Jonathan? I thought
you were trained to always be aware of such things."

"I heard you. I was waiting for you to decide if you
were going to stay."

She had not decided, but she had to now, didn't she?
He had weighted the decision in his favor by letting her
watch him. He still did, standing there half-naked, his body
sculpted by firelight. The memory of his taut arms surrounding her—embracing, supporting, commanding—sent thrills
full of yearning down her core. Not only for pleasure, but
also for the safety and comfort she experienced with him.

Only deadening sorrow awaited her if she returned to her
bed. She much preferred the way she had come alive in this
other chamber. There was still much unresolved between her
and him, but she guessed that he understood some of what
she was feeling now, in ways that Daphne never would.

"I will stay tonight, I suppose." She walked over to the
bed and climbed in.

He stripped off the rest of his clothes and joined her. He gathered her into his embracing arm and tucked her against him.

"You have not cried, have you?" he said. "All the way here you did not, and you have not since, I think."

"Tears will not change anything. It is what it is."

"Perhaps you should anyway. It does not speak well of us, when we begin to accept loss without grieving."

She thought the advice both odd and potentially wise. Maybe with time that deadening response became alluring because it protected one from grief. Perhaps it left remnants that built up over time, until one had trouble feeling anything at all, ever.

"Do you weep when you grieve, Jonathan?" She could not imagine it.

"Men do not weep so much when they grieve. They get drunk instead. Or they look for a fight and thrash or get thrashed."

"Then you cannot give advice to me. If you can conquer disappointments without weeping, why should it be different for me?"

"Because you have no experience with getting foxed or with fisticuffs?"

She had to laugh. It felt strange to have that bubble up out of the void inside her.

He kissed her crown. "I last wept about five years ago. I was on the coast, and a mishap in a mission killed a boy who was guiding me. I was so accustomed to the risks that I barely thought about them by then. I had seen enough death that it hardly touched me. But that boy—it was like a shock, how it affected me. Like it penetrated a soul sheathed in iron."

"It must have been horrible."

"His death was. My response, however— I am embarrassed to confess that I savored it, Celia, because it meant I had not turned to stone. In that moment I was thoroughly, starkly alive again, in ways I had not known for too long."

She turned her face up to his. "Is this the personal thing from five years ago that you studied the crests for?"

One of his eyes opened and looked at her. "You are too clever, or else I am too careless with you."

She snuggled back down. "I will not tell anyone. I really don't know anything, do I?"

She received no response on that. Instead he checked that the bedclothes covered her back and shoulders well. "You should sleep now. The day has been long and hard for you."

"I dare not. Daphne may find us together in the morning and she will not take it well."

"No one will enter this chamber in the morning, Celia. No one will find us together. Daphne sees more than you think with those gray eyes of hers. I think she put me in this chamber hoping that my friendship might succeed in helping you find yourself again, after she felt hers had failed."

Had she arranged this? Possibly so. Daphne had a talent for comprehending human hearts well.

Celia did not sleep quickly, however. The gentle stimulation of pressing against Jonathan kept a hum in her blood, for one thing. His confidence and advice played in her head, for another. The more she thought about that, the more it troubled her.

"Jonathan, are you asleep?" she whispered.

"Mmm."

"Jonathan, what you experienced when that boy died—

Have you never felt it again? Have you never felt starkly alive since?" She thought that very sad.

He sighed. "I had intended to be a citadel of restraint with you tonight, for several reasons. However, since you refuse to sleep—" He flipped her onto her back, and settled his body so that his hips fit between her spread thighs.

Thoughts of his advice and revelations flew from her mind then. Warmth surrounded her and flowed inside, and pleasure's light glistened in her spirit.

He kissed her sweetly, carefully, as if testing for unknown fragilities. He drew her into passion slowly, and the pleasure came like a gentle, fresh breeze. After he entered her, he did not move at first, but only filled her while he pressed slow kisses to her lips and neck.

"Yes, to your last question," he said, while brushing her lips with his. "I have felt starkly alive since that night on the coast. The first time I kissed you, and the first time I had you. Right now, and every other time we have shared this. These affairs always have a story, you said, and that is mine." He kissed her more firmly, as though he claimed more than her mouth. He began moving in her. "I will not give it up easily, Celia."

She was in no condition to ask him to. His care made the pleasure touch her heart. Even the end came softly and poignantly in a mutual release that reconciled their passion, even if they had not buried the reasons for that row. The pleasure and excitement existed in its own world, apparently, or else her need for him ruled her more than she had guessed.

She woke to sunlight, and to a better prospect on the day before. The hurt and humiliation had become a dull ache overnight, one that could be contained. Daphne commented on how good it was to see her recovered.

After breakfast Jonathan hitched her mare to the front of the cabriolet, and his gelding to its rear, and they returned to London and her house. Marian said not one word when Jonathan entered through the garden door after taking the horses to the stable. She watched while he mounted the stairs to his chamber in the attic.

"Had a pleasant sojourn in the country, did you?" she asked once he had gone up.

"Partly pleasant. Partly not so at all."

"I'm told the country air is beneficial for one's blood. Refreshing, they say. It looks like it did you some good."

"I am very refreshed."

"I'd say Mr. Albrighton appears refreshed too, if I were asked."

"He does, doesn't he?"

Bella looked up from where she scrubbed the hearthstones, confused. "He looked no healthier to me."

Bella had not known why Jonathan had left, or for how long, so his return seemed normal to her.

Marian gazed at Bella's perplexed expression, and sighed again. "Not healthier, Bella. Refreshed. Contented and relaxed, like." She shook her head, and aimed for the front room, dusting feather in hand. "It is amazing how there's some in the world who can't smell what is right in front of their noses. I worry for you sometimes, Bella. I truly do."

"I am told that you did a great service to Miss Pennifold." Hawkeswell's casual observation came out of nowhere. It had absolutely nothing to do with the conversations being enjoyed in Castleford's library.

It effectively ended all the others, however. Two other pairs of eyes joined Hawkeswell's in settling on Jonathan.

Old friends could be a damned nuisance sometimes. "Hardly a great service. I extended a small help. That is all."

"To hear my wife tell it, you probably saved her from dying of fever."

Lights of curiosity danced in one glassy pair of eyes. "You saved a woman? You do your blood proud. Her name is familiar to me too. Do I know her?" Castleford's brow furrowed while he pondered the matter.

Castleford had wandered by the library and seen the rest of them by accident. It being a Friday, Summerhays and Hawkeswell had called on the duke's guest, not the duke, but the duke had inserted himself anyway, despite being thoroughly foxed and half-undressed.

To make a complicated social situation worse, Jonathan was not really the duke's guest anymore. He had come to inform Castleford of that, and to thank him for his generosity. Through the kind of coincidence cooked up by hell, however, Summerhays's and Hawkeswell's cards had arrived before he could do so.

Which had brought all four of them into this library, on an afternoon when Jonathan needed to be doing something else entirely.

"I only ensured that she returned to the house near Cumberworth safely. The ladies' gossip has made it more than it was."

"Pennifold. Pennifold . . ." Castleford muttered, thinking hard.

"They say that delivery was in the earliest hours of the morning. I do not envy your sleeping in that inn in Cumberworth, even if only for a few hours," Hawkeswell said.

"Summerhays and I were stuck there one night and it was too rustic for me. The bedbugs like it, though."

Summerhays smiled slyly. "As I hear it, he did not sleep in an inn."

"No? Is it true? Were you allowed into the cloistered area of the convent?"

That caught Castleford's attention. "Convent? Have you discovered a good country brothel and not told me, Albrighton?"

Silence fell. Everyone looked at him. Castleford smiled back at them, oblivious.

Hawkeswell's lids lowered heavily over his blue eyes. "He is speaking of The Rarest Blooms, Castleford. The house where *my wife* lived for two years, and Summerhays's wife for a spell as well."

"Ah, you were using the word metaphorically, but not metaphorically in *that* way. My apologies, although my misunderstanding was not without cause. You should be more careful."

Summerhays glanced at how Hawkeswell still glared. "Castleford, shouldn't you be in your chambers? Whoever is there must be getting impatient for your attention."

"No one is there. She who was there left hours ago."

"Then should you not be resting up for tonight's exertions?"

"You may have to rest before such things, Summerhays. I am always in fine form." Castleford squinted at nothing while his mind drifted. "Haven't I been to this place, The Rarest Blooms? I seem to remember, vaguely . . ." His eyes opened. "Now I remember. They allowed you to sleep there, Albrighton? Hell, I was not even allowed in the door."

"That is because he aided and protected one of their

members, and you would only seduce and abandon them all if given the chance," Hawkeswell drawled. "And after you did, two of the men sitting here now would pay dearly with their domestic bliss."

"Love has made you almost unbearable, Hawkeswell. What is more, we do not know for a fact that Albrighton did not seduce at least one of them while he was there. I don't know why you assume I would be a scoundrel while he would be a saint."

"Don't you, indeed?"

Jonathan just looked at Castleford. Castleford looked right back, innocently.

"I am not saying that you did seduce any of them, of course," Castleford explained. "I merely point out that they"—he gestured to the other two—"do not know for a fact that you did not."

"Of course he did not," Hawkeswell said. "He would not put two friends' heads on their wives' chopping blocks by misusing one of their dearest friends. Furthermore, Mrs. Joyes, the owner of that house, has a pistol that she is itching to use in just such a circumstance. He was good enough to help Miss Pennifold when a little quest of hers went awry, and we would have heard about it in the worst way if he had behaved badly."

"Pennifold. There it is again. Why is that name nudging me so?" Castleford frowned.

Summerhays pointedly turned the conversation to an upcoming lecture at the Royal Society, but Jonathan suspected that Summerhays had noticed that the only man who could know the truth had not actually denied a seduction.

The two guests took their leave shortly thereafter. Summerhays offered to get Jonathan into that lecture, and Hawkeswell said an invitation to dinner would be forthcoming from his wife. After they departed, Jonathan sat down to take his own leave of the remaining person in the library.

He expressed his appreciation for the duke's hospitality, and explained that he now had chambers to which he would move.

Rather suddenly Castleford did not appear very drunk at all. Sly intelligence showed in the gaze he settled on Jonathan.

"I just remembered where I had heard that name. Have you gotten yourself entangled with that Northrope woman's daughter?"

"I have come to know her, obviously."

"I think perhaps you know her very well, if you are playing white knight to her damsel in distress. I think she is the one who threw you over. If that left you without a bed—" He looked to the door. "Our good friends are going to be angry when they find out. Hawkeswell will thrash you soundly if his wife is the least distressed by this."

"Then perhaps you should not share your unfounded and unproven suspicions with him."

"I will try, but he goads me, and it would be a pleasure to rub his nose in how wrong he is." He stood. "At least I now know why you have been so tediously virtuous. Enjoy whatever it is while you can, since it cannot last long."

"That is not necessarily true."

"With your ambitions, it is most definitely true. I am sure she knows it, and you will be spared a scene. Her mother would have taught her that, along with the rest." He yawned, stretched, and strolled to the door, presumably to rest at last for the upcoming night's games.

He stopped before leaving. "Speaking of your ambitions, Thornridge will be coming up to town soon. The

Tory leadership requires his attendance at some meetings next week. He will not be able to avoid me once he is here, so gird your loins for whatever battle you think to fight."

Chapter Twenty-two

"The morning grows old. I must get up," Celia said between giggles.

Jonathan ignored her and continued the tickling kisses along the curve of her side.

"Why must you rise? Are wagons of plants coming today?" he asked finally, not missing a spot from the effort.

"Not until Tuesday."

"Then you can stay as long as you like."

"It is too decadent, Jonathan. Bella and Marian have been up for hours already."

"They will both understand, especially when they hear you moaning soon."

They probably would understand. There no longer was any pretense about what was going on in this house. Marian even made bawdy jokes about it. That was one of several ways in which things had changed with Jonathan's return.

"It will have to wait for tonight." She threw back the covers. "I have matters to attend to today."

"What matters?" The kisses had reached the side of her breast. His hand on her hip kept her in place.

"I do not only store plants. I also need to find sellers for the summer flowers we will have. I would rather not stand in a market and hawk them myself, so I need to find a man who will take them wholesale." His hand moved off her hip, down to where he could do wicked things to her. She took the opportunity to slip away.

He caught her ankle before she made a total escape. She looked back at him while she balanced on one foot.

"Come back," he cajoled, with a devastating smile. "You know you want to."

Indeed she did, but they had hardly left this bed in the three days since returning from Cumberworth, and there were things she needed to do.

"Tonight, I promise."

"You promise what?"

She laughed, and tried to squirm her ankle free. "Whatever you want. Now, allow me to wash and dress."

He released her. She went to the door and opened it. Two buckets of water waited on the other side. Now, that was new. She could hardly blame Marian. Why carry Jonathan's up to the attic when he woke right here? Still, those two buckets symbolized things that went beyond practical convenience.

She dipped her fingers, then carried both to the washstand. "They are warm. You should use it now, if you are wise."

He swung to sit on the bed's edge. "That is convenient."

"Isn't it? You can shave when you go abovestairs."

"You go first. Cool water does not bother me." He stood and came over. He poked at her cloths and smelled her soap.

She poured water into the basin. "I will tell Marian not to do this in the future. I do not know what she was thinking. It is silly for you to have to wait."

"I do not mind. I think it will be charming to see you wash." He stepped behind her and took the soap. "I can even help."

"I don't think—" But he was already wetting the cloth, his arms circling around to the basin. With languid strokes he wet down her arms, then squeezed the cloth so a drizzle sprayed on her shoulders and chest and formed rivulets down her curves.

He reached for the soap. "This is fun. I have never washed a woman before."

"You are getting the floor all wet."

"I will be more careful." His voice and breath tickled her ear as he reached around to soap his hands. "Whatever I want tonight?" His slippery caresses ran up and down her arms.

"That is what I said." Her voice faltered a bit, due to the distraction this washing was creating. Shoulders now, and back and bottom and— She startled, and looked over her shoulder at him. "You are being most thorough."

"I would not want to serve you poorly." He stroked again. A wonderful tremble traveled to every part of her. Deliberately now, he touched to arouse her, and standing made the sensations incredibly intense. He stepped closer then, and pressed his erection between her thighs and up against her heat.

She had to lean against him for support. Her body pulsed savagely around the pressure and she could barely breathe. He soaped his hands again, and slowly caressed her torso, and finally her breasts.

His chin rested against her temple while his hands moved

in luxurious circles on her breasts. She bit her lip so she would not moan, but it was in her, so loud that the whole street would hear if it escaped.

"Whatever I want. Let me think." He tortured and teased while she squirmed against his hardness. "I want you in one of those satin dresses. You should be in bed already when I come to you. With pillows. Lots of pillows. I want you already aroused when I get there. Like you are now."

She closed her eyes and saw what he described, and herself waiting in erotic anticipation. His fingers squeezed her nipples gently, sending jolts of sensation down her body.

"And then?"

"Whatever I want, as you said." He separated from her then. All of him.

She grasped the edge of the washstand to steady herself. "You aren't just going to leave me like this!"

"I thought you had things to do today."

"Jonathan."

He laughed. His arm circled her body, her feet left the ground, and she landed on the bed. He braced himself over her and thrust into her hard.

He lifted her leg and thrust again, deeper. Marvelous tremors came alive in response to the force of it. She bent her knees to her chest so it could be deeper yet, more filling, more complete. Rising above her on taut arms, his severe face angled so he watched what he did to her, he withdrew slowly and entered hard in a joining that left her gasping, frantic, lifting her hips impatiently.

It turned savage, and the force and power commanded pleasures she could not control. The tremors broke free and flowed all through her in a fast wave of perfect sensation.

It did not end there, but happened again and again, in perfect echoes of fulfillment that made her body cry repeat-
edly. It went on forever, it seemed. Finally his own tremor
broke so physically that it shook the bed.

He collapsed on her with a groaning sigh. She embraced him as closely as she could, sharing all that she
could. She let her soul flow within the bliss, and did not
care if it was reckless to allow herself to love him the way
she did now.

"You plan on dallying every day until almost noon?"
Marian set the plate in front of Jonathan, then
folded her arms. "I need to know, so I don't bother cleaning the pans if I'll be making breakfast again this late."

He tried to appear chagrined. Celia caught his eye
while she tended some plants near the window.

"I expect most days it won't be quite this late. My
apologies if I have disrupted the household."

"Oh, you've disrupted this household plenty, Mr. Albrighton. Come fair weather when the windows are open,
you may be disrupting the whole street."

Marian went back down to the kitchen. Jonathan finished his food, then went over to Celia, who clipped weak
leaves from a broad-leafed plant.

He embraced her from behind as she worked. "I have
disrupted your day as well as the household. It was bad of
me."

"Very bad. Nor have we heard the last of it. Wait until
Bella tells Marian about the mess we made with the water.
There may not be enough rags in this house to mop it all
up."

There had been a lot of washing and caressing and

soapy play besides his first service to her. Her screaming climax on the bed had been a beginning, not an end.

He tucked her warmth against him, and again felt the soft strokes of the cloth as she dried him less than an hour ago. He saw her golden crown lower, and his mind and body knew again the unbearable pleasure she had created with her mouth.

The memory made him harden once more against her. She turned her face so he saw her profile. "I would have thought you'd had enough," she teased.

Not enough. Never enough. He noticed a subtle distraction in her, however, as if for all the intimacy of this embrace, her mind considered other things.

As would his own, when he permitted it. Eventually he must. He was glad for the morning's joy, however, and the excuse to delay all that.

He released her. "Will you be going to Mayfair for these errands you must do? I will take you in the cabriolet, and tether my horse."

"I think that I will wait until tomorrow for those errands, and take care of some household matters closer to home today." She reached up and patted his jaw. "You have not yet shaved, anyway. If I am to accomplish anything today, I must leave sooner than you will be able to."

He kissed her, and went up the stairs to shave and finish dressing, but he paused and looked at Celia through the doorway before the stairwell swallowed him. For all her luminous smiles and intimate gazes, she had left some of her fresh joy in her chamber. Now she pondered that plant while she snipped, as if it contained the answers to life.

*   *   *

Celia stopped her carriage in front of a brick building in the City. A boy lingered near the front door, and offered to walk the horse while she was away. She gave him a few pence, and approached the door while the carriage rolled away.

She plucked a letter from her reticule. It had been waiting when she came down from her bedchamber today. It had arrived in the morning mail, and had been lying there in her house, waiting to ruin a day begun gloriously.

She entered the building and found the chambers of Mr. Harold Watson, Solicitor.

Mr. Watson had requested she call at his chambers at one o'clock. It was now beyond half past one. She rather hoped that she had come too late. She would not mind a few days to prepare for this, although she doubted there were any way to do so.

What was going to happen was inevitable. Jonathan had made sure it would when he seduced her, hadn't he? And she had allowed it, for all her drama in making her big decision. Now, instead of a life of security, she would have the memories of a wonderful passion that gained her nothing, enjoyed for a few weeks when she was young.

Ten years hence, what would she think of the trade she had made, and the affair that resulted? That she had forgiven Jonathan his deception too easily, in order to enjoy the power and excitement? That pleasure had so ruled her that she forgot to be sensible? When she was with him, she set aside thoughts of their inevitable parting so that would not ruin the joy, but she was not so stupid as to ever really forget it.

A clerk ushered her into Mr. Watson's private chamber. She stood there in shock while the door closed behind her. She barely heard the greeting of Mr. Watson, who was a wiry, short man with graying hair and an unfashionable beard. The guest who had been sitting with him commanded all of her attention.

"You did not say in your letter that Mr. Dargent would be here, Mr. Watson."

"I advised him to attend, Miss Pennifold. As his solicitor, it is my duty to attempt an amiable solution to the disagreement about the property."

"There is no disagreement," Anthony said, impatiently. "I keep telling you that. You have seen the papers, Watson. You know my claim is solid."

"Mr. Watson is trying to spare you the scandal if full meaning of that indenture becomes widely known, Anthony. Is that not true, Mr. Watson?"

Mr. Watson's expressive tilt of his head was more acknowledgment than agreement. "It is my experience that if two parties in a dispute speak fairly, a brief can be avoided."

"I don't need a damned brief," Anthony blustered. "I need a damned bailiff to collect a damned debt."

The outburst dismayed poor Mr. Watson. He appeared confused at what to do, now that his sensible strategy had turned out so badly.

"Leave us," Anthony snarled at him. Mr. Watson was only too glad to obey.

"The poor man," Celia observed, once she and Anthony were alone. "He meant well. Did you tell him everything, Anthony? I suppose not. And yet he learned enough to want to spare you embarrassment."

Anthony's jaw twitched. His eyes burned. He was the picture of a man holding on to his temper by one frail thread. "One week, you said. One week and you would let me know. And I have heard *nothing*."

"That was wrong of me. However, surely, when you

heard nothing, the answer must have been obvious. If I had accepted your arrangement, I would have hardly kept it a secret from you. The bills from the dressmakers would have been arriving by now."

He strode around the room in a fit of vexation. "You are being rash, and stupid."

"No, Anthony, I am being honest, with myself as well as you. I could take your money and that fine house. I could play out the drama you envision of a great, if disreputable, love affair. It would be a lie, however, because I do not love you now. Perhaps I did once, but not now."

"You are punishing me; that is all. For not marrying you. For not flying in the face of all that was expected of me, and giving up everything for you."

"I do not blame you for that. I know how it had to be." How it still had to be. The funny ache in her heart and tightness in her throat had nothing to do with Anthony. She conquered the surge of emotion. There would be time enough for that when the time came.

"There is something I must tell you, Anthony. It will perhaps explain what I mean about not lying to you. You think to begin again where we ended five years ago. That is impossible. You have asked about my innocence with unseemly interest since we met again. You should know that it is no longer mine to give you."

He stared at her. She felt a little sorry for him, but his amazement did not speak well for his intelligence. He had not been able to marry her because she was supposed to be that sort of woman, after all. Was he now surprised that she indeed was that sort of woman?

His shock gave way to anger. A very special kind of anger. That of a man jealous when he does not even know his rival's name.

He turned away from her abruptly.

"We should part as old friends, Anthony. Not as two characters in a bad operatic comedy."

He refused to turn around. "We do not have to part at all. You have refused my protection, and I will accept that if I must. You have squandered your innocence on some fool, when I would have taken care of you for life, but it is something that cannot be undone. If I must settle for less, I will eat my pride and do so. Just tell me what you expect for it."

Good heavens, he was asking how to buy her favors, only in less exclusive ways. He wanted to know how to join the queue.

"You will have to settle for nothing, Anthony. I am sorry if I did not make that clear."

He did not move for a long count. Then he abruptly walked to the door and called for Mr. Watson.

"You are to send Mrs. Northrope's executor the claim on that property," he instructed the solicitor. "I expect an inventory of its contents within a week."

"Hello, Uncle."

Edward startled so badly that Jonathan saw the back of his head rise in a little jump. Then Edward twisted his entire torso and looked over the back of the library sofa to the garden doors where Jonathan stood.

"What the——? What are you doing, sneaking in through the garden like that?"

Jonathan strolled over and looked down. Edward's frown faltered. He glanced to the windows and door, and the bell near the mantel that was used to call the servants.

"I wanted to see you, very privately," Jonathan said.

"I think it is time for an honest conversation, about this odd mission you gave me, and about that list that you sought."

"Do you have it?"

"I have it."

Edward thrust out his hand. Jonathan walked around the sofa and sat in a chair.

"I don't have it that way. I have seen it. I know the names. I know the dates." He tapped his temple, to indicate where it was all stored. "It does not exist as a normal list or accounting, and it is doubtful that anyone would even know what they had if they chanced upon it."

"Does the daughter know of it?"

"Celia, Uncle. Miss Pennifold to you. I would appreciate it if you finally remembered her name."

"Does your Miss Pennifold know of it?"

"No. She is ignorant." He lied without hesitation. He had done so often enough in his life, and this lie had as good a reason as any other.

Edward visibly relaxed. He peered over, looking for something. Waiting.

"Those rumors about Mrs. Northrope—was the Marquess of Enderby ever suspected of being a part of her scheme?"

Edward's face fell in shock. "Enderby? That is preposterous."

"Why? There were a few peers enamored of Napoleon. Impressed by all the imperial grandeur, I suppose. He could have been one."

"Enderby? You are mad. Put the notion out of your mind at once. I will not have you impugn him because of a theory you have concocted out of air."

"I never concoct out of air. You taught me better. You know if I am wondering about Enderby, it is because I have reason to."

"You have no reason to wonder about anyone. You were not told to find out who the Northrope woman took secrets from, or gave secrets to, or even if there were any secrets to begin with. You were only to bring me a damned list."

"Enderby is on the list."

Edward threw up his hands in exasperation. "As are many others, I assume. It was not he, I tell you."

"You are sure?"

"Damnation, yes. I am sure."

Jonathan believed him. It was good news. It meant those payments Celia had found in the account book had indeed been for her support. There had been the possibility that, faced with that admission, or the assumptions Jonathan had alluded to in that note he wrote on the stone, Enderby had chosen the paternal lie over the seditious truth.

It appeared not now. Jonathan was glad to be able to put aside a concern that, in confronting Enderby, Celia had given a traitor cause to worry about her knowledge of those payments.

"There is only one way you can be sure, Uncle. You must know the honest truth behind those rumors. If you know Enderby was not involved, you must know who was."

"You are wrong there."

"I do not think so. I think I was not sent to protect the reputations of many men, but to protect that of one. Who are you doing this for? Tell me, or I will go to the Home Office and tell them all about this mission they did not initiate, and about Enderby's payments to Mrs. Northrope."

"You would sully the good name of an innocent man? A man guilty of nothing more than dallying with a whore a few times?"

"I hope that you are not trying to appeal to my conscience. That quiet voice has not whispered in my soul for a long time now. I am not feeling kindly toward Enderby these days, so it would not bother me if he saw a spot of trouble over this."

Edward closed his eyes. He looked old suddenly. Tired. "It is not what you think. It is not quite what I said."

"Why am I not surprised to learn that?"

"I merely simplified matters. It was more complicated. Less neat. You did not need to know about it, and you still do not."

"I insist on knowing. Either you tell me, or I will find out my own way."

Edward sighed deeply. He stood and walked pensively to a shelf and took a cigar from a box. He lit it at the fireplace. Five puffs later, he sighed again.

"Alessandra Northrope was not collecting secrets. She was giving them out. Only they were not accurate. There was a man spying for France, and she was given things to tell him. Some of it was good, but of no real significance. That was so the game would not be seen for what it was. Some of it was bad, however, and designed to throw iron bars into the machinery of French strategy."

The revelation surprised Jonathan. He experienced a good amount of relief too. He did not want to think he had been so blind that he had not seen Alessandra for what she was. He also was glad that Celia would now know the truth about her mother. He could spare her that disillusionment at least.

"His name is not on that list you found, so don't be

wondering about all of them. She was not stupid. She would have left no record of this."

"He was English, then? It wasn't her old French lover?"

Edward ignored that. "You cannot tell her," he said. "Miss Pennifold. You must not."

"Of course." He would, though, and Edward could go to hell. "Did anyone die from the good information that was insignificant? This was a dangerous game."

"No one died. It was handled very carefully. Timing was everything, as you know. She would drop something to this man, something she claimed to have heard another patron say. By the time he got it to his contact, and it worked its way back to France, it was too late to be useful. It made her look good, however. It primed the pump for when she dropped inaccurate things that would cause them big trouble."

"Who worked with her? You?"

He shook his head. "They chose a trustworthy man who was not one of the regulars, so there could be no suspicion of the game. Even I only learned it was done after the war. This was begun by the Home Secretary and the military. It came from the highest levels, and was handled with total discretion."

Yet someone had worked with her. Someone "trustworthy" provided that information for her to drop.

Jonathan stood to leave. He would learn nothing else from Uncle Edward. He had everything he needed now, anyway. "You do not need the list. You were right. None of the men involved in this are on it."

He looked back as he slipped through the French doors to the garden. Edward's expression had shattered, and considerable worry showed in his eyes.

Chapter Twenty-three

L ots of pillows. Celia wondered if the ones she had
accumulated on her bed would be enough. They would
have to do since they were all she had.

The fire toasted the chamber. Wine waited on the table.
The fawn satin caressed her body. The rest would be easy.
He wanted her aroused, and already anticipation titillated
her.

She would escape tonight, in the best way. This chamber might not be hers much longer, but for now it remained her home. No matter what happened in the future,
she would remember this house and this room and this
passion.

She lay on the bed, amid those pillows. Their soft sensuality cradled her weight. She wondered if Mr. Watson
would send someone to do that inventory tomorrow, and
whether all Anthony needed was a bailiff to throw her and
the others out of the house. She would have to find a solicitor, and discover if she could at least delay that.

The day's events should make her sad or worried, but they did not. Refusing Anthony had freed something in her. It had been a decision, she supposed. A better one than the first she had made regarding him. She was very proud of how she had acquitted herself today. She would be sorry to lose the life she had made here, but not regret the reason for it.

Could she have been so strong if she had not come to know Jonathan? If he had not seduced her, and closed that other path? He probably thought he might have set her in the direction of her mother's life with this affair. Instead she had discovered that she did not want to avoid the profound emotions that could arise in such intimacy, even if the final cost was very high.

She wondered what Alessandra would say about that. Nothing good.

Familiar sounds down below said that Jonathan was back in the house. He would be coming to her soon. She closed her eyes while her body responded with a delicious liveliness.

Erotic, not vulgar, Celia. She rearranged her dress in a manner that Alessandra would approve.

The visit to Edward left Jonathan in a black mood. He relived the conversation many times on his way back to Wells Street that night. He saw his uncle's expressions in his head and studied them carefully. He saw the exact moment when Edward had realized that the implications of his tale had not been missed by his nephew.

Jonathan assumed nothing in his manner had revealed his thoughts, but then, Edward knew him better than anyone except maybe Celia now. Well enough, perhaps, to merely assume that the unspoken conclusions would be obvious to the one man to whom they mattered the most.

He entered the house still distracted. He mounted the steps with his mood tossing between a fury waiting to explode and a desolation more profound than he had ever known.

At the first landing he looked down the passageway to Celia's doorway. It would be best not to bring this mood to her. He walked to her door, to make some excuse.

He opened the door to the kind of warm, alluring environment that Celia had such a talent for creating. A low fire burned, and a few candles, and wine waited by the two chairs near the hearth. One of her knitted shawls hung over the arm of one chair, adding a domestic touch. Feminine details, like the little bowl of evergreen clippings, spoke of the comfort to be had here.

The bed spoke of other comforts and a different side of her femininity. She was there already, her body draped over soft mounds of pillows. The light reflected in ripples off the satin on her back, and piled in elegant drifts around her waist. From there down she was naked, her round bottom and shapely, parted legs exposed to view.

It was the most elegantly erotic image he had ever seen.

She rose up on her forearms. The movement made her back dip and her bottom rise. Her gaze acknowledged what she was doing to him.

"Lots of pillows, as you requested. Marian will probably object that I stole hers," she said.

He remembered then, the morning's games, and his demand for satin and pillows. It seemed so long ago now.

"You are so beautiful it is painful sometimes to see you, Celia. You are perfect there, and I want you. However, this would not be a good night for it, after the day I have had."

"Something bad happened? My day was unpleasant too. That makes it a perfect night for it, don't you think? We will forget the insults of the world for a short while." She bent one knee and her foot tapped the air. "Whatever you wanted, remember?"

He cast off his coats and stripped off his cravat. He drank some of the wine while he watched her tease him with that foot and her sultry gaze.

Whatever he wanted. Right now he wanted to release some of this fury before it split him apart. He wanted to bury himself in her until her scent and sighs made him oblivious to this odd sickness of the soul. He wanted her screams to drown out the ugly truth in his head.

He continued undressing. "Pillows and satin and whatever I want. Did you remember the rest?"

"Oh, yes, Jonathan. Can't you tell? I have been ready for a good long while now."

He flipped her, and knelt below her on the bed. He propped her hips high on those pillows and parted her knees wide. He touched her and her hips rose from the sensual shock. He gently caressed her damp folds of delicate flesh.

Soon she whimpered with impatience. "Now," she breathed.

"Not yet." He lowered himself, and lost himself in her taste and scent. He used his tongue until all he heard were her cries and his own blood pounding in his head. The fury finally had its way, making him ruthless. He made her beg, and took too much pleasure in the way he forced a desperate need for him that left her powerless.

He made her climax hard, violently, with thrashes and

trembles that made her scream. Then he rose and flipped her again, so the satin fell down her back and her bottom rose high in an erotic position that stoked his madness. He took her hard, savagely, incapable of restraint, and, good to her word, she let him have whatever he wanted.

"Let us go out to the garden," Celia said. "The evening was fair, and it is probably not very cold."

"You will catch a chill."

"I will wear my most sensible bed dress and my low boots and my cloak. It is more than most women wear to the theater at night."

He rose from bed and reached for his garments.

She took a candle and led the way downstairs to the garden door. Jonathan wore his frock coat but carried his waistcoat and cravat. He left them inside the door. She noticed. He would not be staying with her tonight.

The air was crisp but not too cold. There was enough moon to highlight the plantings.

"Did I hurt you?" he asked after they had strolled a few minutes.

"No. I guessed how it would be when I saw you. I am only sorry that your mood has reclaimed you again. I regret that my body did not give you more than momentary relief, since I do not think you would trust the rest of me to help at all."

"That is not true. Your mere presence helps."

"Well, that is something at least."

They walked on, through patches of shadow and vague light that moved with the clouds.

"Celia, do you remember my telling you about a mission I had on the coast five years ago?"

She nodded. "The one where the boy died."

"That happened because someone revealed I would be there. There had been a betrayal. I have recently been trying to discover who was behind it."

Her heart sank. They were back to the subjects of their row. They had never really talked about any of that again. She had assumed they never would.

"You think it might have been my mother, don't you?"

"I thought it was tied to the rumors about your mother. And it was, only the rumors were wrong and so was the tie."

He told her an odd story, about how Alessandra had worked for the government, giving a man information that she was given, in order to fool the French.

"So she was not a traitor at all, Jonathan. Why, she was a heroine."

"That, she was. It was not without danger either."

"But this is good news."

"For her memory, it is, and I am glad for that. For you. However, one day the man who gave her the information told her to tell her spy about something closer to home. And it was not false information, the way it normally was. She did not know that, and so she passed it on."

And Jonathan was almost killed. A young boy actually died.

"Do you blame her? Is that why—"

"Not at all. I blame the man who misused her trust in order to settle a private matter."

She stopped and embraced him. "You think that you know who it is, don't you?"

He pulled her closer, and wrapped his arms around her. He gazed past her, into the shadows. "Only my cousin would have a motive, and also be a man who might be given the duty to work with her. I saw him arrive there once, at her house. His crest is not among the others, however. I do not think he was ever one of her patrons."

"Are you certain it was he who did this? It is a terrible thing to do out of mere irritation about the existence of a bastard cousin."

"I am sure enough. I will be very sure soon."

She laid her head on his chest. He did not sigh, but she heard something much like it in him. She wanted to think that speaking of it had helped him, but she did not believe it had.

"Repudiation was not enough for him. I am embarrassed to admit that I find that dismaying," he said. "He may not like that we share the same blood, but we do all the same. That he would try to arrange my death—" He finally sounded angry, as if that emotion had won a hard battle over a much sadder one.

"What will you do?"

"Tell him that I know. Make him face it. Then we will have a conversation that he has been avoiding since I was nine years old."

He tucked her under his arm and started back to the house. "And your bad day, Celia? If I have bored you with mine, you must share yours."

"I saw Anthony. And his solicitor." She pointed to the house. "I expect it will not be mine soon. I have been thinking that it is too large anyway. I know what income the plants will bring now. I will speak with an estate agent and see about letting another house." She poked him playfully. "I will make sure it has fine attics."

"How much is this debt that scoundrel holds?"

"Eight hundred pounds. Whoever thought my mother could bargain so well?"

"You make jokes, but I know this saddens you, Celia."

"Whenever I get sad about losing the house, I remember Anthony's face when I told him I would not have him in any way, at any price. I take such joy in his expression that I can't be too miserable."

He did not open the garden door, but instead sat her down on the bench nearby, where he had first kissed her. "Celia, before I was old enough to reject Thornridge's allowance for my silence, a little over a thousand pounds came to me. You will take what you need and be done with the man."

She did not know what to say. Just as well, because she could not speak if she had to. He looked down at her as if he had not just offered something astonishing. Her throat burned and the sweetest emotion squeezed her heart.

He misunderstood her silence. "It is not what you think. It is not payment, such as your mother received."

Of course it was, but with the kindest of intentions and the best kind of protection as a motive.

"I am honored that you have offered this, Jonathan. It is probably all the money you have in the world, and the income from it must be what keeps you in coats and shirts."

He took her hand and helped her up. "Then I will see to it tomorrow."

She stretched up on her toes and kissed him. "No, you will not. I will find another house. Do not try to do it unbeknownst to me either. I will not allow you to become impoverished because of my mother's neglect in repaying Anthony."

He did not argue. He opened the door and handed her over the threshold. "I think that I will stay out here awhile longer, Celia."

"I will say good night, then, Jonathan."

She closed the door, and left him in the dark, no doubt to contemplate the meeting with Thornridge that he planned.

She would contemplate it too, and imagine what might happen if Jonathan confronted that family and demanded their acknowledgment. She doubted Jonathan would begin such a battle unarmed. If he engaged at all, he would expect to win.

She hoped he did. She wanted him to have what he deserved. She pictured him escorting that woman in the park instead of being snubbed by her. If the image made her heartsick, it was not because she did not want the best for him. She just knew that if he walked beside his cousin Lady Chesmont, he could not also walk beside Alessandra Northrope's daughter.

Chapter Twenty-four

Jonathan dipped his pen and scratched in the journal, reconstructing the main points of the lecture he had attended with Summerhays at the Royal Society. It had been a generous invitation, especially since Summerhays did not count chemistry among his interests. Astronomy would have kept him awake, not nodding off like he did yesterday.

He was almost finished when feet thudded rapidly up the back stairs. A knock on his door made him put down the pen. He opened the door to find Bella in high excitement.

"You must come, sir. He is asking for you."

"Who is?"

"There is a man at the door, all powdered he is, and in a uniform. Marian says he is just a servant but—" She thrust a small paper at him. "He told us to give you this, and that he would wait. Celia is not at home and—"

He took the paper and read the only two words on it. *Thornridge. Now.*

Grabbing his coat, he went down to the servant. As

expected, the man was in Castleford's livery. No one else would write two words and just assume the world knew from whom they came.

The footman stepped aside and Jonathan went to the street. Dargent's coach had impressed this neighborhood, but Castleford's had drawn a crowd. Heads angled this way and that, trying to see inside. Boys admired the massive horses that stood in perfect formation.

Jonathan opened a door and hopped inside. "You are creating a scene."

Castleford parted the blinds and looked out. "That is because I could ill afford the time to send for you, and had to come fetch you myself."

"How did you find me?"

"Through an annoying waste of time. I sent to Hawkeswell for your address, only to have my coachman discover it was some printer's shop. Then I remembered about Miss Pennifold. My solicitor knew about her mother's solicitor, who knew about this property, so here I am."

Not only was he here; he was groomed like a duke. One could cut cheese with his collar. A fob on his watch chain sported a ruby that could pay the wages in an entire county for a month.

"What are you looking at?" he demanded.

"Nothing. Only—it is not Tuesday."

"This could not wait for Tuesday. I go to meet a fellow peer at his request over a matter of great concern to him. Considering the seriousness of his letter, it behooves me to be sober and wearing my station, so to speak."

They had left Celia's street behind. Castleford opened the blinds. The light revealed eyes not nearly as serious as his dress and words reflected.

"Thornridge asked to see you, Castleford? I thought this was about me."

"It will be. Once we are inside. After I am received. To ensure that reception, I arranged for him to want to see me more than he knew I wanted to see him."

"How did you manage that?"

Castleford angled his head, as something they passed caught his attention. "I seduced his sister. He learned of it, of course, and seems to think it a personal insult, from the strong words of his letter yesterday. He demanded we speak, so here we are, on our way."

Jonathan looked at him. Castleford looked back, devilishly pleased with his own cleverness.

"You seduced my cousin, Your Grace?" He pictured the woman who had cut him in the park and who, he knew, lived an uneventful life with an unremarkable man. She had not stood a chance.

"Damnation, I suppose she is your cousin, now that you mention it. Unofficially. However, she never speaks to you. It is not as if I seduced your *dear* cousin."

"This was badly done, Castleford."

"At least it *is* done. Do not become tiresome. It will be too ridiculous if you start issuing challenges over a blood relation who denies you exist. Besides, I can hardly have a man serve as my second on one day if I am to duel with him over the same matter the next day."

"Your second now. Are you expecting Thornridge to challenge you over this?"

Castleford shrugged lazily. "Well, I expect someone to challenge someone before the day is out. Don't you?"

* * *

The Earl of Thornridge kept a house on Grosvenor Square that he usually inhabited alone when he was in town. His wife, who had been a celebrated beauty while on the marriage mart, had suddenly decided she did not care for London life once she married. Or so it was claimed. Jonathan assumed that Thornridge had a tendency to jealousy, and it was just easier for him to require his wife stay out of temptation's way.

Considering the reason for this call, it was unlikely Thornridge would change his mind about London's amorous dangers soon.

Only Castleford's card was sent up. Since it was Castleford, the servants did not blink at not receiving Jonathan's. Nor did they question the shadow that accompanied the duke up to the drawing room a little later.

"Are you ready?" Castleford mumbled as they approached the doors. It was clear that he expected a fine show in payment for whatever trouble he had taken with that seduction.

The doors swung ceremoniously. Jonathan decided he was as ready as he would ever be.

Thornridge made no pretense that this was a social call. He waited, his posture strictly straight and his face severe. His welcome of the duke sounded clipped and forced.

Then he saw Jonathan's face. His own turned red.

Despite the distortion that anger brought, Jonathan studied him, fascinated. He had seen Thornridge from a distance over the years. He had been unable to resist making it a point to do so. So the graying hair and thickening form came as no surprise. He had not seen the earl's face this close, however, since he was nine years old.

They looked alike. The resemblance could not be missed. Which perhaps gave another motive to Uncle Edward's offer of the kind of employment that took a man out of London for months at a time.

"What in hell is he doing here?" Thornridge demanded.

"He claimed to have an interest in the matter. You accused me of seducing your sister, and Albrighton here accused me of seducing his cousin. Upon realizing that he and you referred to the same woman, I thought it would be easier to have it out with both of you at once." Castleford strolled over to a settee, sat down, crossed his legs, and gazed up at the earl blandly.

"I'll not have him here. He could not have referred to the same woman, because he is of no relation. His is not—"

"Hell, Thornridge, one has only to see him to know he is *some* relation. Half of society has guessed the truth of it."

"How dare you interfere!"

Castleford feigned confusion. "I am here at your request. You are the one who has raised this other matter about his relationships."

Thornridge turned his back on the duke and glared at Jonathan. "If you think to press your spurious claim today, know now that I will not hear you."

"That is not why I am here. I came to find out if I have to kill you."

Thornridge's expression fell in shock. Behind him Castleford sat straighter, impressed.

"Are you daring to threaten me?" Thornridge roared.

"If I know a man is bent on seeing me dead, I'll be damned if I'll wait for him to make his move."

Still an inch away from full bluster, Thornridge took his measure. "Your implied accusation is preposterous. I have no reason to want you dead."

Of course he did. None of the rest made sense if he did not. "I had a long talk with Uncle Edward recently. Perhaps he was too afraid to tell you about it. He does keep you informed normally, doesn't he? About his efforts on your behalf to keep me busy and away over the years. The end of the war created a challenge there, but even so, he has been resourceful."

Thornridge hardened perceptibly. "He may have mentioned that you had talents that were useful to England. He spared me the particulars."

"That is because you already knew them. Anyway, I now know about Alessandra Northrope's special role during the war. And I know you were the one who told her what bits of information to pass on."

"You know nothing of the kind."

"No one else had a reason to have her pass the information about a mission I went on. Very accurate information. I walked into a trap. I should be dead. Who else but you might want me dead, and possibly have access to the details of my mission, and also have a way to get those details to the enemy?"

"I have no reason to want you dead, so your theory is illogical from beginning to end."

"Of course you do. I was not sure before. For years I thought the odds were less than even that my mother's story of a deathbed marriage with my father was true. Now I know it was."

Thornridge looked as if he would burst. Not only anger tightened his face and braced his posture like a man ready to exchange blows. A good deal of shock and fear flexed through him too.

"You dared speak of killing me. Are you so sure of what you know that you would issue a challenge? If they try you for murder, what you *think* you know will not save you from the noose."

"If I conclude I need to kill you, why should I meet you on the field of honor when you have not been honorable? Fingers may point to me afterward but, I assure you, no evidence will."

His cousin's eyes widened. Jonathan trusted that the mind behind that astonishment was reviewing all those missions where so many moral liberties were taken in the name of the greater good.

Over on the settee, the devil's familiar smiled vaguely in admiration, and almost purred.

Rather suddenly, Thornridge remembered Castleford's presence. "You have just threatened me in front of a witness."

"I only heard a man speaking metaphorically, Thornridge," Castleford said. "Everyone says things like that all the time. I threaten my valet with being drawn and quartered at least once a day."

"Damnation, there was nothing metaphorical about it!"

Castleford's lids lowered. "If you believe that, then perhaps you should give him satisfaction in some other way. Unfortunately, if what he says is true, I doubt an apology will suffice. It would not for me, if I ever learned a man had tried to arrange my death."

"That is a hellish, unfounded accusation on the part of a man looking to make trouble," Thornridge sputtered. He paced away fretfully, brow knitting hard.

Jonathan let his cousin weigh what he would, however he chose. Castleford managed to sprawl a bit on that settee without looking too rude.

Thornridge abruptly turned, now wearing a very different expression. Appeasing. Almost friendly.

"I have perhaps been too harsh. The shock of learning about you back then—such an affair was not in keeping with my uncle's character. There is always the chance that after such a man dies, spurious claims will be made. But, I will admit now, there is a strong resemblance in you. It is time, I think, for amends to be made."

Jonathan had been waiting to hear those words his whole life. His reaction felt almost commonplace now that he did. No glorious excitement or wave of relief broke in him. No anticipation of better days teased at his imagination. All he experienced was a deep, soulful contentment that an ambiguity about who and what he was had been settled. Not completely settled, but settled in the part that mattered most.

He thought of Celia in that instant. He saw her on the portico of Enderby's house, sitting in the rain. He wished that she had received a similar resolution. He wished that he could give it to her.

"We will invite you to the house this season," his cousin said. "We will receive you, and make our acknowledgment of your paternity known. An allowance is in order too, I suppose. A bit more than what you rejected years back. Enough to keep you in some sort of style at least."

"This is all very generous. I do not know what to say."

His cousin missed the sardonic note. Castleford did not, and smirked.

"A good marriage too," his cousin said. "Yes, that will be essential. We will find a girl with a handsome settlement. An alliance with a family of indisputable station and respectability will go far to establishing you, and blunt any rumors that might arise about your duties during the war."

"I prefer to choose my own wife."

"You'll never get the one you need on your own. If we acknowledge you and receive you, we cannot risk being mocked if you wed unsuitably." He smiled broadly, as if he understood the concern. "Do not worry. We will make sure she is pretty."

"Well, now, that is settled," a voice announced from the settee. "Thornridge, perhaps you will address our business at less expansive length."

The earl pivoted, as if surprised to see Castleford there still. "Indeed. I will be very brief. What in hell are you doing, daring to interfere with my sister?"

"I was overcome by her sweet manner. It was very bad of me, I agree. I understand if you want satisfaction, although normally it would be her husband who demands it. However, if we must duel, Albrighton here has agreed to serve as my second. It is why I brought him. Tell him the name of yours, and he will make the arrangements."

"Second? Satisfaction?" Thornridge could not hide his alarm. Having just avoided one threat to his life, he now found himself being cornered into another. "I did not invite you here so I could challenge you, Castleford. Damnation, the days are gone when men dueled over such things. I just wanted to tell you to stay away from my sister in the future."

Castleford stood. "You could have written a letter for that. However, I will make every effort to avoid her in the future. We will leave you now, so that you can begin your plans for welcoming Albrighton onto his irregular branch of the family tree."

Jonathan received a final glare from his cousin for that. Something between a smile and a sneer formed. "To be expected that of the two of us, you decided to blame *me* for the enemy getting that information about you on the coast. I'm the one who had what you wanted, after all, even though Uncle was the traitor."

Jonathan did not miss a step as that revelation followed him to the door, even though the parting shot stunned him more than any pistol ball could.

"You are quiet for a man whose fortunes have just been reversed," Castleford said.

Jonathan had wanted to take his leave of the duke on the street outside his cousin's house, but Castleford in his unpredictable way had insisted on returning him to the spot where he had found him.

"It is a victory that inspires reflection, not celebration, I am discovering. And it is not without its costs."

"The curtailment of freedom, you mean. The obligation to be respectable and boring. The day will come when you will be nostalgic for your old obscure insignificance, I predict. The lower you are in our elevated world, the more suffocating that world can be. I am glad I was born at the very top, let me tell you."

"I may choose to remain obscure and insignificant. My cousin's intentions for my life are more detailed than I like."

"It sounded predictable enough to me. Since you did not balk at the allowance or the connections, it must be his thoughts on marriage that impose too far."

Indeed they did. He had no interest in that kind of marriage, no matter what the woman's settlement. Had his desire or need for either money or respectability extended that far, he could have lured such a woman himself.

The duke's eyes closed then, leaving Jonathan to his

thoughts. The coach eventually stopped in front of Celia's house. Jonathan stepped out.

"Are you not even slightly tempted to go for it all, Albrighton?"

Jonathan looked back in the coach. Rather suddenly Castleford appeared alert.

"He all but admitted it," Castleford said. "If he tried to do you in, he felt threatened by you, and a bastard is no threat. Surely you want to know the truth now."

Jonathan instinctively glanced over his shoulder, at the house and the window on the second floor.

"I am not sure that I do want to know, or that I can. My uncle claimed to be looking for the truth for years."

"It sounded to me that your uncle serves a master with no interest in your learning anything. That business at the very end was intriguing."

"I ask that you not repeat it. My cousin was just looking to cause trouble between me and the one relative who admitted I existed all these years. As for the rest, my mother did not tell me much, other than the earl married her on his deathbed. That is all. I wondered if it was true, and now I think it is, but that is not the same thing as being able to prove it." He closed the carriage door. "I thank you for your aid today. I trust that seducing my cousin did not inconvenience you too much."

Castleford laughed. He stuck his head to the window. "I would tell you all about it, but since she is now officially your cousin, that would be inappropriate."

"Most inappropriate."

Castleford looked at the house. "Even if you embrace Thornridge's plans, you do not have to give her up. Miss Pennifold will understand. She probably expects nothing more than what she now has."

He signaled to his coachman to go. Jonathan walked to the house.

Castleford was probably correct. Celia Pennifold expected no more. She had learned through hard experience years ago that her mother's lessons about how men of society made marriages were all too accurate. She might even encourage him to grab Thornridge's match. She might well agree to continue as a mistress.

It was the way these things were done, after all. The way it was supposed to be.

L aughter punctuated the night silence. A thick slice of light pierced the darkness. Three men came out of Brooks together, and wandered off to find carriages and horses.

Jonathan waited in the shadows. All men were creatures of habit, and the man he waited for was tied to habits just like the rest. Jonathan had learned most of them out of curiosity more than anything else. There had always been the chance, however, that the information would be useful.

He checked his pocket watch by the light of a nearby lamp. Unless something had happened to disrupt the pattern tonight, Uncle Edward would leave the club soon. Then he would walk down this street, to hire a hackney coach to take him home. Edward did not like the bother of waiting for his carriage to be prepared, and used it of an evening only when he attended a dinner party or the theater or a ball.

Jonathan positioned himself near a building that Edward would pass. He made no effort to hide. No one ever found him suspicious. He looked too much a gentleman to cause alarm.

The club's door opened again. Edward's face and hair appeared in the light. He said something to the servant, doffed his hat, and walked.

He noticed Jonathan as he approached. His pace slowed considerably. His grasp of that walking stick tightened.

"Lurking in the dark for old times' sake, Jon? Getting nostalgic?"

Jonathan fell into step next to him. He chose the side with the walking stick, so Edward could not raise it easily. "I thought that I would see you tonight without imposing on your household."

Edward gazed around, assessing their isolation.

"I am finished with that mission, Edward. I spoke with Thornridge too. I know he is the one who gave Alessandra the information for the government. I thought you were protecting him with this curiosity about her accounts and list of patrons. He shared that you were actually protecting yourself. You were correct when you said Alessandra would not be so stupid as to include her spy's name in her accounts and such. You just needed to be certain."

Edward stopped, right there on the street, in the dark between two streetlamps. "Will I be needing my pistol, Jonathan?"

He did not mean for protection, or for a duel. "I don't know. Will you?"

"Not unless you or your cousin exposes me publicly. The rest already know. The Home Office. The ministers. Nothing was said to me, but I am sure they know. I suppose nothing was done because this traitor became useful to them."

"At least you do not try to make excuses. I will give you that. You call it what it was."

"I always knew what it was."

"Then why did you do it? Money?"

Edward walked on, his posture less correct, his gait a bit weary. "Hardly. It was a woman. God help me."

Jonathan guessed he was supposed to express shock in the pause that followed. Instead he found the response fascinating.

"I had known her for ten years. Loved her for most of them. They had her in prison. I thought I could spare her." Edward shrugged. "Alessandra accepted me as a patron, and I encouraged her to be indiscreet about the things her other clients said in passing. Little did I guess she saw my interest as suspicious, and went to the Home Office. They made sure the indiscretions continued."

"You had access to much better information than she could ever hear in bed."

"Passing on what I knew in my governmental capacity would expose me too clearly and quickly. I thought to satisfy them this other way and not truly be a traitor, I suppose. I took solace when most of the information proved useless or worse."

"Except once."

Edward tensed. "I assumed the details of your mission were also inaccurate because I would surely know if such a mission were planned. After the disastrous results, I realized someone had seen a pattern and suspected me. Used me. The last few years it became an elegant game. I pretended I did not know they knew, and passed on what they fed me."

"You make it sound almost patriotic."

"Damnation, I know what it was. What I was. But little

harm resulted from what I did. Sending them bad information proved to be a useful tactic. I never compromised you, or any of the others I worked with. At least not knowingly. I swear to that."

They stopped at a corner, and faced each other in the dark mist. There really wasn't anything more to ask or say. Jonathan did not even experience much anger. He thought it ironic, however, even scandalous, that Edward had not had to answer for this in any way, either public or private, before this night.

"Did you not worry that one day someone would hand me or another man a mission, and you would not be the puppeteer, but the prey?"

Edward exhaled deeply, the way a man does when he is trying to control a strong emotion. "Has that happened now, Jonathan? Or are you here independently?"

"The war is long over, Uncle. If men are still sent on those kinds of missions, I do not want to know about it. As for me acting for personal reasons—" He did not try to pretend that Edward was blameless. This man had assumed there was no mission on the coast, however. It was another man who made sure there was. "My cousin has made you beholden to him with this. He knows everything, and he holds your fate, your good name, and maybe even your freedom in his hands. I expect being his lackey and living in fear that he will expose you is punishment enough. You do not have to worry that I need my own revenge."

They passed under a streetlamp then, and Edward's face was visible. Slack from relief, ashen from fear, his expression spoke of his torture the last five minutes. Once they left the pool of light and were back in the dark, Jonathan stopped walking. Edward kept on, his stick dragging the ground like a lame third leg.

"Was she spared, Uncle? The woman for whom you did this?"

Edward turned and looked at him. "She survived. She is living near Nice with an artist now." He turned and walked on, until the night absorbed him.

Jonathan walked the other way. Whoever thought Edward would betray his country because of his love for a woman? As reasons for being a traitor went, however, it was at least one that Jonathan understood.

Chapter Twenty-five

"It is odd, that is all," Celia said. "I have found two other houses that will do, but my inheritance of this one remains in limbo."

"Perhaps it is Mr. Dargent's plan to leave you unsettled and worried. It gives him an eternal claim on your attention," Daphne said.

They stood in the middle of the garden, after a long stroll along its beds with Verity and Audrianna. Now Audrianna was at a table on the terrace, writing down all the improvements they had decided would be made, and Verity was writing down lists of plants. No one would recognize those two now as the ladies they were. Spring's mud decorated their hems and boots, and the simplest bonnets shielded their complexions from the sun.

"Anthony knows it cannot remain unresolved forever, Daphne. He needs to make his claim on it or lose that claim. I want to believe he had a change of heart, but I fear I am wasting all of your time with today's planning."

"It is never a waste to spend time with friends. This is mostly an excuse for that."

They strolled to the terrace. Audrianna set down her pen as they arrived. "It is all here, but you must do your drawings, Celia. And I fear it is more work than women can manage."

"I could send over some of our gardeners," Verity said while she focused on penning her lists. "But perhaps Mr. Albrighton will insist on helping. He is most eager to be of service to you, Celia." She glanced up. "Carpentry and such."

A little stillness fell among them. Not a long one. A five-count at most, but it was there, unmistakably.

Verity's bonnet could not hide her insinuating smile as she bent over her lists. Daphne suddenly appeared almost too composed.

Celia glared at Audrianna, who turned bright red.

"It slipped out," she confessed. "I all but forgot you had told me privately. We were talking about how he stayed in Daphne's house, while you did too, and Daphne made one of her bad jokes about trifles, and I—well, I—" She appeared miserable and contrite, but also ready to laugh.

Daphne's arm came around her shoulders. "We do not judge, Celia. If you are content, we are as well."

Content. An odd word. She supposed she was content. Certainly things with Jonathan had been very good this last week. Not only the sensuality, which now seemed imbued with new emotions. Also the little things, such as how he looked at her in the morning, and the kisses he gave her in passing.

So why did nostalgia sometimes color her contentment, as if she lived a memory? It was much like she felt as she moved through this house that she soon might lose.

"Since we all know, and now you know that we all know, I have an invitation," Audrianna said. "We are going to the theater tonight, Celia. Verity and Hawkeswell are joining us in our box. And, I believe, so is Mr. Albrighton. I want you to come as well."

"I do not think that Jonathan will welcome my attendance, Audrianna. He expects to settle things with Thornridge soon. This is not a good moment for his name to be linked to mine, if he hopes to realize those expectations."

Her friends exchanged glances. They understood, of course. These dear women accepted her, but they also did not pretend that her birth and history did not matter.

"You will only be sitting in a box with him, Celia," Verity said. "Why don't you allow Mr. Albrighton to decide if he thinks that will interfere with his expectations?"

Verity asked Daphne for help with one of the lists then. Audrianna tilted her head back, so the sun could find her face. "The scents out here are so rich. Don't you agree, Celia? One can smell nature coming alive again."

"Your condition probably makes you more sensitive to it all than most others, Audrianna, but I agree that spring stirs all the senses toward hope, with its promise of new beginnings."

He found Celia on the terrace, sitting on the bench near the garden door. The sun had begun its descent and the breeze had cooled. She had removed her bonnet. A sketchbook rested on her lap but she did not draw.

He angled his head to see the page she had been working on. "The ladies and you have planned changes out here, I see."

"It was an excuse to see each other." She gestured to the sketch. "This will never see fruition. Eventually Mr. Watson will send someone to do that inventory."

He sat beside her. "I do not think so, Celia. I am almost sure he will never come."

She looked at him, puzzled. Then her expression cleared. "Jonathan, did you give Anthony that money?"

"I did not. I was obedient to your wishes."

"Thank you. I could not bear the thought of your doing that."

He took the sketchbook, and paged backward to see what else she had drawn. "I did speak to Anthony, however. Several days ago."

Out of the corner of his eye, he saw her curious skepticism.

"Did you, now?"

"Mmm."

"What did you say?"

"Let me see if I remember. The usual greeting. A request for a private word. A reminder that I was an old friend of your family, that sort of thing. It was very cordial. I may have suggested that no gentleman would try to coerce a woman into his bed by the means he was using. Yes, I do believe that came up too. I think that I may have indicated that I would not take it well if he made any further moves against the property."

"Since no move has been made, you appear to have been persuasive."

"I have been told that the ability to persuade is one of my talents."

Her fingertips cupped his chin and she turned his head so he faced her. "Jonathan, did you hurt him?"

"Of course not. His arm may have been a bit stiff for a

few days, due to my enthusiasm for the conversation, which somewhat exceeded his. However, I did not hurt him, in the way a man would use that word."

"Did you threaten him?"

"Only a man with a guilty conscience would take what I said as a threat. I did suggest he might want to ask some mutual acquaintances about me. If he did, and they led him to think better of his plan, it had nothing to do with me." He imagined Dargent seeking out the men with whom his father had consulted during the war. Anthony probably had not slept well since.

Celia looked in his eyes. "I should scold you. My mother essentially took offers for me, and he made the best one. As much as I dislike him now, *he* was not the one to break the rules of that game."

"He has done well enough without the money this long, and will continue that way. Nor did he make the best offer. He just had the right family, and your innocent love. But it is done now. If Mr. Watson has not written to arrange that inventory by now, he never will."

She frowned halfway through his response. Frowned so deeply that he doubted she heard the rest of it. He realized why. It was not like him to err like that. How like Celia to not miss it.

"How do you know he did not make the best offer? Did my mother confide about that to you?"

"It is a small thing, Celia, and long in the past. What is important is that you can build your gardens and put down your own roots here if you choose."

He tapped at her drawing. She looked at it and smiled. Then the frown formed again. She scrutinized him, suspiciously.

Such were the wages of being distracted by a lovely

woman. Of being so comfortable that one did not parse every word three times over before speaking. "Celia, I know he did not offer the most because I offered more. It is not what you think. I was leaving town for God knew how long."

Her expression fell in astonishment. "You? What on earth for, if you were leaving town?"

Why indeed? Looking back, it appeared a futile, noble gesture. At the time, it had seemed the right thing to do. "It was as good a use of the money as any, and I expected to have more eventually. You were still too innocent, Celia. Too much a child. I thought I would delay it a couple of years. That is all." He shrugged. "Your mother thought differently, and explained that I would not be an appropriate protector for you at any time, and no matter what my intentions."

"She was correct. You would not have been."

She spoke only the belief she lived. The rules she knew. Yet he did not care for the knot of unsuitability that she assumed, even though his meeting with Thornridge had only proven she was right about that.

Her eyes watered and her smile trembled. "You cannot know how this touches me, Jonathan. You could have told me before. I would not have misunderstood, and thought it meant you had tried to buy me when I was a girl." She half laughed and half cried, and her eyes glistened even while she smiled. "There I was, thinking Anthony was going to save me in the name of love, and the mysterious Mr. Albrighton tried to do so in the name of common decency. Is it any wonder that I love you, Jonathan?"

She sniffed and dabbed at her eyes with her handkerchief, perhaps unaware of what she had just said. He was not. He watched her joy in this small revelation of something long ago. Dusk was gathering, but not around this bench.

He still was not appropriate for her. If she ever wanted a protector, she could do far better than him.

Unless she loved him. She would set aside her own best interests then. He could probably have all that Thornridge offered, and Celia too, just as Castleford had predicted.

"It is good to hear you say that you love me, Celia. It is good that we talk of that, and how love has become a part of what is between us."

Her breath caught in midsniff. She looked at him almost fearfully, with a question in her eyes.

He had to smile, but her expression touched him with its sadness. "I am speaking of my love too, darling. You are more worthy of being loved than you will ever know."

She truly wept then, with tears that made her eyes luminous a thousand times over.

He took her in his arms. "It is past time, I think, to decide which story it will be, Celia."

Her head rested against him. She breathed deeply for control. "The one we have started, I think. My friends accept it, the ones who matter, that is. Once you talk to Thornridge, once he accepts how it must be with you, it will also be the only story allowed. Only I don't want any gifts, Jonathan. I don't want it to be *that* sort of affair."

"There is much wisdom in what you say. Only I am not accustomed to normal sorts of stories for myself. Nor are you, as you have proven." He tilted her head back so he could kiss her lips. "I said I would not give you up easily. Not any part of what we share. I will never risk losing this love you now say you have for me. I think that we should marry, Celia, so I am sure you are mine forever."

A lovely joy suffused her expression. Then the Celia who had been educated by Alessandra looked at him with love and kindness, but too much worldly realism. "Thank you for that, Jonathan. I am honored, and flattered, and I will never forget this moment. It cannot be, however. Once you convince your cousin to do the right thing, you will have to live a very normal sort of life. More normal than most, I should think."

"I have already met with him. I have already weighed my choices. I do not propose on an impulse, Celia. I know what I gain, and what I may lose."

She studied his eyes. "You mean it, don't you? You are serious."

"I am as serious as I have ever been."

Another long gaze, full of cautious joy. Then the most beautiful expression softened her face, and the caution left her. She threw her arms around his neck and kissed him hard.

She angled back to look up at the house's windows, and the last fiery rays of the setting sun limned her side and profile with an orange red glow. With naughty glee in her eyes, she stood and climbed onto his lap, facing him with her bent legs flanking her hips.

"Kiss me," she whispered. "Kiss me, then fill me, so this wonder and sweet astonishment that I feel does not break my heart from sheer happiness."

He kissed her. She snuggled closer, then raised her skirt and petticoat. Within moments he was in her, bound to her, rocking in a slow rhythm toward ecstasy while her soft cries chanted her love and pulled him into her brilliance.

*   *   *

They went to the theater that night. Celia wore her mother's ermine-trimmed mantlet over a restrained white dress decorated tastefully with lace. Jonathan hired a coach and called for her as if he did not live in the attic.

He always looked like a gentleman. There was never any question of his station, even though he officially did not have it. His bearing and confidence communicated the truth, she decided, as she sat across from him in the coach. Tonight, however, his normal informality was gone, and his crisply groomed appearance would stand up to any scrutiny.

The joy of the afternoon stayed with them both. They laughed and joked in the coach, and were still wearing their hearts on their sleeves when they arrived at the box. Jonathan made no pretense that he merely escorted a friend of the ladies, and the ladies noticed. Celia was glad that her secret was already out with them because she could not have hidden her love tonight if she had to.

Summerhays welcomed them warmly alongside his wife. Lord Hawkeswell appeared surprised by their arrival.

"He is not being especially discreet," Audrianna said in her ear while they found their seats to watch the play.

No, he was not. Not in the way he looked at her, and not in the way he addressed her. Everything remained very proper but he did not hide the signs of intimacy that said they belonged together.

He sat beside her. No one in their party made any attempt to stop that. She noticed other eyes in boxes across the way turn in their direction. She saw people notice the two bastards in Summerhays's box who had no business being there.

He is mad. Utterly mad. The voice spoke in her head while the play unfolded onstage, and the "he" in question sometimes looked at her with a smoldering, possessive attention that suggested he saw little of the histrionics down below. *He sacrifices your future as well as his own. Better to be a wealthy mistress than an impoverished wife.*

She recognized Alessandra's voice. That ghost had tried to ruin her happiness while she prepared for tonight, but she had banished it. Now, in the theater, with the world that he challenged looking on, she could not escape Mama's scold.

Not impoverished, she wanted to say back. *He is not without devices or income. I will be a partner in The Rarest Blooms. We will not starve.*

It is romantic and noble and good now, in the first excitement of a new passion. Ten years hence, when you both long for the comforts of life that he rejects, it will be too late to undo it if you marry. He gives up too much, and so do you.

A hand touched hers. Not Jonathan's hand. Audrianna sat on the other side of her, and her white-gloved fingers entwined Celia's own. She bent her head close.

"You look troubled now, Celia, and you were so happy when you arrived."

Celia gazed across the theater. Heads still turned sometimes, to watch her. Audrianna's attention followed in that direction.

"You may think they all know who you are, but I think most are just admiring your beauty," she said.

"I think that unlikely."

"That is because you have never understood just how beautiful you are. All the same, I wish Castleford had come the way he was supposed to. Our plan was to have him here. Then no one would have given more than passing notice to anyone else in the box. Alas, he sent word to

Sebastian this morning that he had to depart London at once and could not attend."

"It was probably just an excuse, when he learned about the rest of your party."

Audrianna found that amusing. "He would never trouble himself to avoid you, Celia, and you are the only one he does not know. He is friends with all the gentlemen, and has shown a peculiar kindness to Verity and me."

Her husband claimed Audrianna's attention then, and she released Celia's hand.

The little conversation had silenced the scolds. They interfered no more. Celia watched the play, never forgetting the exciting and handsome man by her side who was announcing his interest in her in such a public way. She also looked on her friends with great affection, touched by their care for her.

This had all been arranged, she guessed. By Jonathan and Summerhays and maybe even the ladies. Her presence here, in this most respectable box owned by a marquess, had been a calculated step, so that Jonathan could show the world that he loved the woman known as Celia Pennifold, and did not care if an accident of birth had also made her Alessandra Northrope's daughter.

Chapter Twenty-six

She grasped the windowsill for support. The first sign of sun peeked over the rooftops beyond the garden, giving dawn's mist an ethereal beauty. Heavenly scents of renewal flowed over her on the refreshing breeze that cooled and teased her skin.

Jonathan's hard strength curved over hers. His arm surrounded her from behind and supported, while his hand cupped her breast. His hold on her flank held her steady to his thrusts.

Pleasure inundated her. Transformed her. All of her senses heightened at once, so she observed more and felt more and heard the subtlest sounds. The trembles of fulfillment beckoned where they joined, then grew intense and spread until her entire being reached toward the pending moment of release with exquisite anticipation.

It broke in her with unbearable force and went on and on while he thrust harder, deeper, faster. The tremble of ecstasy was all through her, filling her, then outside of her too, into the mist and the light and the sounds, and into him as well, she was sure, until more than their bodies joined.

He pulled her to him and wrapped her in an embrace so complete that he bound her length to his. They floated together in an aftermath echoing with the beauty of this precious intimacy.

"The wagons will be coming soon," she muttered when her feet finally felt the ground again and their breathing had calmed. "I must go and dress."

He pressed a kiss to the crook of her neck and stayed there, as if he did not want to lose the scent of her. His hold loosened, finally. "I will help, so it does not take long."

She went to her chamber and washed and dressed. Before she went down the stairs, she opened a door next to her own. The chamber within was hardly luxurious, but of good size, and much more convenient than that one in the attic.

She would move Jonathan down here. It was past time to make that change. He was not a tenant anymore, and would soon be the master of this house.

Pacing its length, she judged what other furniture it would need. In the midst of her contemplation, she heard Marian calling up the stairs for Jonathan, alerting him to callers.

Celia returned to her own room and looked out the open window to see two men tying their horses' reins to a post. Their voices carried up the building to her.

"I only said he is too free in sending us on errands like footmen," Hawkeswell said.

"He did not send us. He requested that we help."

"He is being far too sly for me. If this is revealed to be some besotted game—"

"Give the devil his due, Hawkeswell. When he sets his mind to a task, he can be tenacious in seeing it through, for good or ill."

Hawkeswell stepped to the door. "It is the ill that I fear." He looked at the building, then up and down the street. "What is this place? Albrighton lives here?"

"According to my wife, yes. I should tell you that this is Miss Pennifold's house."

Hawkeswell's head snapped around. "Is it indeed? If your wife knows, mine surely does too. Am I the only one who was not aware of this affair?"

"I expect so. Although I don't know how you missed it. He looked like he wanted to devour her at the theater last week." Summerhays raised his fist. The knock sounded down below. The two men's crowns passed below her, into the house. Male voices exchanged greetings, then spoke more quietly.

Celia left her room, and descended the stairs. The conversation stopped when they heard her footfalls.

She stepped down, to where she could see them standing just inside the door, and they could see her. Hawkeswell looked like a man ill at ease with his mission. Summerhays appeared to have been placating the other two.

Jonathan looked angry. Furious. She had never seen him quite like this before.

He looked at her, then glared at Summerhays. She excused herself, and walked to the back of the house.

"Go back and tell him no." Jonathan made no effort to lower his voice. She heard every word. "He should not have interfered. I did not ask him to."

"He is not a man who thinks he requires permission for anything, let alone interferences," Hawkeswell said. "I would be just as vexed as you are. I agree he went too far."

"Whether he should have done it or not, it is done," Summerhays said. "You should at least find out what he has learned."

"I don't give a damn what he has learned."

"Well, you should," Summerhays said. "For your future, and that of your children, you should."

None of them spoke then. Celia set about moving the few plants still on the shelves to one side. A good deal of time ticked by. Perhaps they were whispering, so the household could not hear them. So she could not.

"I will admit that Summerhays has a point, Albrighton," Hawkeswell said. "You can tell him to go to hell afterward, but you may as well hear him out."

Another protracted silence, then boot steps came down the passageway. Jonathan entered the back sitting room and closed the door. He was still angry, but perhaps not as indignant as before.

"What is it?" she asked.

He sighed impatiently. "A man I know has sought some information on my behalf, without my permission. He now wants to share it. If I do not go to him, he may well come here someday when in his cups and make a scene."

"An earl and the brother of a marquess serve as this man's messengers? Would this man be Castleford? He is notorious for scenes and drunkenness, and you are friends."

He laughed a little. "Friends. I suppose you could say we are friends, of a sort."

"I do not know everything about the world, Jonathan, but I do know that if a duke has done something in the name of friendship, it would be foolish to be ungracious."

She left her plants and went to him. "What has this one done for you?"

He gazed down so thoughtfully. So gently. It frightened her. He looked at her much like a man might look at his beloved before leaving on a long journey.

"He sought information about my birth, Celia. He looked for the proof of whether I was a bastard or not."

She needed a few moments to understand what he said. Then the fullness of the meaning shocked her.

"Did you know it was even possible that you were not?"

"My mother claimed the earl married her, but it could have been a tale told to make a young child feel better about his lot."

Confused reactions jumbled in her. "Does he know she claimed this? Thornridge? Is that why he tried to—"

"Yes."

He continued looking at her in that kind way. His gaze invited her to confide the foreboding growing thickly beneath her heart.

I am going to lose you. You are mad, but not that mad. No man will give up such as this, when it is handed to him as a gift of fate.

She smiled as brightly as she could. "This is wonderful, Jonathan. If he has learned something so important that he sends for you at this hour, I think that the best news waits for you."

He did not disagree. A grip of anguish squeezed her heart with his silence.

"Come with me, Celia."

She longed to, if only to be with him a little longer before everything changed. She would not be able to bear it, however. She could not listen with composure while a duke explained that the wrong man was known as Thorn-ridge.

"I cannot. The wagons. Remember?"

"Of course." He touched her face, and dipped to kiss her. "I will return soon. Probably in time to help as I promised."

Then he was gone, his boots striding toward the men who waited, and toward his true destiny.

"What do you mean, His Grace is in bed?" Hawkeswell bit out the question so fiercely that the servant stepped back a pace in alarm.

"Just what I said, m'lord. He gave orders that he is not to be disturbed until noon."

Summerhays checked his pocket watch. "Forty minutes."

"The hell you say," Hawkeswell snapped. "His messenger woke *me* at nine o'clock with the urgent demand that I collect you and Albrighton and attend him forthwith on this matter of critical interest to Parliament and the nation. I'll be damned if—" He noticed the servant pacing back more, his ass aiming for the door. "Where are you going?"

"Nowhere, m'lord! Does m'lord require something?"

"Reassurance. Please tell me that the duke is at least in bed alone, and that I am not being inconvenienced due to a hasty debauch."

"I could not say, m'lord."

Hawkeswell gave the man a good glare.

"I have not been in his apartment," the man hastily added.

"Hawkeswell," Summerhays chided.

"Go up and tell his valet to immediately inform the

duke that the Earl of Hawkeswell is here, on their matter of mutual urgency." Hawkeswell gestured the servant away. He turned to Summerhays after the door closed on the pleasant, airy room off the drawing room where they waited. "It would be just like him, and you know it. To send me riding all over town, and realize it left him a few hours to slip in a quick one."

"As it were," Jonathan said.

Hawkeswell pivoted in his direction. "Damnation, he made a joke, Summerhays. It was even a little bawdy. You are feeling better, Albrighton? Not so angry anymore?"

"Not so angry."

"I expect a half hour contemplating the chance of being an earl can cure most men of righteous indignation. Even you."

Contemplation had gone far to ease his annoyance. Short of holding a pistol to Thornridge's head, he doubted Castleford had been able to learn anything of real use. He would listen to the duke explain how clever he had been thus far, thank him for his efforts, warn him off interfering in the future, and be on his way back to Celia.

"If Castleford has learned anything useful, you could have too," Summerhays mused. "Yet you never did. Which must mean you never tried."

"I relied on someone else to look into it, all the while doubting there was anything to learn." An error on the first count, and the second too, it had turned out. "I assumed if there were anything to it, Thornridge would settle half a loaf on me through acknowledgment, to discourage my claims to more."

"Instead he sought to make you invisible."

Thoroughly. "I have become rather comfortable with invisible as a result."

"He does not want the tedious parts, is what he means," Hawkeswell said to Summerhays. "He does not want the responsibilities. Well, you don't get to decide and choose, Albrighton. If you are born to it, you are stuck with it."

"I doubt that is true. The evidence would have to pass muster with the most critical and suspicious examiners. It could take years. It isn't that I don't want it, Hawkeswell. I don't want to devote my life to fighting for it, and making every other choice with an eye to being acceptable for it."

The door opened again. A different servant entered, one with more braid and decoration on his livery. Hawkeswell's manner had summoned forth an officer of the army.

"His Grace commanded that you be brought to his apartment, m'lord. If all of you would follow me."

"I am most displeased," Castleford announced as they filed into his dressing room. His valet, who had been buttoning a deep blue brocade morning robe on him, froze and glanced up dolefully.

"Not with you, man. Get on with it," Castleford snapped. He glared over the valet's head at Hawkeswell. "I have been on a horse for a week, and only dragged my sore ass home long after midnight this morning. Is it too much to ask for a few hours' sleep?"

Hawkeswell appeared a bit chagrined, but not too much so. "Why not use your coach and spare your ass? That is what I do on long journeys."

"I needed to move fast." He shooed the valet away impatiently before all those buttons were done. He threw himself onto a sofa and propped his head on one hand. Self-satisfaction replaced annoyance. "They should have used me during the war, not you, Albrighton. I have a knack for this investigating business. My analytical powers even impressed me this week."

"Being a duke probably helps too."

"In investigating? Probably so."

"Also in impressing yourself, and in convincing yourself you have the right to interfere."

Castleford looked at Summerhays. "These two are both piquish today, aren't they?"

"Perhaps you could explain why you requested our presence, and they would be less so."

"Requested, hell," Hawkeswell muttered.

Castleford ignored him. "It is done, Albrighton. I know everything, and have the proof that your cousin usurped your title."

Jonathan laughed. "Forgive me, but I am sure you exaggerate."

"Not at all. Everything I needed was in the one sentence your mother gave you. She said the last earl had married her on his deathbed. That meant that either he had a special license—and my solicitor called at Doctors' Commons and assures me none is on record—or they married in Scotland, or it was the sentimental, meaningless gesture of a man in love with his pregnant mistress."

"Most likely the last, unfortunately," Summerhays said.

"My assumption too, but I decided to look into the second, just in case." He gazed ever so blandly at Jonathan. "Did you know that your estate includes a charming hunting lodge right over the Scottish border? You must promise to have us all there during grouse season. We will drink and shoot and have a fine time. Hawkeswell can come too, if he promises not to act like a child's nurse and scold all the time."

An odd sensation blossomed in Jonathan's chest. Castleford was only being his smug, conceited self in speaking as if the matter were settled. And yet—something in the duke's eyes suggested he really believed it.

"And?" Hawkeswell prompted with irritation.

"So I went there. Hence my sore ass. I did not want to waste too much time on this and thought riding cross-country would be best. I asked some polite and discreet questions and—"

"You are incapable of being discreet, so you are already turning this tale to make yourself look better," Hawkeswell said.

Castleford sighed. He gave Summerhays his attention. "He really is annoying today. More than usual. Do you know why?"

"When he came for me, he was grousing about your very loud and very insistent servant pulling him out of bed at a very inconvenient moment."

Castleford's face fell. "My apologies, Grayson. No wonder you are out of sorts. It never entered my mind that married men took their pleasure in the daylight. I specifically waited until after dawn to send my man, for that very reason."

That hardly appeased the married man in question. If anything, his glare darkened. "Continue, please. When you last broke your story, you were riding your sorry ass along the Scottish border, I believe, flouting your title and prerogatives, holding guns to men's heads to learn what you wanted."

"Damnation, one would think you were there with me. Well, the long and the short of it is I found them, so whatever I did worked."

"Them?" Jonathan asked.

"The witnesses. Both still alive, thank God."

That silenced everyone for a long, astonished moment.

"If your questions were not polite, or if you threw money around, there is no telling if they spoke truthfully, Castleford," Summerhays said. "Even if they did, they may change their tale if Thornridge finds out this happened, and either threatens or pays them off."

"He had already paid them off. Which is why I brought them back with me. I thought about how your cousin tried to get you killed, Albrighton, and decided these two fellows might come to no good once you go after that inheritance."

Two pair of eyes swung their attention to Jonathan. Silence fell. Castleford looked around, perplexed at no longer being the center of the party. Then he realized why.

"Ah. They did not know about that, did they? I appear to have been indiscreet, Albrighton." He shrugged. "Just as well. It must all come out in the end now."

"These witnesses. Where are they?" Jonathan asked. His voice sounded far away to his own ears. The day had become unreal, as though he stood inside an invisible mist that subtly but unmistakably altered his perception.

"Hmmm. Where did I put them? I remember the older one smelled, which is why I rode my horse and avoided the hired carriage." He stood. "I clear forget what I told the steward to do with them. Let us go find out."

He led the way. Jonathan brought up the rear. A throbbing pulse in his head and chest spoke of an excitement that he could not quiet.

If there were witnesses, and Castleford had found them, that changed everything.

Chapter Twenty-seven

Daphne closed the account book. She opened her reticule and extracted some pound notes. "I am confident it will be more in the future, Celia. In this short time the efficiencies of bringing the plants here have already improved our trade. With your arrangement with Mr. Bolton for summer flowers, and the contacts you are cultivating for fruits in winter, we will indeed flourish as you predicted."

Celia tucked the money into a pocket on her apron. Color surrounded them everywhere. The wagons had brought many pots of forced blooms that would bring early spring scents and brightness to dozens of homes in the next few days.

She could take no joy in them, or even in Daphne's company. Jonathan had been gone a long while now. More than five hours. She was beginning to wonder if he would ever come back.

That was stupid. Of course he would. He would return and look at her in that new way, that nostalgic gaze of this morning. He would explain how his expectations meant he could not marry just any woman. He would . . .

She hoped he was hearing the very best news. She truly did. It excited her that such a miracle of good fortune might befall him. But side by side with that joy was this grief, and she could not make it go away.

"I am glad my plan is working, Daphne. I am only sorry that it ties me here now. I would like to return to Cumberworth with you today, but these pots must be dealt with."

"Why would you want to come with me? Your life is here now. So is your lover."

Celia said nothing to that. Daphne understood too well, in her quick way.

"So that is why you have been oddly quiet today," she said. "You are heartsick. Has he been cruel to you?"

"Not at all. This love has been wonderful. Beautiful. So moving that I forget myself." She had to smile at the memories of all the ways he touched her heart. "The last part, the forgetting myself—it has been a mistake, I think."

Daphne reached over and placed her hand over Celia's sympathetically. She asked for no particulars, but offered what comfort her friendship might provide. She probably guessed, however. She probably agreed that Celia should never forget who she was, since no one else would.

No sound came from the garden, but they both turned their attention to the window at the same time. Shadows moved near the shrubbery, and Jonathan started down the garden path. Celia grasped the hand covering hers without thinking.

Daphne stood and came around to embrace her. "I will

go now. Come to us if you want, and leave word for Mr. Drummond on how to deliver the plants. Verity and Audrianna are not far away at all too, if you need either counsel or consolation in the days ahead."

She kissed Celia's cheek in parting, and was out the front door just as Jonathan came in the back one.

He smelled hyacinth before he saw any of the flowers. It penetrated the wall and door as he approached. Only one bloom showed through the window, however. The fairest and rarest bloom of them all, with golden hair and pale skin and eyes that could capture the stars.

She smiled when he entered. She kissed him in greeting, then swept her arms toward the dense tapestry of vibrant colors and green textures draping those shelves.

"Spring has thoroughly come to one chamber in London," she said.

"Why would people purchase from you what they will have in abundance for free in a couple of weeks?"

"Those little shoots outside are like a tease. They make people impatient. When fairer weather begins, they cannot wait. Even one pot is enough for some, although there are those who insist on thirty."

He admired the blooms while she gave a little lesson on their names and varieties. She spoke quickly, as if both impatient with the small talk but also afraid to allow a moment for another topic to start.

Eventually she stopped. They stood side by side, looking at the indoor garden. He felt excitement in her, and even the tension of arousal that they always shared at some level when together. Sorrow touched all of it, however, and his heart as well.

"Are you not curious about what transpired with Castleford, Celia?"

"I have thought about little else since you left. Was it good news?"

"The best news. He had only to ask and people rushed to tell him all they knew. He learned what it could have taken me a lifetime to learn, if at all. He found witnesses who are terrified of my cousin, and well paid for silence. Castleford managed to terrify them better, and they admitted the truth."

She embraced him. "I am so happy for you, Jonathan. More than you can know or guess. I watched you walk up the garden path and thought, *Of course he is an earl. How could anyone ever have met him and not known at once.* Your cousin no doubt did. You may have only been nine years in age, but he probably knew on seeing you that the title was not really his."

Possibly. Or perhaps the determination of a woman sitting on his step for days suggested as much. But the witnesses, both retainers at that hunting lodge, had been paid from the start, even before his cousin reached his majority. The whole family had been in on it, most likely. Even Uncle Edward.

He shut away the loss he felt over that relationship and its long deceptions. He sat, and pulled Celia onto his lap so he could hold the comfort of her feminine warmth. Flowers surrounded his view of her face. Her smile expressed joy, but her eyes showed something else.

"You probably should find other chambers now," she said.

"If you want. We will find a house closer to your friends."

She licked her lips and tried hard to appear sensible,

not distraught. "You should make the move alone, Jonathan. You must not give anyone cause to question your character while this is being settled."

"That could be years. My cousin will do all he can to stop it."

"You must behave very correctly or he may succeed in stopping it. He has many friends, and—"

He silenced her with a kiss. "I think that you have spent the hours I was gone applying Alessandra's lessons to my fate, and concluding I cannot have you now. Is that true, Celia?"

"It cannot be what we had planned. You know that. You cannot marry such as me. As for having my love—until you marry—"

"I'll be damned if I will marry another, and only marry the woman I love on my deathbed, the way my father did." He cupped her soft face with his hand. "I did not return for so long because I went to Doctors' Commons, to ask for a special license. Summerhays was good enough to use his influence, and it should be forthcoming in a few days. You and I will wed at once, so it is done before any of the rest of this starts."

"You are talking like a madman now. These people have rules about such things."

"Celia, every lord in the realm has an interest in making sure the only people to become peers are those born to it, and that a title does not pass down wrongly because of fraud. That is the foremost rule. There is a process for looking into claims like this. My birth will be what matters, that and the legality of that marriage. They do not give a damn about my character. I could be insane and fornicate with sheep every day, and it would make no difference."

She began to speak. He touched his fingers to her lips to stop any more recitations of Alessandra's practicalities. "And if anyone should look at my life, they will find that I am married to a good woman who has always been honest in her love and passion."

Love was in her gaze, but hesitation too. "You cannot know all of this for certain, Jonathan. What if you are wrong?"

"You are the light of my life, Celia, in ways you will never understand. I told you once that I would never give you up easily. Now I could never give you up at all, not even to be Thornridge."

The caution left her, and the worldly, practical knowing disappeared from her eyes. She circled his neck with her arms and laughed.

"I will argue no further, since you are so determined. I am proud that you love me this much, and that you will be mine in truth. This is exciting but also frightening, Jonathan. So frightening it is a wonder you did not walk away from it. They may have to give you that inheritance, but they do not have to accept us."

"We already know some will accept us. They already do. As for the rest, we will live as we like and not worry too much about them."

She kissed him. Beautifully. Expertly. She laid her fair cheek against his and breathed her contentment. "I cannot hold all this happiness in me, Jonathan. My heart is so full of love that I think it will burst. I am too joyful to weep, but I don't know what else to do with all this emotion."

He stood, lifting her in his arms. He carried her toward the stairs. "I do."

Epilogue

Celia sat on the bench near the garden door, basking in the day's warm sun. Down the garden path, near the shrubbery, April's tulips displayed their happy colors while they swayed in the fresh breeze.

She waited for Jonathan's return. He had gone to another meeting about his petition. Thornridge had said he would contest the claim on the title, as expected. Also the legality of the marriage, and the right of any inheritance. It would indeed drag out, and be the talk of the season. All kinds of legalities would complicate the matter, most of which Celia did not understand. The articles in the newspapers opined, however, that Jonathan was likely to receive the estate at least.

In the meantime they would live in this house, and she was not sorry for that. She had grown fond of it, and proud of her partnership with Daphne. This was a fine garden too, she decided, gazing out at the new beds that had been dug, and other improvements. There would be room for children here.

Her hand instinctively went to her body as she thought that. She could not help laughing. She and Jonathan had wed none too soon.

Jonathan entered the garden then, and walked toward her. He appeared happy, but then, he often did now. He smiled as he sat beside her, stretched out his legs, and crossed his boots.

"Are you warm enough here?" he asked. "You should take care. The sun is warm, but the air is still chilled."

"I am fine."

He embraced her shoulders with his arm anyway, to provide more warmth. She rested her head on his shoulder.

"It went well?" she asked.

"Well enough. Also boring and tedious, as I expected. There were twenty lawyers there, a bishop, two dukes, three earls, and more vellum than I have seen in my life combined."

"It sounds horrible."

"Not horrible, but it will be lengthy. As best I can tell, first I go to the Church courts about the marriage. Then I go to other courts about the inheritance, once the marriage is upheld. Then I go to the House of Lords. My cousin's lawyers kept saying 'once a peer, always a peer.' The High Chancellor opined that tradition did not apply to men who usurped a title through criminal acts. One bishop disagreed. The other said the Lords may consider such crimes treasonous. And so it went, all afternoon." He laughed. "I will probably be dead before it is completely done."

"You do not appear too concerned about that."

"That is because I am exaggerating. It will be some years, however. Also, what happened as I left those chambers is more on my mind, and cause for my mood." He smiled slyly. "My cousin's solicitor approached me and asked to have a word with me."

"Whatever for?"

"To discuss my allowance."

She straightened and looked at him, perplexed. "He wants to give you money?"

"Hell of a thing, isn't it? I don't think he *wants* to. I think he believes it would look bad if he did not now. Everyone knows I am his uncle's son one way or another. Perhaps he fears that if he does not make this gesture, the bigger question will be badly influenced against him." He shrugged, and closed his eyes.

"Or, perhaps he sees the estate slipping out of his hands eventually, and wants to encourage you to be as generous as he, when it is yours."

"How cynical of you, Celia." He kissed her nose. "I am sure it is just his good heart at work."

She nestled against him again. "How much was this allowance he offered?"

His eyes remained closed and turned to the sun. "A respectable amount."

"How respectable?"

"A lot."

She smacked on his shoulder. "*How much?*"

"Two thousand."

"A year?"

"Mmm."

"That is a handsome income, Jonathan."

"I thought so. Had the solicitor approached me before the meeting, I might have taken it. Having just left hours of droning tedium, I decided I deserved more and countered with seven thousand. We settled in the middle."

More than four thousand pounds a year. "What will we do with it?"

"We could buy you a new wardrobe, I suppose. And some jewels."

"A carriage would be nice, with a matched pair."

"See, if we put our minds to it, we will manage to run through it in no time." He hooked his arm around her neck and drew her close so he could kiss her. "You can have it all, to do as you wish, Celia. I have what I want right here." He touched her belly, then her breast, in a caress.

A discreet cough at the garden door made them both turn. Bella stood there, flushing hotly from what she had witnessed. "My apologies. But there is a man here, to see you, Celia. He is in the sitting room. I've his card here."

Jonathan stood to take the card. He read it, and raised his eyebrows. He handed it to Celia.

Mr. Mappleton had called.

Mr. Mappleton was all smiles when they greeted him. He bowed a little deeper than he ever had in the past to Celia, and made some flattering, ingratiating comments to Jonathan. Celia assumed that Mr. Mappleton had been reading the papers about her husband's considerable expectations.

When they all sat, the solicitor smiled some more. "I have come for several reasons. I hope you do not mind. I thought to spare you the visit to my chambers."

"That is considerate of you." She had always liked Mr. Mappleton. He had been a faithful helper to her mother.

"Yes, well, first, I want to inform you that the estate is settled. All is in order. There have been no further claims on it, so this house is yours free and clear."

"That is good to know." She resisted glancing at Jonathan, who had ensured there would be no further claim.

"I also come as an emissary," Mr. Mappleton said, more seriously. "It is my sincere hope that you will hear me out. My words are verbatim, from the gentleman who asked I speak them."

"Which gentleman?" Jonathan asked.

"I am not at liberty to say, sir. I was assured that Miss Pennifold—Mrs. Albrighton—would know the source and meaning." His eyes sparkled mischievously. "I think it would not be a betrayal of my charge if I said this was a *most* esteemed gentleman."

"Let us hear it, then," Jonathan said.

"I am asked to tell you, Mrs. Albrighton, that if you call again, you will be received. That is the entire message."

Jonathan caught her eye. He did not appear joyed by the overture. Actually, he appeared much as she felt. It would be some time before she called on Enderby again, no matter what second thoughts he recently had. She would someday, though. He was her father, wasn't he?

"Thank you, Mr. Mappleton. I understand, and appreciate your service in this," she said.

"Now that is done. There is only one more thing." He reached in his coat and brought forth a letter. "This was left in my possession by your mother. The instructions were to give it to you, if you ever married for love." He looked at her, then Jonathan, and blushed. "As if I could know for sure! I said as much to her. She assured me that her daughter would answer the question honestly if I put it to her."

He suddenly appeared dismayed. "Perhaps I need to ask this of the lady privately, Mr. Albrighton. Yes, that would be best, I suppose. How careless of me. I am not accustomed to such a peculiar mission and—"

"Do not distress yourself, sir," Celia said. "My husband's presence does not constrain my honesty on this of all questions. I most certainly married for love, I assure you."

Mr. Mappleton looked at her kindly. "Yes, I believe you did, dear lady." He ceremoniously offered her the letter.

He took his leave then. Celia sat with the letter on her lap. The paper appeared fresh enough. It must have been written not all that long ago.

"Aren't you going to read it?" Jonathan asked.

"I do not know if I want to. It contains a scold for this marriage, I am sure, and for being reckless with my future."

Jonathan scowled. "If so, it is cruel and selfish that she reaches out from the grave to distress you. I would have thought better of her."

She fingered the paper with trepidation, then quickly opened it.

She read its contents once, and blinked hard, confused by the words. She read it a second time. Her heart filled as she did. Emotions overwhelmed her. She began weeping uncontrollably.

Jonathan gathered her into an embrace. He took the letter and crushed it in his fist. "We will burn it, and if any more come, you are not to read them. I will not see you so distraught merely because she could not accept that her plans for you were not your plans for yourself."

She shook her head, and struggled for composure. "It is not what you think, my love. Not selfish or cruel. It is a lovely letter." She took it from his clenched hand, and unfolded it. She smoothed the sheet on her lap. "You must read it with me. You must."

Head to head, and bound by his embracing arm, they read the letter together.

My dear, dear Celia,

If you are reading this, it means that you have married. Furthermore you have discarded everything I ever taught you by choosing your husband for the least practical reason. You have risked your future, your security, your heart, and even your person, in the name of an emotion that for most women proves transient and fickle.

I want you to know that I understand. I too loved once. Although it led to heartbreak, it was a glorious passion while it could last. If you have embraced the opportunity to know something similar forever, I can hardly object. Indeed, it is my sincere hope as I write this letter that you will someday read it, because that will mean that you not only found a man worthy of your love, but one wise enough to recognize the true beauty that is within you, and who is also willing to risk as much as you do, in order to have you in his life.

I pray that you will remember me, Celia, and when your children are of an age to understand, perhaps you will tell them about me. You would have made the most magnificent courtesan London has ever seen, daughter, but I weep with joy at the thought that you may find happiness on this other path.

You have my love, and my blessing.
Alessandra

You won't want to miss the breathtaking finale of
Madeline Hunter's magnificent quartet . . .

Dangerous in Diamonds

On sale in May 2011 from Jove Books

There is only one man who can shake
Daphne's composure.
And there is only one woman who can resist
Castleford's outrageous brand of seduction.

Penguin Group (USA) Inc.
is proud to present

GREAT READS—GUARANTEED

We are so confident you will love
this book that we are offering a
100% money-back guarantee!

If you are not 100% satisfied with
this publication, Penguin Group (USA) Inc.
will refund your money!
Simply return the book before
December 5, 2010 for a full refund.

M712G0510

The "mast　　　　　　　　　　　　thor

MADELINE HUNTER

presents the first book in
a magnificent historical romance quartet

Ravishing
in Red

Audrianna Kelmsleigh is unattached, independent—and
armed. Her adversary is Lord Sebastian Summerhays. What
they have in common is Audrianna's father, who died in a
scandalous conspiracy—a deserved death, in Sebastian's eyes.
Audrianna vows to clear her father's name, never expecting
to fall in love with the man devoted to destroying it ...

*Booklist

9T1009